winter's KiSS

The Ex Games
Jennifer Echols

and

The Twelve Dates of Christmas
Catherine Hapka

Simon Pulse

New York   London   Toronto   Sydney   New Delhi

SIMON PULSE

An imprint of Simon & Schuster Children's Publishing Division

1230 Avenue of the Americas, New York, NY 10020

This Simon Pulse paperback edition January 2012

The Ex Games copyright © 2009 by Jennifer Echols

The Twelve Dates of Christmas copyright © 2008 by Catherine Hapka

All rights reserved, including the right of reproduction in whole or in part in any form.

SIMON PULSE and colophon are registered trademarks of Simon & Schuster, Inc.

For information about special discounts for bulk purchases, please contact Simon & Schuster Special Sales at 1-866-506-1949 or business@simonandschuster.com.

The Simon & Schuster Speakers Bureau can bring authors to your live event. For more information or to book an event contact the Simon & Schuster Speakers Bureau at 1-866-248-3049 or visit our website at www.simonspeakers.com.

Designed by Mike Rosamilia

The text of this book was set in Garamond 3.

Manufactured in the United States of America

2 4 6 8 10 9 7 5 3 1

Library of Congress Control Number 2011937694

ISBN 978-1-4424-5040-0

ISBN 978-1-4424-5074-5 (eBook)

These books were previously published individually by Simon Pulse.

winter's
KiSS

More romantic comedies:

♥ ♥ ♥

Royally Crushed
by Niki Burnham

Endless Summer
by Jennifer Echols

Love, Love, Love
by Deborah Reber
and Caroline Goode

A Funny Thing About Love
by Erin Downing

The Ex Games

For Amy

seat belt

('sēt belt) *n.* **1.** a trick in which a snowboarder reaches across the body and grabs the board while getting air **2.** what Hayden needs to fasten, because Nick is about to take her for a ride

At the groan of a door opening, I looked up from my chemistry notebook. I'd been diagramming molecules so I wouldn't have any homework to actually take home. But as I'd stared at the white paper, it had dissolved into a snowy slalom course. The hydrogen and oxygen atoms had transformed into gates for me to snowboard between. My red pen had traced my path, curving back and forth, *swish, swish, swish,* down the page. I could almost feel the icy wind on my cheeks and smell the pine trees. I couldn't *wait* to get out of school and head for the mountain.

Until I saw it was Nick coming out the door of Ms. Abernathy's room and into the hall. At six feet tall, he filled the doorway with his model-perfect looks and cocky attitude. He flicked his dark hair out of his eyes with his pinkie, looked down at me, and grinned brilliantly.

My first thought was, *Oh no: fuel for the fire.* About a month ago, one of my best friends had hooked up with one of Nick's best friends. Then, a few weeks ago, my other best friend and Nick's other best friend had gotten together. It was fate. Nick and I were next, right?

Wrong. Everybody in our class remembered that Nick and I had been a couple four years ago, in seventh grade. They gleefully recalled our breakup and the resulting brouhaha. They watched us now for our entertainment value, dying to know whether we'd go out again. Unfortunately for them, they needed to stick to DVDs and Wii to fill up their spare time. Nick and I weren't going to happen.

My second thought was, *Ah, those deep brown eyes.*

Maybe snowboarding could wait a little longer, after all.

"Fancy meeting you here, Hoyden." He closed the door behind him, too hard. He must have gotten in trouble for talking again, and Ms. Abernathy had sent him out in the hall.

Join the club. From my seat against the cement block wall of our high school's science wing, I gazed up at him—way, *way* up, because I was on the floor—and tried my best to glare. The first time he'd called me *Hoyden*, years ago, I'd sneaked a peek in the dictionary to look up what it meant: a noisy girl. Not exactly flattering. Not exactly a lie, either. But I couldn't let him know I felt flattered that he'd taken the time to look up a word in the dictionary to insult me with. Because that would make me insane, desperate, and in unrequited love.

He slapped his forehead. "*Oh*, I'm sorry, I meant *Hayden*. I get confused." He had a way of saying *oh* so innocently, like he had no idea he'd insulted me. Sometimes new girls bought his act, at least for their first few weeks at our school. They were taken by the idea of hooking up with Nick Krieger, who occasionally was featured in teen heart-throb magazines as the heir to the Krieger Meats and Meat Products fortune. And Nick obliged these girls—for a few dates, until he dumped them.

I knew his pattern all too well. When I'd first moved to Snowfall, Colorado, I had *been* one of those girls. He'd made me feel like a princess for a whole month. No, better—like a cool, hip teenage girl who dated! The fantasy culminated with one deep kiss shared in the back row of the movie theater with half our English class watching us. It didn't end well, thus the aforementioned brouhaha.

I blinked the stars out of my eyes. "Fancy seeing *you* here, Ex."

He gave me his smile of sexy confidence, dropped his backpack, and sank to the floor beside me. "What do you think of Davis and Liz?"

My heart had absolutely no reason to skip a beat. He was *not* asking me out. He was asking me my opinion of my friend Liz and his friend Davis as a couple. That did not necessarily mean he was heeding public opinion that he and I were next to get together. Liz and Davis were a legitimate topic of gossip.

I managed to say breezily, "Oh, they'll get along great until they discuss where to go on a date. Then he'll insist they go where she wants to go. She'll insist they go where *he* wants to go. They'll end up sitting in her driveway all night, fighting to the death over who can be more thoughtful and polite."

Nick chuckled, a low rumble in his chest. Because he'd sat down so close to me and our arms were touching, sort of, under layers and layers of clothing, I felt the vibration of his voice. But again, my heart had no reason—repeat, *no* reason—to skip two beats, or possibly three, just because

I'd made Nick laugh. He made everybody feel this good about their stupid jokes.

"And what's up with Gavin and Chloe?" he asked next.

"Chloe and Gavin are an accident waiting to happen." I couldn't understand this mismatch between the class president and the class bad boy, and it was a relief finally to voice my concerns, even if it *was* to Nick. "They're both too strong-willed to make it together long. You watch. They're adorable together now, but before long they'll have an argument that makes our tween-love Armageddon look like a happy childhood memory."

Suddenly it occurred to me that I'd said way too much, and Nick would likely repeat this unflattering characterization to Gavin, who would take it right back to Chloe. I really did hold this opinion of Chloe and Gavin's chances at true love, but I'd never intended to share it! I lost my inhibitions when I looked into Nick's dark eyes, damn him.

I slid my arm around him conspiratorially—not as titillating as it sounds, because his parka was very puffy—and cooed, "But that's just between you and me. I know how good you are at keeping secrets."

He pursed his lips and gazed at me reproachfully for throwing our seventh-grade history in his face, times two. Back then he'd brought our tween-love Armageddon on himself by letting our whole class in on his secret while he kept me in the dark.

Not that I was bitter.

But instead of jabbing back at me, he slipped his arm around me, too. And I was *not* wearing a puffy parka, only a couple of T-shirts, both of which had ridden up a little in the back. I knew this without looking because I felt the heat of his fingers on my bare skin, above the waistband of my jeans. My face probably turned a few shades redder than my hair.

"Now, Hoyden," he reprimanded me, "Valentine's Day is a week from tomorrow. We don't want to ruin that special day for Gavin and Chloe or Davis and Liz. We should put aside our differences for the sake of the kids."

I couldn't help bursting into unladylike laughter.

I expected him to remove his hand from my hip in revulsion at my outburst, but he kept it there. I knew he was only toying with me, I *knew* this, but I sure did enjoy it. If the principal had walked by just then and sensed what I was thinking, I would have gotten detention.

"Four years is a long time for us to be separated," he crooned. "We've both had a chance to think about what we really want from our relationship."

This was true. Over the four years since we'd been together, I'd come to the heartbreaking realization that no boy in my school was as hot as Nick, nobody was as much fun, and nobody was nearly as much of an ass. For instance, he'd generated fire-crotch comments about me as I passed his table in the lunchroom yesterday.

Remember when another heir called a certain red-haired actress a fire-crotch on camera? No? Well, *I* remember. Redheads across America sucked in a collective gasp, because we *knew*. The jokes boys made to us about Raggedy Ann, the Wendy's girl, and Pippi Longstocking would finally stop, as we'd always hoped, only to be replaced by something infinitely worse.

So when I heard *fire-crotch* whispered in the lunchroom, I assumed it was meant for me. Nick was the first suspect I glanced at. His mouth was closed as he listened to the conversation at the lunch table. However, when there was commentary around school about me, Nick was always in the vicinity. He might not have made the comment, but I knew in my heart he was responsible.

Now I chose not to relay my thoughts on our four-year-long trial separation, lest he take his warm hand off my hip. Instead, I played along. "Are you saying you didn't sign the papers, so our divorce was never finalized?"

"I'm saying maybe we should call off the court proceedings and try a reconciliation." A strand of his dark hair came untucked from behind his ear, and he jerked his head back to swing the hair out of his eyes. Oooh, I *loved* it when he did that! I had something of a Nick problem.

His hair fell right back into his eyes. Sometimes when this happened, he followed up the head jerk with the pinkie flick, but not this time. He watched me, waiting for me to say something. Oops. I'd forgotten I was staring at him in awe.

A reconciliation? He was probably just teasing me, as usual. But what if this was his veiled way of asking me on a date? What if he was feeling me out to see whether I wanted to go with him before he asked me directly? This was how Nick worked. He had to win. He never took a bet that wasn't a sure thing.

And if he'd been listening to everyone in class prodding him to ask me out, the timing was perfect, if I did say so myself. He was between girlfriends (not that I kept up with his dating status) and therefore free to get together with me. Everett Walsh, my boyfriend of two months, had broken up with me last week because his mama thought I was brazen (no!). Therefore I was free to get together with Nick.

Playing it cool, I relaxed against the wall and gave his puffy parka a squeeze, which he probably couldn't feel through the padding. With my other hand, I found his fingers in his lap and touched the engraving on his signet ring, which he'd told me back in seventh grade was the Krieger family crest. It depicted bloodthirsty lions and the antlers of the hapless deer they'd attacked and devoured—which seemed apt for our relationship in seventh grade, but *not* for our relationship now, in eleventh. I was no deer in the headlights. Not anymore. Coyly I said, "I'll mention it to my lawyer." Ha!

He eyed me uneasily, like I was a chemistry lab experiment gone awry and foaming over. But Nick was never truly uneasy. He was just taken aback that I hadn't fallen at his feet. Then he asked, "What are you doing for winter break?"

Winter break was next week. We lived in a ski resort town. It seemed cruel to lock us up in school the *entire* winter. They let us out for a week every February, since the base might or might not start to melt by spring break in April.

Was he just making convo, whiling away our last few minutes of incarceration at school, or did he really want to know what I was doing during our days off? Again I got the distinct and astonishing impression that he wanted to ask me out. Perhaps I should notify Ms. Abernathy of a safety hazard in her chemistry classroom. Obviously I had inhaled hallucinatory gas just before she kicked me out.

"I'm boarding with my brother today," I said, counting on my fingers. "Tomorrow I'm boarding with Liz. Actually,

Liz skis rather than boards, but she keeps up with me pretty well. I'm boarding with some friends coming from Aspen on Sunday, the cheerleading squad on Monday—"

Nick laughed. "Basically, anyone who will board with you."

"I guess I get around," I agreed. "I'm on the mountain a lot. Most people get tired of boarding after a while, which I do not understand at *all*. And then on Tuesday, I've entered that big snowboarding competition."

"Really!" He sounded interested and surprised, but his hand underneath my hand let me know he was more interested in throwing me into a hot tizzy than in anything I had to say. He slid his hand, and my hand with it, from his lap and over to my thigh. "You're going off the jump? Did you get over your fear of heights?"

So he'd been listening to me after all.

My friends knew I'd broken my leg rappelling when I was twelve. That actually led, in a roundabout way, to my family's move from Tennessee to Colorado. My dad was a nurse, and he got so interested in my physical rehab that he and my mom decided to open a health club. Only they didn't think they could make it fly in Tennessee. The best place for a privately owned health club specializing in physical rehab was a town with a lot of rich people and broken legs.

Though my own leg had healed by the time we moved, I was still so shell-shocked from my fall that I never would have tried snowboarding if my parents hadn't made me go with my little brother, Josh, to keep him from killing himself on the mountain. Josh was a big part of the reason I'd gotten pretty good. *Any* girl would get pretty good trying to keep up with a boy snowboarder three years younger who was half insane.

And that's how I became the world's only snowboarder with the ability to land a frontside 900 in the half-pipe *and* with a crippling fear of heights. Not a good combination if I wanted to compete nationally.

"This competition's different," I said. Growing warmer, I watched Nick's fingers massaging the soft denim of my jeans. "For once, the only events are the slalom and the half-pipe. No big air or slopestyle or anything that would involve a jump. Chloe and Liz swore they'd never forgive me if I didn't enter this one."

"You've got a chance," Nick assured me. "I've seen you around on the slopes. You're good compared with most of the regulars on the mountain."

I shrugged—a small, dainty shrug, not a big shrug that would dislodge his hand from my hip and his other hand from my thigh. "Thanks, but I expect some random chick from Aspen to sweep in and kick my ass." And when that happened, I sure could use someone to comfort me in the agony of defeat, *hint hint*. But Nick was only toying with me. Nick was only toying with me. I could repeat this mantra a million times in my head, yet no matter how strong my willpower, his fingers rubbing across my jeans threatened to turn me into a nervous gigglefest. Sometimes I wished I were one of those cheerleaders/prom queens/rich socialite snowbunnies who seemed to interest Nick for a day or two at a time. I wondered if any of them had given in to Nick's fingers rubbing across their jeans, and whether I would too, if he asked.

"Anyway, those are all my plans so far," I threw in there despite myself. What I meant was: I am free for the rest of the week, *hint hint*. I wanted to kick myself.

"Are you going to the Poser concert on Valentine's Day?" He eased his hand out from under mine and put his on top. His fingers massaged my fingers ever so gently.

Nick was only toying with me. "That's everybody's million-dollar question, isn't it?" I said. "Or rather, their seventy-two-dollar question. I don't want to pass up a once-in-a-lifetime opportunity to see Poser, but tickets are so expensive." I may have spoken a bit too loudly so he could hear me over my heart, which was no longer skipping beats. It was hammering out a beat faster than Poser's drummer.

Nick nodded. "Especially if you're buying two because you want to ask someone to go with you."

I gaped at him. I know I did. He watched me with dark, supposedly serious eyes while I gaped at him in shock. Was he laughing at me inside?

We both started as the door burst open. Ms. Abernathy glowered down at us with her fists on her hips. "Miss O'Malley. Mr. Krieger. When I send you into the hall for talking, you do not *talk* in the *hall*!"

"*Oh,*" Nick said in his innocent voice.

I was deathly afraid I would laugh at this if I opened my mouth. I absolutely could not allow myself to fall in love with Nick all over again. But it was downright impossible to avoid. He bent his head until Ms. Abernathy couldn't see his face, and he winked at me.

Saved by the bell! We all three jumped as the signal rang close above our heads. On a normal day the class would have flowed politely around Ms. Abernathy standing in the doorway. They might even have waited until she moved. But this bell let us out of school for winter break. Ms. Abernathy got caught in the current of students pouring out of her classroom and down the hall. If she floated as far as the next wing, maybe a history teacher would throw her a rope and tow her to safety.

Chloe and Liz shoved their way out of the room and

glanced around the crowded hall until they saw me against the wall on the floor. Clearly they were dying to know whether I'd survived being sent out in the hall with my ex. Both of them focused on the space between me and Nick. I looked down in confusion, wondering what they were staring at.

Nick was still holding my hand.

I tried to pull my hand away. He squeezed even tighter. I turned to him with my eyes wide. What in the world was he thinking? After the insults Nick and I had thrown at each other in public over the years, we would have been the laughingstock of the school if we *really* fell for each other.

And now he was holding my hand in public!

He wouldn't look at me, though I pulled hard to free myself from his grasp. He just squeezed my hand and grinned up at the gathering crowd like he didn't care who saw us.

Which was *everyone*. Davis sauntered out of the classroom and slid his arm around Liz. Unlike the train wreck that was Chloe and Gavin as a couple, Liz and Davis were the two kindest people I knew. They deserved each other, in a good way. But even Davis had a comment as he casually glanced down at Nick and me and did a double take at our hands. "That's something you don't see every day," he understated to Liz. "Usually at about this time, Nick is going around the lab, collecting whatever particulate has dropped out of the solution so he can throw it at Hayden."

"We didn't do an experiment today, just diagrammed molecules. Nothing to throw," Nick said in a reasonable tone, as if he and I were not sitting on the floor, surrounded by a two-deep crowd of our classmates. They had all filed out of chemistry class and joined the circle. They peeked over one another's shoulders to see what Nick and I were up to this time.

Then Gavin exploded out of the classroom, and I knew Nick and I were in trouble. He whacked into Chloe so hard, he would have knocked her off her feet if he hadn't grabbed her at the same time. Over her squeals, he yelled at Nick, "I knew it!" while pointing at our hands.

"Oooooh," said the crowd, shifting closer around us, totally forgetting they were supposed to be *going home* for *winter break*. If Davis, Liz, Gavin, and Chloe hadn't made up the front row, the rest of the class would have overrun us like zombies.

"I was just shaking Hayden's hand, wishing her luck in the snowboarding competition Tuesday." Nick stood, still gripping my hand, pulling me up with him.

"See you tonight," Davis mouthed in Liz's ear. Then he turned to Nick and said, "Come on. I'll fill you in on what

Ms. Abernathy said after you got ejected from the game."
Of course Nick didn't give a damn what Ms. Abernathy
said in the last ten minutes of class before winter break.
But that was Davis, always smoothing things over.

Nick *finally* let go of my hand. "See you around,
Hoyden." He pinned me with one last dark look and a
curious smile. Then he and Davis made their way through
the crowd, shoving some of the more obnoxious gawking
boys, who elbowed them back.

But a few folks still stared at me: Liz, Chloe, and
worst of all, Gavin. One corner of his mouth turned up
in a mischievous grin. Gavin was tall, muscular, and
Japanese, with even longer hair than Nick. I would have
thought he was adorable if I didn't want to kill him most
of the time for constantly goading Nick and me about
each other. I certainly understood what Chloe saw in him,
even though he drove her crazy too.

Gavin turned to her. "Give me some gum."

"No."

Liz and I dodged out of the way as Gavin backed Chloe
against the lockers and shoved both his hands into the front
pockets of her jeans. You might think the class president
would find a way to stop this sort of manhandling, but
actually she didn't seem to mind too much.

By now the crowd had dispersed. Nick and Davis

were walking down the hall together, getting smaller and smaller until I couldn't see them anymore past a knot of freshman girls squealing about the Poser concert and how they were working extra shifts at the souvenir shop to pay for the expensive tickets. Go home, people. I resisted the urge to stand on my tiptoes for one more peek at Nick. If I didn't run into him on the slopes, this might be the last I saw of him for ten whole days.

"I don't have any gum!" Chloe squealed through fits of giggling, trying to push Gavin off. "Gavin!" She finally shoved him away.

He jogged down the hall to catch up with Nick and Davis, holding the paper-wrapped stick of gum aloft triumphantly.

"That was my last piece!" Chloe called.

I never would have admitted that Gavin's gum theft made me jealous. Nick was bad for me, I knew. He was the last person on earth I wanted to steal my gum. Still, I stepped to one side so I could see him behind the Poser fangirls. I watched him turn with Gavin and Davis and disappear down the stairs, and I couldn't help but feel like a little kid on Halloween night, standing in the doorway in my witch costume with my plastic cauldron for trick-or-treat candy, watching the rain come down. Such sweet promise, and now I was out of luck. Damn.

Chloe stared after the boys too. I assumed she really wanted that gum. Then she looked at me. "Oh my God, did Nick ask you out? It sounded like he was asking you out, but we couldn't quite tell. Ms. Abernathy finally came to check on you because the whole first row got up from their desks and pressed their ears to the door."

I answered honestly. "For a second there, I thought he was going to ask me out."

"But he didn't?" Liz wailed.

To hide my disappointment, I bent down to stuff my chemistry notebook into my backpack as I shook my head.

"At least you got a *see you around*," Chloe pointed out. "Normally if he bothered to say good-bye to you at all, he would do it by popping your bra."

"True," I acknowledged. And then I realized what was going on here. Chloe and Liz had been hinting that I should go out with Nick now that they were dating Nick's friends, but at the moment they seemed even more eager and giddy about it than usual. I straightened, folded my arms across my chest, and glared at Chloe and then Liz. "Please do not tell me you put Nick up to asking me to the Poser concert."

Chloe stared right back at me. But Liz, the weakest link, glanced nervously at Chloe like they were busted.

"Come on now." I stamped one foot. "Even y'all aren't

going to the Poser concert with Gavin and Davis. It's too expensive."

"Nick has more money than God," Chloe pointed out.

I turned on Liz. "You really want me to go out with him after I told you he made that fire-crotch comment about me?" Liz was all about people being respectful of one another. We were in school with teenage boys and this was asking a lot, I know.

"That *did* sound disrespectful," she admitted. "Are you sure he didn't mean it in a friendly way?"

Incredible. Even Liz's sense of chivalry and honor was crushed under the juggernaut called Wouldn't It Be Cute/Ironic If Nick and Hayden Dated Again.

"What if he *did* ask you out?" Liz bounced excitedly, and her dark curls bounced with her. "Oh my God, what if you saw him on the slopes over the break and he asked you to the Poser concert? What would you say?"

I considered this. Part of me wanted to think Nick had changed in the past four years. I would jump at the chance to go out with the boy I'd made up in my head. In real life Nick was adorable, funny, and smart, but in my fantasies he had the additional fictional component of honestly wanting to go out with me.

Another part of me remembered his dis four years ago as freshly as if it were yesterday. When I recalled that awful night, the image of Honest Nick dissolved, even from my imagination. That Nick was too good to be true. I couldn't say yes to Nick, because I was scared to death he would hurt me again.

"It doesn't matter," I declared, "because he's not going to ask me out. If he really liked me, he wouldn't have treated me the way he did back in the day. So stop trying to throw us together."

"Okay," Liz and Chloe said in unison. Again, too eager, too giddy. The three of us turned and made our own way down the hall. We discussed how low Poser tickets would have to go before we sprung for them, but the subject had changed too easily. I was left with the nagging feeling that, despite their promise, they were not through playing Cupid with me and Nick.

fakie

I know what you're thinking. Girlfriend has fallen out of the stoopid tree and bonked her head against every branch on the way down. If Nick had such beautiful dark eyes and a low, rumbly voice and a perfect ass (did I mention his ass?), then why would I hold a grudge for something he did in the seventh grade?

Well, there was no mortification like seventh-grade

mortification—just like my mom said there was no hunger like pregnancy hunger. Normal people got hungry, but pregnant women were driven toward food like starving wild animals, and a Big Mac never tasted so decadent to anyone. Clearly my mother had completed her research on this topic way before I broke my leg and my family turned health-conscious and vegetarian.

Not that I planned to find out about pregnancy hunger myself before I turned thirty. I had too much snowboarding to do first. But I was an expert on seventh-grade mortification. At that age you already worried that every step you took and every word out of your mouth would send your so-called "friends" into fits of laughter, because they hadn't quite outgrown the cruelty peculiar to sixth graders. If something truly mortifying happened to you on top of this, your heart began to shrink. And if, in addition, you were the new girl at school who wanted desperately to fit in, then in eleventh grade you would still be mad.

I moved to Snowfall about this time of year, terrified I'd make some blunder and everyone would hate me for the rest of middle school and high school. Or that these strangers would hear about the broken leg I'd just completed rehab for and would view me as the crippled girl and feel sorry for me, just like the kids did back in Tennessee. *Snowfall*—funny name for a ski resort town, at least the falling part. It made me worry I would take my dog for a walk one afternoon and slip into an icy crevice, never to be heard from again. The only evidence that I'd ever existed would be Doofus the Irish setter, trotting happily home, dragging his leash.

Instead, the opposite happened. Seconds after I handed my enrollment slip to the teacher and snuck into an empty desk in the back of English class, Nick picked up his books and moved to the desk beside mine.

I remembered every detail of that first five minutes with him, as if each minute were packed with a whole day's worth of emotion and color. Even back then, Nick was a head taller than most of the other boys in the class, and *so* handsome. He looked vaguely familiar in a way I couldn't quite place.

But what struck me most was how comfortable he seemed with me. The thirteen-year-old boys I'd known in Tennessee were split down the middle: Either they wouldn't make eye contact because they weren't interested in girls yet and played way too much Nintendo, or they were interested in girls and expressed this by making comments about their boobs. Unlike those immature boys, Nick talked to me as if we were friends. And he was funny. And he was hot. And I was the vulnerable new girl. I never had a chance.

Back then we weren't very mobile, of course. A seventh-grade "date" looked exactly like every other seventh grader's weekend outing: pizza at Mile-High Pie, the dive for locals only, and then whatever movie was playing at the theater down the street. Only, if you were on a little baby "date," you did all this while hanging with a boy, and the rest of the seventh-grade girls gazed at you in awe. And if your relationship were truly serious, you sat in the back row of the theater and kissed. I went on three "dates" with Nick, with no macking so far. The girls in my class squealed every time they saw me, beside themselves over the possibility that our fourth time might be sealed with a kiss.

On that fourth date, Mile-High Pie was packed with teenagers wearing hip winter sports gear even if they didn't ski or board. February in Tennessee was cold and brown, but Snowfall sparkled with excitement at the height of the ski season, like a beach town in summertime. I sat in a booth with Nick, surrounded by colored lights twinkling in the windows and decades of teen graffiti layered on the walls: VIOLET LOVES RANDY. ZACH + KAREN. That's what Nick and I were: Nick + Hayden. He watched me attentively, smiled at me, laughed at my jokes, and ignored Gavin elbowing him.

After a while we moved with the teenage crowd to the movie theater. Do you remember a Will Smith romantic comedy about a player who makes all the right moves to sneak into a woman's heart? IRONY. Maybe you could tell me the details sometime, because I wasn't paying much attention.

A tall, beautiful blonde named Chloe, obviously the prima donna of the class, was having a very public argument with two different boys who liked her. Because I was new, I had a hard time puzzling it out. There was a lot of high drama before the film started, middle schoolers yelling accusations at each other, like a Disney Channel version of *COPS*, and Chloe was comfortable at the center of it. I thought the attention had finally moved away from Nick and me, and we were safe from everyone's eyes in the back row.

The second the lights dimmed, he put his arm around me. We weren't wearing puffy parkas, either—we'd draped them over the backs of the seats when we'd come in—so the heat and weight of his arm imprinted themselves along my shoulders and the back of my neck. By the first love scene in the movie, he was leaning toward me.

I figured he wouldn't really kiss me. He would want to. He would mean to. But I couldn't possibly be lucky enough for this to happen for real, even though I *was* wearing my four-leaf clover earrings. The fire alarm would sound in the theater, or the roof would collapse under the weight of the snow. (I hadn't gotten used to two feet of snow blanketing everything.) The fact that we were hot for each other would be obvious to everyone, but like a pair of unfortunate saps on a TV sitcom, we wouldn't kiss for another two seasons.

And then he kissed me. His arm tightened around my shoulders, his other big hand cradled my cheek, and his warm lips touched mine. We kissed for a long time. I didn't make him stop. If this had happened in Tennessee, I would have known the boy just wanted to brag to his friends afterward. Nick made me think he honestly liked me and wanted to touch me.

My first kiss.

Obviously not his. He knew what he was doing.

I blink away tears thinking about this now. Such a perfect night, the sweetest reward after two years of embarrassment at school in Tennessee and excruciating pain 24/7. I'm feeling sorry for myself, I know, but I can't help crying for poor little thirteen-year-old me at the moment Nick kissed me. Because the castle in the air he'd built for me over the past month was about to come crashing down in the snow.

A girl named Liz bounced into the seat beside me and whispered that I should come to the bathroom with her and Chloe. This surprised me, because I'd never heard Liz's voice before—she was a quiet little librarian in class—and also because I'd begun to think no one dared disturb the mature teen bliss that Nick and I embodied. But I really did need to pee. I had needed to pee since the movie began. In seventh grade you do not admit to boys that you need to pee, so this was the perfect excuse to relieve myself while retaining my image as a peeless goddess.

When I came out of the stall, Chloe was peeking under the other doors to make sure the bathroom was empty. Liz stood in the center of the tiled room with her arms folded. I felt a flash of panic that maybe Colorado middle schools traditionally welcomed new students with a swirly. Or that Nick was on the list of boyfriends Chloe was balancing. I'd had my fun with him in the back row, and now she wanted payback. But Chloe didn't *look* bent on revenge. For the first time all month, she was silent, waiting, deferring to Liz.

By junior year Liz let her dark curly hair float around her shoulders. But back in seventh grade, she was still pulling it off her face with combs and clips with little monkey faces on them. The monkey faces laughed at me as she dropped the bomb. She told me Nick was from a famously rich family. Hadn't I seen the TV commercials last year in which Nick and his parents stood beside a huge rock fireplace and his father invited the camera to try Krieger Meats and Meat Products, from their family to yours?

That's why Nick looked familiar!

Liz said that at the beginning of the year, Nick and Gavin had argued about whether Nick's family money was the only reason he got any girl he wanted. So a month ago, when the English teacher let the class know a new girl was starting school, Nick bet Gavin he could get a date with the girl that weekend, sight unseen, without her knowing anything about his money. To make it fair, Nick and Gavin swore everyone in the class to secrecy.

I was not, as I'd thought, a cool teen. I was not Nick's dream girl. I was a bet.

And Liz and Chloe, feeling guilty, thought I should know. Now that Nick had kissed me, the bet had gone too far.

They also thought I would respond to this info by hugging them and crying in the bathroom, I'm pretty sure. They didn't expect me to flounce back into the theater and scream at Nick for what he'd done to me.

In the flickering light of the movie screen, he looked horrified. I held out hope that he would apologize and explain it was all a misunderstanding. Maybe I was a little starstruck after all. I couldn't believe the heir to the Krieger fortune had actually come on to me, even if his heart wasn't totally in it. He'd been so sweet to me for the past month. His kiss had felt real. I wanted him to like me for real.

After he'd gaped at me and I'd held my breath for a few moments, Gavin prompted him, "Well?"

Nick blinked and said in his faux-innocent voice, "I don't know what you're talking about, Hoyden. I mean, Hayden."

The theater burst into laughter, and *not* at Will Smith.

I stomped out. Liz and Chloe followed me, which sealed our friendship forever. Liz had told me what was up when no one else would, and Chloe was willing to leave her own intrigue behind, at least for the moment, to comfort me. We all trudged through the snow back to my house, made hot chocolate, and bitched about boys.

But the second the girls weren't looking, I escaped to my room, opened my dictionary, and looked up *hoyden*.

And here we still were. In the four years since, every date I'd been on, every party, every school field trip, I remembered on two levels: how it went with my boyfriend at the time, and what Nick was doing in the background, with another girl, on the other side of the room or the other end of the bus. In other words, I was addicted to Nick.

Now the stage was set. I'd been boyfriendless for about a week, ever since the Incident with Everett Walsh's mama. Nick had dumped Fiona Lewis last week after three dates, which was one more date than he usually lasted in a relationship. I'd been watching him in class: *check*. I'd been dreaming about him at night: *check check*. He'd flirted with me in class for the past four years, but he'd never sat down with me in the hall and treated me to the low rumbly voice and hinted about the Poser concert. Now I wished I could resist him, especially since I suspected he'd started the fire-crotch discussion in the lunchroom on Thursday just to see if he could seduce me after insulting me. Exactly how easy was Hayden, anyway? Nick's inquiring mind wanted to know.

I was afraid he was about to find out. Despite myself, and despite Liz's lectures about disrespect, my blood raced through my veins every time I thought about his hand on my hand in the hall (not to mention my thigh). I didn't think I would answer yes if I ran into him during winter break and he asked me out. I *couldn't* answer yes. Still, I hoped against hope that he'd ask the question.

But I also hoped he'd wait until after Tuesday, because he was distracting me enough already. I had more important things to worry about than Nick. Tuesday I had an appointment with a snowboard.

I inhaled through my nose and felt my lungs fill with air. My blood spread the life-giving oxygen throughout my body.

I exhaled through my mouth and felt gravity pull the energy from my heart down through my legs, through my boots and snowboard, through the snow, to the rocks below. I was one with the mountain.

"Good luck, Hayden!" Liz squealed. I opened my eyes to find her in the crowd of spectators behind the ropes on one side of the snowy course. I spotted her right away because she was bouncing. Her dark curls flew into the eyes of people around her.

Chloe put one hand on Liz's shoulder to hold her down. "Hush, Hayden's doing one of her yoga things. Let her concentrate."

No chance of that now. Bouncing friends tended to break my concentration. At least my brother, Josh, and his friends weren't around. I'd checked in on them between my events, and all four of them were kicking butt in the fifteen-and-under boys' competition held on another course at the same time as my eighteen-and-under girls' contest. If they'd been here, they wouldn't have squealed like Liz. They would have made up a rap with beatboxing and very embarrassing pushing-up-the-house hand movements.

It's Hayden
What?
She's a maven
What?
On the ski slope

What?
Give it up, folks
What?
Got the board slide
What?
Got the frontside
What?
Got the mad skillz
What?
For a sick ride
What?

It was sad that I could predict their lyrics. I boarded with them *way* too much.

The warning buzzer sounded. In a few seconds I would begin my slalom run in my first-ever official competition. I'd run hundreds of casual races against friends and challenged my brother to comps in the half-pipe, but nothing like this. It was so strange to stand on my board as a competitor rather than as a spectator. I recognized the sensation of adrenaline bubbling through my veins. I felt it every time I stood behind the ropes and watched someone else start a slalom. The feeling was magnified by a thousand now that I didn't have to picture myself in the racer's place. I was really here.

And all because of Liz and Chloe. They'd told me I was good enough to compete. When I'd seen this competition advertised, I'd ignored it as usual. They'd pointed out to me that this one had no jump, nothing higher than the half-pipe wall, so I had no excuse not to try it. I wouldn't have been here without them. I winked at them on the sidelines, lowered my goggles, and slid my board forward to the starting line.

Deep breath. One with the mountain.

As a final touch, I twisted one of my four-leaf clover earrings. My dad had given them to me the day I got the cast off my leg, as an amulet for better luck in the future.

And then I was flying down the slalom course, staying tight and tucking in, dodging around the gates as fast as possible. I knew my time would be good because I was in the zone. My body went on automatic, feeling exactly what to do when. I enjoyed the bright sparkling day, the white snow, the spectators in crazy-colored gear lining both sides of the course, the too-blue sky. There was no feeling in the world like this, having a body that worked.

Then I hit my usual snag. For most people, the hardest part of this course was the moguls. For me, it was the straightaway past Nick's house. His parents' mansion had an enormous front yard and a daunting front gate to scare away paparazzi and beggars. But the backyard bordered the slopes so the Kriegers could sit on their deck and watch the skiers. Every time I boarded past, no matter what trick I tried or who I was with, I glanced over at the deck while attempting to look like I wasn't looking, just in case Nick was there. He never was.

Until now. I thought I couldn't feel any more adrenaline than was already pumping through my body in my first boarding competition ever. Apparently my body kept some adrenaline in reserve, because I flushed with a new rush at the realization that he was watching me. I could *not* let Nick distract me. It probably wasn't even him but his father. Or was it? I'd seen Mr. Krieger at my parents' health club. He had blond hair, not dark hair like Nick. And why would Mr. Krieger wear Nick's puffy parka?

Okay, Nick probably didn't recognize me from a distance. Though my red hair and hot-pink snowboard made me hard to miss. Okay, he might recognize me, but he hadn't *meant* to watch me. He was out on the deck to fetch a few more logs for the fire inside. The fact that he'd come outside at exactly the moment I took my turn in the competition was just a big coincidence. An almost impossible coincidence, actually.

Believe it or not, every bit of this flashed through my mind in one second. My questions about Nick (*Is he looking at me? Is he looking at me on purpose? What does it meeeeeeeean???*) were familiar to me after four years. I had become very efficient. I thought them and then pushed them to the back of my mind before they made me fall down. I was one with the mountain. My body worked perfectly. I skimmed around the gates, torn between excitement that I could see the finish line and disappointment that I'd finished so fast. I always hated for a run to end.

I made a wide circle to slow down and skidded to a stop. Almost before the final curtain of snow I'd kicked up had fallen out of the sky, I was squinting at my time on the scoreboard.

"Holy shit," I whispered. I was in the lead! Three chicks waited to take their turns, but I was so far ahead of them after my half-pipe score, they'd have to really hightail it down the mountain to beat my overall score now.

What if I *won*? I'd dreamed about placing, but I'd never expected to *win*!

And then, so predictably that I wanted to hold myself down and rub my face with snow as punishment, I glanced way up the slope at Nick's deck to see if he was still watching me.

He was gone.

And *then* I heard the cheers and applause of the spectators for me, with Liz and Chloe's screams ringing above the noise even though they were near the top of the course, easing their way down through the crowd and the snow. I turned away from Nick's empty deck, unlatched my boots from my board, and hiked over to the sidelines to meet the girls. I had two friends who I knew for sure had come out to support me, and who weren't the least bit embarrassed to let everyone know it. They were the ones who were really important.

Besides, if I won this competition, I would be in big trouble, and Nick Krieger would be the least of my worries.

"So, what's next?" Liz asked the instant she plopped down beside me on the seat of the bus. "Are you registering tomorrow for that amateur comp in Aspen a couple of weeks from now?"

I'd been afraid of this. After the competition, Chloe had walked back to her parents' hotel. The bus would wind through the snowy streets from the ski resort to my house and then to Liz's. This ten-minute ride was my only chance to convince Liz to drop this idea of pushing me into more competitions, before she dragged Chloe onto the bandwagon with her.

I'd been so thrilled when Josh won third place in his boys' division. And I was absolutely ecstatic when the other times in my girls' division came in and I found out I'd WON THE WHOLE SHEBANG! It still hadn't quite sunk in. And now it never would. Because almost the second I realized I'd won, I started worrying about what came now.

"We already checked the Aspen contest," I reminded Liz, careful to keep my voice even. "It requires a big air event."

Liz spoke carefully too, using the fingertip of her glove to trace graffiti on the back of the bus seat, rather than looking at me. "Chloe and I thought that after you won the competition today—and we knew you would—you'd realize how good you are, and you'd start entering everything in sight."

"You and Chloe thought wrong." I stared past Liz's dark curly hair, out the bus window so streaked with salt that shops flashing by outside were just blurs of color.

"Let me put it this way," Liz said, looking directly at me now. "What am I doing after high school?"

"Getting a bachelor's in English from the University of Colorado and a master's in library science from the University of Denver," I recited. Liz and Chloe both had been very consistent in their career plans since I'd known them.

"And what's Chloe doing?" Liz prompted me.

"Going to Georgetown and getting into politics."

"And what are you doing?"

"Boarding," I muttered. I should have seen this convo coming, and now she'd backed me into a corner, even though I was sitting on the aisle.

"Unless you're planning on living with your parents forever, how are you going to board all day when you haven't gone pro? And how are you going pro when you won't enter any competitions to get there?"

She was right, of course. I'd known I would have to face this reality sooner or later. I wanted it to be later, after this year's snow season was over.

She persisted. "The prize for winning first place in the competition is lessons with Daisy Delaney, right?"

"Right." I felt myself grinning all over again at the thought. Daisy Delaney held a silver medal in the Olympics, an X Games title, and two world championships in women's snowboarding. Last December I got a big head after landing the 900, and I called the office of the Aspen slopes where she worked to inquire about lessons. I didn't want to miss an opportunity to develop in the sport if lessons with this stellar athlete were in my reach.

They weren't. The waiting list for lessons with her was three years long. And the cost was out of my league. But now I'd won this very prize: ten lessons with her.

"This is your opportunity to impress someone who can pull strings for you," Liz said. "I've heard of three Colorado girls Daisy Delaney's coached who've gone pro. But potential sponsors will want to photograph you snowboarding off a cliff. And after Daisy Delaney spends the morning drilling you on spins, she'll expect the two of you to leave the main slopes and shred the back bowls. You're not going to tell her, 'No thanks, I don't go off cliffs. Don't bother coaching me in slopestyle or big air, either, because I don't board off anything higher than my own head.'"

Liz was mocking me. *Liz*, who never said an unkind thing to anyone, was mocking *me*, one of her best friends! I gazed reprovingly at her and hoped my hurt look would shock her into an apology.

She folded her arms as best she could in her thick coat, and she raised her eyebrows at me under her dark curls and blue knitted hat. She was right again. Fear of heights would be a little hard to explain to a snowboarding coach who might want to take a chance on me.

I just didn't want to hear it.

The bus squealed to a stop, which snapped us out of our stare-down. We both glanced around and realized we'd reached my street. "We'll continue this discussion tonight," she told me in an authoritative voice, as if I didn't already have a mother.

"Give it a rest, would you, Liz?" I wailed. "I appreciate what you're doing, I really do. But Chloe invited us over tonight so we can celebrate my win. At least let me enjoy the thrill of victory, okay? We can talk about how it's ruined my life tomorrow."

As I stood, I saw Josh crouched in the seat behind us. I'd thought he'd sat in the back of the bus. Maybe he had, but then he'd worked his way up the aisle for eavesdropping. When we locked eyes and he realized he was busted, he dashed past me down the aisle as best he could in snowboarding boots and disappeared through the door.

"Oh God, there's been a security breach," I gasped to Liz. "See you tonight."

"See you," she sang after me, her authoritative tone totally gone. In fact, she sounded eager and giddy, just as she and Chloe had last Friday in the hall when we'd discussed Nick. I had a feeling she and Chloe were not going to leave my fear of heights alone.

And neither was Josh. I did my best to dash after him, clunking down the bus stairs into the crisp air. He'd already pulled his snowboard out of the rack on the side of the bus and was hiking up the icy sidewalk. I slid my own board from the rack and chased him. "Hey!" I hollered. "James Bond! What's the big idea?"

He stopped on the slick sidewalk and whirled around to face me. "You're supposed to take me with you," he snarled.

"Pardon?" I played dumb to put off the inevitable, because I had a good idea what he meant.

"That's what siblings do for each other, like Elijah and Hannah Teter, and Molly and Mason Aguirre. You're supposed to make it as a pro snowboarder, then reach back and help me do the same."

I stared blankly at him, waiting for him to acknowledge the irony of *him* scolding *me*, when I was older than him. I moved closer so I could stare down my nose at him. This didn't work. He was almost as tall as me. He'd shot up a few inches lately and was about to catch up to me. And he was standing above me on the sloped sidewalk.

His dark eyes were shaped like mine. He had a scattering of freckles like I did, but not as prominent, even though I tried to even mine out with makeup. And he used to have hair almost as bright red as mine, but now his hair was dark brown. Flashes of red echoed in the strands only when he moved his head in the sunlight reflecting off the snowdrifts in our neighbors' yards. He'd outgrown his red hair as easily as his peanut allergy. He actually wasn't bad-looking. Eventually he might even land his crush, Gavin's sister Tia. My hair, in contrast, was as red as the day I was born. As red as Shaun White's, the greatest snowboarder ever. Strangers on the slopes were always calling to me that I could be his little sister.

But I wasn't. "I'm no Hannah Teter," I insisted, "or Molly Aguirre, either."

"You *could* be," Josh insisted. "You're supposed to have a fear of heights for a little while after you break your leg. You're not supposed to have it *four years* after you start snowboarding. And you definitely can't let it ruin your chance of impressing Daisy Delaney. I'm not going to let you." He spun on the ice and stomped up the sidewalk again, dragging his board.

"What are you going to do, *tell* on me because I won a snowboarding contest?"

"That's exactly what I'm going to do," he called haughtily over his shoulder.

Uh-oh. I definitely did not want my parents butting into my business, especially not about this. "You had better not!" I shouted after him. "Do you hear me, O'Malley? I will tell Gavin's sister you slept with a stuffed bunny rabbit until you were in middle school, so help me God!"

Josh dropped his board, slid down to me, and clamped his hand over my mouth. "Shhhh! Mr. Big Ears was very special."

It took me a full ten seconds to push Josh off me. I hoped no more buses passed by, because the tourists inside would probably grip the poles in the middle of the bus and edge a bit farther from the crazy locals. Last winter I would have beat Josh away with no problem. He was growing fast. I wouldn't be able to overpower him much longer, so we needed to solve this issue before then.

Avoidance was so much easier. I'd had enough of him and Liz both dragging me down in the midst of my happy afternoon. "Don't tell them," I said again between gasps. I bent his fingers backward to make him let me go.

"Ow!" he barked, rubbing his fingers, face bright red underneath his freckles. I shouldn't have bent his fingers back. This was another thing Josh and I had in common: a bad temper. We might seem good-natured to the point of ditzy, but push us too far and we'd snap. I was using yoga to work on this. Judging from our current convo, Josh was not.

He bent to snag his board and jogged up the slippery slope. He wanted to beat me home. What would he tell Mom when he got there?

"Josh!" I shouted, jogging after him as best I could. I tripped over my board and lost my grip. It zipped back down the sidewalk, past two houses, and crashed into a mailbox. At least I knew I'd done a good job of waxing it last night. I trotted after it and called pitifully to Josh as I picked it up. "Little bro, I love you so much!"

Way up the hill, he disappeared inside our house.

1440

(fôr tĕn 'fôr tĕ) *n.* **1.** a quadruple spin, nearly impossible to pull off **2.** Hayden's fear of heights, nearly impossible to hide

When I finally made it into the mudroom, panting with exertion and hot under five layers of clothing, Josh had only pulled off his boots. He sat on the bench and playfully grabbed at Doofus's snout. He hadn't spilled anything to Mom yet. Whew.

I extracted myself from my parka. "You are, seriously, my favorite brother."

Josh scratched Doofus's ears and seemed to be telling the dog rather than me, "I'm your *only* brother. And you bent my fingers back and hurt them." He poked out his bottom lip.

"I will kiss your fingers and make them better, kissy kissy," I threatened him. That got him up pretty quickly. He kicked off the rest of his snow clothes and skidded into the kitchen in his long johns and socks. I stripped down to my long johns, too—tripped over Doofus—and scrambled after Josh, angry already about what he might tell Mom, depending on how mischievous he felt.

Mom was giving him a big hug, wearing her yoga leotard from work, holding the large kitchen knife she'd just been chopping dinner with. If they weren't my family I might have been frightened. "Well, how'd you do?" she asked, pulling back to look him in the face.

"I won third place in the junior boys' division!" Josh exclaimed with wide, innocent eyes like an adorable woodland creature in a Disney cartoon. I wondered what he was up to. I wanted to slap him. But then I would be forced to explain to my mom why I'd slapped the adorable woodland creature.

"That's great, honey!" She wrapped him in another hug. He was facing me now. He gave me a wink and a thumbs-up. Ugh!

Mom eased out of the hug with him but kept her hands on his shoulders. "Why are you acting like a parody of yourself?" she asked him.

Josh blinked at her. "That's just a function of being a teenager. I feel so empty inside. What's for dinner?" He slipped out from under her hands and wandered to the refrigerator.

Mom turned to me, and the big grin she'd worn for Josh sagged a little. She didn't expect much from my first snowboard competition. "And how'd you do, honey?"

"I did okay."

"I'll give you five seconds," Josh called from behind the refrigerator door.

Mom looked at Josh, then back at me. "What? What is it?"

I looked into her eyes, dark like Josh's and mine. I took in her long red hair tamed into a braid down her back, her freckles that made her look younger than forty-six. At least, I thought so, and I hoped so, because clearly I was going to look just like her. Maybe she'd take my side, whatever Josh was about to tell her. She knew how hard my injury had been on me.

"Actually . . . ," I said slowly.

With each of my syllables, her right eyebrow arched higher.

"I won," I finished.

"Oh my God, that's great, you won!" With her braid bouncing as she jumped up and down, she looked and sounded a lot like Liz—except for, you know, the knife. "That means you're a lot better at snowboarding than I thought! You've finally gotten over your fear of heights! And—wait a minute—why didn't you want to tell me?" Abruptly she stopped jumping. "What's the prize?"

Josh walked over with a stalk of celery sticking out of his mouth. He took the knife from Mom's hand and set it on the counter. Then he said around the celery, "Lessons with Daisy Delaney."

"Daisy Delaney!" Mom gasped. "Hayden! I am old and out of it, as you're so fond of telling me, but even *I* know who Daisy Delaney is. That's some prize!"

"But guess what?" Josh went on, removing the celery from his mouth so he could rub this in as thoroughly as possible. "Hayden's been avoiding comps all this time because they have jumps in them. Her fear of heights is so bad that Daisy Delaney's going to think she's a beginner."

Mom turned back to me, and her other eyebrow went up. "Really?"

"She won't set foot on the gondola," Josh blathered on. "She won't even get on the regular ski lifts that go too high off the ground. She sticks to the low, short lifts, which means she's been boarding for four years and she's never even seen half the mountain."

"That half of the mountain is nothing but jumps and cliffs. I don't *want* to see it," I insisted.

"This is bullshit!" Josh shouted over me. "Mom, she's supposed to take me with her. Like Elijah and Hannah Teter. Like Molly and Mason Aguirre."

"Who?" Mom shouted back.

"One sibling goes pro and helps the other along." Josh gestured dramatically with the celery. "You could have *two* pro snowboarders in the family. We would buy you a new minivan. You want a new minivan, don't you?"

"Tempting," Mom told him drily. She turned and gave me a long look. "Well, Hayden? You've said you want to become a professional snowboarder, but your father and I assumed you wouldn't be able to do that because of your fear of heights. We thought eventually you'd give up, go to college, and major in . . ." Her voice trailed off.

And no wonder. Currently I had a C in chemistry, a C in history, and a D in algebra. Ms. Abernathy wasn't the only teacher sending me out in the hall for talking.

"But if you're good enough to win a contest in Snowfall," Mom went on, "and you have a foot in the door with Daisy Delaney, you have as good a chance of going pro as anybody. Do you want help getting over your fear of heights? We could take you to the doctor—"

"Yeah, that's just what I need, to miss my days snowboarding so I can sit in some doctor's office and go through more rehab." My voice rose and thinned until it petered out at the end, and *rehab* was a whisper. My fear of doctors might actually have been worse than my fear of heights, judging from my shallow breaths.

Mom must have noticed, because she put her hand on my shoulder. "Or a counselor of some kind?"

"Absolutely not."

"Don't let her get away with this." Josh pointed at my mother with the celery. "She is a foolish, foolish young girl."

Mom rolled her eyes at Josh. "Lay off her, would you? If she doesn't want help with her phobia, she'll work through it on her own, or she won't go pro. It's not something we can decide for her. Get your own lessons with Daisy Delaney. I'm going to call your father and tell him the good news. Where's my phone?" She padded out of the kitchen in her bare feet, braid swinging gently against her back. Then there was a screech and a dog yelp. She must have tripped over Doofus lying on the floor in the living room. "I'm okay!" she called.

I was holding my breath. When I realized this and forced myself to breathe again, I smelled smoke. Mom had left dinner burning. I dashed to the stove to stir the tofu.

I didn't look at Josh, but out of the corner of my eye I could see him standing at the counter, stuffing his face with handfuls of organic rice crisps out of the bag. Finally I said, "You owe me."

"I don't owe you anything." He sidled over and tried to stick a rice crisp in my ear. "You're supposed to take me with you. That's what siblings do."

I batted his hand away and shook the tofu-y spatula at him. "If I ever do go pro, I have no obligation to take you with me. Younger siblings have to earn that kind of favor. You *told* on me for winning a contest, you ass! You owe me. And you know what I want in return."

He scowled at me. "Not the pants."

I nodded gravely. "Give me your pants."

These were no magical traveling pants. They were only my little brother's broken-in jeans that fit me perfectly and that he almost never let me wear. I'd even tried on the identical size and style at the store, but they weren't the same.

He knew how I loved them, too, so he sabotaged them just to irk me. Once he tore a hole in the butt so my panties would show. This might have been an accident, but I was pretty sure the edges of the hole were cut, not frayed. I got revenge on him by patching up the hole with a little red heart. Infuriatingly, he wore them like that out in public, as if I didn't have enough social problems without a little brother with hearts sewn onto his behind.

This time, as I stood in my bedroom and looked the jeans over, just in case, before pulling them on, I saw that he'd written BOY TOY in big block letters across the butt in permanent marker, right next to the heart patch. Never mind that *he* would have to wear them to school like that. It was worth it to him if he embarrassed *me*. Gah, he might have made it to the eighth grade, but he was still such a little brother! When we were fifty he'd still be stuffing my snow boots with wet macaroni.

But I had to wear the jeans tonight while I had the chance, and the marker would probably take years to wash out. That was okay. I enjoyed feeling like I looked good, but I wouldn't be trying to impress anyone with my outfit tonight. For winning the competition, Chloe and Liz were throwing me a "party" at Chloe's parents' hotel. What this really meant was that Chloe would suck face with Gavin, Liz would suck face with Davis, and I would keep the onion dip company. No one would notice my BOY TOY butt. It was sweet of Chloe and Liz to *intend* to celebrate my win and show me a good time, even if I knew it wouldn't work out that way.

So after dinner I rode the bus back into town, waved to

the doorman at the front entrance of the hotel, and made my way downstairs into the kitchen adjoining the banquet room. A beautiful cake frosted with CONGRATULATIONS HAYDEN! waited on the counter, and a chick wailed lonely emo lyrics from the stereo. But the room was empty.

"Hello?" I called, my voice echoing above the music.

There was a scream, and then a door opened. Chloe stepped out of the pantry, smoothing her hands through her mussed blond hair. "Hey girl! Oh my God, you look so awesome in those jeans!"

"Thanks. Josh let me borrow them. You'll never see them again unless I find something else to coerce him with, but it'll be two years before he's old enough to drive down to Denver and buy crack."

"I'm serious." She looked me up and down. "You could be a model."

"Selling what? Hamburgers, like the Wendy's girl? I have red hair and freckles."

"Think about Lindsay Lohan."

"I'd rather not," I muttered as Chloe turned me around backward and lifted up my coat to admire my ass.

Then she gasped. "Oh my God, 'boy toy'?"

"That's me, fast and loose." This came out sounding more wistful than I'd intended, and I hoped she didn't guess I was thinking about Nick. "Speaking of which, I take it you and Gavin are rearranging the soup cans?" I nodded toward the pantry.

"Ah . . . yeah." Her cheeks tinged pink. "We're almost through with our inventory."

"You *are*?" I exclaimed.

"I mean, that didn't come out right." She blushed more deeply. It was hilarious to see Chloe flustered, which happened only once a year or so. She must *really* like Gavin, which I still found bizarre.

"We'll be out in a sec," she said. "Liz and Davis are in the hot tub."

They certainly were. The back of the kitchen was a wall of windows overlooking the hotel's heated pool and hot tub. Steam rose from the water and wisped into the night. Over Chloe's shoulder I could see Liz and Davis deep in the hot tub, seeking refuge from the frigid winter air, kissing slowly. I didn't have the heart to interrupt. Knowing them, it had taken them half an hour to work up the courage to touch each other at all.

"No hurry." I winked to show Chloe my support for taking inventory with Gavin. It was very important that a winter resort hotel never run out of soup. She backed into the pantry and closed the door.

I examined my cake on the counter again. CONGRATULA-TIONS HAYDEN! The only thing worse than being abandoned at my own victory party was letting my friends know I cared about this, and making them feel bad about it so they stayed with me instead of stealing the alone-time they really wanted with their boyfriends. You know what it was like? It was exactly like being grateful to my friends in Tennessee for continuing to hang out with me when I was in a wheelchair, but knowing all along that they'd rather ditch me.

I missed Everett Walsh for the first time since we'd broken up last week.

Suddenly I realized I was staring at Liz and Davis again, his dark hand stroking her porcelain complexion. Okay, I would *not* stare at my friends making out like I was love-starved. From the hot tub my gaze traveled up, over the faux-rustic shops of downtown Snowfall and the white lights strung in the bare trees. The dark mountain looming over the town was visible in the night only because starlight reflected on the snowy slopes. I'd always regarded that mountain as my friend. It had given me years of highs induced by sun and speed. It had helped me regain so much of the confidence I'd lost when I'd broken my leg. Tonight, for the first time ever, the mountain looked cold and menacing. I shivered.

I knew one way to warm up, besides the hot tub and the pool. I hurried to the locker room to change into the bikini and flip-flops I'd brought to enjoy the hotel amenities. Then I dashed back through the cold banquet room. The door into the hallway squealed, letting anyone in the sauna know I was coming.

A few times over the years, Chloe and I had surprised hotel guests in compromising situations in the sauna. Tonight I might walk in on a beer-fueled boys' night out for a group of middle-aged men, in which case I would make an excuse and back out of the sauna. But now that the hallway door had developed this squeak, at least I knew I wouldn't interrupt folks in the middle of something they shouldn't be doing in a public place.

As I pushed open the sauna door and stepped into the eucalyptus-scented steam, I saw I wouldn't be alone. The other occupant had heard me coming and was wrapping his towel more modestly around his bathing suit. I could still back out of the small, dark space. I hesitated to slide onto the bench across from him until I got a good look at him.

I squinted through the mist and finally realized it was—"Nick! I mean, Ex!"

"Hayden! I mean, Hoyden!" He sounded as surprised to see me as I was to see him. His eyes slid to my bare tummy. "You have a body like a rock."

Right back at ya, I could have said. I'd known Nick

was built. His family had a membership at my parents' health club, and sometimes he came in to lift weights. His favorites were the arm curl machine and the abdominal machine, where he would lift hard for long minutes and then fight for a few last painful crunches. Not that I made a habit of standing there and staring at him as he worked out. That would be creepy. I watched him on the surveillance cameras behind the reception desk.

Even though he never worked out with his shirt off, I could have predicted that what I saw now had been hiding under his tee: six-pack abs with beads of sweat sliding down them, like a disembodied torso in a workout machine infomercial. But I was surprised at how thin he was. There wasn't an ounce of fat on him anywhere. I watched the muscles of his upper arms move underneath his skin as he leaned forward and put his hands on his knees. I had the strange sensation I was seeing a different person, a real person, rather than the model-handsome perfection who had sashayed his way through my school and my fantasies for the last four years. Suddenly he was less a superhero and more a boy my age, caught off guard in the sauna.

I liked this Nick even better.

And *he* approved of *my* body, too.

Or did he? Did a girl want to be a rock? Was this a compliment? I draped my towel across the bench opposite him and sat down. "What kind of rock?" I asked casually. "Granite is rough. Mica is shiny and flaky." Whoops. I was feeding him jokes. I might as well have sat there and insulted myself. Nick didn't even need to participate.

Both of those sound right, he would have said if we were trading insults across the chemistry classroom. Instead he said, "Come over here and give me a closer look."

Nick was hot, and his voice was honey. We were alone in a cloud of steam. I wanted so badly to close the five feet of space between us by hopping down from my bench and jumping onto his.

But there was no way. That's what I'd do if I were still the new girl at school who wasn't wise to him yet. I said, "You're the one who wants the look. *You* come over *here.*"

His gaze slid up my body to my face. His eyes locked with mine and held me there. Would he give in to this battle of wills? Or did he figure that if it led to contact with a girl, he always won?

Yeah, he sure was acting like he had the upper hand. Still holding me in place with his eyes, slowly he stepped down from his bench. He stepped up onto my bench and settled beside me on my towel. And he slid one hand onto the bare skin of my tummy.

I tried not to flinch. I told myself he didn't mean anything by it—he was just the school's biggest flirt—so there was no reason to make him unhand me. In fact, I'd found through experience that people who didn't flinch seemed to fare better with Nick, because he wasn't sure what to do with them. And I *had* told him to come over here.

Besides, it was just my tummy, my innocent tummy that I showed to the general public every summer at the pool. But Nick had never touched my bare tummy before, and my body screamed at me to *pay attention, this was serious,* just as when he'd touched my bare hip in the school hall last Friday. However dark and dangerous I'd considered Nick before, he was about to get a lot worse.

Or better. "The smooth white stone that statues are carved from," he clarified, brushing his warm fingertips across my skin. "Marble."

I did my best to keep my tummy absolutely still so he wouldn't feel how fast I was breathing. This required me to take very small breaths of heavy hot sauna air through my nose. No wonder what I said next sounded strained: "Marble? With black veins? Sounds attractive."

He smiled a little. "Statues don't talk."

"Yeah, I wasn't buying this sexy rock metaphor anyway."

His eyebrows went up and his face opened into that *who, me?* innocent expression of his, even as his pointer finger dipped inside my belly button. "I'm trying to be nice to you."

"I can tell." Something needed to be done about this belly button issue. I didn't push his hand away because . . . well . . . I wanted it there. But I couldn't just leave it there without acknowledging it, either. That would show weakness, telling Nick he could do whatever he wanted with me and I would just sit there and take it. That would be every girl he'd ever dated. Instead, I put my hand on top of his and pressed gently, like I approved.

Which I did.

I think I surprised him. Oooh, I *loved* this! His nostrils flared a little, and his big hand under my hand spread all the way across my tummy, stroking there slowly. Something was definitely going to happen, and I was going to let it.

But while he was off balance, I needed information from him. Now that I'd gotten over the surprise of seeing him at Chloe's hotel, it occurred to me just how out of place he was. "What are you doing here?"

"Chloe invited me."

"She *did*?" I squeaked. I hoped he didn't assume I'd put her up to it. I *knew* I couldn't trust Chloe and Liz to quit the Cupid business!

For once, being a very bad actress served me well. Nick could see I was floored by this info. He explained, "Chloe asked Gavin to invite me to your victory party. Didn't they tell you?"

"I didn't see Gavin," I said slowly, still puzzling this out. "I only talked to Chloe for a minute. I don't think they know you're here."

"Maybe they don't," he admitted. "I came in and saw Davis and Liz making out in the hot tub, and I heard these groans coming from the pantry. What are Gavin and Chloe doing in there anyway?" he asked in his *I'm so innocent* voice.

I laughed. "Chloe said they were taking inventory."

Nick chuckled. "Gavin wishes. Last I heard, he had no idea how many boxes of cereal were in that pantry."

"Oh!" I gave him a little shove that would have been playful if we'd been in the school hall. But here, alone in the sauna, it was my hand on his hard bare chest. I swallowed and tried to pretend I shoved half-naked boys in the sauna every day of the week. "You guys have big mouths."

"Like Chloe didn't tell you every move Gavin tried to make on her while they watched basketball on TV at his house last night. Or *didn't* watch basketball."

He had me there.

"So, Gavin and Chloe are otherwise occupied," Nick mused. "Davis and Liz are in the hot tub. You and I are alone. We might as well make the best of it."

As if I weren't hot enough already, I felt the heat rising through me, burning every inch of my skin. I blushed so hard that my face burned at the thought that my fantasies for four years, and specifically my dreams since last Friday in the hall, were about to come true.

A small space had opened between us when I'd shoved him. Now he closed that space again. His long, muscular leg touched my leg inch for inch—stuck to it, in fact, in the shadowy wet room. His long fingers found my bare tummy again and splayed wide across it, with his hot palm centered on my belly button.

"I love saunas, don't you?" he purred, leaning close to my face. "The heat." A lock of his dark hair stuck to my wet cheek. "The steam."

My heart knocked so hard against my chest that I could hardly stand it. "The scent of eucalyptus," I suggested before I thought about whether this added to the romance of the situation. "Smells like a bottle of my granddaddy's Old Spice that's been fermenting in his attic since 1969." I cringed. I just couldn't leave it alone and enjoy the moment, could I?

Nick pressed his lips together to keep from laughing. He nodded sagely. "I'll never think about this scent quite the same way, that's for sure." But Nick had a one-track mind, and even my lame jokes couldn't distract him. One of his hands still moved on my tummy. The other picked up my hand and moved it to his thigh.

Talk about a body like a rock.

I wanted to do this—had wanted it forever—but somehow

I had thought there would be more preamble to it, more than fifteen minutes of flirting in the school hall. Even though I'd admittedly accepted every advance he made on me, picking up my hand and putting it on his thigh seemed mighty forward of him. I didn't take the radical step of *removing* my hand, but I did open my mouth to act all indignant.

He put two fingers to my lips to stop me from talking. He knew me pretty well. His mouth close to my ear, he growled, "You know, you and I *are* exes."

"So?" I asked around his fingers. My skin tingled with excitement, or possibly eucalyptus poisoning.

He leaned so close, I could feel his breath on my cheek, cool compared with the hot air. "If we weren't exes," he whispered, "it might be different. But we are. We won't do anything we haven't done before. What could it hurt?" His dark eyes looked deep into mine for a few more seconds. Slowly he peeled his fingers away from my lips like he was afraid of what would escape my mouth.

What came to mind: *Oooh, yes, please, thank you.* But I couldn't let him know how much I wanted this. Sarcasm, I needed some sarcasm. "What a bunch of bull," I breathed. "Haven't you learned *anything* since the seventh grade?"

"One way to find out," he purred, moving in. He slipped his hand around the back of my neck, and then—

invert

('in vərt) *n.* **1.** a handstand on the lip of the half-pipe course **2.** Hayden turning the tables on Nick

—I hesitated.

I *never* hesitated. Hesitating in the slalom could cost me the race. Hesitating in the half-pipe could earn me a concussion. Hesitating on a jump could get me killed—and since I did have a tendency to hesitate there, I did not go off jumps.

And I knew better than to hesitate with Nick. That

would show weakness, and he would swoop in and take advantage of me. Better to keep him off guard if I could.

Yet here we were, inches away from each other in the hot shadowy sauna, breathing hard, looking into each other's eyes, with my hand on his chest to keep him from coming any closer. He glanced to my lips, then focused on my eyes again, genuinely perplexed. Like he wasn't Nick at all but that boy my age, someone without filthy rich parents, someone unsure and terrified of messing this up.

Someone like me. I was terrified of messing this up, too. Which was exactly why I held him off. I *wanted* to believe he was unsure and vulnerable like me. But those old suspicions about Nick resurfaced. I'd waited too long for this, and I wanted to make sure we were doing it right.

"What's up?" he prompted me, cluing me in that I'd guessed correctly about him. Not a gentle *What's the matter, dear Hayden?* but a sharp *What's up?* like a boy growing impatient while bowling a girl over.

"Uh, I don't know," I stammered. "I just don't get a good vibe about this."

"You don't get a good *vibe?*" Although Nick controlled his emotions carefully, I could tell he was mad. This frightened me a little. I held the dubious honor of being the one person who could make cool, collected Nick lose his temper.

I wanted to be honest with him and give good reasons

for balking, so I wouldn't hurt his feelings just in case he was being straight with me after all. I said slowly, "Well, for starters, from some of the things you said in the hall on Friday, I was thinking you might ask me to the Poser concert, but you haven't said another word about it."

I watched him closely as I said this. He watched me too, his dark eyes giving away nothing but anger.

I swallowed. "You've said Chloe invited you here for my victory party. I saw you out on your deck during the competition, so I know you remembered it was going on. But you haven't asked me anything about the contest, either."

His lips parted. I watched his soft lips (at least, I remembered them from seventh grade as soft) and waited for him to explain himself. But after a moment he closed his mouth again, and his dark eyes glinted harder.

I had desperately wanted to be wrong about Nick. I had wished he honestly liked me. But his silence and his anger were convincing me otherwise. That made *me* angry. And when I got angry, I was anything but silent.

"You've pretty much ignored me for the past four years, except to insult me or to throw something at me. Then suddenly you want to make out just when our friends get together? You don't act like you're very fond of me. You act like I'm convenient. You would have made out with any chick you happened upon in the sauna, from the hotel maid to the lady in room 3B. I'm not sure I *do* want to end our trial separation. We have irreconcilable differences." By the time I got all of this out, I was shouting at him. I'd known I was angry at him, but I hadn't realized I'd been storing up *that* much resentment for four years.

Apparently, neither had he. His hand suddenly tensed on my tummy, and I suppressed the urge to say *oof*. Nick and I had been pressing into each other on the bench, our thighs touching. Our heads were coming closer together with every word we uttered. If someone had interrupted us just then (which they wouldn't, because we would hear the hall door squeak first), they would think we were about to kiss. They would never understand how much tension rode on every word as Nick looked into my eyes and the following words slid out of his mouth and straight into my heart like slivers of glass: "You have a lot of freaking nerve." He sat back against the wooden wall, sliding his hand off my tummy and his thigh out from under my hand (nooooo!).

Clearly I couldn't read Nick as well as I'd thought. I hadn't wanted to make him angry if he really did care about me. I'd only wanted him to get his hands off me if I didn't mean anything to him. Now that it appeared I *did* mean something, and I'd hurt his feelings, my goal now was to get his hands back *on* me. "I'm not trying to make you mad," I said quickly. "I'm not even saying I'm right. This just seems very sudden, and I wanted to talk about it with you a little mo—"

"Forget it, Hayden." His skin glowed with sweat in the low light of the sauna, and his dark hair stuck to his forehead in wet black wisps. He breathed hard like the football team had just given him a good workout. Or like *I* had. And he looked like I'd slapped him.

But even without the hurt expression on his handsome face, I would have known I'd seriously wounded him because he called me *Hayden* instead of *Hoyden*. Like my mother using my full name, Hayden Christine O'Malley, it meant I was in big trouble.

He went on, "I can't believe you would say something like that to me." He folded his big arms on his bare chest. "I mean, even if you don't care about *me*, I can't believe you would be that much of a bitch to *anyone*. That's just cruel."

The thing to do then was to make a snappy comeback and stomp out of the sauna, never to return. I got called the B-word a lot, undeservedly in my opinion, just because I had red hair and I said what I thought, perhaps a tad too loudly.

But all I could do was sit there on the bench, staring at Nick with my mouth open and tears in my eyes. I couldn't get over the feeling of seeing him for the first time tonight as younger and vulnerable, more like me. It hurt that I had hurt him. It hurt more that he had hurt me back.

Outside the sauna, the hall door squealed open. Someone was coming.

"Great," I breathed. Chloe had invited Nick over here tonight because he'd held my hand in the hall and she'd thought there was more to come. Even once I explained to Chloe that we officially hated each other now and that nothing had happened between us, Nick and I would not live down getting caught together in the sauna. All my friends would tease me about Nick even more, and I would *never* be able to get him off my mind.

Strangely, Nick didn't seem the least bit concerned about Gavin catching us and teasing us in class forevermore. He still stared at me like I'd slapped him. Okay, I'd slapped him a lot in class over the years, when he had shot spitballs at me or tried to write his name on my arm. This time he stared at me like I'd slapped him when he didn't deserve it.

The sauna door swung open. "*There* you are," Chloe exclaimed at me with her fists on her hips. Her eyes slid to Nick.

Gavin appeared over her shoulder. "And there *you* are," he called to Nick. His eyes slid to me.

Liz and Davis crowded the doorway, too. All four of them now wore bathing suits, which meant they'd intended to join us in the sauna. Suddenly it was way too hot and I couldn't breathe.

"God, it's like a *sauna* in here," I muttered at the same time Nick mumbled, "I was just leaving. This place is full of hot air." Too late I realized we were pushing through our friends in the doorway at the same time. We couldn't have acted more guilty.

I reached the hallway free and clear. Someone big padded behind me—Nick, I assumed—but I didn't look back. I burst through the squealing door, slipped into the women's locker room, and rushed under a cold shower with my bikini still on. "Eek!" Maybe if I stood there long enough, the lingering lust I felt for Nick would wash away, along with the regret that we hadn't kissed in the sauna.

The cold water bouncing off my skull only gave me a headache. I'd rejected Nick, yes. But the more I thought about it, the more his reaction seemed completely uncalled-for. I'd been called the B-word before, but never by Nick.

I turned off the water and pushed through the door on the opposite side of the locker room, into the cold night. I dashed for the heated pool, jumping in without looking first to see who I'd be sharing it with. Of course, Nick sat alone on the submerged stairs with his elbows behind him on the wall, watching me as I came up for air. Everyone else must be inside.

He didn't take the opportunity to leap across the pool and push me under, as he usually would have. He just stared me down, frowning, and flicked his wet hair out of his eyes with his pinkie. When I was little I'd spent a lot of time at the Tennessee Aquarium in Chattanooga. Now it was like Nick and I were separated by one of those foot-thick walls of specially tempered glass. We could see each other. We could even long for each other. But even if we both had put our hands up to the glass, we could never have touched. The glass between us was smooth and cold.

"Congratulations to you," the voices of the others sang from behind the slowly moving door. Gavin held it open for Chloe, who paraded out with the cake, and Liz, who carried paper plates and forks and napkins. As soon as everyone was clear of the door, Gavin and Davis made a run for the pool and jumped in to avoid the frigid air just like I had, but the girls sang on. "Congratulations, dear Hayden, congratulations to you!"

Liz's dark hair had kinked into tight curls from the hot tub, and Chloe had carefully pinned up her long blond hair to keep it from getting wet in the pool. Chloe and Liz looked so adorable in their own ways, and so happy to be celebrating my victory, that I remembered for the first time in an hour this night was for *me*, not them, and definitely not Nick. I should enjoy it. Like Josh had warned me, my little baby snowboarding career might end in a stupendous crash when I took my first lesson with Daisy Delaney and she discovered I was afraid of heights. This night was all I knew I had.

"Thank y'all so much," I said, meaning it. I ignored Gavin echoing *y'all*, making fun of my Tennessee accent. I also ignored the fact that Nick was *not* echoing *y'all* like he usually would.

"You're-hur-hur welcome," Chloe said, teeth chattering as she set down the cake at the edge of the pool. Liz set down the plates, too. They waded into the pool, cut the cake from there, and passed around big slices. White cake with white icing, a pure sugar rush—not something I normally would have included in my health-conscious diet, but exactly what I needed when, frankly, this strange episode with Nick had gotten me down.

Liz handed me a plate, careful not to drip pool water on it. I was just taking my first bite when Nick spoke to me in a voice so kind, I knew something ugly was coming. "So, Hayden. What was your time on the slalom?"

"A minute seventeen," I told him, stuffing the next bite of cake into my mouth while watching him warily.

"That's funny," he said between bites. "Didn't you come in first in the girls' division? Because that's three seconds slower than the third-place time for the boys' division in your age group."

Everyone in the pool looked at me. They expected a rebuttal.

For once, I didn't have one.

Chloe extended her hand toward Nick. "Give me back that cake."

He held it away from her. "No, it's good."

"Give it. I don't like where you're going with this."

"No, I'm hungry." Wisely, he waded into the deeper end of the pool, where Chloe would not follow him if she wanted to keep her hair dry. Holding his cake and fork at chest-level above the surface of the water, he looked straight at me and said, "I just think that unless you compete with everyone, it's not really a competition." His dark eyes dropped to his plate, and he shoveled a big bite of cake into his mouth. He had basically told me my win today didn't matter, *and* I was not quite as important as cake.

I opened my mouth to holler at him. I was so angry, I had no idea what I would have said.

Luckily all I got out was a noise like *nyah* before Chloe interrupted me. "That's ridiculous. Girls and boys compete separately in almost every sport. You don't have girls on your football team."

"That's because girls would suck," Gavin offered. Nick

waded back across the pool so they could bump fists. As he passed, the movement of his big body splashed water on my cake.

I slid my plate onto the pool deck and opened my mouth to lay into Nick with the insult he deserved.

But all I got out was something that sounded like *yerg* before Liz talked over me. "Basic physics. The average boy is bigger than the average girl. Girls don't play football with boys because they'd get crushed. Girls have slower times than boys in the slalom because they're not as heavy. You should have seen Hayden's 900 in the half-pipe. Not a single boy did a 900 today, not even the guy who came in first in the oldest boys' division."

"That's because he's not that good," Nick countered. "Even *I* could beat that guy."

"Besides," Davis spoke up, "this was a local competition. You never know who'll show up for those. It would be different if she stepped up to a higher level. The men's Olympics are an event. The women's Olympics are a bathroom break."

"They are not!" I gasped, instinctively coming to the defense of snowboarding chicks, my idols. *Et tu, Brute?* I thought. This was getting ugly if even Davis, usually such a gentleman, was making light of my win.

Liz must have been thinking the same thing. After her

big logical speech, she just gaped at him like she couldn't believe he'd said this.

Chloe was the one who shouted, "The three of you really mean Hayden didn't accomplish anything today? You weren't even there to watch her!"

Nick was, I thought. He was there on his deck. He'd made note of the slalom times. Now he cut his eyes at me, letting me know this had flashed through his mind, too.

"We didn't have to see her," he said. "Any snowboarder knows this about the sport. Women aren't anything compared with men. Hayden won lessons with Daisy Delaney, right? Pit Daisy Delaney against Shaun White. He'd crush her. Hell, pit Daisy Delaney against Mason Aguirre."

"Yeah!" Gavin took up the challenge. "Did you see the X Games on TV a couple of weeks ago? The guys stick 1260s on the slopestyle. They throw down back-to-back 1080s in the half-pipe or it's not even considered a run. The girls are lucky if they land a 900." He then created a range of Daisy Delaney slap-downs with every famous male snowboarder he could think of. Davis laughed, and he quietly offered suggestions when Gavin ran out of ideas. Chloe kept breaking in with protests, and Liz kept saying, "But . . ." From their separate places around the pool, all four of them waded closer as the talk got more heated, until they surrounded Nick and me on all sides.

But I didn't really hear them anymore. I stared at Nick in front of me. He stared back. We'd set this argument in motion, and now it kept rolling without us. No one seemed to notice we'd dropped out. I watched him, hoping I'd get some sign he was just kidding.

He watched me, too. But he never winked or made any move to break the tension. Everything he'd said about girls versus boys, he'd meant.

"So, you think you could have beaten the first-place guy?" I asked Nick.

He knew I'd said something. But he was listening to Gavin, and he couldn't hear me over the guffaws. With a last dark look at me, he turned toward the other boys and laughed.

I was angry now, truly angry. I'd worked hard to win that competition, and it *did* mean something. I slogged through the warm water and cold air, stopping right in front of him, my tummy only inches from his knees where he sat on the stairs. I said again, "Nick, you really think you could have beaten the first-place guy today if you'd only bothered to enter the competition?"

"Absolutely," he told me, still not looking or sounding like himself. He made cocky statements all the time, accepting challenges and taking bets. But his voice always held an ironic tone, like he was half-kidding and didn't believe it himself. This time he sounded like he believed it.

Or maybe the difference was in me, not him. Maybe after four years, I'd finally fallen out of love with him.

"Let's do it, then." I reached forward and poked his bare chest with two fingers like we were actors in a gangster movie. "You and me, on the slopes, head-to-head, the slalom and the half-pipe. I will kick." *Poke.* "Your." *Poke.* "Ass."

"Oooooh," the boys said. The moaning was so loud that I could have sworn Chloe and even Liz chimed in.

But all I saw was Nick in front of me, not budging a millimeter as I poked him, eyes frowning and lips curled in a tight smile. Quietly he told me, "Remember, you asked for it."

I did *not* ask for this attack. But I didn't dare defend myself or even hint at what had transpired between us in the sauna. The madder I got, the more he'd know I cared that he'd called me a bitch, and the worse I would hurt.

"Want to make it interesting?" Gavin asked, wading over. "Let's do this thing on Saturday. After Nick wins, the girls treat the guys to the Poser concert that night."

"You mean when Hayden wins, the boys treat the girls," Chloe corrected him. "That sounds fair."

"It's *not* fair," Davis protested. "After Nick wins, you'll just say conditions were different when Hayden came down, and that's what made her slower. Like, it started snowing."

"Or it *stopped* snowing," Gavin said.

"Or the wind was harder," Davis said.

"Or the wind was *softer*," Gavin said. "Girls will whine about anything."

"Fine!" Liz broke in, obviously agitated. She never spoke this loudly, much less broke in. "Instead of a slalom where they come down one at a time, they'll come down together, like in a boardercross."

"It's still not fair," Gavin pointed out. "No matter how high Nick goes in the half-pipe, you'll say, 'But Hayden landed a 900!'" He ended in a high-pitched voice that none of us girls had used since the second grade.

"Leave it to me," Chloe said ominously. "I'll find three impartial judges. Even *you* won't be able to complain." She used one finger on her right hand to pretend to scribble a note to herself on the palm of her left hand. Then she put her hands down and glared around the pool. "In the meantime, we've had just about enough of you guys and your sexist attitudes. Find your own way out. Come on, ladies." She picked up the cake, and Liz obediently gathered the plates.

I still crouched in the warm pool in front of Nick, stunned. Whether the girls treated the boys to Poser tickets or the boys treated the girls, we'd be paired off: Liz with Davis, Chloe with Gavin. Did this mean Nick and I had . . . a date?

That was *so* not going to happen.

Dazed, I moved past him up the stairs, following Chloe. Nick caught me by the wrist. Our hands were wet and I could have slipped out of his grasp, but I didn't. I stopped beside him on the stairs, shivering in the cold air, waiting breathlessly for him to break the date Chloe and Gavin had arranged for us, or to make a snide comment about it.

"We need a tiebreaker," he said, loudly enough for everyone to hear, but looking only at me. "Not that I'm saying I won't win the boardercross *and* the half-pipe. But I want to make sure I win fair and square. Just in case, we need to add a third event. Like a big air."

"Done," Chloe said quickly. "We'll bury you. Come on, Hayden."

Funny, I must have been riding waves of adrenaline the whole afternoon and night. I'd exerted myself on the slopes in the competition, but I hadn't felt the least bit sore. Now I suddenly felt it. My muscles were sore and tired, my eyes strained, and my brain hurt just thinking about the jump at the slopes, the one stunt I hadn't tried and didn't plan to. But Nick was right. This whole argument was about who was the better boarder overall. How could I be better than him if I couldn't go off a jump, one of the biggest parts of this sport?

"Good idea," I heard Gavin say as I sloshed out of the pool.

"No problemo," Davis said knowingly. The *smack* of their high five echoed against the wall of the hotel.

Before I closed the hotel door behind me, I stole one more glance back at Nick. Maybe he hadn't meant to set me up to fail. Maybe he'd momentarily forgotten I was afraid of heights. But no, he turned around on the steps and looked straight at me, still wearing that small smile. He flicked his wet hair out of his eyes with his pinkie, as if to show me yet again how little he thought of me. He knew exactly what he'd done.

comp

(kämp) *n.* **1.** a snowboarding contest **2.** Hayden vs. Nick

Heart racing and mind whirling, I walked into the locker room and changed into my clothes, hardly hearing Chloe and Liz's discussion echoing against the tile walls about what pigs boys could be. I was calculating how to fix this terrible situation. Maybe I could do the jump this time, and then I wouldn't have to worry about Daisy Delaney challenging me in the back bowls. Maybe all I'd ever needed to get over my fear of heights was the tall, dark, and hunky heir to a meat fortune to insult me and make fun of me. But gosh, it sure would be easier if I could *talk* my way out of this whole contest. "What?" I said.

Liz was standing in front of me. She looked a bit frazzled with her damp curls in her face. Obviously she'd been trying to get my attention for a while. "I *said*, have you seen your butt?"

"Is that a rhetorical question?" I craned my neck to take a gander at my backside.

Chloe clarified, "She means you have 'boy toy' written across the back of your jeans."

"Oh." I nodded. "They're Josh's."

"You say that as if it explains everything." Liz cocked her head to one side and considered me while buttoning her cardigan. "My stepbrothers don't write 'boy toy' across the back of their jeans. They only say the entire alphabet while burping."

"That's nothing. Josh can recite the Gettysburg Address. Listen, y'all." I pulled my hair free from the collar of my sweater. The long strands were damp, reminding me I'd just been in the pool with Nick. I could *still* be in the pool with Nick if he weren't such an ass. "I want to call off this contest."

Chloe's eyes narrowed. "Don't you dare."

Liz's eyes got big as she wailed, "Hayden, you can't!"

"I want to call it off." I took a deep breath before I warned them, "Otherwise, plan to buy Poser tickets for the boys. There's no way I'll win."

"Of course you'll win!" Chloe exclaimed. "You'll probably beat Nick in that race thing—"

"Boardercross," I corrected her. Chloe owned a snowboard, and that's about as far as her knowledge of the sport went.

"—and you'll blow him away in the trick part."

"Half-pipe. And then there's the jump."

They both just stared at me with their arms folded. They'd been pushing me to get over my fear of heights and go pro, so this was no way to argue myself out of my new corner.

I started over. "Okay, here's the real deal. I regret what I lost with Everett Walsh—"

"Come off it," Chloe said. "Tell us another."

I swallowed. "—and I want to make sure y'all aren't making a huge mistake. I mean, I'm mad, too, but I'm always mad at Nick. Maybe you're blowing this out of proportion with Gavin and Davis. I know both of you looked forward to seeing them tonight. Your evening with them got off to an excellent start. And now you're sending them home early, all because of this stupid challenge? I wish I'd never said anything." At least *that* part was the truth.

"Gavin told me a dumb-blonde joke last week when he made a ninety-eight on the chemistry test and I made a ninety-seven," Chloe said.

"That's just Gavin." I couldn't believe I was defending that jerk, but I really did think Chloe was overreacting. "Gavin would make fun of you for a hair out of place. He's just feeling around for material."

"He can't feel *there*," she said vehemently. "He can make jokes, and I'll giggle and pretend he's actually funny, up to a point. But if he tries to tell me I'm less of a person because I'm a girl? Or *you* are? That's where I draw the line." She pulled her bag from a locker and slammed the metal door.

"But you can't blame Davis," I reasoned, turning to Liz. "He didn't start it."

"He didn't stop it," Liz said, not looking up from tying her boots. "He was so disrespectful of you on your big day."

"But he didn't mean anything by it," I pointed out, "unlike Gavin, and definitely unlike Nick. Davis is naturally a sweet-natured person. He's just been hanging around Nick and Gavin too long. It's a wonder they don't have him stealing candy from babies, or blasting rap music out of his car stereo in front of the retirement home."

Liz stood, shaking her head. For a moment I hoped some water had dripped down her face from her damp curls—but no. She had tears in her eyes. "My boyfriend can't treat my friends that way."

"Oh God!" I exclaimed, really desperate now. "Look at me." I stood in front of both of them. To Liz I said, "You and Davis are adorable together." I moved to Chloe. "And you and Gavin are—"

She raised her eyebrows at me.

"—*interesting* together. You can't let my fight with Nick ruin your relationships with your hot boyfriends. Come on, now. My fight with Nick has been going on for years. It's like this black hole, with gravity so strong that not even light can escape, sucking in winter breaks and dates and whole relationships, until the world—are you listening to me?" When I'd started waxing poetic, Chloe's attention had wandered around the room. I grabbed her chin and turned her face to me again. "Until the very world is devoid of love!"

"It's not *that* bad," Nick's voice came faintly through the locker room wall.

We all looked at one another.

"Let's go up to my apartment," Chloe said. "Forget them. I have something in my room that will cheer us up, and it's *much* better than boys."

Chloe was serious about putting the boys in Time Out for the time being, and Liz seemed serious, too. Now that I knew Nick was in the locker room next door, I listened for him and wondered whether the boys would eventually follow us to Chloe's family's apartment at the back of the building, overlooking the ski slopes. Chloe and Liz clomped up the stairs like they weren't giving the boys a second thought.

I slowed on the steps. Chloe and Liz reached the top of the staircase and pushed into the hall above me, leaving the door to close slowly and bump shut behind them. I was alone. I turned around and watched the door at the bottom of the staircase, waiting for Nick to appear. Wishing he would materialize so I could yell at him and get this weight off my chest.

I'd been so in love with him for that magical month in seventh grade, and so devastated to find out I was a joke to him. He must have sensed that I still liked him more than I was letting on, and now he was acting mean about it. *Why?* What had I ever done to him? I wanted to be furious with him about the girl snowboarder comments, the jump challenge, *everything*, but it just didn't make any sense.

I stood there so long, staring a hole in the closed door at the bottom of the stairs, willing it to open and Nick to walk in and explain himself to me, that I got dizzy in the long white room. The dread of snowboarding off that jump came back to me in a rush. I clung to the railing to keep from falling down the stairs.

"Hayden!" Liz called from the hall.

"Coming!" I shook my head to clear it, then ran up the stairs to my friends without looking back again.

In Chloe's bedroom, she and Liz sat on Chloe's fluffy pink king-size bed, waiting expectantly. Uh-oh. Sure enough, the second I closed the door behind me, they both squealed, "Did you and Nick make out?"

I sighed. "For a second there, I thought we were going to."

"But you didn't?" Chloe wailed.

I flopped onto the foot of the bed and stretched out on my back. "No. We had an argument, and he called me a bitch."

"What!" Liz exclaimed. "That's so disrespectful!"

"That doesn't sound like Nick," Chloe said. "What exactly led up to this?"

Thinking back, I sat up with an enormous groan. The whole evening had been so confusing and frustrating and *mortifying*. Not like the seventh grade, but close. "I walked in on him in the sauna. We joked around. You know how we do."

Liz and Chloe nodded. Chloe motioned for me to hurry up with my story.

"I thought he was going to kiss me, and I stopped him." I put up a hand to Chloe's chest just as I had to Nick's. Then, when I realized what I was doing, I hastily jerked my hand away. "Sorry. Didn't mean to feel you up."

"It's quite all right," Chloe said.

"Why did you stop him?" Liz shrieked impatiently.

I rubbed my temple. My headache from the cold shower hadn't quite dissipated. "I don't know. It seemed like that was all he wanted, and I couldn't let him take advantage of me."

"Maybe he thought that's all *you* wanted from *him*," Chloe suggested.

I frowned at this disturbing possibility. "Maybe. It's hard to have a heart-to-heart with someone who throws stuff at you and calls you a fire-crotch and a bitch."

"Is that all that happened?" Liz prompted me. "You stopped him from kissing you, and he called you a bitch?"

"No," I admitted. "I told him I didn't want to kiss him because he hadn't asked me to the Poser concert. He hadn't asked me about winning the competition. He acted like I was just a convenient catch because all of y'all are dating. I told him we had irreconcilable differences."

Chloe gasped. "Like in a divorce? Hayden, why did you say that?"

I supposed it *did* sound ugly, now that I thought about it. But not *that* ugly. "We were both making divorce jokes in the hall last Friday. He started it."

"Hayden." Liz leaned forward and took me by both shoulders, bracing me for the bad news she was about to break. "Nick's mother left his father on Sunday."

"What!" I hollered, jumping off the bed to pace the floor.

"He told Gavin and Davis," Chloe said, "and they told Liz and me. Nick must have thought you knew. If *I* were him, and you blew me off and made divorce jokes, I guess I would have called you a bitch, too."

I stopped pacing and put my hands in my hair to keep from throttling her. "Jesus, Chloe! Why did you invite him over here in the middle of his family troubles?"

"He's friends with Gavin and Davis," she said. "He needed to get out of the house and forget about it for a night. He needs all our support right now."

Guilt trip.

"And you didn't have a date tonight because you broke up with Everett," Chloe said.

I took my hands out of my hair so I wouldn't tear it out. "Everett and his mama broke up with *me*, thank you very much."

"You shouldn't have made out with him in his mother's scrapbooking room," Liz said sagely.

"We're seventeen," I snapped, "and Everett and I had been dating for two months when that happened. What were we supposed to do, eat dinner with his family and keep our hands on the table where everyone could see them? I mean, you and Davis are Mr. and Mrs. Polite Reserve, and even you were macking in the hot tub an hour ago." I picked up a pink fuzzy pillow that had fallen from the bed and threw it at Liz.

"You *were?*" Chloe gushed. "You *what?* Hello, I need the details of Liz and Davis."

"Hayden!" Liz squealed, ducking behind Chloe. "I'm not saying you shouldn't have made out with Everett. I'm saying you shouldn't have done it in his mother's scrapbooking room. Location, location, location. You might have disorganized her supplies. Some people are very particular about their chipboard getting mixed up with their cardstock."

I closed my eyes, inhaled through my nose, and felt my lungs fill with air. My blood spread the life-giving oxygen throughout my body.

"Watch out," Chloe whispered to Liz. "She's doing yoga."

My eyes snapped open. So much for controlling my temper. "Why the hell didn't you tell me Nick's mother left before I went into the sauna with him?" I hollered at Chloe.

"We didn't know he was here!" Liz came to Chloe's defense.

"And if we'd warned you about him *before* he got here," Chloe explained, "you would have known he was coming. We didn't want you to leave. The two of you are surprisingly hard to throw together, let me tell you."

"I'm not buying it," I informed Chloe. "You were distracted. You had your mind on taking inventory."

Liz giggled, turned red, and fell back on the pillows.

"Taking inventory requires enormous concentration!" Chloe said with a straight face, but she was blushing, too.

I was glad for them, really. I was happy they'd had fun with their boyfriends, at least for a little while, and I hoped they didn't push this bet too far.

At the same time, I was very angry with them for contributing to this terrible mix-up with Nick. As supportive as Chloe and Liz usually were to me, I couldn't help thinking at that moment that I had Very Bad Friends.

Liz sat up again and wiped her eyes. "Do you want me to tell Davis to tell Nick that you didn't know anything about his parents when you were in the sauna with him?"

I shook my head no. "It sounds too much like a debauched game of Telephone. This whole thing seems very seventh grade. Besides, it's actually good this happened. Nick is a smooth talker. It took him getting furious for me to find out how he really feels about me. I don't want or need a boyfriend who thinks so little of my snowboarding skills and questions the very relevance of women's athletics. I'll admit, I may have carried a torch for him all these years. He just blew it out. So consult me the next time you want to play Cupid for me. And don't choose me a boy with four or five girls in a holding pattern. Nick Krieger is all wrong for me. Stop throwing us together."

Chloe and Liz stared at me from the bed.

"Okay?" I prompted them.

"Okay," they agreed, way too agreeably. Even after tonight's disaster, I got the feeling they were not through with Nick and me yet.

"I'm glad this happened, too," Liz said quickly. "It'll give you the push you need to get over your fear of heights."

"Yeah, about that bet." I rubbed my temple again, massaging away the headache that throbbed harder than ever. "I'm sorry, y'all, but there's no way I'm going off that jump. I'll buy the Poser tickets for you." I had been saving for another snowboard—they didn't last forever, the way I abused the half-pipe—but fair was fair.

"Oh," Liz cried sympathetically, "you don't have to do—"

"You will not lose this bet!" Chloe insisted. "We are showing up those boys, and you are going off that jump. I'll board with you tomorrow and coach you."

Now *there* was some motivation to get over this problem quickly. Chloe was a notorious betty. On the rare occasion when she graced the slopes with her presence, boys zoomed toward her because she was so cute in her pink snowsuit, then zoomed away again as she lost control and threatened to crash into them. She'd made the local snowboarding news a few years ago when she lost control at the bottom of the main run, boarded right through the open door of the ski lodge, skidded to a stop at the entrance to the café, and asked for a table for one.

"I'm working at the city library tomorrow," Liz said, "but I'll ski with you and coach you on Thursday."

"Have you actually tried to go off the jump and failed," Chloe asked me, "or do you not even try?"

"I don't even try." I didn't like to look at the thing. I averted my eyes when Josh and his friends jumped off.

"So, now you'll try," she decreed. "What's the worst that could happen?"

I opened my mouth to describe the worst that could happen. I could freeze up ten yards from the precipice, and all four spots where my leg had been broken would throb deep inside, even though I'd been healed for years. I would relive my rappelling accident. A series of sickening jerks as every safety belt and harness failed, one by one, and let me fall.

"Hayden, what's the matter?" Liz called. "You look like you saw a ghost."

I looked at her and then at Chloe, biting my lip to keep from crying. I didn't want to let them down, but this was a lot of pressure for what was supposed to be a carefree winter break.

Chloe clapped her hands, snapping me out of it. "I almost forgot what I found to show you! It's so good, it'll make this whole night worthwhile."

The three of us settled on her bed and ate CONGRATULA-TIONS HAYDEN! cake straight out of the box with our forks while she passed around this secret treasure that was better than boys (as if). She'd been cleaning out her closet—some people *did* clean out their closets, I supposed—when she'd come across a teen fashion mag–style quiz with twenty questions that she'd written and all three of us had answered back in seventh grade. Our handwriting was young and loopy. We'd dotted the *i*'s with stars and flowers and hearts.

1. If you accidentally got locked inside the school for an entire weekend with a blizzard coming, and the only way you could survive was to share body heat with the boy trapped inside with you, who would you want it to be?

Hayden: Barry Yates
Chloe: Ollie Cattrall

"Ollie Cattrall," Chloe mused. "Right after we wrote this, he moved to Massachusetts. I should look him up on Facebook."

"Chloe!" Liz exclaimed, horrified.

"And then he would post a comment on *my* page," Chloe explained, "and Gavin would see it. This would show

Gavin he's not the only man interested in me, and he might treat me a little nicer."

"Or," I pointed out, "this would show him that Ollie Cattrall, who lives two thousand miles away, either is being polite to you or is hitting on you because he cannot get a date at his own school. Which makes one wonder if he had to take his Facebook picture carefully in very low lighting."

She glared at me. "Moving on."

Liz: Davis Goggins

"Awww," Chloe and I both said. I reached out to pinch Liz's cheek. She and Davis hadn't been dating long, but it was so sweet she'd thought about him that way back in seventh grade. Almost as if they were destined to be together.

"I'm not sure anymore," Liz grumbled. "Ask me again after he pays for my Poser ticket."

2. If you were suddenly transported to the 1800s and you had to marry a boy in our class to be saved from an arranged marriage with an evil viscount,

(Chloe read a lot of historical romances.)

who would you want to marry?

Hayden: Mark Jones

Chloe: Scotty Yarbrough

Liz: Everett Walsh

"Everett Walsh!" Chloe exclaimed. I fell off the bed laughing.

Liz folded her arms and tried to scowl at us, but I could tell she was having a hard time keeping a straight face. "What's wrong with Everett Walsh?" she sputtered. "I didn't know when we wrote this in seventh grade that Hayden would hook up with him later. I saw him first."

"He's so straitlaced," Chloe said. "Not exactly the ideal hero of a romance."

"Watch out for his mama," I advised Liz.

"I was answering the question you asked," Liz told Chloe self-righteously. "If your family threatened you with an arranged marriage in the 1800s, you'd want someone on your side who was very mature and organized, who could approach the situation logically and help you out of it. In the 1800s, Everett Walsh would have been a barrister. He'd be perfect for the job."

"I'd rather have the evil viscount," I said.

We stayed late at Chloe's, giggling over the other eighteen questions. The night was so fun, and I loved reliving these memories with Liz and Chloe. I hoped we stayed friends forever and would someday look back fondly on *this* night, just as we were looking back on *that* night four years ago. And I hoped we wouldn't remember this as the night we foolishly cut those cute boys loose.

Because although the night was fun, this quiz definitely was *not* better than boys. I didn't admit it to Liz and Chloe, but I remembered exactly what I'd been thinking when I took this quiz in seventh grade. I'd been hoping I wouldn't go to hell for the little white lies I was telling. I would have been mortified to say so, but when I'd picked Barry Yates or Mark Jones or any boy for the rest of the quiz, I'd always meant Nick.

"Hayden Christine O'Malley!"

I started awake. White morning sunlight reflected off the snow outside and bounced through my bedroom window. My body still felt sore and my mind was wiped out from the contest and the argument with Nick yesterday. For my dad to be hollering at me like that, I must have been so tired when I came in last night that I left dishes on the kitchen counter instead of putting them in the dishwasher, or—worse—I forgot to let Doofus out. That really *would* be a mess to clean up.

I reached out from under the covers, opened my bedroom door, and called down the stairs, "Yes, honored father?"

"Get down here."

I jumped out of bed, eager to please. That was the only way I knew how to take the edge off the punishment he chose to hand down. Luckily, I glanced in the mirror, because I'd slept in a Burton Snowboards T-shirt. This would not help me look innocent at *all*. I pulled that off and pawed through my dresser for something more ladylike and less . . . dangerous. Hello Kitty!

I galloped downstairs—tripped over Doofus at the foot of the staircase—and slipped into my chair at the kitchen table. A plate of whole wheat pancakes and tofu bacon was waiting for me. I hoped the steam and the giant innocent face of a kitten on my T-shirt would blunt whatever blow was coming.

My dad had his back to me at the stove. Mom had already left to open the health club. Across the table from me, Josh put his fork down and made a small twisting motion with his fingers. I wasn't sure, but he seemed to be telling me I was screwed.

Dad set his own plate at the table and sat down. He drew out the torture, taking a bite, chewing slowly, staring a hole through me without speaking.

Finally I said, "Good morning, respected padre."

"Hmph," he said. "Your brother tells me that by giving in to your acrophobia, thereby ruining your chances of a professional snowboarding career, you are also sabotaging *his* chances of having the same sort of career through no special effort on his part. Shame on you! You're grounded."

I sniffed. "Did you really wake me up early during my winter break just so you could make a sarcastic comment to Josh?"

Josh stuck out his tongue at me, then took a huge bite of pancake.

Dad pointed at me with his fork. "Yes, sorry. If I'd waited until you woke up on your own to make that sarcastic comment, I might have been late for work."

I yawned.

"But while we're on the subject, Josh is right. His motivation is self-serving, but he's right about your phobia. If you really want a pro boarding career, sounds to me like you'd better get over your fear or throw away your chance to impress Daisy Delaney. No pressure."

I grumbled, "You have no idea."

Though my stomach hurt, somehow I swallowed breakfast. Thirty minutes later, Josh and I pulled on our layers of boarding clothes—tripped over Doofus—and headed outside for the bus. But when I opened the mudroom door and looked down at the doormat, I stopped short. Josh ran smack into me and nearly brought us both down. *"Forward,"* he said. "Most people walk *forward*. What is it?"

I picked up the local newspaper and held it out to him, speechless for once. It was rolled, but on the part we could see, a huge headline proclaimed, SNOWBOARDING COMPETITION . . . And a huge photo showed me in midair, snowboard and parka and red hair bright against the blue sky.

Then I pulled the newspaper back from Josh and took another look. "I've never seen myself snowboard before. Check my excellent form! I would be ecstatic, except that my life is crumbling around me and stuff."

"Your life isn't crumbling around you. Just go off the damn jump." Josh grabbed the paper from me and slid off the rubber band. Unrolled, the news was even worse. The whole headline was SNOWBOARDING COMPETITION SHOWCASES LOCAL TALENT, and the caption under the photo read SNOWFALL HIGH SCHOOL JUNIOR HAYDEN O'MALLEY LANDS A FRONTSIDE 900 IN THE HALF-PIPE TO WIN THE GIRLS' 16 TO 18 DIVISION.

"Give me that, you little traitor." I grabbed the paper back. "I've got to hide this from Mom and Dad. You want them to make me spend my whole winter break in some shrink's office?"

"If it helps you get over your phobia, yeah. Anyway, if you hide the paper, Dad will just call the newspaper office to deliver another copy. And I don't know who you're calling little."

I knew one way to solve this argument. I carefully tore

the whole article out of the front page, then rolled up the newspaper and slid the rubber band back on. "Doofus," I whispered. Poor Doofus, behind us in the mudroom, stood up in a rush of jingling dog tags and slobber. I slipped the paper into his mouth and whispered, "Take this to Dad."

Doofus wagged his tail and trotted into the kitchen. We heard Dad say, "Did you bring me the paper? Good dog. Wait a minute. Bad dog!"

Josh softly closed the door behind us. "You've got to do something, Hayden. You just *can't* throw away this opportunity with Daisy."

"If it's a choice between that and me falling to my death, I sure as hell can!" I shrieked. As if in answer, ear-splitting brakes squealed downhill. "And now we're going to miss the bus!"

We waved our arms and skidded down the icy sidewalk with our snowboards as fast as we could. The bus driver was used to us and waited. Hardly anybody rode the bus this early—only a couple of other die-hard locals on winter break. We called hi to them in the back and sat down up front.

I heaved a deep sigh. "You're not the only one gunning for me to go off the jump. Now I've got Liz and Chloe on my case." Briefly I recounted my ugly convo with Nick last night and explained our snowboarding challenge—leaving out that I'd supposedly made Nick feel worse about his parents' separation on purpose, which was actually an accident.

Josh was staring at me with his brows down, perplexed. "Nick Krieger, of Krieger Meats and Meat Products?"

I nodded. "Yeah, *that* Nick Krieger."

"Why is Nick Krieger telling you that girl snowboarders are no good and your win doesn't mean anything? Does he like you or something? Make sure he knows we're vegetarian. Mom and Dad would die if they had to pay your dowry in kielbasa."

I gaped at Josh in disbelief. "What do you mean, does Nick like me? Is that how *you* flirt with girls you like? Tell them they're bad at stuff? Is that how you flirt with Gavin's sister?"

He blinked innocently. "Is that wrong?"

"I wouldn't say 'wrong.' I would say 'not the most efficient way of asking a girl to the middle school Christmas dance.'"

He wrinkled his nose and moved his mouth, imitating my scolding, so I knew I'd guessed correctly about the last time he'd bombed asking out Gavin's sister.

"Stop it." I slapped at him. "And tell me the truth. Do you agree with Nick that I'll never be as good as a boy, so there's no use trying?"

"Keep in mind that I have seen the answer key. I know

what I'm supposed to say to stop you from hitting me."

"Uh-huh."

He leaned back against the salt-streaked window and considered me. "You are the most physically fit person I have ever met. I mean, I'm physically fit, too. I probably work out in the health club almost as much as you do. But I have been known to sneak a Pop-Tart out of the vending machine at school."

I gasped and put my hands to my mouth in mock horror.

"I know. It was whole grain, but still. You, on the other hand, are serious about keeping your body in top shape. You have a lot of natural athletic ability. And you got hurt all those years ago, which gives you extra drive like nobody else on the slopes."

I couldn't believe all this was coming out of Josh's mouth. Normally he was such a dork, but he did have his moments of depth. Right now he was looking me in the eye, letting me know he understood what a serious problem this was for me. I felt so much better just knowing that he cared.

"If you want to be a professional snowboarder," he went on, "the only thing holding you back is you. And I can help you there." He put his arm around me and squeezed way too hard on purpose. "Just leave it in the hands of me and my posse."

lemon grab

('le mən grab) *n.* **1.** a trick in which the rider grabs both ends of the snowboard **2.** what Hayden feels like she's doing every time she talks to Nick

"AY-BATTA-BATTA-BATTA-BATTA-BATTA!" yelled Josh's fourteen-year-old friends. I ignored them and sped across the snow toward the jump.

"Schwing!" finished Josh. He made a batting motion with both arms.

I saw this out of the corner of my eye. I'd lost my focus on the end of the jump. There was no way I could go off the jump *now*. Hating the feeling of relief that washed through me, I slid to a stop next to the boys. I was careful to slice the bank with my snowboard, sending a wave of snow straight over them.

"Hey!" Josh protested. He shook snow off his hat. "I thought we were supposed to help you go off the jump. We were trying to distract you from your fear." He wiggled his gloved fingertips at me on *fear*.

"You're just giving her another excuse not to go off," Chloe said through her pink glove. She sat on a snowboarding trick rail nearby, chin in her hand, almost as frustrated with me as I was with myself.

In the boys' defense, they *had* stayed here with me for over an hour while Chloe coached me in getting over my fear of heights. I was asking a lot of all of them. I needed to end this *now*. Looking around at the blinding white slopes glittering in the bright sunshine, I tried to remember why this was so important. I needed to do this jump so I would believe in myself. To impress Daisy Delaney.

To show up Nick.

"Okay." I curled my arms up like a bodybuilder. "Cheer me on here."

"Yaaaaay." Chloe and the four boys cheered and clapped with zero enthusiasm.

"I can do this," I insisted. "How many failed attempts is that?"

"Nine," Chloe said through her glove.

"There's no way I'm going to fail at this ten times in a row. I'm Hayden O'Malley! I won the Snowfall Amateur Challenge!"

"Wooooo," they moaned, no more excited than they'd been before.

"I shouldn't have to convince you to cheer for me." I reached down for a clod of snow and pelted Josh with it. Bull's-eye: It got him right on the goggles. "What happened to leaving it in the hands of you and your posse?"

He took off his goggles and wiped them on his snow pants. "That still seemed like a good idea, back on failed attempt number three."

"I'll show you," I grumbled. Anger was good for me when I tried something new with my board. Possibly Josh knew this and was acting like a butt on purpose. I tried not to think too much about that, or to remember how nice he'd been on the bus. I released my back boot from the binding and pushed myself along like I was riding a skateboard, up the hill and away from the edge of the jump. From here I could get a running start. Ideally, I would pick up enough speed that if I *did* chicken out at the last minute, it would be too late.

It was a gorgeous late morning with a cloudless, bright blue sky. No fog, no haze, so I could see all the way to the buildings of Snowfall at the bottom of the mountain, even pick out the festive red banners flying beneath the streetlamps.

That was a long way down.

I squeezed my eyes shut and inhaled through my nose. My blood spread the life-giving oxygen throughout my body.

I exhaled through my mouth and felt gravity pull the energy from my heart—

"No excuses this time!" Chloe's voice sounded hollow, like she was calling through her cupped hands.

—down through my legs, through my boots and snowboard, through the snow, to the rocks below. I was one with the mountain.

"Daisy Delaney would be halfway down the mountain by now!" called Josh.

"Yeah!" came the voice of one of Josh's friends. "You expect Daisy Delaney to wait for you to meditate every time you go off a cliff?"

So much for re-centering. Anger seemed to be a better motivator after all. I was a little angry at Chloe, plenty angry at Josh, and mega-angry at Nick for making me feel like a second-class snowboarder. Most of all, I was angry at myself for not being able to do this. I would show us all.

I burst into action, leaning down the hill to put all my weight into increasing my speed.

Snow arced away from me, and dark snowy trees flashed past. The jump came closer. I pictured how ecstatic I would feel when I finally made this happen. The jump loomed closer. I pictured myself going off the end.

I panicked. I skidded to a halt at the last second. Clumps of snow launched from the edge in slow motion and burst into smithereens on the snowpack below.

And then I realized I was still falling, following the momentum of my snowboard and slipping over the edge. I grabbed for anything, but there was nothing solid to grab. The jump was made of layers of packed snow. My slick waterproof mittens slipped on the edge. I banged my snowboard against the jump to free my feet from the bindings so I could get some traction with my boots, anything to keep from falling. Normally the catches were touchy, sometimes releasing at unfortunate times during the middle of a forceful trick—but now they wouldn't pop open, and my snowboard was a dead weight pulling me down. I was back in my wheelchair already.

No way! I would not break a leg again. I would not be an invalid. My arms ached from holding myself on the precipice. I was tiring myself out and doing myself no good. I inhaled through my nose and felt my lungs fill with air. My blood spread the life-giving oxygen throughout my body. I exhaled through my—

"Hayden!" Chloe screamed. "Stop doing yoga and climb your ass up the jump!" Her voice jogged like she was maneuvering toward me as fast as she could in her gear, falling in the snow.

I could hold on until she and the boys got to me. I slipped another inch, but that just sent another wave of adrenaline through my arms, helping me tighten my grip. I could hold on—

Strong hands circled both my wrists and pulled a little, then slid down to my upper arms and pulled harder. Thank God that Chloe had reached me in time. But now I was afraid I was too heavy for her and would pull her over with me. I looked up to tell her to let me go if she felt herself falling.

It was Nick. Goggles and snow half-covered his face. I recognized him by his jaw—which he set in a grimace as I watched. Maybe I was too heavy for *him*.

But then Chloe did arrive, leaning over the lip of the jump to grab one of my legs. Josh grabbed the end of my snowboard. Together they all hauled me up over the edge, then collapsed around me on the jump.

"Are you okay?" Chloe shrieked, kneeling over me. I nodded, panting, and patted her pink glove. She and Josh's friends plopped down with us in the snow.

"Y'all, thank you," I breathed. I lay on my back, staring up at the bright blue empty sky. Compared with the blue shadows below the lip of the jump, it was so bright and white up here. Thousands upon thousands of people must be skiing on the mountain today, but the snow muffled sound. All I heard was the seven of us struggling to get our breath back. Nick breathed closest to me, inhaling long and deep and exhaling big clouds of water vapor, like he was truly shaken by the idea of me falling and relieved he'd come to my rescue.

No, come on. He would have rescued anyone. He wouldn't let anybody fall off the end of the jump, even a stranger. In fact, he might not even recognize me. True, how many redheaded snowboarders could there be in Snowfall? But surely he didn't have me on the brain like I did him. In my puffy, figure-erasing snowboarding clothes, I was basically in drag.

And then he grumbled, "Get on the other side of me."

The snow squeaked under my head as I turned toward him. Was he talking to me?

He stood, grabbed the edge of my jacket in one hand and the edge of my snow pants in the other, and slid me five feet across the snow. He sat down again between me and the edge of the jump, like he was protecting me from rolling off. "Either do the jump or don't, Hoyden. In-between is very bad."

Some tourists up the hill yelled at us to get the hell

out of the way. The boys scooted off one side of the jump, and Nick and I scooted off the other. Chloe stayed in the middle for a moment more. Clearly she preferred not to spend quality time alone with my brother and his friends. But when I made a small motion down by my side for her to join Nick and me, she shook her head and made a talking motion with her hand.

She wanted Nick and me to *talk*? Great. I huffed out one last sigh left over from my breathless moment hanging off the jump, and searched my mind for what I wanted to say to him. That I was sorry for insulting him about his parents splitting up, when I really didn't know? This would be difficult to explain, and I found myself hoping Chloe and/or Liz had played Telephone and passed this message along after all.

I looked up at him. He still had his goggles on, and so did I. If we removed them, we would be able to see each other better, but we would also see the face-divots that came with several hours of wearing goggles. So I left mine on, and so did he. When I tried to look into his eyes, all I saw was a reflection of snow, trees, and sky.

"You're welcome for saving your life." He grinned at me for the first time, and his playboy smile was all the more dazzling because that's all of him I could see—that and his strong chin—like he was a masked superhero. "Did Chloe say you were doing yoga?"

"Yeah, I help my mom teach a class at the health club," I said sheepishly. Nick could make me feel so happy about my own jokes, or so sheepish about the things that defined me. I loved and hated that about him.

"Does yoga help you levitate? Because it sure wasn't helping you climb back up that jump."

"It helps me stay focused so I can concentrate on tricks. It keeps me limber so I don't get hurt on hard landings. I could show you some stretches, now that you've decided you're this big boarder." Too late I realized this sounded like a come-on. *Yeah, Hayden,* he would say, *I want you to show me some*—wink—*stretches!*—nudge nudge.

"Stretches!" he barked in exactly the outraged tone he would use to say, *Pink sequined football uniforms!* "What good would that do?"

Now I was offended, which was strange because he hadn't even tried to offend me, for once. But stretches were a big part of my life. "Typical. High school boys think the only speed for exercise is full throttle, with nothing between complete rest and heavy exertion. You're going to pull a muscle if you don't warm up enough."

"I warm up."

"Come on." I whacked his chest playfully, sugarcoating what I viewed as serious information. My insulated hand bounced off his insulated body. "I've seen the football team start practice. You're in full pads so you can hardly move, and you stretch what the coach tells you, when he says. You can't stretch right with a team. You're not listening to your own body."

"And *you* are? Tell me what my body's saying now." He flicked his long hair away from his goggles with his gloved pinkie. *God*, how I loved it when he did that. But he was plotting, scheming, turning my own words against me, making fun of me. He was *so hot*, even in goggles and waterproof layers, and I wished *so badly* he hadn't called me a bitch yesterday and insinuated I was a betty.

"No, you're right." I nodded. "What was I thinking? Yoga would be too hard for you. You're not subtle."

I almost cackled as his lips parted in surprise. Now that I'd discovered Nick's button, it was so easy to push! Just challenge him on *anything*. Tell him he couldn't do something. Press the button and watch him steam in the frigid air.

He leaned very close to me, his lips inches from my forehead. "Neither are you," he growled.

I flushed so hot that I was afraid he could see *me* steaming. What did he mean? Could he tell how much I liked him, after everything that had happened?

As quickly as he'd leaned toward me, he stepped away and glanced uphill. I turned to see what he was looking at. Gavin and Davis zigzagged down the mountain, barely missing each other each time they traded sides. As they approached the jump, they never hesitated. They both sped straight up the ramp and off the edge. Gavin recognized Chloe at the last second and called to her as he descended. Davis did a frontside 360, almost as if he'd seen me beside the jump and was mocking me, which was impossible because Davis did not mock people. Until last night, that is.

Then they were gone. Snowflakes sparkled in the air where they'd been.

Nick reached out and pulled my hair. "Don't worry," he whispered. "I won't tell Gavin and Davis about your incident with the jump just now."

I laughed shortly. "You mean you won't embarrass and belittle me? Thanks, Nick. It's too late. You took care of that last night."

He studied me for a second. At least, I thought he did, though all I could see were his mirrored goggles. Then his waterproof fabric zipped against my waterproof fabric as he slipped his arm around my shoulders. "Have fun out here with your boyfriends." He nodded across the slope to Josh and his posse, who were taking turns jibbing on the trick rail while the others pelted them with snowballs. Chloe protected her hairdo with both arms over her head.

I shrugged off his arm. "That's right. Fourteen-year-old

boys have better taste than you. They think I'm *hot*." I licked my fingertip and stuck it on my butt. "*Tsssss.*"

And with that, I propelled myself across the slope and skidded to a stop at one end of the trick rail. "Quick," I told the boys, "act like you think I'm hot."

Chloe cracked up. Josh stared blankly at me. His friends blushed deep red, but they weren't claiming it.

"Thanks for your support," I told them. "Look without looking like you're looking. Is Nick gone?"

Chloe gazed past my shoulder to watch uphill. "He's hiking farther up so he can get some air. Here he goes."

"Nice speed," Josh murmured. All the boys tracked Nick behind me with their eyes. "Nice air." Josh turned to me. "You're toast."

I *felt* like toast, burning with anger inside my water-proof layers. "I am *not*," I insisted. "I might be lightly browned on one side. But it's only Wednesday. The comp isn't until Saturday. Right now let's go to the half-pipe and end this on a high note. Okay?"

I turned and boarded through the trees beside the jump without waiting for them. My enthusiasm was stretched to the limit, having to cheer on my own cheerleaders. Behind me Josh broke into a rap about me. His friends joined in with beats and sound effects. I wasn't sure whether this was supposed to boost my spirits or not.

Hayden, she's a red-haired lass
Doing nose-grabs by the score
Gonna kick some Krieger ass
Maybe she needs one day more
Wants to snowboard off the jump
Not today, she's filled with sorrow
Scared she'll lose her steeze and biff
Gonna kick some ass tomorrow.

This was not exactly the vote of confidence I was looking for. I was already angry at myself for being chicken. I was glad I had something else to concentrate on—staying on the trail and not skidding into a tree—because otherwise, I might have burst into tears.

As soon as we cleared the woods and emerged onto the wide slope down to the half-pipe, Josh boarded even with me. "Your bet is only for Poser tickets, right?" he called.

And for my self-esteem, but that was splitting hairs. "Yeah, that's all."

"Because if it was for more than that, I'd be sweet-talking Nick right now and doing everything I could to pull out."

"Oh, no you don't!" Chloe squealed. I think she meant to board between us and shove Josh away for effect. However, she didn't have enough control to do this, so she just crossed in front of him and fell in his path, which was somewhat anticlimactic. She shouted up at him, "*You* need to decide whether you stand with your sister or with the sexist pigs!" Even on her butt in the snow, Chloe was a formidable force.

"Yes, ma'am." Josh saluted with his mitten to his goggles, then slid around us to catch up with his friends, who had moved farther down the slope to the half-pipe. This was the part of the ski resort where everyone from my school came to see and be seen. The ski lodge sat at the foot of Main Street, the main wide slope. The half-pipe ended another big run on one side of Main Street. Kids busting ass in the pipe served as après-ski entertainment for adults drinking beer (and teenagers sneaking beer) on the deck at the lodge.

I stopped at the bottom of the half-pipe with twenty or thirty other skiers and boarders who were watching the show. Then I turned to catch Chloe as she came down the hill. Over the years, on the rare occasions when she boarded with me, catching her had proven a more effective method of stopping her than teaching her to stop herself, which she could not seem to get the hang of.

In front of us, the guy who'd come in second place in the older boys' division yesterday sped through the pipe, which was basically the bottom half of a tube buried in the snow—an enormous tube with eighteen-foot sides. He boarded up one wall, launched into the air, and rotated his body in a backside 720. Then he landed easily and slid like butter down the wall, accelerating across the flat to launch himself up the opposite wall, back and forth until he ran out of pipe. He boarded out toward us. Seeing me on the edge of the crowd, he called, "Hayden O'Malley! My girlfriend and I have a bet for Poser tickets on you and Krieger. Be sure you lose that comp for me!"

Now that I looked around, there were a *lot* of people from school hanging out here, and all of them seemed to have heard about Nick and me. They murmured behind their hands or called out, "Dis!" and "Drama!" I even heard some girls close by discussing whether Nick and I were hooking up, as if I were deaf.

"You might as well fork over your seventy-two dollars right now!" Chloe yelled after the offending guy, but he was already halfway to the lift back up to the top of the pipe. To me she murmured, "You go almost as high as he does in the half-pipe. I don't want to scare you or anything. But you're sliding up the wall and going way up in the air, upside down half the time, and you're not the least bit scared of *that.* What's so different about the jump?"

I knew exactly what was so different, because I'd discussed this at length with Josh years ago when we first discovered I Did Not Do Jumps. "In the half-pipe I'm starting out in the flat, going up the wall and into the air, and then coming back down," I explained. "To me that's a lot different from the jump, which is basically a controlled fall off a very high wall. It sounds a little too much like equipment failure when you're rappelling."

"But you're *not* rappelling," Chloe pointed out, "and you don't have any equipment to fail you. Well, you have your snowboard, maybe, but no ropes or pulleys or whatever's supposed to hold you up. I have studied this in great detail today. While you were *not* going off the jump, everybody in Snowfall *did* go off it. My dentist. My mailman. An entire second-grade class."

"What's your encouraging and helpful point, coach?" I prompted her.

"The jump's just mind over matter. It's *not* like you're falling off a cliff. When you go off the jump, you've got so much momentum that you fall gently, and the ground keeps sloping gently away from you as you go, so you have a longer ride." She demonstrated with her pink-gloved hands. One of them was the jump and the gentle slope. The other one was me, going off the jump and then falling to my death.

As if I needed instruction on this. As if I didn't live here in Snowfall and stare in awe at the jump every day of my life. "Thanks for the tip, professor. Okay, watch this." I turned around so I could see the jump behind us through the trees, and I put out my hands to spin Chloe around on her board. We watched a little kid go off the jump. "See how he loses his balance and moves his arms in wild circles like he's rolling down the windows on an old car? That means he's lost most of his balance and all of his control. I'm not going off anything where I might lose control. Ever. Again."

Chloe pushed her goggles off her face. Then she put both hands on the sides of my head and lifted my goggles so her blue eyes stared straight into my eyes. "Then you know exactly what you have to do. You have to take back control."

Midafternoon, I left the mountain. No loss there, since I didn't need any more practice at *not* going off the jump. I was scheduled to help my mom with yoga class. I didn't have the certification yet to teach yoga by myself. But we had a lot of elderly and disabled members at the health club, and my mom liked me to hang in the back of the class in case anyone needed special assistance. One time last year, she had to stop instruction when somebody got totally stuck in the Downward-Facing Dog.

On the hour, I walked into the main classroom and knelt in front of the stereo. I adjusted the music from the heinous Sweatin'-to-the-Oldies aerobics beat for the class before ours to the calming *ohm*-like chords for yoga, complete with running water and chirping birds in the background. Out of the corner of my eye, I recognized all the regulars for this class and waved to them as they came in: new moms trying to lose the baby weight, a couple of men in rehab after skiing accidents, and old folks maneuvering slowly through the door, some with canes or walkers. Then came a few folks I didn't know, probably tourists who'd bought a temporary membership for their week or two in town. And then Nick.

Okay, it probably wasn't him. I was so angry with him that I had him on the brain and I was seeing him everywhere, just like I thought I saw him watching me from his deck during the competition yesterday. Oh, wait, that really *had* been him.

Anyway, I forgot all about phantom Nick when my mom bustled in. She liked to stay at the front desk, greeting guests, until the very last second, which was another reason she needed me there—to socialize before class and to set up the equipment for her. As I handed her the headset mic that would project her voice around the mirrored studio, she looked me up and down. "Well? Did you go off the jump?"

"Did she ever!" called an elderly lady at the back of the class. "Congratulations, Hayden! We saw your picture in the newspaper." Several people broke into applause.

My mother raised one eyebrow at me. "I haven't seen the paper today. Were you in the paper?"

"Uhhhhh." Without answering, I turned and hurried toward the back of the room, weaving around bodies on yoga mats in the center of the polished wood floor, thinking unkind thoughts about well-meaning old people who wanted to push me into being successful.

My mom got settled on the raised platform at the front of the class. She made her voice soothing as she coaxed everyone into Child's Pose. They curled into balls with their foreheads down on their mats and their arms out in front of them. I skirted one last mat to curl up on mine. Listening to my mom, I relaxed heavily into the pose. There was a reason I was so into yoga. I was high-strung (news flash!). Yoga helped me focus and keep a handle on what was important, so I didn't wig out over the small stuff. Only the big stuff.

Speaking of which, I followed my mom's instructions and slowly rose into Mountain Pose (that's standing up, if you want to get technical) and opened into Warrior One with one foot ahead. At the same time the man beside me, obviously a novice, got confused and held Warrior One with his other foot ahead. Mom moved us into Warrior Two, so our arms opened toward each other and I was able to glance at him out of curiosity without being obvious.

It really *was* Nick.

goofy

('gü fē) *adj.* **1.** riding the snowboard with your right foot forward, unlike most people **2.** Hayden, trying to act sophisticated

As I've said, Nick was no stranger to the health club. I'd whiled away many a shift behind the front desk, watching his love/hate relationship with the abdominal machine unfold on the surveillance cameras.

But he'd never, ever come to my mom's yoga class. When he'd showed up at the jump a few hours ago, I'd felt befuddled. Not angry, though. Not about *that*. He had as much right to the mountain as the rest of us, and he'd only happened upon us by accident.

Now I was angry. I supposed he had as much right as I did to use the health club, too, since his family was paying for a membership. I'd even told him this afternoon that I helped my mom with yoga. But after a fight like the one we'd had last night, he did *not* have a right to follow me to my family's business, to my *job*, insulting me.

He grinned at me and shook his dark hair out of his eyes. He was still holding Warrior Two and he didn't have a pinkie free to flick it. "You offered to show me some stretches," he murmured.

Not quietly enough. As my mom brought us up and around into Reverse Warrior with our arms pointed toward the ceiling, her calming yoga voice rose a notch.

The smart response would have been to ignore Nick—though this had never worked for me in the past. Instead, I said in a stage whisper, "You shouldn't have poked fun at my offer before, if it sounds like a good idea now."

"Return to Warrior Two," my mom intoned. "Bree-eeeathe. You are strong like a warrior, with strong and stable roots down into the floor."

"I was being subtle." He wasn't facing me now. He directed his words forward, over his fingertips pointing ahead, with his perfect body in the perfect Warrior

Two Pose. Except for, you know, the talking.

I did *not* speak over my perfectly pointed fingertips. Screw Warrior Two. I turned my head toward Nick, and it was all I could do to keep my arms out rather than putting my hands on my hips as I scolded him. "You don't care about yoga. You're here because I told you that you couldn't do it, and you can't *stand* to pass up a challenge."

My mom's soothing voice rose a bit more. "Open your body toward the wall, then sink into Triangle. Feel the stretch. Breeeeeathe. Continue to send strong and stable roots into the ground." This was her code for me to make sure the elderly people were not about to fall down.

I folded over into Triangle Pose. With my head hanging down, I looked through my legs straddled wide on the mat. The old folks appeared to me like they had pretty stable roots, or as stable as possible for hundred-year-olds doing yoga.

I glanced up at Nick, whose head was very close to mine. His face was turning red.

"The Triangle Pose is not for everyone," I said drily.

Nick eyed me uneasily. Or maybe that was just the blood rushing to his head. Then he said, "You invited me here."

I shook my head, and my ponytails brushed the wood floor. "You misunderstood me. You were making fun of me for not going off the jump. Suggesting that you do yoga was my *subtle* way of telling you to go to hell."

"From here, move your hand behind your foot for Reverse Triangle. Breeeeeathe." My mom was practically shouting into her headset now. She might as well change the *ohm*-like yoga music with chirping birds to a nice, relaxing polka.

Reverse Triangle put Nick's head away from me, behind his muscular thigh. But even from several feet away, I heard him exclaim, "Ouch!"

"You think that hurt?" I asked out of the corner of my mouth. "Wait until Half Moon."

"Half Moon *does* hurt," someone nearby agreed. It was hard to tell who, with everyone upside-down.

"And roll up into Mountain Pose, with hands to heart's center." My mom stood, closed her eyes, and placed her hands in the prayer position on her chest. "Breeeeeathe and relax as two teenagers take a walk, leaving the haven of the yoga studio in peeeeeace and quiet." She opened one eye and lifted her eyebrow at me.

"Come on," I whispered to Nick. As my mom's voice droned on, I rolled up my yoga mat and whacked Nick in the back of the head with it. He looked up from his obviously painful Reverse Triangle and glared at me. Finally, he took the hint and rolled up his own mat. We wandered among the adults balancing precariously and dumped our mats into the bin by the door.

As soon as the door closed behind us, I whirled to face him in the hall. "Thanks, Nick. I've never been kicked out of my own yoga class before. My mom will probably dock me forty-five minutes of minimum wage."

He tilted his head to look at me from a different angle, and the scowl he'd been wearing since I'd whacked him in the head melted away. His words melted me in turn as he grinned brilliantly at me and said, "I really like your hair that way."

Without meaning to, I self-consciously reached for my hair. Around the health club, my mother always wore her red hair in one ponytail or one long braid down her back. I used to, too. But since I'd grown as tall as her, people mistook us for each other. I couldn't walk through the hall without middle-aged women stopping me to recount their hot flashes last night or to complain that the baby had the croup.

But I needed to pull my hair up for yoga, so I wore it in two ponytails. At first I worried the style was too little-girlish for me. Then, because of some of the looks I was getting from men at the health club who weren't regulars, I'd started to wonder whether the hairstyle had the opposite effect, reminding them of Britney Spears's schoolgirl getup.

Nick was giving me the same look. And this time,

instead of being taken aback or feeling squicky about it, my heart raced and my face grew hot, my body's response to the call of Nick. The yoga music and my mother's soothing voice filtered through the door, reminding us we weren't exactly alone, and occasionally a lady in sequined track pants speed-walked past us in the wide hallway that doubled as an indoor track. But I couldn't stop glancing at Nick's soft lips. If a dark corner had been available, I would have kissed him right then, despite everything he'd said to me last night.

No, I would *not* let him charm me. I said, "Nick, for real. Why are you here? You didn't suddenly decide to pop into my mother's yoga class after four years of health club membership."

He still grinned at me with his head tilted, like he found me so amusing and did not take me seriously at *all*. Then he folded his arms on his chest, so his biceps strained at the sleeves of his T-shirt, courtesy of the arm curl machine. "Why can't I tell you you're pretty? You've got issues, Hoyden." He turned and walked into the men's locker room. The door closed gently behind him.

I stood in the hallway, listening to the muffled drone of my mother's voice, the slow yoga chords filtering through the studio walls, and the swish of the speed-walker's pants somewhere around the corner. I stared at the men's locker room door like my x-ray vision would switch on any second. Ugh, mistake—lots of our members came to the health club to get back into shape, with good reason. Still I stared at the door, wondering what in the world was up with Nick. If he liked me, why was he mean to me? If he didn't like me, why did he show up here? Was it possible that Josh was right, and Nick's dis last night was a sign he actually had a thing for me? Again, this seemed very seventh grade. Maybe he was a case of arrested development.

Not in his biceps, of course. Or his abs. *Emotionally* arrested development.

The door burst open and I tensed like a rabbit, ready to bolt before Nick saw me staring at the door where he'd disappeared.

It wasn't even him. He hadn't had nearly enough time to shower. It was two regulars who walked out laughing and called a hello to me as they passed.

Swallowing the lump in my throat, I skittered into the women's locker room before Nick really did catch me staring. I'd wasted enough of my winter break worrying about Nick. I had plenty more to enjoy: no homework, meeting Chloe and Liz at Mile-High Pie for supper in a few minutes, lots of slope time, and a renewed push tomorrow to master the jump. Not for Nick's sake, but for mine.

As the locker room door thumped shut behind me, I

pictured the lid closing on this box of troubles I'd opened with Nick's name on it. Unfortunately, when I emerged from the locker room again a few minutes later, ready for Mile-High Pie, Nick was standing in the hall in jeans and his puffy parka, talking with my mother.

Yoga class had let out. My mother was all about chatting up the members, even the teenagers, even the ones she kicked out of her classes (apparently). I ducked around them, into the crowd spilling out of the studio. Better let my mother cool down for a few hours before I faced her about interrupting her Reverse Triangle. I flounced down the staircase. With every step down, I felt myself relaxing a little more, looking forward to a few hours out with my girlfriends, away from Nick.

And then my mom called, "Have fun on your date, Hayden!"

Another step down and I thought, *Good. Mom is mistaken and has led Nick to believe I'm going on a date.*

One more step down and I thought, *Oh no, Mom has led Nick to believe I'm going on a date!* No matter how I tried to convince myself otherwise, obviously I still held out hope for Nick and me getting together this winter break. I turned around on the stair, wondering what I could say to let Nick know I was still unengaged, without letting him know I wanted him to know.

Nick ran smack into me.

"Ooof!" he hollered, grabbing me around the waist to keep me from falling down the rest of the staircase.

That's when I realized Mom thought Nick and I were going on a date *together*.

Quickly Nick let me go. He looked huge, frowning down at me from the step above. "Why are you stopping in the middle of the stairs?"

"Why are you tailgating me?"

He put his hand behind me, at butt level, without touching me. "*What* is *that*?" he demanded.

I bent a little and slapped my butt. "Something the heir to a meat fortune should know all about. USDA grade-A prime, baby." I straightened. "Just kidding. Really, it's my butt."

He put his hands on his hips, and from below I noticed his strong superhero chin again. He grumbled, "Why do you have 'boy toy' written across your butt?"

"Oh!" I put my hand over the words, realizing that I probably should have been embarrassed about this sooner. "These are my little brother's jeans. He wrote it to annoy me. Or to get me a date. Speaking of which, what did you say to my mother to make her think we're going on a date?"

He shrugged. "I just told her we're both going to

Mile-High Pie. Aren't you meeting Chloe and Liz there? I'm meeting Gavin and Davis."

More of Chloe and Liz's matchmaking, no doubt.

"Did you tell my mother that you called me a bitch last night, too?" I asked him. "Because that's the best way I know to win parents over."

For a split second, he looked uncomfortable. Almost immediately, he recovered and went back on the offensive. "You shouldn't wear those jeans. People might think something."

I stamped my foot on the stair. "Like what? I want to show off my fire-crotch? What do you care? God! Stop following me." My hair was down now, and I felt it smack into his chest as I whirled around and flounced down the rest of the stairs, across the lobby, and into the cold night.

I mean, *really* cold. The temperature must have dropped twenty degrees since I came off the slopes that afternoon. The formerly slushy snow on the lesser-used sections of the sidewalks had frozen over and now crunched under my boots. I tucked my nose deep into my scarf against a sudden gust of freezing wind. Mile-High Pie was only a few blocks away, but this walk seemed to stretch in front of me forever. Cold and anger were not a good mix.

"Hayden," Nick called from behind me.

Oh, good! Just what this walk needed: a double-shot

of ex to go with that cold and anger. Shaking my head, I crossed the icy street.

"Hayden." His voice was sharper, angry now, and it echoed against the two-story storefronts closed for the night. I could tell from the direction of his voice that he was crossing the street after me.

"Don't you mean Hoyden?" I called over my shoulder.

Heavy steps cracked behind me, closer and closer. Nick rounded in front of me and stood in my path, his breath puffing white into the black night. "I never called you that."

"You call me Hoyden all the time!"

He frowned at me and said, "Fire-crotch."

"Take a number." I tried to walk around him.

He caught me by the elbow. "Would you hold up for a minute and listen to me?" His dark eyes focused on me, hardly blinking when the wind gusted in his face. He put on a very convincing act of disbelief and outrage. "I mean, I did *not* call you a fire-crotch. I was afraid you overheard that in the lunchroom last week. *Everett Walsh* called you a fire-crotch as you walked by. I told Everett Walsh that he should watch his mouth. Then Everett said, 'Oh, you're one to talk, you say stuff like that about Hayden all the time,' and I said, 'I would *never* make a comment about her *crotch*. No.' We nearly got into it right there in the lunchroom, but you conveniently missed *that* part."

I certainly had. And I wasn't buying it. Nick, standing up for me? "Let me get this straight. Your lunchroom speech went a little something like this." I put my hands out in front of me like I was a Roman orator enunciating for the crowd. "'I, Nick Krieger, defender of women, would never denounce the crotch. I am *above* the crotch.'"

He gaped at me. Other boys might not look so hot while gaping. Nick looked adorable in the soft light of the streetlamps, against a backdrop of small town and snow.

I put my hands down.

He watched me silently for a few moments more. "You don't think very well of me," he finally said.

I shrugged. "I don't blame you for being confused and thinking, 'Gosh, I called Hayden a fire-crotch and she's *mad*? What's up with *that*?' There was a time in my life when you could have called me a fire-crotch in front of a bunch of people, and I would have just laughed. I wanted any kind of attention I could get from you. In eighth grade, ninth grade, tenth grade, when you insulted me and other girls said it was just because you liked me, I believed it. But I guess everybody reaches a point when they're done with that, and they want to be respected. This is definitely unfortunate for the purposes of teen love—I mean, look at Gavin. But there it is."

"You don't want to be with me because you think I don't respect you."

"I *know* you don't respect me."

"Because you don't believe me that I didn't call you a fire-crotch?"

"You don't have a good track record for telling me the truth." I walked around him and nuzzled my nose into my scarf again, heading into the wind.

His boots crunched behind me.

"And stop following me!" I yelled over my shoulder.

"I'm not following you. Stop walking in front of me." The crunches sounded louder and louder again until he jogged past me and kept jogging until he was fifty feet ahead of me on the sidewalk. He disappeared around the corner. I was left with nothing but my anger and the cold again.

When I finally reached the restaurant and swung open the door, of course the first thing I saw was Nick hanging his parka on the coatrack, revealing how adorable he looked in his sweater and scarf underneath. And Fiona Lewis was calling to him from the ancient Galaga arcade game. His *other* ex. Drat!

"Haaaaaydeeeeen!" moaned Josh and his peeps from the nearest booth. Double drat! Just what I needed when I was trying to get the upper hand in this ongoing argument with Nick: the undying friendship of four fourteen-year-old boys.

On hearing my name, Nick looked up at me, then nodded toward the posse with a smirk. "Your boyfriends are calling you." He glanced toward Fiona.

"You act like that's not possible," I heard myself say coyly, even though my brain was waving frantically at me, screaming, *Stop, Hayden, don't go there!*

Nick turned back to me, and his eyes flew wide in surprise. "I act like *what's* not possible?"

"You act like I would never go out with any of them." Which I wouldn't. They were like brothers to me. Especially my brother. And they still watched cartoons. It was just that Nick acted so *disdainful*, as if I could never have anyone if it weren't for him or Everett Walsh throwing me a bone.

"Nick, quick, help, I'm about to die!" Fiona squealed.

Ah, triple drat. A real live ex-girlfriend and damsel in space-distress totally trumped fourteen-year-old boys, no matter how many of them there were. Nick dashed over to her and took over mission command. I hung my own coat on the rack and dragged myself to the boys' booth.

But you know what? They all grinned at me in welcome, and Josh even scooted over to make room for me on the bench. At least I knew who my true friends were. Feeling grateful and loved, I sat down.

THPPPPTHPPPPTHPPPPT! I farted. Or so it seemed.

The boys died laughing. I pulled the whoopee cushion

out from under me and flung it on the table, which only sent them into another paroxysm.

"Nick——Krieger—is—behind—you," Josh gasped between giggles. "He totally heard it over Galaga. Do you still want us to look without looking like we're looking?" This sent them into yet another laughing fit.

"But don't worry," one of his friends said. "We'll act like we think you're hot." They all snorted and dabbed at their eyes faux-girlishly with paper napkins from the holder. Then, as if on cue, they started their rhythmic heavy breathing, and I knew one of Josh's raps was coming. The people in the booths around us turned to look, if they weren't already staring at us outright because of the whoopee cushion.

Hayden C. O'Malley was your
Average girl
Thought she'd give the boarding, jibbing,
Riding a whirl
Thought she'd have some trouble kicking
Nick Krieger's ass
But her secret weapon is she's
Cooking with gas . . .

Not every one of Josh's raps was a success, and this one trailed off to dissolve in a morass of laughter and fart noises. I laughed along with them, because it was funny, and because I was that much of a Loser.

But of course the whole time I was preoccupied, wondering whether Nick had gone home with Fiona yet. On the one hand, I hoped that the two of them got extra points and extra lives in the bonus round, and that they were sticking around for another hundred thousand points. On the other hand, Nick overhearing Josh's rap would not be my shining moment.

"Do you think y'all could hold it down?" I finally asked the boys. "I appreciate your art, but there's a difference between rapping about me on the slopes, and rapping about me in a restaurant where other people are trying to eat. The latter is very prepubescent."

"*Pre*pubescent!" Josh gasped. "*Pre*pubescent!"

"I am totally pubescent," one of his friends said.

Another said haughtily, "I will have you know that my mom and I are going to Aspen to shop for training bras this weekend."

I rolled my eyes. "Later." I slid off the bench and stood.

"Hey, we're helping you go off the jump again tomorrow, right?" Josh asked, using the word *helping* very loosely.

"Yeah," another boy said, "eleventh time's the charm."

I looked toward the Galaga machine. Fiona was still there, yet Nick was gone. Probably just to order her a drink. Ordinarily, I would have bounced all over the restaurant searching for him so I could flirt him out of Fiona's pink-nailed grasp. But the whoopee cushion had taken the wind out of my sails.

As I walked through an open doorway decorated with broken skis and snowboards, here he was again, sitting in a booth, handsome face lit softly by the dim overhead lamps and the Christmas lights outlining the ceiling. Colors danced in his dark hair as he laughed with Gavin and Davis and . . . Chloe and Liz.

Sure enough, Chloe and Liz had invited me here, Gavin and Davis had invited Nick, and they were all playing Cupid again. Even after the fiasco last night! But I knew for sure that either way, the couples were back together, at least for tonight. Chloe and Gavin sat on one side of the booth, and I saw the backs of Liz and Davis on the other side. Nick had squeezed onto the end of the bench next to Gavin, which left only one place for me.

My feet felt like they had boots and bindings and two separate snowboards attached to them as I dragged myself closer and closer to the table of doom. Nick looked up at me. He didn't sneer at me and turn away to make a joke about me to the table at large. He watched me coming, dragging my phantom snowboards across the room. I held his gaze. I knew he was about to humiliate me (again), but

I would hold my head high while he did it. I slid onto the bench next to Davis, across the table from Nick.

"Hayden!" Chloe said. "Where've you been?"

I jerked my head in the direction of my brother. "Josh."

Here it came. Nick offered another explanation with a smug grin. "Hayden's having gastrointestinal issues."

"You are?" Liz asked with real concern.

"Must be the tofu," I muttered. When Liz continued to stare at me with wide eyes, I reached around Davis and patted her hand. "No, I'm not. Nick is kidding. Isn't he hilarious?" I gave him a sickly smile.

He pointed at himself like, *Who, me?*

Conversation at the table went on without us. Gavin related the details of the trip to Japan his family was planning for next summer to visit relatives they hadn't seen in years. Even if Liz and Chloe hadn't completely made up with Davis and Gavin, it was so obvious they were couples, because they sat next to each other in the booth. I felt a flash of jealousy. Maybe it was just that the bet for Poser tickets loomed over me, but I couldn't shake the idea of all six of us triple-dating.

What if Nick and I were a real couple for once, out in the open? Nick and I would slide together onto the bench on one side of the booth, and all our friends would take it for granted. He'd been cruel to hint around at asking me out when he didn't mean it, because now I couldn't get it off my mind.

As if he knew what I was thinking, he startled me by pushing the big plate of community nachos in front of me. "No wonder you're so skinny," he said quietly. "Why aren't you eating?"

"Hayden's a vegetarian," Liz called across the table.

"Oh yeah, I forgot." Nick gave me a perplexed look, like he'd just found out I was a nun or a spy.

"How can you have gone to school with her for four years and not known that?" Liz challenged him. "Why do you think she's the only person who brings her lunch on pepperoni pizza day at school?"

Davis could not get his brain around it. "Is it some Tennessee granola health club thing?"

"Just a granola health club thing," I explained. "My family didn't go vegetarian until right before we left Tennessee." Luckily, I wasn't the least bit self-conscious about being a vegetarian, because I knew it was good for me. If I'd been self-conscious, I might have begun to get uncomfortable right about then. With one short, unpainted fingernail, I traced a heart carved into the thick wooden table.

It was Gavin's turn to look perplexed. "You're from Tennessee?"

"Of course she's from Tennessee," Nick said. "Why do you think we always make fun of her accent?"

Gavin shrugged. "Because it's there?"

Davis laughed and choked on his water. Liz pounded him on the back while Chloe commented, "Somebody's being made fun of and you come running, no matter who or why, right?"

Gavin and Davis simultaneously said, "Right."

"But I forgot you were a vegetarian," Nick repeated to me. "I offered you nachos exactly like that in seventh grade, at this very table. You said you were a vegetarian and I nearly died of embarrassment for offering you meat."

"And meat products," Gavin couldn't help chiming in.

But after Gavin's comment, conversation stopped, and everyone stared at Nick. Nick? Dying of embarrassment?

He must have realized he'd blown his suave cover, because his face turned bright red.

Nick? Turning red?

"Excuse me," I said, sliding off the bench. "I'm going to the ladies' room." I was a peeless goddess no longer. That was so seventh grade. Now I was in eleventh grade, and I peed. Though of course I didn't need to at the moment. I needed to confer with my girlfriends.

"Me, too!" Chloe and Liz both said. The boys stood to let them out. Gavin and Davis grumbled about girls always having to go to the bathroom together. Nick never took his eyes off me. He knew my need to pee was a total put-on.

jib

(jib) *v.* **1.** to board around and over obstacles **2.** such as Nick

Without waiting for the girls, I rushed between the booths and down a dark hall to the tiny women's bathroom, which was wallpapered with women's wipeouts. Big photographs cut out of the newspaper, pictures cut from magazines, and snapshots showed women on skis (and a few more recent shots of women on snowboards) taking hard spills and kicking up snow. Usually I found the bathroom highly amusing. Today, as soon as I opened the door, I stopped short. The walls were sending me a message.

But I didn't stand there in awe for long, because Chloe burst through the door behind me. I hollered at her, "You're trying to set me up with Nick again!"

"We are *not*," Chloe insisted, moving over to let Liz through the door. "We thought about what you said last night. You're right. We don't want to throw away what we have with Gavin and Davis. So we thought we'd meet them here and reconcile. *Without* giving up those Poser tickets."

I folded my arms. "And you just happened to forget about that when you invited me, too? And Gavin and Davis just happened to forget they were meeting you when they invited Nick?"

Chloe tossed her blond hair and said, "Yes."

"No," Liz sighed, "we *are* trying to set you and Nick up."

Chloe glared at Liz. "Remind me never to embezzle any funds with you. The least bit of pressure and you crack!"

"It's not right to hide it from her." Liz turned to me. "I definitely have misgivings about you getting together with Nick after that fire-crotch business in the lunchroom on Thursday."

"Ah, update," I said, turning a bit red myself. "He said I was wrong about that. I didn't believe him at the time, but . . ." Something in Nick's dreamy expression when he'd mentioned the seventh grade just now had made me wonder. Was it possible that he *had* defended me against Everett Walsh? It was all sort of medieval and chivalrous and romantic if I didn't think too hard about it.

Liz nodded. "See, we may have been underestimating Nick. I feel responsible." She leaned back against the wall. Her shoulders just covered an enlargement of a girl snowboarder in the midst of a spectacular face-plant. "Gavin and every other boy in school ribbing Nick about you . . . that all started in seventh grade. Remember that awful night at the Will Smith movie, right after you'd moved here?"

"Vaguely." I rubbed my thumb across two chicks crashing into each other on skis as if I were getting bored with this convo.

"*I* remember," Chloe called out. "I was trying to balance a couple of boyfriends at once. I had a *lot* to learn about cheating."

Liz stared blankly at Chloe for a moment, then turned back to me.

"Will Smith movie," I reminded her.

Liz shook her curls. "Right. I've always regretted telling you that Nick and Gavin had a bet about you. Nick had asked everyone not to tell you. Nobody wanted to go against what Nick said. But I couldn't leave you out there alone, not knowing." She shifted uncomfortably against the wall, like the snowboard in the picture was jabbing her between the shoulder blades. "I've been the butt of jokes before."

I looked from Liz to Chloe and back to Liz. "Then why do you regret telling me?"

"I'm not sure anymore that he meant it as a joke," Liz said.

"How else could he have meant it?" I shrieked. I looked to Chloe for help in talking Liz out of this insanity. But Chloe just poofed up her blond hair in the mirror, almost as if she agreed with Liz about this.

Liz shrugged. "I know Nick has a funny way of showing it, but I honestly think he's got it bad for you. Chloe thinks so, too."

Chloe nodded her affirmation. "So do Gavin and Davis. Seventh grade to eleventh grade—that's a long time to go out of your way to be mean to somebody you can't stand."

I didn't say it, but surely Liz and Chloe felt what I felt: a vibration shaking the bathroom and speeding up my heart rate at the thought that Nick really liked me. I could *not* fall for this and get hurt again, but Nick was so tempting. I wished it were true.

Feeling dizzy, I backed against the wall beside Liz for support. "This is why I wanted to talk to you chicks in here. I'm sure that, against my instructions, you told Davis and Gavin to tell Nick that I didn't know his parents were separated, right?"

They eyed each other and nodded.

"But has he apologized for calling me a bitch? No. He came to my mother's yoga class just now, and we argued about that. Then we argued about the fire-crotch business. Now he's sitting across from me at a booth in Mile-High Pie, waxing poetic about the seventh grade. He's basically followed me around all day and poked at me, without an apology in sight." I whacked the back of my head on the pictures of snowboarders in mid-fall.

Liz gazed at me, wide-eyed and awestruck. "Wow. He's *definitely* smitten. He wants to apologize, but he doesn't know how to approach you because *you're* mad, which makes him madder and madder."

"You know what I think?" Chloe asked. She was going to tell me whether I wanted to know or not. "I think you've both built up enormous amounts of sexual tension since your session in the sauna was cut short last night, and you won't get along until you let it out. You need to make out with him. Take control."

Before I could pursue this astonishing idea with her, three senior girls pushed through the bathroom doorway and squealed when they saw me. "Hayden O'Malley!" one of them said. "I had a huge fight with my boyfriend about you, and we both joined the bet over Poser tickets. I think every couple in the school has made that bet with each other. You'd better show that boy up."

"I heard you and Nick are actually hooking up," another girl said. "Is that true?"

Chloe nodded at me encouragingly. Liz motioned with her head toward the door.

"I'm not sure. Let me get back to you." I swung open the bathroom door and walked into the restaurant again. This was my evening out: bopping back and forth, away from whichever convo made me the most uncomfortable.

I walked back to the booth and stood next to Nick. He was leaning forward, listening to what Davis and Gavin were saying. I waited for them to finish. I stood naked beside him—wearing BOY TOY jeans, a long-sleeved shirt, and a short-sleeved PowderRoom.net T-shirt over that, but feeling naked nevertheless—for several long seconds.

When he finally noticed me, he looked up quickly like he'd been waiting on edge for my return. He set down his pizza, crumpled his napkin in his hands, and even slid his half-filled plate toward the center of the table like *I* was the main course now and he was making room for me. "So, Hoyden."

I noticed the Christmas lights glinting in his dark hair

again, reflecting in his dark eyes. It took me a moment to remember I had something to tell him. Nick had that effect on me.

I bent down and cupped my hand around his ear—such an intimate gesture on its own. The coarse strands of his hair brushed my fingers as I whispered, "Chloe and Liz think we need to make out."

I jumped away at his sudden movement. He leaped up from the table and grabbed my hand. "I'll get my coat."

"What's your hurry?" Gavin called after us, but Nick didn't stop pulling me through the room. Booth after booth of loving couples flashed by, along with the wooden columns that divided the booths, each covered in years of graffiti: ALEX LOVES TAYLOR. CATHY + DAN. SYDNEY ♥S BRANDON. We flew at light speed through the restaurant, going back in time to that magical seventh-grade night, and I couldn't help giggling.

I did have some misgivings as we approached the door. But Fiona had left the Galaga machine. I never should have felt jealous about her. If Nick went out with her again, that would have been *four* dates, which was unheard of for him. And Josh and his posse had left their table. They must have gone down to the movie theater, where they could humiliate middle school girls with the whoopee cushion. I made a mental note to explain to Josh that this would not bring him any closer to a date with Gavin's sister, either.

Nick looked for his coat on the rack. I snagged mine and shrugged it on without stopping. I swung open the front door of the restaurant. The frigid night wind blew snow into my eyes.

"Hayden," Nick called to me.

"Close the door!" hollered the couples in the booths nearest us.

I let go of the door handle, then turned to Nick in the warm room. When he just stood there, staring down at me, I walked back to him.

"On second thought," he said, "I don't know about this."

I was *not* going to get dissed again. I said brightly, "Oh, don't be scared. It's easy!" I jerked his puffy parka down from the rack and held it open for him. "Try one arm at a time."

Glaring at me, he took the coat and shrugged it on. "Close the door!" shouted the couples around us as we walked outside.

Now that my eyes were used to the lights indoors, the night was black, except for the streetlights glowing yellow, and the dark blue mountain looming over the downtown buildings. Blinking the snowflakes out of my eyes, I took Nick's warm bare hand in mine and dragged him along the narrow path down a sidewalk that had been cleared of snow. I turned in at the alley between Mile-High Pie and an antiques store next door, closed for the night. The snow was deep here, and the alley was empty and dark.

"Hayden," he said softly. He slumped a bit against the brick wall and—oooh—did the pinkie-flick to his hair. But it wasn't to get me hot. In fact, he'd cooled quite a bit since I'd first whispered in his ear.

"Let's talk." I reached up to touch his shoulder, showing him I had no hard feelings that he'd lost the mood. "Gavin and Davis told you I didn't know about your parents when I made those comments last night, right?"

He nodded shortly. His hair fell back into his eyes. "Right."

"But you still haven't apologized for calling me a bitch and dissing my contest win."

"I know, and I'm sorry."

Chloe had been right! When I let Nick control our conversation, we followed each other around, throwing insults all night. Yet the second I took control, I finally got the apology I'd needed to forgive him.

Or so I thought. Then he added, "But what you said to me in the sauna was really mean, considering."

I folded my arms across my thick coat. "I understand that, *now*. But I know, and now you know, that I *didn't* understand what was going on at your house when I said that."

"Right."

I studied his handsome face. Even now, the uneducated observer would say he looked happy. Only I saw his slightly narrowed eyes and heard the edge in his voice. "You're still mad at me anyway," I said. *"I'm sorry I called you a bitch, but* doesn't count as an apology."

He put up one hand to wipe away the tiny snowflakes sticking and melting in the stubble on his chin. "You don't know how mad I was at you in the first place. I think I've done really well to back down as far as I have. Chloe and Liz say I should ask you out. Everybody in school had been telling me that, actually. But when it came down to it, in the hall last Friday, you made that comment about your lawyer. I thought you might say no and rub my face in it."

Exactly what I'd thought. If he might lose, he didn't want to play.

"My parents argued the whole weekend," he said. "I was pretty much home for the entire thing, except when I was boarding. It's been coming on for a while, but I couldn't help thinking I'd brought it on somehow by making those divorce jokes to you in the hall on Friday."

"Oh." I might believe in a little karma to go with my yoga, but Nick hadn't done anything to deserve *that*. I wanted to wrap my arms around him to comfort him. I didn't touch him, though. I didn't dare.

He splayed his hands on his jeans and rubbed his thighs like he could hardly stand to stay in his own skin any longer. "Then, in the sauna, I got a second chance to ask you out. I was really into what we were doing—or, as it turns out, not doing."

"You never did ask me out," I reminded him.

"I was *going* to. I thought we would get together. And then, when you said I never take you anywhere, and I take you for granted, and I ignore you except when it's convenient, you sounded almost exactly like my mother yelling at my father right before she left."

That hurt. I knew I hadn't said those things to him. But coming off a whole weekend of listening to his parents bicker, that's what he must have heard when I'd said he hadn't asked me to the Poser concert, he hadn't congratulated me on winning the boarding contest, and he only wanted to be with me now that our friends were together. I actually grimaced at a pain in my stomach at the thought I'd hurt him so much. "Nick—"

He waved away what I was about to say. "I'm sorry. I know that's not what you wanted to hear, and it's definitely not sexy, but I wanted you to understand what happened. I'd told Gavin and Davis some of what went down with my parents, so I figured you could have known. If you were throwing that back in my face, you were a different person than I thought. I've probably never been that angry at anyone in my life. Except my dad." He bit his lip, looking so unsure and so much younger, for once, than seventeen. "I know that's not fair to you. I'm going through kind of a tough time right now, and I might not be thinking straight."

"It's okay." I shuffled forward through the snow to hug him, whether he wanted to be hugged or not. As Chloe had said, Nick needed my support. As a friend. All our arguments seemed silly now, compared with what he'd been going through at home.

To my surprise, he put both his arms around me and hugged me closer, until I had to step toward him on the icy pavement. His body curved around me. I felt his hot breath in my hair, and I shivered.

"Are you cold? Here." He unzipped his jacket, then unzipped mine—my heart was doing flips as his hands passed down my chest, unzipping me—and he pulled me even farther forward, into his body heat.

I'd been shivering from the feelings he stirred in me every time he looked at me, not from the cold. But I certainly was not going to clue him in if he wanted to share bodily warmth. Sometimes it was best to leave well enough alone. His 98.6-degree body was an 80-degree contrast to the cold night all around me. My heart sped up, pumping my confused blood so hard through my veins that I could hear it in my ears.

"So Chloe and Liz think we should make out." He spoke just above a whisper. The low notes of his voice made my insides quiver.

I looked way up at him, into his dark eyes. "Well, last night we didn't finish what we started." I put my hands in his hair and drew his face down toward mine, enjoying every second of anticipation, feeling the aura of heat around him. I kissed his neck, just below his chin.

In yoga class, I could see when people started to let go of their busy schedules and relax into the stretches. Now I could feel Nick leave Mile-High Pie behind, and the snowy street, and the cold mountain, and relax into this little cloud of warmth with me. "God, Hayden," he breathed.

I kissed my way across his neck. He blindly fumbled under my jacket until his hot hand slid inside my T-shirt. He took my chin in his other hand and turned my face toward his, looking me all over, my eyes, my hair, my lips. I thought for a moment he was going to tell me to stop.

And then he kissed me, softly at first, then more firmly and deeply. He was not going to tell me to stop. His second thoughts were gone. He was fully committed, at least to this make-out session. His tongue swept deep inside my mouth. He gathered fistfuls of my T-shirt on either side of my waist and held me tight. For long minutes, as the cold wind teased us outside our cocoon of coats, we warmed each other and breathed each other.

It went on for thirty minutes, I would say. I'm really not sure. Time flew when I was having fun, but my brain recorded every tiny detail of his mouth on mine like we were moving in slow motion in the hot air. Like I was falling off a cliff.

Finally, when I was absorbed in the sensations of my own body and his, and I'd totally forgotten anything but the two of us in this hot moment, he brought me back. He took his hands away, broke the kiss, and stood up straight. Snow squeaked under his boots as he shifted his weight. "Do you realize we've been standing here making out in the snow and the fifteen-degree weather for five minutes?"

"Five?" I asked in a daze, touching my tingling lips and staring dumbly up at him.

"Can we go to your house?" he purred in a sexy voice.

Boy, could we! I couldn't wait to get him into my warm living room. I wasn't ready for the tingles to end, and Nick's lips on mine *plus* climate control sounded too good to be true. But I wanted to get one thing straight first. "Does this mean we're calling off the bet?"

He frowned down at me. "Of course we're not calling off the bet. You owe me a Poser ticket. Did you only come out here to get me to call off the bet?"

I sighed and looked up at the stars in exasperation. But I stopped short of walking away from him, just in case he came to his senses and decided to kiss me again. I found one of his hands and held it, gently stroking his palm with my thumb, toying with his signet ring. Feeling a little like Fiona or some other girl from my school whose voice seemed to pitch an octave higher whenever she wanted something from a boy, I asked, "Why do you want to be with me if you think so little of me?"

"I'm not sure I do want to be with you." He slid his hand out of mine. Devastating as that was, he floored me with what he did next. He faced me again and gave me the brilliant smile with the movie-star expression he always wore around school. As if none of this had happened at all. He walked by me, away from the wall, through the deep snow to the sidewalk, and disappeared around the corner of the building.

I stared into the space where he'd been, an alley entrance filled with tiny snowflakes. My tummy still swirled with tingles like the snowflakes in the air. How could Nick and I be over as suddenly as we'd started? Sure, I'd wanted him to call off the bet now that we were together. I'd expected him to. But that's not why I'd come out here with him. Truly wheedling something out of a boy, Fiona-style, required planning and organizational skills that I did not possess.

"Hoyden," Nick called from around the corner.

I shuffled after him through the snow. He had one hand on the door of Mile-High Pie, prepared to open it for me.

"I'm going home," I told him. No way was I sitting at a booth in Mile-High Pie again tonight. When I got home I would call Chloe and then Liz. They would ask if Nick and I had gotten together. I would say that for a second there, I thought we were going to, but . . . then I asked him to forfeit a challenge. I could explain all this to them on the phone, but I did not want to rehash it at the table, or in the bathroom. Mile-High Pie was a dangerous place.

"Got a ride?" he asked in exactly the polite but distant tone he would use on some ninth grader he hardly knew.

"Bus." I gestured toward the familiar squeaks as the bus lumbered around the corner several blocks down.

"Okay, then. See you around, Hoyden." He pulled the door open.

"Close the door!" called the couples as he stepped inside.

I watched him through the glass door as he hung up his puffy parka, then wove between the tables and slipped into the booth where we'd been sitting. He nodded at something

Gavin said to him. But Nick's shoulders were hunched, and he looked so defeated that I wanted to hug him again. I wished I didn't feel so strongly that he shouldn't have challenged me to this comp. I wished he would run back out to me, tell me it was all a joke, and make out with me against the wall like he was supposed to.

Watching Nick's defeated pose, I realized that wasn't going to happen. Nick might have enjoyed making out with me. He might even want to be with me. But more than anything, Nick wanted to win. And winning me over wasn't enough.

"Hayden! Yoo-hoo, Hayden O'Malley! Are you and Nick Krieger finally hooking up?"

"How are these people recognizing me?" I muttered to Liz beside me. We'd just slid away from the top of a ski lift, one I could stand to ride because it never rose too far from the ground, when we were overtaken by sophomores. It was snowing—not a pleasant light shower with the sun occasionally breaking through the clouds, either, but a heavy, constant dump from overcast skies that made visibility almost nil. Without admitting it, I'd had an eye out for Nick all day, and I figured Liz had been looking for Davis, but we'd never recognized them in the thick white air. Yet these sophomores were the fifth group of boarders from our school to pick me out that afternoon. My hair must glow in the dark.

"Dish, Hayden," exclaimed a gossip-seeking girl who skied directly into my path. "It would be sooooo cute if you and Nick got together after he sealed your backpack inside that plaster of Paris volcano last year."

Liz giggled and elbowed me. "I'd forgotten all about that one!"

"But my friends say no way," the girl went on. "Nick hates you. Which is it?"

I shrugged. "I guess you'll have to ask Nick." And if she found out, I hoped she'd pass that info along to *me*.

"Practice hard," said another girl shooting past on her board. She called backward to me, "I've got a Poser ticket riding on you."

"Me, too!" said another girl accelerating down the white slopes. "Me, too! Me, too!" more of them called, until the air was as thick with pressure as it was with snowflakes.

Liz knew what I was thinking. "Let it go," she advised me. "We're taking the afternoon off, remember?"

We'd worked hard all morning at getting me to go off the jump, with no success, despite the "help" of Josh and his posse. On the bright side, if I never became a professional snowboarder and never opened that door for Josh, he already had a whole album's worth of raps about me, my boarding, and my gastrointestinal issues. Maybe he could sign a record contract.

But Liz and I had made a pact that no matter what happened this morning, we would let loose this afternoon and have fun on the mountain. Much as I loved Chloe, she was a pain to board with, because I was forever slowing down so she could keep up, or helping her right herself and innocent bystanders after she crashed into the ski-lift line. To be honest, I was relieved she'd said she couldn't board with us today because she had "a pressing matter to attend to," even though her tone of voice made me suspicious she was meddling in my business again. Liz was a different story completely. On her skis, Liz kept up with me.

"Why don't we go down Main Street?" She gestured to the enormous slope in front of us with the ski lodge a tiny dot at the bottom. "And then we'll have time to take the lift up for one last run before it gets dark."

"Race ya," I said, getting a five-second head start on her before she could put her goggles down.

We crisscrossed the expanse of snow. She leaped over moguls and crash-landed on the other side, her falls cushioned by six inches of fresh powder. I used the moguls to launch me into lazy 360s. We giggled and shouted and nearly ran into each other a dozen times on our way down.

Despite the slow powder conditions and the snow plastering my goggles so I had to stop and wipe them every few minutes, this was what snowboarding was really about for me. Speeding downhill in a race was fun, and I loved pushing my body to land new stunts with steeze. But the real joy came in messing around with friends, exploring, trying new things without worrying about how they'd look, and knowing I could come back and do it all again tomorrow.

"Boy alert!" Liz called as we reached the bottom of Main Street and passed the half-pipe. I stopped beside her, shook the snow out of my hair (gingerly, because the ends of my hair were heavy with ice), and pulled off my goggles so I could see. Sure enough, Nick, Davis, and Gavin stood in line on the side of the pipe, waiting their turns and watching another guy bust ass on a 720 attempt.

"Oooh," said the crowd around the pipe.

"Oooh," echoed the people braving the snow to drink beer or hot chocolate out on the deck of the ski lodge. They were far enough away that their voices reached us a split second later.

"Do you want to go and say hi to the boys?" Liz asked me. She was so sweet to ask me first. I *knew* she wanted some Davis time since she hadn't seen him all day, but I'd told her how things had ended last night between me and Nick.

"Sure," I told her. "I have to go back to school with Nick on Monday. No point in avoiding him now." She took off her skis and I kicked off my board below the pipe, and we hiked up behind the boys in the center of the crowd of spectators lining the lip.

"Davis," Liz called.

He looked back toward us, ducked his head so he could see us among the other spectators, and waved at us. Then he turned around to the half-pipe again. He and Gavin both leaned their heads in toward Nick so all three of them could share a laugh. I heard their cackles echo against the far side of the half-pipe. The whole crowd sighed, "Oooh." And then I heard Nick say, "Fire-crotch."

biff

(bif) *n.* **1.** crash **2.** somebody bites it

Thinking back on it later, I realized I must have dropped my board without any regard to how far away it might have slid down the slope. I must have climbed to the rim of the half-pipe with surprising nimbleness, considering my usual trouble maneuvering in my boarding boots. I must have pushed five people aside. But all I remember is shoving Nick in the back and screaming, "Liar!"

He spun around with his dark eyes wide. It was the only time I'd ever seen him startled.

"Did you call me a fire-crotch in the lunchroom, Nick?" I shouted. "Did you? Does it really matter if you didn't, when you called me one just now? You have got a lot of freaking nerve!" Panting, I managed to stop myself from saying anything else, because so many people around us were leaning in, listening, murmuring about the bet and the Poser concert.

But what I'd said didn't begin to tap how furious I was with him, and how hurt I was. He'd stood there in the snow at Mile-High Pie last night and made me feel sorry for him! He'd made me feel terrible for something I didn't even do, after he'd lied to me to my face! And then he'd kissed me, and I'd let him!

Mortifying.

Now his lips parted. I waited to hear the next lie. I almost hoped it was a good one, so at least I'd have an entertaining story to share with my friends about what an ass he was.

But Davis spoke up first in a reasonable tone, like a psychiatrist soothing a loony. "We weren't talking about you, Hayden."

Gavin jerked his thumb over his shoulder. "The kid in the pipe just busted his nuts on the deck."

I glared at Gavin, showing him I didn't buy his ridiculous story. Then, just to make sure he was lying, too, I stuck my head between him and Nick and peered into the pipe. A freshman lay at the bottom of the course, holding his crotch. As I watched, he slowly stood and used his board as a crutch to hobble out of the pipe. The spectators cheered like he was an injured football player walking off the field during a game.

Nick was watching me. Not glaring. Just watching me with an expression beyond hurt.

I took a breath, and couldn't think of anything to say.

"Come on, Nick," Gavin called. "You're up. Better get your head in the game, if you know what I mean."

Nick still watched me as he passed. Then all three boys turned their backs on me as they hiked above the pipe. Nick stepped onto his board and lowered his goggles.

"Here's your board," Liz said behind me.

"Thanks." Absently I gripped the snowboard she slipped into my mitten. "I guess you heard all that."

"I guess everyone between here and Aspen heard it," she murmured. "Why didn't you tell him you were sorry?"

"I—," I began. Truth was, I'd opened my mouth to apologize, since that was the logical thing to do after such a stupid mistake. But I'd still been so angry over something he hadn't really done, I couldn't get the words out.

So angry that I would have belittled what he loved or challenged him to a stupid contest if I'd had the chance.

"Nick Krieger," the crowd sighed, collectively recognizing Nick as he hopped onto the slope and sped toward the deck.

He dropped into the pipe and picked up incredible momentum down the side and across the flat, almost as if the pipe weren't filled with powder. The opposite wall launched him so high, I definitely would have lost my balance and rolled down the windows if I were him. Nick just grabbed his board in a method air, like it was nothing. He hung in the sky for an impossible second, then slid down the side.

"Oooh," said the crowd, followed a moment later by an "oooh" from the ski lodge.

He hit the same height in his next trick, a 360. He couldn't do my tricks, but he went much higher, and he was so heavy and powerful that the pipe seemed to grind and bend underneath him. I could feel it in my teeth.

"Oooh," said the crowd.

He crossed the flat again and launched his third trick, a 540. I could tell the split second after he hit his apex that what he'd intended to do didn't match his rotation.

"That's not going to end well," Liz whispered as Nick headed for the snow without completing the last revolution.

I'd seen a lot of crashes, courtesy of Josh and his peeps. I pictured this one in my head before it happened.

I couldn't watch. The snow in the air had thickened, but even so, I could see his dark silhouette headed downward. I closed my eyes.

"Biff!" yelled the crowd in unison.

I opened my eyes and gasped. "He's not moving."

Liz grabbed my padded arm.

I waited for Gavin and Davis to move from their places at the top of the course. A gray snow cloud of testosterone always hung over the half-pipe course, making boys try tricks they couldn't land and pretend not to be hurt when they were. Nick would be embarrassed if his friends went down to check on him. He would be horrified if I did. But *somebody* had to go. Nick got hit in football games all autumn long, and he was used to it. If he wasn't getting up, he was really hurt.

Finally, Gavin and Davis maneuvered their boards to the edge of the course and tipped over into the pipe, skidding to a stop just above Nick's dark, motionless body.

Through the thick snow, I saw him slowly rise.

I gasped again, and realized I'd been holding my breath.

He kicked off his snowboard and hoisted it behind his back to carry it home. The boarders around me on the lip of the course cheered for him.

"Thank God!" Liz exclaimed. "He can't be hurt too badly if he's walking away." She turned to me with her dark eyebrows raised in question. "Want to go after him?"

I did, desperately. I squinted through the snow after the dim retreating shapes of the three boys, Gavin and Davis sliding on their boards, Nick limping a little. "Better let him cool down first."

Liz puffed out a little sigh of relief. "Still want to get in that last run?"

"No. If it's okay with you, let's call it a night." I'd thought I wanted to squeeze every minute of boarding I could out of winter break. I'd never been the person to turn down one last run. And I should have been ecstatic that my snowboarding challenge with Nick was over now because he'd been injured.

But for once, my heart just wasn't in boarding. My heart was with Nick.

This was how my life worked: Something great happened simultaneously with something very bad. I won lessons with Daisy Delaney, but I had to snowboard off a cliff to get any benefit from them. I found the perfect pair of jeans, but they didn't belong to me, and they had BOY TOY written across the butt. Now my ugly bet with Nick had ended, so maybe we could finally get together. But oops—I had just screamed at him in front of a live audience, *and* he was probably crippled.

That night after supper I sat on my bed, staring at the cell phone in my hand. I'd already called Liz and Chloe. Both of them had promised to meet me on the slopes the next day just for fun, since the comp was obviously off after Nick's injury. More importantly, they said Davis and Gavin did not have an update on Nick's condition. Boys, it seemed, did not check on each other like girls.

Which was precisely my problem. I couldn't stand the thought of Nick hurting in his house without his mother home. Maybe his dad wasn't home, either. They might not even know he'd fallen. I had to make sure he was okay.

Nick had been angry enough at the half-pipe that he'd probably hang up on me when I called. Or worse, he'd be very polite, like he was at school to people he didn't know.

But his well-being was more important than my pride. I'd just entered his number from the school handbook into my cell phone. All I had to do was press the green button and the call would go through.

Good: I would find out whether Nick was okay.

Bad: Nick would view me as one of those girls at school who chased him, even after they'd gone on two dates and he'd called it quits.

Nick's number waited impatiently on the screen, tapping

its foot. I could press the red button to cancel the call. Without pressing anything, I set the phone down on my bedside table, crossed my arms, and glared at it.

Good: Nick wouldn't think I was chasing him.

Bad: Nick would die alone in his house from complications related to his stupendous wipeout. The guilt of knowing I could have saved his life if not for my outsized ego would be too much for me to bear. I would retreat from public life. I would join a nearby convent and knit potholders from strands of my own hair. No, I would crochet Christmas ornaments in the shape of delicate snowflakes. Red snowflakes! They would be sold in the souvenir shops around town. I would support a whole orphanage from the proceeds of snowflakes I crocheted from my hair. All the townspeople of Snowfall would tell tourists the story of Crazy Sister Hayden and the tragedy of her lost love.

Or I could call Nick. Jesus! I snatched up the phone and pressed the green button.

His phone switched straight to voice mail. Great, I hadn't found out whether he was dying, *and* if he recovered later, he would see my number on his phone and roll his eyes.

Damage control: *Beeeeep!* "Hey, Nick, it's Hayden. Just, ah, wanted to know how a crash like that feels." Wait, I was trying to get him to call me back, right? He would not return my call after a message like that. "Actually, just wondering whether you're ready to make out again and then have another argument." He might not return that call, either. "Actually, I remembered your mother isn't home, and I wanted to make sure you're okay. Please give me a call back."

Pressed red button. Set phone on nightstand. Folded arms. Glared at phone. Picked it up. "Freaking stupid young love!" I hollered, slamming it into the pillows on my bed. Doofus jumped up, startled.

Ah-ha.

I slipped into long underwear, layered on the BOY TOY jeans and shirts and sweaters and coats and hats, and waddled stiffly downstairs to find Doofus's leash. By now Josh and Mom were video-bowling. I hoped they were so absorbed that I could escape from the house just by calling a good-bye into the den as I passed the doorway.

But no. "Hayden," Mom called. "Where are you going all bundled up?"

"I'm taking Doofus for a walk," I said brightly.

"I already took Doofus for a walk," Josh said.

I stared at him. He stared right back at me while Mom took her turn bowling. I could have explained that I wanted to walk without Doofus and get some air. But it would be pretty unusual—one might even go so far as to say unheard of—for me to take a hike on a winter night when I was exhausted from boarding all day.

I could also come right out and tell both of them that Nick had fallen on the slopes today and I wanted to check on him. But then Mom would suggest I take the car to his house. And then I could never pull off the charade that I just happened by his mansion while walking my dog.

Besides, it was the principle of the thing—the very idea that Josh saw I wanted to walk Doofus and he was going out of his way to foil me, like a normal little brother. This made me angry. Did he *want* Nick to die on the floor of his bathroom from an overdose of mentholated rub? Did he *want* me to spend the last eighty years of my lifespan in a convent? Maybe he was mad that I was trying to sneak out of the house wearing his jeans for the third day in a row.

"I am taking Doofus for *another* walk," I said clearly, daring him to defy me.

"That would not be good for Doofus." Josh folded his arms. "Mom, that would not be good for Doofus."

Oh! Dragging Mom into this was low. Not to mention Doofus. "Since when is going for a walk not good for a dog?" I challenged Josh.

"He's an *old* dog!" Josh protested.

"He's *four*!" I pointed out.

"That's twenty-eight in dog years! He's practically thirty!"

"Strike!" Mom squealed amid the noise of electronic pins falling. Then she shook her game remote at both of us in turn. "I'm not stupid, you know. And I'm not as out of it as you assume. I know the two of you are really arguing about something else. It's those jeans again, isn't it?" She nodded to me. "I should cut them in half and give each of you a leg. Why does either of you want to wear jeans with 'boy toy' written across the seat anyway?"

"I thought that was the fashion," Josh said. "Grandma wears a pair of sweatpants with 'hot mama' written across the ass."

"That is *different*," Mom hissed. "She wears them around the *kitchen*."

I sniffed indignantly. "I *said*," I announced, "I am going for a walk with my dog. My beloved canine and I are taking a turn around our fair community. No activity could be more wholesome for a young girl and her pet. And if you have a problem with that, well! What is this world coming to? Come along, dear Doofus." I stuck my nose in the air and stalked past them, but the effect was lost. Somewhere around "our fair community," Mom and Josh both had lost interest and turned back to the TV.

Or so I thought. But just as I was about to step outside, Josh appeared in the doorway between the kitchen and the mudroom. "What the hell are you doing?" he demanded.

I said self-righteously, "I am taking my loyal canine for a w—"

"You're going to Nick's, aren't you?" he whispered. "Do you think that's a good idea? I heard you yelled at him for no reason at the half-pipe, right before he busted ass."

I swallowed. Good news traveled fast. "So?"

"So, why are you going over there? Best-case scenario, you make out with him again and then have another fight."

Good news about *everything* traveled fast. I scowled at Josh. "It's better than not knowing whether he's hurt."

"Is it?" Josh leaned against the doorframe and folded his arms. He'd never looked so much like my father, and it was time to put him in his place.

"Way better, and someday you will be old enough to understand." I reached forward to pat him on the head. He dodged my hand and came after me across the mudroom, bent on revenge. Doofus and I escaped out the door and ran all the way across the snowy yard. I wouldn't have put it past Josh to chase me outside in his socks, but behind me the mudroom had turned dark.

Doofus and I headed toward town. The sidewalk was icy as always but not nearly as slippery, now that I wore good walking boots rather than snowboarding boots. And the night was gorgeous, deep purple all around with the lights of downtown glowing from the valley, and a sky full of stars. We skirted the touristy area, with its streets full of happy families and laughing couples in love, and headed up the mountain.

Nick's street was close to the center of town, but I couldn't recall ever driving up it in my mom's car. It allowed access to only ten mansions overlooking the slopes, the homes of nobody I knew except Nick. And somehow I had always resisted driving very slowly back and forth in front of his house. Willpower? No. I figured his front gate was equipped with security cameras and I would just be embarrassing myself. And this street was definitely not on the bus line.

Doofus and I hiked up the sidewalk. Since there was no one around, I dropped Doofus's leash. He pranced in the snowdrifts and bit the snow and rolled in it until ice clumped and froze in his tail. He promptly trotted back to me, wagging his tail, and whacked me with the ice.

"Ouch! Sweet doggie." We'd passed two mansions and had reached Nick's. It was big and beautiful and distant amid the snow falling gently in the night. Through the cold landscape, warm light glowed from a second-story window. If he'd died alone in his big, empty house, at least he hadn't died in the cold dark.

I couldn't leave without knowing. With a sigh, I pressed the button on the imposing gate. Doofus and I both jumped at the buzz. I backed up to give the gate room in case it opened out.

It stayed shut.

After a few moments, I pressed the button again. The gate didn't move, and the lights of the house stared at me across the snowy plain.

"Fine. Come on, Doofus." I led the way back down the hill to the narrow passage between the Kriegers' fence and the fence next door. Mistake: The unshoveled snow was knee-deep. I kept right on wading through it. "This is because I'm a good person," I assured Doofus. "I am going to heaven, though hopefully not by way of the convent." Doofus pranced happily around me.

Finally I reached the back corner of Nick's enormous yard, where even the passage between the Kriegers' fence and their neighbors' was shut off from the ski slopes by another, higher fence. "Okay, this isn't good. I'm sorry, Doofus, but I have to leave you out here while I go save the day. I'll only be a minute." I looked around for a tree to tie Doofus's leash to, one that he would not pull out by its roots.

Something moved swiftly in the corner of my eye. Mountain lion! I gasped and whirled around.

It was only Doofus, climbing Nick's fence. He'd leapt to the top and hooked his front paws over the wood. Now his back legs scrabbled against the smooth planks, searching for a claw-hold to push him over.

"Bad dog," I sighed. He'd disappeared.

Well, if I'd had any thoughts of chickening out on my mission, they were gone now. I jumped to the top of the fence, hauled myself over, and dropped to the snowy ground.

And froze with horror. The mountain lion was *here* in the fenced yard with us where we couldn't escape. *Growling* at us. Except for the square rectangular glow of a glass door on the deck, I saw nothing but blackness. But I heard the growl, too close.

"Doofus!" I screamed, needlessly. He barreled toward me and hit me in the chest, yelping. I'm not sure whether I dragged him or he dragged me, but somehow we dashed up the wooden steps to the snow-covered deck and headed straight for the door. I didn't even have time to pray it was unlocked. The sharp claws of the mountain lion nicked my calves above my boots, through my long underwear and jeans. I yanked open the door and picked Doofus up bodily. We collapsed inside in a mound of Polartec and fur and backed against the door until it clicked closed.

We both started away from the door as the mountain lion leaped against it, howling, all fangs and claws and wild eyes.

Very small wild eyes. Four of them.

It wasn't a mountain lion at all. It was two tabbies.

There were a few seconds of stillness, just Doofus and me panting in the large, quiet room, and bemusement that I had exploded with my wet dog into a filthy-rich family's grand home. We faced a huge rock fireplace that I recognized from the Krieger Meats and Meat Products TV commercial so many years ago, with Nick giving the camera his winning smile, his mother blinking pleasantly into the camera, and Mr. Krieger inviting the public to taste Krieger Meats, from their family to yours. Happier times for Nick and his parents.

Feeling a pang for all of them, I gave Doofus's wet, cold fur a stroke. I wasn't sure what to do now. I still needed to find out whether Nick was okay. And there were still attack cats on the prowl.

I was about to detangle myself from Doofus and survey the damage we'd done to Nick's palace when I caught another movement out of the corner of my eye. Someone was lying on a leather couch facing away from me. A blond head eased ominously into view. Nick's father! Oh, no! He would take me for a stalker. Now Nick would *really* think I was chasing him!

Or not. Mr. Krieger took out one earbud. He cackled in a high-pitched witch voice, "I'll get you, my pretty, and your little dog Toto, too!"

"Uh, Doofus," I corrected him.

He pursed his lips quizzically. "Come on. It wasn't *that* bad a joke."

I didn't bother to explain. I wouldn't need to get along with Mr. Krieger in the future. Something told me I would never find myself eating Thanksgiving dinner with these people—and wait until the owner of Krieger Meats and Meat Products found out I was a vegetarian! I just wanted to satisfy myself that Nick was okay, and then get out. "Hi, there!" I beamed. "Did you order a redhead and a dog?"

"Hayden O'Malley," he purred.

"Yes, sir." He knew who I was? Doofus was licking my face.

Mr. Krieger pulled out his other earbud. "I know all about your challenge with Nick. My money's on you, literally. Nick's a quitter."

I blinked at him, not sure what to say to that. I'd never heard a parent say something so mean about his child— and something so untrue. I reminded myself that his wife had left him the previous weekend, and he was probably not in the best of moods. If Nick had hidden his injury from his dad and hadn't yet told him the challenge was over, I didn't want to be the one to clue his dad in and mess things up worse for Nick. I said carefully, "Yeah, the girls at school are always pushing him down on the playground and telling him not to be such a baby."

Mr. Krieger sat up straighter on the couch and glared at me. Great. I was definitely not getting invited for Thanksgiving now. At least I'd made my point, and I thought he'd heard me.

"Is he in?" I prompted Mr. Krieger.

He swept his hand dramatically toward a wide staircase, then reinserted his earbuds and sank back onto the couch, dismissing me. I supposed this meant I was invited in? Or at least, not thrown out? Doofus and I righted ourselves and walked past the couch and up the stairs. Doofus's claws clicked on the stone and echoed against the vaulted ceilings.

On the second story, windows overlooking the ski slopes lined one side of the vast hallway. The other side was an endless stretch of doors. I headed toward the open door with light flooding out onto the Navajo rug. But I stopped short when I heard Nick talking inside. There was a pause, and then he talked again. He must be on the phone, which is why my own call had gone straight to his voice mail.

"I love you, too," I heard him say. "'Bye."

My heart stopped. Had he been on the phone with Fiona? Or some new snow bunny I hadn't yet heard about? Whoever his new girlfriend was . . . it wasn't me.

shred

(shred) *v.* **1.** to tear up the slopes **2.** or Hayden's
heart

Before I could react, he called, "Come in."

I froze like a rabbit, just as I had outside the men's
locker room at the health club yesterday. This time Nick
really *had* caught me.

I couldn't very well run away. Mr. Krieger knew I was
there. Finally, I sauntered forward and lounged in the doorway with my arms crossed on my chest. After all, *I'd* caught

Nick telling someone he loved her. Someone other than me.

He lay with his legs on his king-size bed and his body folded forward off the edge, toward the floor, in what looked suspiciously like a cockamamy approximation of a Downward-Facing Dog. The football players in the huge posters all around the room seemed to rush toward him, taunting him, while he lay helpless in the center of the circle and tried in vain to stretch his back.

I'd discovered so many new sides of Nick in the past few days, and now I was seeing another. His dark hair had been long the whole time I'd known him. I'd never glimpsed the nape of his neck, but here it was, bare to me as his hair touched the floor. Doofus sauntered over and licked Nick's face. Squinting against the dog slobber, Nick grumbled, "You may be a lot of things, Hayden, but quiet isn't one of them."

I sniffed. "Oh, yeah? You weren't very quiet on the phone just now, either."

He eyed me. Even from his upside-down viewpoint, he must have been able to see I was jealous. "That was my mom," he explained.

My heart started beating again, painfully. I kept my face carefully neutral, hiding how freaking relieved I felt that he hadn't given up on us and moved along to another girl. Not yet, anyway.

"She's staying with my grandmother in Phoenix." Nick sat up on his bed with a groan, looking hurt and adorable in a tight T-shirt and track pants, his hair a disaster. "What are you doing here?"

"I just happened to be in the neighborhood, walking my dog . . ." This was sounding lame. ". . . several miles from my home, in the middle of the night, in the snow. And I found myself in your backyard."

His eyes flew wide open. "With the cats?"

"If that's what you call them."

"You came over because you feel guilty for yelling at me at the half-pipe."

I did. He didn't have to sound so smug about it, though. "I do feel sort of guilty for yelling at you at the half-pipe," I admitted, "but—"

"But—," he broke in sarcastically.

"But," I continued over him, "I've had good reason in the past to think you'd called me a name like that to your friends."

"What's your good reason? That I *didn't* call you a fire-crotch last week in the lunchroom?"

He had me there, but I wasn't ready to admit defeat. Nick was just as guilty as I was. "You're one to talk. You walked around mad at me for something *I* didn't mean to do for a whole day, until I persuaded you otherwise."

"And then *I* apologized," he pointed out. One side of his mouth cocked up in a mischievous grin. "And then I slipped you the tongue."

We both cracked up then, with spontaneous exclamations of "The tongue!" I was glad we'd broken the ice. At the same time, it seemed like we were laughing about a relationship we'd had long ago, rather than last night. Maybe we had nothing in common now that the bet was off.

I hoped not. To show him that a sequel to "the tongue" was not out of the question, I crossed his room, shedding layers of outerwear as I went, and sat beside him on the bed. "Seriously, I came over to make sure you're okay. Did you go to the doctor?"

"I'm not hurt," he said flatly.

I rolled my eyes in exasperation. "I was there this afternoon, Nick. I saw you fall. You were lying immobile in the snow."

"Yeah. I didn't get enough—"

"—rotation in the 540," we said simultaneously.

We paused, watching each other. All our problems fell away. Just for a moment we were friends, fellow snowboarders, discussing a mistake we'd both made a million times. This was not my imagination. Nick felt it, too. He looked deep into my eyes. His own eyes were impossibly dark with the lights of his room reflecting as little halos.

And then he looked away, flicking his hair out of his face with his pinkie. "So anyway, after I busted ass, I'm lying there in the snow. My life flashed before my eyes."

"Why?" I asked, horrified, scooting closer.

"Not my whole life, I guess. My personal life. I've been kind of down about my parents, and I was mad at you for yelling at me, and then I wondered why we're doing this stupid comp anyway. Gavin's been breathing down my neck about winning him Poser tickets and putting Chloe in her place. All I ever wanted to do this winter break was have fun and board and relax."

"Amen." I sighed. Thank God the comp was over. "I was worried about you. I called your cell and rang the bell at the gate. You didn't hear it?"

"It rings downstairs, and my dad . . ." Nick stared into space, and his voice trailed off.

I could have finished this sentence for him. *My dad . . . is lying on the couch, listening to the middle-aged person's equivalent of emo songs on his iPod, because my mother left him.* Journey, or something. Duran Duran.

Finally Nick focused on me again. His long, dark lashes blinked slowly. He looked lost. A more accurate end to his sentence: *My dad . . . is lost himself, and I don't know whether my parents are coming back.*

I wanted to reach out to him then, to touch his stubbled cheek with my fingertips. We were alone in his bedroom, after all. On his bed. His mom was gone. His dad probably didn't care what we did. Doofus stretched into a different position on Nick's carpet, sending a wave of wet dog odor toward us only occasionally. We could have made out.

But maybe Josh actually had a point, and it wasn't good for Nick and me to keep making out and arguing. Perhaps making out was *not* the answer to all our problems, oddly enough. And I'd come over to check on Nick, not to seduce him. Shaking my head to clear it, I said, "I know what will make you feel better."

"I'm not hurt," he insisted.

"Obviously you are, or I wouldn't have walked in on you doing half-assed yoga." I stretched out on his bed and hung forward over the side, just as I'd found him. "Come on, I'll do it with you."

Grumbling, Nick bent over the side with me. We hung that way for about ten seconds of quiet before he said, "It's not working."

"That's your problem, like I told you yesterday. You don't hold the stretch long enough, and besides, you do it while listening to"—I felt behind me on the bed for his MP3 player and peered at the screen—"alt metal." I tossed it across the room into a leather armchair. "Try this with me. Inhale through your nose, and let your legs melt into the bed. Exhale through your mouth, and let your body and your arms fall toward the floor." I led him through a few more long breaths that way, until I could see from the corner of my eye that he'd relaxed, like when we'd made out last night.

I reminded myself yet again that this was not the time for making out. I was making up with Nick for exploding at him in public about the fire-crotch comment. As he stretched with his eyes closed, he looked so young and vulnerable, so *normal*, that I ached to reach out and feel around on his back for the bruise where he'd fallen, or to change my voice from soothing to sexy. But I'd come here on a mission to make Nick feel better. And I was pretty sure making out with me was not what Nick needed right now. I took him through a whole series of easy poses, moving from the bed to the floor.

Finally we sat up. Nick slouched glassy-eyed against his leather armchair. I relaxed in the Lotus Pose, invigorated from the stretches.

"I feel better," he said languidly.

"I'm glad."

"No, really better," he said like he couldn't believe it now that he was waking up a little.

"Keep stretching every day and take it seriously, and you won't be as likely to get hurt boarding. Now I'd better go." I nodded at the clock on his bedside table. "I told my mom I was taking Doofus for a walk. We could have walked to Leadville by now."

He stood up unsteadily, leaning on the chair. "I'll drive you home."

I wasn't sure this was a good idea. I had a lot of anxiety about him being polite to me. It would probably be best to give him more time to cool off after I'd yelled at him at the half-pipe.

On the other hand, I *really* did not want to walk back home through the freezing night or make Doofus do it, either. He'd been through enough. "Is your SUV parked outside, or is it in the garage?" I asked hopefully. "Doofus and I would rather not face your attack cats again."

"There's a cat door in the back of the house. They can come inside any time they want. Don't worry. I'll protect you." He slid a machine gun from his dresser—a red-and-blue plastic water gun.

"My hero," I breathed as he pointed his gun into the hall and looked both ways before stealthily motioning for me and Doofus to follow, like he was the star of an action-adventure flick. With me giggling at him and him shushing me as if I really were his airheaded heroine, we made it downstairs and stepped from an enormous, gleaming kitchen into a three-car garage.

His SUV, so familiar to me from seeing it parked every day at school since he'd gotten his license last year, looked out of place in the vast space next to a Porsche. The SUV seemed so . . . normal. Like Nick: normal but not. He didn't mind an Irish setter dripping melted snow on his bedroom carpet or hopping into the back of his SUV. Yet his SUV was parked in the garage of a mansion.

You know what else was perfectly normal? The missing third car. His parents had separated, just like Liz's parents had divorced three years before. The Krieger Meats and Meat Products fortune did not solve everything. I tried not to stare back at the empty space on the other side of the Porsche as the garage door tipped out of the way and the SUV pulled into the light snow.

Snowflakes zoomed around in the headlight beams, defining them far out in front of us, almost all the way down the hill to the gate. Nick turned on the windshield wipers, but he hardly needed them. The snowflakes weren't substantial. The breeze of the wipers shooed them away like fireflies during a Tennessee summer.

He pushed another button, and the gate majestically opened for us before we even reached it. He didn't mean any-thing by this motion, I reminded myself. He drove through the gate a few times a day. He didn't give it a second thought. He had no idea that, to me, he seemed to be rubbing in how rich he was and how powerful his parents were. This was what had separated us in the seventh grade, when he'd half-believed Gavin that a girl wouldn't date him without his family status behind him. This was what separated us still.

And yet, in a strange way, I'd never felt closer to him. The SUV crunched through gravel onto the main road, where it swished through slushy snow. But inside it was warm, and a rock ballad from the Poser CD whispered about true love lost. This should have been a date. Instead of him taking me home after I came to check on him and got run inside by killer cats, he should have been taking me back to my house after we'd watched a movie together at his. He would come inside. My parents would go to bed, and Josh would take a hint and abandon video-bowling to go upstairs and read a book. (I could dream, couldn't I?) Nick and I would be alone with the smoldering embers of a fire. And then we would—

"—get out?" he was asking me.

I blinked at him across the dark SUV. "I beg your pardon?" I hoped to God I hadn't been discussing any of this out loud.

"Are. You. Going. To. Get. Out?" he asked more distinctly. We'd already parked in front of my house, with the

SUV's heater still bathing us in warmth against the snowy night outside. "You haven't said a word the whole five-minute drive here. Are you sick?" He reached across the cab and put his hot hand on my forehead.

I laughed and pulled his hand down. But I didn't let it go. I kept it there in both my hands, on my knee. And he didn't pull it away. We watched each other for a quiet moment.

"I'm glad this happened," he said softly.

He was so handsome in the soft and snowy moonlight. I wanted him to be talking about our relationship: He was glad we'd finally gotten together. But after everything that had passed between us this week, doubts still lurked at the back of my mind about whether he seriously liked me, or he intended to date me twice and dump me like all his other girlfriends, or the whole thing was just a joke to him. I hoped it was for real, and I didn't want to talk about it too much and ruin the lovely illusion that we were a couple. So I said noncommittally, "Me too."

"Because I've been trying to get you back since the seventh grade."

I must have given him a very skeptical look.

He laughed at my expression. "Yeah, I have a funny way of showing it. I know. But you're always on my mind. You're in the front of my mind, on the tip of my tongue. So if someone breaks a beaker in chemistry class, I raise my hand and tell

Ms. Abernathy you did it. If somebody brings a copy of *Playboy* to class, I stuff it in your locker."

"Oh!" I thought back to the January issue. "I wondered where that came from."

"And if Everett Walsh tells the lunch table what a wicked kisser you are and how far he would have gotten with you if his mother hadn't come in—"

I stamped my foot on the floorboard of the SUV. "That is so not true! He'd already gotten as far as he was going. He's not *that* cute, and I had to go home and study for algebra."

"—it drives me insane to the point that I tell him to shut up or I'll make him shut up right there in front of everybody. Because *I* am supposed to be your boyfriend, and *my* mother is supposed to hate you, and you're supposed to be making out with *me*."

Twisted as this declaration was, it was the sweetest thing a boy had ever said to me. I dwelled on the soft lips that had formed the statement, and on the meaning of his words. "Okay." I scooted across the seat and nibbled the very edge of his superhero chin.

"Ah," he gasped, moving both hands from the steering wheel to the seat to brace himself. "I didn't mean *now*. I meant in general. Your dad will come out of your house and kill me."

"He won't," I murmured against Nick's neck. "He came

home while I was gone and went to bed early because he's so pooped." I glanced at my watch to make sure. "Yeah. He teaches four Pilates classes on Thursdays." Then, just to be mean, I did a real number on Nick's neck, like I would want *him* to move his mouth on *my* neck. I had to be careful or I would give him a hickey. Served him right for playing hard to get.

"Damn it," he grunted in frustration. He put his hand in my hair and pulled my head back. Our eyes met for a second. I saw how frustrated he was, and how hot for me, and something else between his dark brows.

And then *he* kissed *me*. His mouth was on mine, covering mine and making me feel small. His tongue swept inside. He pulled my nape with his big hand to adjust me to exactly where he wanted me. The air in the SUV flashed too hot and then cold as he kissed me. His other hand slid up my thigh.

I would never have admitted this to anyone, and I would only put up with it for so long. But this was the part of a relationship with Nick I'd dreamed about and longed for: Nick in control of me.

He murmured against *my* neck, "See? We can't do this in an SUV on your street in the open." His tone was triumphant, as if he'd conquered me. *Yeah!*

"You win," I sighed. Then I opened my eyes.

He gazed down at me, wearing the most beautiful smile.

Nick Krieger was not putting on a brave face for the public. He was not faking. He was genuinely happy.

With me!

And then, it turned out that *I* won, because I got what I wanted. He kissed me for several long minutes.

Finally, he slid his hand from my nape down to my shoulder and squeezed there for a second, catching his breath. "Come on. I'll walk you to the door." Before I could argue about that (after all, who *really* wants a gentleman for a boyfriend, besides Liz?), he walked around the SUV and opened the hatchback to let out Doofus, whom I had forgotten about completely.

I resented Doofus a little. First he'd jumped into my arms when the cats attacked and made me smell like dog. Now, if it weren't for him, I could have hung around outside, chatting Nick up until he agreed to get back in the SUV and make out with me for a few more minutes. As it was, Doofus would be tugging on his leash the whole time and trying to pull my arm out of its socket.

To my surprise, as I watched in the rearview mirror, Doofus leaped out of the SUV, dragging his leash. I tensed, prepared to lunge from the SUV after him. I pictured chasing him all over the neighborhood. I'd had enough snowy walks for one night, not to mention snowy runs to escape death at the paws of wild animals.

Fortunately, he didn't run away from my house. He ran toward it. He must have been hungry. He ran straight for the fence—at this point, I suspected brain damage from our fall through the Kriegers' back door—and hooked his paws over the top of the fence, just as he had at Nick's house. He scrabbled with his back paws until his big red dog-booty disappeared over the fence.

If he could come and go over the fence as he pleased, there was no telling what he did all around the neighborhood while we weren't watching. Suddenly, it seemed the O'Malleys were having a hard time keeping track of their dog *and* their daughter.

Nick seemed to be thinking the same thing as he opened the passenger door for me. "Did you see that?"

"Yep," I laughed, swinging his hand as we walked across the snowy lawn toward the mudroom door.

"This *is* your house, right?"

"Either that, or some naked hot-tubbers behind that fence just got the surprise of their lives." We'd reached the door. I leaned back against it, looking way up at him, thinking the strangest thoughts, such as, *Nick Krieger is finally my boyfriend!*

"I'm boarding with Liz and Chloe tomorrow," I said. "Maybe I could come over to your house again afterward and check on you?" I raised my eyebrows to *hint hint* what

I meant by *checking on him*. With any luck, his father would be as uninvolved and dismissive as he'd been tonight. Nick needed more yoga in his bedroom, and possibly a physical.

"I'm boarding, too," he said, "but that doesn't mean you can't check on me afterward." He raised his eyebrows too, *hint hint*.

It wasn't funny when he did it. "What do you mean, you're boarding?" I asked suspiciously. "You're hurt."

"I keep telling you, I'm not hurt that badly. It's no worse than a football hit, and I get those all the time and keep playing. I have to beat you in a comp in two days."

I put my hands on my hips and looked up at him. "The comp is canceled because you're injured!"

He shook his head stubbornly. "I'm not injured. The comp is not canceled. Everybody in town knows about our bet. I can't quit now. My dad would kill me. My dad has actually bet *against* me. Winners never quit."

Exasperated, I ran my hands through my hair. "Nick, I understand you want to impress your dad, but it's not worth risking your health."

"My he—" he began. Then he took a step backward into the snow, and his broad shoulders sagged in defeat. "That's the only reason you came over, isn't it? Just like going outside with me last night. You want me to call off the comp because you're so scared of that jump."

I hadn't even thought of the jump all night. I'd thought only of Nick. Now those fears flooded back to me, paired with his unfair accusation. I nearly started crying right there against the mudroom door. But I managed to say "No" while looking into his eyes. "I am not a liar."

We glared at each other in the starlight, clouds of our frozen breath mingling in the space between us. I realized then that the pain of crushing on him would continue for the whole year and a half of high school I had left. We would not get together, no matter how hard Chloe and Liz wished it. We couldn't. Try as we might, Nick and I could not find a way to graduate from the seventh grade.

"Whatever." Stomping through the snow toward his SUV, he called over his shoulder, "See you at the comp on Saturday. And by the way"—he opened the door and slid inside—"I did get your message about making out and then having an argument. I guess you got what you wanted. Now don't call me again." He slammed the door. Snow bounced off the hood from the shock wave. He cranked the engine and drove away down my street. Even after he'd turned the corner and disappeared, the strains of the Poser love song still reached me in the quiet snowy night.

betty

('be tē) *n.* **1.** a girl who isn't used to snowboarding and is liable to have a fatal accident any second **2.** Chloe

I dragged myself downstairs the next morning, hardly excited about boarding with Liz and Chloe. The sitch with Nick, or lack thereof, was so depressing.

Mom and Dad busied themselves with breakfast so they could get out the door and head for Boulder, where they would be spending the night. Personally, I wouldn't have picked Friday the thirteenth for my date night. But tomorrow night, the real Valentine's Day, they'd be running Parents' Night Out for members of the health club. In years past, they'd made me work Parents' Night Out with them. This year they'd let me off babysitting because they figured I might have fancy teenage Valentine's Day plans, maybe even a Poser concert. If only they knew.

Josh watched me as I walked in and sat down. Then he watched the TV on the counter for a few seconds. Then he looked straight at me. I stuck out my tongue at him. He looked at the TV, then widened his eyes at me. Finally I got it. I turned to see what on TV could possibly be so important.

Me. Snowboarding! The local access channel cycled through the same few items over and over: birthday announcements, club meetings, a recording of the latest city council meeting, a film of Everett Walsh leading the high school Scholars' Bowl to annihilate Telluride. Now the channel listed the scores from the Snowfall Amateur Challenge in front of footage of me in the half-pipe. Hey, nice form.

My mom headed toward me with a plate of oatmeal and fruit—tripped over Doofus—and managed not to spill anything. Athleticism obviously ran in the family. She sat down and followed my gaze to the TV. "Hayden, your dad and I heard you have some kind of snowboarding bet with your boyfriend, Nick."

I choked on a strawberry and glared at Josh, who shrugged. He hadn't ratted on me. So I told my mom, "Nick is not my boyfriend. He may have charmed you at the health club the other day, and we did indeed both go to Mile-High Pie afterward, but we were not there *together*." At least, not at first. "Don't adults have adult bets to gossip about?"

"Are you kidding?" my dad asked—tripping over Doofus—and sitting down at his place with his breakfast intact on his plate. Good save. "He was your little friend when we first moved here, right? It's a battle of the exes. Bets about golf aren't nearly that juicy."

Mom went on, "Word on the street—"

Josh snorted.

"—is that you won't win because of your fear of heights. Now, with your lessons with Daisy Delaney coming up soon, haven't you changed your mind? Don't you want me to make an appointment for you with a doctor who can help you get over your phobia?"

"Yes," said Josh.

"No!" I shouted. I ignored the three of them eyeing one another over my outburst. Me, I eyed my image on TV, landing a 900 like it was nothing. Nick was right. I was chicken, and it was now or never.

* * *

"So think back to that moment," Chloe coaxed me, "when your mom was offering you help. Picture her face when you go off this jump all by yourself."

"Yeah, it was weird that she mentioned the bet this morning," I said flatly. "If I didn't know she had to work Valentine's night, I'd say she had a bet for Poser tickets herself. No pressure." After eight hours on the slopes, the last two at the jump, I was getting a little tired of Chloe's motivational speeches.

Liz must have sensed I was about to blow. She nudged the tips of her skis between my board and Chloe's in the snow. "Let's review the progress we *have* made today. We've done the boardercross, and though we're not sure Hayden can beat Nick there, we're satisfied she's going as fast as she can go."

"Unless I eat a lot of meats and meat products to gain weight between now and tomorrow morning," I interjected.

"Yuck," Liz said at the same time as Chloe put her glove on my cheek and turned my head to face her. "Focus!"

"We've done the half-pipe," Liz continued, "and we're confident Hayden will kick Nick's butt there."

"Yes, but only if we employ careful strategy, as in rock-paper-scissors," I said. "My 720 totally beats Nick falling down, like paper covers rock. Unless the rock is a boy, in which case the boy always wins."

"Hayden—," Liz began.

"I am getting sick of your attitude, Hayden," Chloe talked over Liz. "We've been up here all day with you. All we have left is to get you off this jump. Every time you try, you have some excuse: wind in your face, bug in your ear, panties up your butt—"

"I was not making that up," I broke in. "Imagine trying a trick with uncomfortable underwear." I squirmed, rocking back and forth on my board to make my point.

"Or you make some stupid joke!" Chloe hollered at me. Her voice echoed against the rocky slope of the mountain overhead.

I stealthily looked around in my goggles to see if any boarders I knew had heard, but it was getting late, and the slopes were empty except for us.

"I'm beginning to think you don't *want* to get over your fear of heights," she said.

Suddenly, the mountain was quiet, except for the wind swishing through the tree branches and swaying their loads of snow. A few storm clouds approached from over the next peak. "I *do* want to get over my fear of heights," I said.

"You don't," Chloe insisted. "You're in your comfort zone. As long as everything stays right here, exactly the same, you can handle it. Guess what, Hayden? If you stay right here without ever trying anything new, you know where you'll be ten years from now?"

"In a convent?" I guessed.

"I seriously doubt *that*," Liz said.

"Right here." Chloe grabbed one of Liz's ski poles and planted it in the snow. "Here. In Snowfall. Still trying to go off this jump. Not at the X Games. Not at the Olympics. Here."

"I like it here," I whispered.

"Obviously," Chloe said.

"Let's end this on a high note," Liz suggested. "Chloe, why don't you tell her about the surprise?"

I rolled my eyes. "Did you set me and Nick up so we can make out and then have a huge fight?"

"Better!" Chloe jerked her head and arms wide in a dramatic flourish. A few rhinestones from her goggles went flying, lost forever, white against white in the deep snow. "Remember how I promised to get three unbiased judges for the comp? And remember how I couldn't board with you yesterday because I had something to take care of?"

"You didn't," I breathed.

"I did! I got Daisy Delaney to come over from Aspen, *and* her boyfriend, who's also a pro. That way the boys can't say you won just because the girl voted for the girl. All I had to do was give her and her boyfriend a complimentary night at the hotel. Though it probably didn't hurt that I also gave her some background on your challenge with your ex." She wagged her eyebrows at me, making her goggles move up and down. The bling remaining around the rim glittered in the sun. "One of the resort's snowboard instructors gladly offered to serve as the third judge when I told him Daisy Delaney was coming. The resort photographer may be there to capture the event on film. And—oh yeah—the newspaper."

"Isn't this great?" Liz prompted me gently, patting my padded arm.

"No pressure," I growled.

"Honestly, you need to get used to it," Liz said ominously. "A professional snowboarding career is nothing but pressure."

"Honestly," I yelled so loudly that she released my arm in surprise, "the two of you are not helping!" I turned on Chloe. "Didn't you advise me to take control? Well, how am I supposed to do that if the two of you manipulate every facet of my life?"

"Another excuse," Chloe declared. "I can't *believe* you made me *snowboard* today for this. My cheeks are chapped, and for what? Come on, Liz." Under her wooly rainbow hat, her blond ponytail flipped around, dissing me, as she boarded away.

I turned to Liz. "Well? What are you waiting for? Go on, Liz."

Liz reached out to pluck her ski pole from where Chloe had poked it into the snow. "I think you're just tired," she said gently.

"How could I be tired? I haven't done anything. That's the whole problem." Actually, I was bone-tired, just as I'd felt a few times this week when Nick had made me feel bad about myself. I hadn't gone off the jump, but *thinking* about going off the jump and gathering all my energy only to pull out at the last second had totally drained me.

And then I started to cry.

"I'm sorry, Hayden," Liz said instantly. "I shouldn't have let Chloe pick those judges." She skied over to hug me.

"No, I'm sorry," I sobbed. "I'm making everybody mad at each other and now at me, and for what? For nothing!"

"It's not for nothing," Liz said soothingly. "Let's ask the boys for an extension. We'll do the comp on Sunday instead of tomorrow. Daisy won't care that she missed it, since she'll get a free hotel room anyway. Chloe and I will come back to the mountain with you tomorrow and work with you until you go off the jump. We'll figure something out."

"The Poser concert is tomorrow night, so Sunday will be too late for the bet," I cried. "Plus, the boys would never let us do that. They want me to fail anyway, so why would they give me another chance to succeed? Plus, it would just be an extra day for me to screw up, and to lose one more friend. Let's face it, I'm done." My goggles had fogged up inside with my tears. I tore them off, along with my hat. The wind was shockingly cold on my bare, wet face. "Totally useless, totally done."

"Hayden!" Chloe screamed from somewhere downhill.

Liz and I glanced at each other for only a second, then whipped around in a rush of powder. Chloe had been headed to the pass through the trees onto Main Street. I feared the worst, and I knew Liz did, too. People around here only half-laughed at Sonny Bono jokes. Skiers and boarders were killed every year running into trees, not just betties like Chloe but also experienced boarders. I slid across the snow as fast as I could, throwing all my weight into it. I stopped sideways at the edge of the stand of trees and sent a wave of snow arcing into the dark trunks.

Chloe was in the trees all right, way down the slope from us. I picked out her pink clothes right away against the white. She must have hit a mogul in the snowy path and veered into the trees. She was sitting upright, though, and none of her limbs pointed the wrong way. Ugh ugh ugh, I shrugged off that thought and called to her. "Are you okay?"

"Okay," she called back. "Just stuck. My board's buried and kind of pinned against this tree and my boot won't come loose. Aren't your boots supposed to pop out of your bindings when you suffer a major biff?"

This was not the time to point out to Chloe that her "major biff" was likely a low-speed slide of ultrabetty-ness. And if she hadn't been able to free her boots by now, I wouldn't be able to talk her through it. I would have to show her.

"Hold on!" I called, popping off my board. The snow between the trees was piled up much higher than the snow on the slopes, which the sun melted and skiers wore down all day. There was no telling what lurked underneath the snow in the woods. Most likely, it wasn't safe to board across. Boarding boots weren't the safest footwear for hiking, either, but I couldn't leave Chloe. Darkness was falling.

"You want me to go with you?" Liz asked, stopping on her skis behind me.

"Nah, but bring my board if I'm able to haul her out the other side. And see if you can find my goggles and my hat. I dropped them somewhere." I put one boot into the soft snow at the very edge of the slope and sank much farther than I'd imagined, up to my hip.

"Watch that first step!" Liz called.

I didn't even retort, I was so focused on Chloe downhill from me. Every step I took was deeper than the last, and it grew harder to bring my other foot around. Once I sank into a snowdrift all the way to the ground and slipped on the rocks underneath, like disappearing under the surface of a frozen lake.

"Hayden, are you still there?" Chloe screamed.

"I'm still here!" At least, I thought I was. The daylight vanished even more quickly here under the bare trees, and the white all around disoriented me.

"Do you want me to call the boys?" Liz suggested from way above me.

"Do *not* call Nick Krieger!" I shouted. "God, would he love this."

"I've got Davis in my cell phone!" Liz called. "Gavin, too."

"Absolutely not! If you call Davis *or* Gavin, Nick will be attached!"

Chloe squealed, "Yes, please, Liz! Gavin would be excellent right now! No offense, Hayden, but don't join the ski patrol anytime soon."

"Ingrate!" I yelled. "I'll show you. I'm about to save the day, in just a minute here." I'd reached a patch where the snow was shallower, only knee-deep again. I seemed to be on an outcropping of rock, because my boots slid around beneath me worse than ever. Luckily, I'd almost reached Chloe. She was ten yards downhill from me.

"Tick-tock!" she said. Through the low-hanging branches between us, I could see her haughty expression, like she was *still angry* with me.

Now *I* was mad. Even though they were water-resistant, my boarding clothes weren't meant to be immersed in snow. I was freezing. I expected at least a *little* gratitude from this diva. "Apologize for what you said to me at the jump!" I demanded.

"Never!" she cried, sitting up straighter in her snowdrift.

"You are really testing me, Chloe," I muttered as I took one tentative step into even lighter snow cover. Now I could actually see the icy rocks underneath. "I am trying pretty hard to remember how nice you were to me that night with Nick in seventh graaaaade!" My boot slipped out from under me and I skidded straight into the claw-like branches in front of me. I managed to turn my head in time to avoid getting an eye poked out, and I waited until my body stopped and settled against the springy branches.

"Oh God!" Chloe squealed. "Are you okay?"

"Yep." I thought so. My face stung, and the thought crossed my mind that I was scarred for life. But I was sure the pain came from skidding across the snow on my cheek, not from a branch cutting me. I had a hard time extricating myself from the tree, though, and my head was getting cold. Finally, slowly, I rose up to kneel in the snow and asked Chloe, "Am I all in one piece?"

Her eyes flew wide open. I knew it was *really* bad when she almost screamed, but she slapped her hand over her mouth in time. She said, too calmly, "Hayden, put pressure on your ear."

"Put pressure on my ear," I puzzled out. "Why?" I touched my ear. It was wet, but so was the rest of me by now. Then I looked at my mitten. It glistened with blood.

"Call Josh," I whispered before I passed out.

"Hayden, that's going to take one stitch." Thank God for Josh. He sounded far off, even though I could feel his hands on my face. I couldn't quite make my way back to consciousness. Not while stitches were the topic of conversation.

"She's too heavy for me to carry," Josh said.

I tried to insult him back, but I didn't make a sound.

"Should I call the ski patrol?" Liz asked.

"No, they'll make a huge deal, and our parents will wig out and come home. They're over in Boulder for their first night out of town alone in a year. This is no biggie. She did the same thing when she gashed her arm at the skateboard park last summer. We just need to get her down the mountain. Call Nick."

"No!" I tried to exclaim but didn't. Wait—if Chloe was still lodged against the tree, dying of hypothermia, did it really matter who got called? Any hero would do.

"Hayden," said Nick.

My cheeks tingled with cold, and when I opened my eyes, all I saw was a blue glow. I must have face-planted. "Get Chloe," I told the snow. "She's stuck."

"Gavin and Davis have her." Nick's hands were on my shoulder and my waist. He rolled me onto my back. Now my wet face froze all over again in the cold wind. I opened my eyes.

Even though he was kneeling beside me in the snow, he towered above me like a movie superhero. Beyond his strong shoulders and the snowy trees, the sky glowed orange, and a few low clouds sugared him with snow. As I watched, he unzipped and pulled off his parka, then unbuttoned and tossed off his flannel shirt. He pulled his T-shirt over his head and shook his hair out of his eyes. Leaning over me with his chest bare, he pressed his wadded-up T-shirt to my ear. It was his Poser T-shirt that he wore to school at least twice a week, and he was willingly stanching my blood with it. He must be in love.

More likely, I was having a wet dream. They'd told us during sex-ed week in PE that this might happen to girls as well as to boys. It had never happened to me. And now, just when I'd given up hope because I was seventeen and the puberty thing was pretty much done, here was Nick Krieger tenderly touching my face with the sun setting behind him and snowflakes sliding off his bare shoulders.

"Hayden," he said again, gently. "Are you sure you didn't hit your head?"

"I don't think so." It came out as a whisper. I cleared my throat. "I think it's just my ear." Now that his T-shirt was warming my skin, I could tell the insistent sting came from my earlobe rather than from the cold.

He moved the T-shirt aside and leaned closer, examining my ear. Oooh, it would be so much more romantic if he looked into my eyes rather than fixating on my ear. Shouldn't I be able to make this happen? What was the world coming to, that I couldn't even control what Nick did in my own wet dream?

He poked my ear.

"Ow, ow, ow!" I squealed, and then felt faint again, out of breath. This was no wet dream. It was reality after all.

He let out a disgusted sigh. "Hayden, Josh is right. The doctor might not even put a stitch in that. What's the matter with you? Do you faint at the sight of blood?"

Oh, no. There was no way I would let him get the upper hand, even if I *was* lying on my back in the snow and he was kneeling over me. I laughed. "Of *course* I don't faint at the sight of blood. I jump onto the dance floor and do the Soulja Boy. Get the hell off me, Dr. McDreamy."

He sat back in surprise. I rolled over to all fours and stood up slowly, letting his T-shirt slide off my ear, since my injury was so minor. The woods seemed to tilt sharply to the left.

"Hayden," said Nick. "Take it easy."

"What for? This would never have happened to a boy, right? A boy could break his leg and keep on boarding. So could I." Or maybe not, but at least I could hike out of the trees on my own power after I scratched my ear. It wasn't until I looked down to check my footing that I realized I was still bleeding. *Plop, plop, plop,* neat red circles that burrowed warm holes into the snow.

"Well?" Chloe called from far off. "Is she okay?"

"No, but is she ever?" Nick lifted me. One of his arms cradled my head against the wad of his T-shirt. He hooked his other strong arm under my knees. His chest felt intensely warm against me. I opened my eyes and saw his chest was still bare. He'd put his flannel shirt and parka back on without fastening them.

He seemed good for a few steps. Then he hit a soft patch of snow. His foot sank, and he staggered. Josh trudged forward to help, struggling with three snowboards—his, Nick's, and mine, I supposed. If Nick fell while carrying me, even if it was due to loose powder, he would blame it on my unwieldiness or my girth. Together with Josh's joke, I would never, ever live it down.

"Let go," I said. "I can walk." At least, that's what I meant to say, but it came out slurred.

"Shut up." Nick took a few more steps. Now we were on Main Street, where the snow pack was solid. His strides were more sure.

"We can't leave the snow all bloody," I told the underside of his chin, shadowed with stubble. "It will scare the tourists."

"The new snow will cover it up." He looked down at me. "Shhh."

Something in his *shhh* tugged at my heart. He kept watching me, not examining my ear for medical emergencies but looking into my eyes, for a few more steps. I couldn't read his look. He was kind of blurry, for one thing, and I was kind of dizzy. I thought he looked . . . concerned. Sympathetic. Determined to rescue me from danger. I wished that was what he felt. But it couldn't have been. I was misreading him.

What did he really think of me? He probably assumed I was faking loss of consciousness. Maybe he even thought

I'd cut my ear on purpose, all to get out of the comp with-out admitting defeat. If he hated me, so be it, but I'd be damned if he hated me by mistake.

"I broke my leg," I breathed.

He stopped short in the snow and glanced down at me again, alarmed this time. His eyes traveled across my body. "I don't think so, Hayden. Where does it hurt?"

I shook my head, which made him squeeze me more tightly to his chest.

"I mean, when I broke my leg before. I broke it in four places. It bled a *lot*. I didn't walk for a year." I said all this in one gasp, rushing through so I didn't pass out again just from thinking about the way my leg had looked when I'd hit the rocks. I hadn't felt anything at first. I was scared I was paralyzed. When the pain hit me a few seconds later, I was actually relieved. And then, not. I'd never felt pain like that, or seen that much blood.

"Hey, don't cry." He sounded horrified. I couldn't see him anymore through the tears, and I was glad.

"Is she crying?" Gavin called from behind us. "Let me see."

"Just go," I sobbed to Nick. "Get me out of here."

"Gavin, be a little more sensitive," Nick grumbled. "Jesus."

"*You're* telling *me* to be *sensitive*?" Gavin called, and then Chloe was scolding him. The snow was heavier now. The clumps of snowflakes were so big that they squeaked as they hit the ground, like rubber-soled shoes on a gym floor. I hated snow like this, even though it would mean wicked boarding in a few days. Snow like this reminded me of a Laura Ingalls Wilder book I'd read when I was little, about plucky Laura stranded in the Western wilderness when the locusts descended, a cloud of millions of locusts stripping the crops clean in a matter of hours. Nothing had filled the air like this in Tennessee.

"You're shaking," Nick said gently. "Are you cold?" He hugged me closer to his warm skin.

"Is she going into shock?" Davis suggested.

"No," I said, "I just . . . I know we're headed to the gondola." In answer, the groans of metal cable against metal gear reached me from across the slope. "I don't ride the gondola." I tried to stop shuddering.

"It's the best way to get you down the hill. You'll have to walk, too, or they'll call the ski patrol." Nick eased me down from his arms, and I stood against him as he buttoned his shirt and zipped his coat. "Okay. Lean on me. Hide that bloody T-shirt and move your hair over your ear."

As we hiked across the snow to the gondola station ahead, I stuffed the Poser shirt into my pocket, then reached up and tentatively touched my ear. "Oh my God, what happened to my luck?"

"Your clover earring?" Nick asked. His low voice sounded even deeper with my head on his chest. I caught a little chill at the nearness of him, shiver upon shiver.

"It got pulled out of your earlobe, Hayden," Chloe offered. "That's why you're bleeding." As we continued to walk, I felt Nick move. I didn't have to look. I knew he moved his hand across his neck, telling Chloe to shut up.

Good idea. A new wave of dizziness hit me. I wasn't sure anymore whether it was the thought of blood or the fear of heights. Either way, I was going to pass out again, here in front of the gondola station for the park officials to see. "I lost my luck," I murmured, waiting with Nick for the next gondola, watching the huge cable slide through the huge gears, listening to the shriek of the machine. "My dad gave me that luck."

"You can make your own luck!" Josh called from behind us in line.

"Right!" I exclaimed with new purpose. I needed to get my mind off my phobias and act like a halfway sane person on the gondola. The gondola car slung around the curve of the station and paused just long enough for all of us to pile on. I had my eyes closed and let Nick guide me, but I did step on and slide beside him onto the plastic bench. Like we were a couple.

sick

(sik) *adj.* **1.** good **2.** cool **3.** gnarly **4.** Hayden

The nurse knocked softly on the door of the examining room and wheeled in a shiny silver tray displaying neatly arranged instruments of torture. She handed me a paper cup of water and then a smaller paper cup, shaking it to rattle the pill inside. "Mmmmmm, guess what I okayed with your mother over the phone? It's to calm you down. Take that, then stare at this tray, and call to me when stitches seem like a good idea." She bustled out. I was left with no one for company but the smiling photos of other patients on the bulletin board across the room. Clearly *they* did not need stitches.

Sometimes I was glad my doctor and his staff had a sense of humor. This was one of the times when I was not. Still, I took the pill. Anything was better than yo-yo fainting and waking up to a new humiliation. And after five minutes, or perhaps five hours, I realized I was counting the smiling faces of patients on the bulletin board for the three hundredth time. "Nurse!"

Nick grinned at me from across the wide cab of his SUV, then glanced back at the snowy road, then smiled over at me again. He looked so handsome and mature as the glow of streetlights passed over him and faded.

He said, "You're loaded."

I remembered being carried into Liz's den. If I hadn't talked to my mom on the phone pre-pill and agreed to spend the night with Liz so her mom could watch me, I might not have known where I was. It occurred to me that I should be embarrassed, sleeping in a room full of awake boys. But I wasn't embarrassed, and that was *delicious*. To hell with teen angst. I went back to sleep.

Then I heard gunshots. An action movie was playing on Liz's TV. I recognized Will Smith's voice. Funny, I must have associated the sound of Will Smith with the smell and sensation of Nick. I could have sworn Nick was with me, just as in seventh grade when we'd snuggled together during that fateful romantic-comedy movie. I inhaled him, sighed happily, and sank back into wistful dreams of him.

I woke, but I didn't want to be awake. I kept my eyes closed and listened for what had changed to wake me. The gunshots and explosions in the movie had grown surprisingly soothing after a while. Now they'd given way to the sweeping theme song as the credits rolled, and soft voices around me.

"Is she still asleep?" Liz asked from somewhere across the room.

Closer by, Gavin answered, "If she wasn't, there's no way she could have been quiet this long." A *smack* sounded as Chloe slapped him for insulting me.

Nick's voice was closer still, down at my feet. He was sharing the sofa with me. There must have been nowhere else for him to sit in the room. "I knew she broke her leg before she moved here, but I never realized it was that big a deal."

Oh, no, I really *had* spilled all that to him while woozy!

Stupendous. Luckily, I was lying on my side with my face to the back of the sofa, so I wouldn't give myself away with fluttering eyelashes or a grimace. Chloe and Liz confirmed and cooed, and I felt myself drifting off again.

Then something moved on my ankle. I nearly jumped out of my skin. And still another wave of adrenaline rushed through me as I realized what was happening. Nick wasn't just sharing the sofa with me because there was nowhere else to sit in Liz's den. My feet were in his lap. His hand was around my ankle. He was *rubbing my ankle*, his fingertips tracing slow circles around my ankle bone.

Technically, he wasn't even touching me, unless you counted the pressure of his fingers through my sock. It was ridiculous for me to go tense under his hand, hardly daring to breathe, waiting for the next stroke of his fingers. Except that this meant something. I doubted anyone could see Nick touching me from across the darkened room. Nick wasn't doing this for his friends, showing them how he could tease me to get the upper hand with me. He wasn't even doing this for me. He thought I was asleep. He was doing it for himself. He was stroking me, comforting me, putting a protective hand on me, because he wanted to. Even after he'd said he was finished with me.

The conversation moved on to Will Smith and the movie. The TV switched from teen drama to basketball and back as

Chloe and Gavin snatched the remote away from each other. I tried to relax a bit and enjoy Nick's hand on my ankle while I had it, because I might not ever experience this strangely intense connection with him again. But I resigned myself to the torture of remaining wide awake and perfectly still for a few more hours until everyone went home.

I started awake, jerking upright this time. The shadowy room was empty. They must have turned off the satellite box but not the TV, and after a few minutes of silence it had burst into static and had woken me. I relaxed against the pillows on the sofa, but the static wouldn't let me ease back to sleep. It was like my brain, loud and scrambled and panicky.

I peeled myself from the sofa, switched off the TV, and padded through the silent house to the hall bathroom. I squeezed my eyes shut and flicked on the light. Then I opened my eyes slowly to protect them from the glare, but also because I dreaded seeing what I had looked like to Nick while he lugged me around all evening. I couldn't avoid the mirror right in front of me.

My face was pale, my eyes smudged with dark circles underneath, as if I'd spent the last few hours fainting and then sleeping fitfully. Go figure. My normally straight hair had been so teased by hats and goggles and pillows and Nick that it had grown big and frizzy. And my ear—I pushed back my hair to examine the tiny bandage on my earlobe. *This* had caused all the trouble? I felt like a fool.

Frowning at myself, I reached up and fingered my other earlobe and the one lucky earring I had left. I wasn't a fool. Hysterical, yes. Maladjusted, definitely. But not a fool. My broken leg had been a devastating injury. So had my encounter with Nick four years ago. I'd known this, but only now was I realizing just how badly I'd been hurt.

Sighing, I washed my face. I was squeezing toothpaste onto the toothbrush Liz's mom kept there for me, because I always forgot mine, when I heard voices outside. I stepped over to the window and pushed aside the curtain, then backed up a pace when the cold night air leaking around the windowsill touched my skin.

Nick and Gavin were talking at the end of the driveway— or what I assumed, from the tire tracks, was the driveway under a blanket of fresh snow. Streetlights glinted on Nick's dark and Gavin's black hair. Then Gavin got into his car, and Nick hiked through the snow toward his SUV.

"Oh, mo," I mumbled through toothpaste. I couldn't let him get away. Not now.

I swished, spat, and ran for the front door, pausing only to shove my feet into galoshes owned by some unknown member of Liz's family. Her stepdad, I decided as I tried to run down the snowy front steps. The galoshes were so big, it was like wading in a Tennessee river.

I was too late anyway. They were gone. Gavin's tires spun briefly and his car pulled away, taillights reflecting red and long on the snow. But no—Nick's SUV still sat idling in the street at the end of the driveway. And as I waded closer, I saw he was in the driver's seat of the dark cab, slowly, repeatedly banging his head on the steering wheel.

He must not have heard me approach over the hum of the engine. I walked all the way up to the passenger-side window and stood there, watching him, waiting for him to notice me. He would see that I had caught him banging his head on his steering wheel, and this was something I could tease him about and hold over his head for the next few months at school.

But I was getting cold in my foreign galoshes and only two layers of clothes in the freezing night. As Nick kept hitting his head, I realized the two of us weren't in that place anymore, the one where we made fun of each other and had a fight and left it at that. We'd been driving in circles, having wrecks and backing over each other, but somehow we'd come way past that place in the last week. I knocked on the window.

He stopped with his head halfway to the steering wheel for another whack, and he turned to me with his eyes wide behind his dark hair. Immediately, he slid across the seat and pulled the handle to open the door for me.

Leaving the galoshes outside in the snow, I gratefully slid inside the warm cab and shut the door softly so it wouldn't wake the neighborhood. Nick took off his parka and draped it around my shoulders. He didn't have to say, "You shouldn't be out here without a coat," or "You shouldn't be awake now after the terrible day you had." I could see all this in his eyes. He wasn't concerned with making a joke at my expense. He was concerned about *me*.

"What were you and Gavin talking about?"

Nick rolled his eyes and let out a frustrated sigh. "He thinks I've wanted to be with you all these years, and his proof is the way I acted when you got hurt today. He says good friends shouldn't lie to each other. He's really lording it over me, too. Such an ass."

"Is he right?" I whispered.

Nick's dark eyes drilled into me, and the set of his jaw hardened. He slipped one hand onto my waist, underneath the parka.

"Uh," I protested.

He put his other hand on the opposite side of my waist.

"Nick," I said.

He slid me toward him across the seat.

"You," I whispered, looking into his eyes.

He was about to kiss me. His lips brushed mine. He pressed down on me with his chest, bent me backward until I lay down across the seat, and he lay on top of me. He closed his eyes, and the tip of his nose touched mine in an Eskimo kiss. Then he opened his eyes, stared hard at me, and went still. "You want to make out and then have an argument?" he whispered.

"Yes," I said. It would be worth it.

"You sure?"

I swallowed. "Absolutely."

"Then tell me what happened when you broke your leg, and why you're so terrified of heights after all this time."

I looked up into his dark eyes. I wanted to say something, but his weight was heavy on my chest, and I could hardly breathe.

"I broke my leg." Suddenly the story gushed out of me. "I was eleven. I loved outdoorsy sports. My parents let me go to adventure camp up in the mountains in Tennessee. My first day there, I fell."

That moment had flashed through my mind so many times since, it was as much a part of me as my lungs or my heart or my red hair, and I couldn't describe it to Nick. The long fall, with repeated jerks upward as safety mechanisms caught me and then failed. Realizing I was on the ground. Wondering why I wasn't hurt. Trying to stand. Seeing all the blood, and then my leg. The slowly growing horror that continued to build over the next few days until I reached my breaking point.

Between our bodies and the seat of the SUV, Nick squeezed my hand.

I gasped. "In Tennessee I was known as the girl who came in a wheelchair to the Valentine's dance. The girl whose friends had to go out of their way to include her when they went to a concert or the mall. At first, I counted myself lucky to have friends like that. But a couple of times I overheard them arguing about why they always had to invite me when it was such a pain to find the wheelchair ramps everywhere we went. They said it would be so much easier to flirt with boys if they weren't always worried about *me*.

"And then, one day when I'd made it out of the wheelchair and onto crutches, I gimped into the room and caught them imitating me. I didn't see enough of it that I recognized myself, but I could tell from everyone else's stricken expressions that they thought I had. It was so foreign. I used to be in charge of things, like Chloe. I was president of the fifth-grade class. And I used to make good grades like Chloe and Liz. Gosh, it's hard to think back that far. Fifth-grade math must have been a lot easier than eleventh-grade math."

"You think?" Nick's words were dry, but his tone was gentle.

"I had never been that girl people made fun of. I didn't want to be that girl. I am not that girl."

He watched me, wishing he had never asked this question, wondering what possessed him to break up with somebody easy like Fiona.

But no—with tentative fingers, he brushed a strand of my hair away from my forehead.

And for just a moment, I really wasn't that girl. I had never been that girl. I was that cool teenager again, who moved to a new town and found a new boyfriend. The girl who started over.

I sniffled. "By the time we moved here, I was walking without a limp. People had no idea. I was only the new girl, the red-haired girl, the girl who Nick Krieger made a fool of."

If Nick hadn't been holding my hand, I would have slapped it over my mouth. This *was* what I thought, but it's not what I'd intended to share with Nick right then.

His eyes widened in shock. Sorrow moved across his face, and then worry. "I wanted to tell you, Hayden. Yes, I had a bet with Gavin in seventh grade, and you wandered into it. But I really liked you. I wished Liz had never told you about the bet, and we could have stayed together."

"Why didn't you come clean with me when you figured out you liked me?"

He sighed, a short, disdainful puff through his nose. "I was thirteen."

I wasn't buying it. "You had a bet. You couldn't lose a bet. If you have a choice between me and winning, you'll choose winning every time. It's still true."

The worried expression on his face morphed into anger. He let go of my hand and sat up, his chest heavier on mine just before his weight lifted from me completely. "You are *not* going to put this on me," he barked.

"I'm not trying to put anything on you." I backed across the seat and scooted up to sit against the door.

"You can blame me or your fall or whatever you want for not being able to go off that jump. But the bottom line is, some people are competitors and some people aren't. There's no way you're suddenly going to decide at age seventeen to become a competitor. You don't have it in you. You're just scared."

I would have been mad at Nick for saying this to me at any time. But right now, after I'd spent the night fainting and I desperately needed comfort, I was downright bitter. "Me!" I lashed out. "You're one to talk. You're scared to tell your father that you made a mistake, agreeing to this challenge with me. *You're* the coward." I opened the door to a swirl of frigid air, remembered I was still wearing Nick's parka, and struggled out of it.

"That's bullshit." He grabbed the back of the parka, but I got the distinct impression he was not trying to be a gentleman by helping me out of it. He just wanted his parka back. "When you feel cornered, you'll just fling whatever you've got at people, and you don't care who gets hurt with what."

"I am not scared." I slid down from the truck seat into Liz's stepdad's galoshes, then turned to face Nick one last time. "I am not scared of boarding *or* you, and I will prove it to you tomorrow. If you think I'm going easy on you in the comp just because you have a debilitating injury from yesterday—"

"That's what you think," he snarked. "I've been doing yoga."

"—you have another think coming. You will buy me those Poser tickets. And I'm not even taking you. You will hand the tickets over to me, and I'll take someone else."

"Who? Your little brother's friends?"

"No, Everett Walsh." I closed the door softly behind me so as not to alarm sleeping adults, because I was that mature.

Even through the door and the rolled up window, I could clearly hear every filthy word Nick uttered, ending with, "Everett [cuss word] Walsh."

I opened the passenger door. "Ask not for whom the

fire-crotch burns; it burns for thee!" I'd meant this to be an insult. Then I realized it sounded like I wanted Nick. Or like I had a feminine problem.

"Shut up," Nick said. "I'm waiting for you to go in the house."

"Fine." I slammed his door, forgetting all about courtesy to sleeping adults this time. But as I hiked back through the yard to Liz's front porch, I was so proud of myself for not crying. I never shed a tear.

Not until I opened the front door and heard his truck ease away. Just as he'd promised, he'd idled there all that time, watching me, waiting to make sure I got inside the house okay. Like a gentleman.

I closed the door softly, turned the dead bolt, and managed to slip out of the galoshes and line them up against the wall as I'd found them. Only then, with everything else in order, did the tears spill out of me. I wanted to scream, but there was no way I'd startle everyone in the house like that. Holding the sobs inside hurt my ribs. I collapsed on the floor, hugging my knees, rocking back and forth on the carpet. I felt empty, lost, and totally alone in the dark house.

I wished I could start over in a new town, with new friends. I would do everything right this time.

No, wait. That's exactly the chance I'd had four years ago, and now I'd blown it.

Besides, just thinking about leaving Liz and Chloe and Nick behind, I missed them already.

I was exhausted, even after so many hours of fainting and drug-induced sleep. My first instinct was to lie back on the carpet where I sat. But that might alarm Liz's mom when she woke up to make breakfast. She would trip over me like I was Doofus. The obvious choice was the den sofa, which I could see from my seat on the floor. But Nick's scent would linger there. Thoughts of him touching me might have lulled me to sleep earlier this evening. They would keep me wide awake now.

In the end I dragged myself down the hall and up the stairs to Liz's room. Chloe snored softly in one twin bed. Liz was sprawled across the other. Lifting Liz's covers, I tried to coax her over so I could slide in next to her. With gentle prodding, she wouldn't budge. It was exactly like the last time I'd had a nightmare about falling and had wandered down to get in bed with my mother. Liz finally groaned and gave me some room. I lay down beside her, relaxed into her warmth, and felt comforted just lying next to her, even if she didn't know I was there.

She rolled over and spooned against me, fitting her front to my back. She draped her arm across me and hugged. "You okay?" she whispered dreamily.

I nodded. "I thought Nick and I were going to make out."

"Surprise."

"And then we had a fight. If you and Chloe could throw us together, I would really appreciate it, because I don't know how to fix this anymore."

"Tell us about it in the morning."

I nodded again, then felt myself sobbing, shaking against Liz. She held me more tightly as I cried myself to sleep.

steeze

(stēz) *n.* **1.** style and ease **2.** you've either got it or you don't

After a big breakfast at Liz's house and more bitching with her and Chloe about what pigs boys could be, I rode the bus home to change into clean boarding clothes. I walked into the mudroom—tripped over Doofus—and found Josh stepping into his boarding boots. "Hey!" I greeted him cheerfully. "Thanks for coming to my rescue yesterday, and for calling me fat."

"You're going to be sorry you were snide to me when you see what I've got for you." He lifted the folded garment next to him and shook it out.

The BOY TOY jeans!

"What do you mean?" I exclaimed. "They're mine *forever*?"

"Yes. They're to help you make your own luck. The catch is, if you want them forever, you have to wear them to the comp today."

"But I'll get soaked!" I wailed.

"Don't fall."

I took the jeans from him and hugged them close. "Thank you, Josh. This means so much to me. I know you've joked about me going pro and taking you with me, but are you actually *for* me in this comp? I figured you'd have a bet with Gavin's sister that I'd lose."

He shook his head. "I went ahead and bought her and me both a ticket. Might as well. That's one bet I know I'd lose."

"Aww, Josh, that's so awesome of you!" I wrapped my arms around him and hugged him hard.

He didn't hug me back. He stiffened and said, "Ew, ew, ew."

I let him go and stepped back to look him in the eye.

"Ew," he said again. But one corner of his mouth crooked upward in a smile.

It was nice to have at least one boy behind me.

* * *

"Hayden O'Malley!"

I looked up from the sink and peered around the women's bathroom in the ski lodge. Chicks stood inside and outside stalls, in various states of undress. Waterproof layers were hard to get in and out of, and snowboarders definitely were not peeless goddesses. Finally I saw the girl who had called my name. She stood in the doorway, long blond hair twisted into hippie twirls and braids.

"Daisy Delaney!" I hollered.

"I'd recognize you anywhere!" she yelled over the chatter in the bathroom. "They're playing your steeziness over and over on local TV! Girl, you're famous!" She crossed the room and leaned forward to hug me by way of introduction.

We talked for a few minutes about the local competition I'd won and the tricks I'd landed. Then she said, "After your comp is over, my boyfriend and I are shredding the back bowls. Want to hang? We can get a head start on your lessons next week, see where you are. I can give you some pointers." She chuckled. "Maybe *you* can give *me* some pointers."

"The back bowls? Sure!" I felt confident that she wouldn't find out what a chicken I was, because after the comp, if I hadn't gone off the jump, I would be dead of shame. And if I *had* gone off the jump, I would be just plain dead.

"Your friend Chloe told me this comp is with your ex," she said. "What's *that* about? Are you hooking up again or what?"

"Not anymore," I said wistfully. "Can I ask you something? This whole argument started because he said I couldn't beat an average boy snowboarder. Does it bother you that your boyfriend has landed a 1260 in competition and you haven't?"

"So this is a girl-power thing?" Daisy mused.

"It's a lot more complicated than that, but that's how it started."

She shrugged as best she could in her puffy outerwear. "I might land a 1080. I might not. But I'm sure not going to give up boarding just because the odds are stacked against me to be the best boarder ever. I mean, there are short people who play professional basketball."

"True."

"And on a personal level, my boyfriend and I love each other enough, and we have enough respect for each other, that we're bigger than that."

I laughed. "Nick and I are not bigger than that. We are very, very small."

Daisy nodded. "And then, of course, there's the fact that

I'm prettier than my boyfriend. He may fly higher, but I look better doing it." She turned around backward. "I mean, even in these snow pants, check out my ass."

We both cackled, and everyone in the bathroom stared at us. I decided right then that Daisy was going to be fun to hang out with, and I could learn a lot from her.

When I'd envisioned the comp with Nick, I'd pictured exactly this strong sunshine and bright blue sky. Beyond that, my predictions were all wrong. I'd thought my friends and Nick's friends would be waiting for us at the bottom of Main Street. I hadn't imagined a crowd of several hundred people, as many as had watched the local competition last Tuesday. They rang bells for Nick and me because they couldn't clap in their mittens, cheering for us as we boarded over to the ski lift.

I also hadn't realized I'd have to ride up on the lift with Nick, just the two of us. But it was the last Saturday of winter break. The slopes were crowded. Nobody got to ride a lift alone. And he was right behind me in line. Nick and me riding up together right then was like George W. Bush and Barack Obama riding to Obama's inauguration in the same limo. Relaxed!

We didn't say a word to each other the whole time we shuffled through the long line in the shed. Finally it was our turn. We slid into position in the path of the chair. It swept us off our feet and up into the air, and Nick pulled the guard bar down across our laps.

After the voices echoing in the shed, the cold air around us was silent, except for the ski-lift cable clanking overhead and the *swish* of skiers dodging moguls below us.

I looked up at Nick beside me. He had his goggles down already. I couldn't see his eyes behind those damn reflective lenses.

I took in a sharp breath of freezing air. "I'm not saying this because I'm scared, or because I want to get out of anything. But I want you to know that I'm sorry for what happened between us last night. We've said a lot of ugly things to each other in the past week, and we didn't mean most of them." I raised my voice as we neared a pole supporting the lift, and the cable clanked louder and louder through the pulleys. "At least, *I* didn't. If we can just get past all this, I think we're both bigger than that."

Now I found I was shouting, even though the noise of the cable had died away. Even more deafening was Nick's silence. He didn't look down at me, didn't say a word as we passed four more poles and boarded off the lift. I could see a muscle working under his skin in his strong superhero jaw, but his mouth stayed closed.

We slid to the top of a narrow slope that curved into

the forest. "Hey," Nick called to a kid boarding by. "We're racing. Say go, would you?"

The kid turned to us, and his eyes widened. "Oh my God, you're Nick Krieger and Hayden O'Malley, aren't you? Is this the comp everybody's been talking about? Are you guys hooking up?"

"Just say go!" Nick and I both yelled.

"Go!" the kid shouted.

I pointed myself downhill and boarded as fast as I could. But it was no use. A field of rumble strips slowed me down like speed bumps for a car. Nick was so much bigger than me that he blazed straight across them like they weren't there. Soon the slope took a turn into the forest and he disappeared behind the trees. He was gone, baby.

I was boarding by myself. I kept going as fast as I could, crouching down into the frigid wind and squinting through the water on my goggles, just so the spectators at the bottom didn't tire of waiting for me, give up, and go home, thinking I'd forfeited. No way.

The trees fell away on either side of me, and the slope opened up wide. At the bottom of the course where it merged with Main Street, I picked out Nick, one of the tallest boys, already standing in the crowd with his arms crossed, watching for me as if he'd been waiting all day. Then the three judges with their heads together. Then a gaggle of girls with Liz and Chloe in front, gloves over their mouths, watching for me.

So I did what the most stylish boardercross riders do when they're not winning but they know they've got the silver in the bag. I hit the last roller and cranked it into a front flip, a little steeze for the fangirls. The second I landed, the girls hit me with an ear-splitting squeal laced with frantic bell-ringing. I couldn't help breaking into the widest smile. I skidded to a stop in front of them.

Daisy leaned over to bump fists with me. "Girl has attitude. *Way* to *lose!*"

I laughed nervously and said, "Thanks." I wasn't sure if this was a compliment.

Liz guided Chloe over so Chloe didn't lose her balance and hurt anyone. They both gave me big hugs, and Chloe shook me by the shoulders. "We're down but we're not out. Go back up there and give him hell."

"Thanks, coach!" I slid away from the crowd and over to the lift again, following Nick. I didn't want to linger with Chloe and Liz, because I knew the crowd was waiting expectantly. But if I'd had more time, I would have asked for coaching on the sitch with Nick.

We moved through the line in the shadowy shed and launched into the sunshine in the chair again. I prepared for another cold, silent ride. His goggles were up this time, but I didn't look over at him and try to read the expression in his eyes. I was afraid it would break my heart.

"I'm sorry, too," he said.

At first I thought it was wishful thinking on my part, and I'd misheard him. But then he slid his glove onto my thigh. Even through the BOY TOY jeans, I felt those familiar tingles shooting up my leg.

"You *are*?" I exclaimed. "Why didn't you say something before? I was all worried!"

"I didn't want you to think I was apologizing because of the comp. You know, we want this to be fair and square so we don't have to go through it again."

"Then why are you copping to it now?"

"Because I don't want you to think I hate you. I don't hate you. I definitely don't." He squeezed my thigh.

"But you still think I'm not a competitor," I muttered. I was trying to be bigger than this, but there was no getting around it. If Nick and I were going to ease toward being together again, I wanted him to respect me.

"No, I do." He turned to me for the first time, and his dark eyes searched my eyes. "Did you know the local TV channel broadcasts your 900 in an endless loop? It's a bunch of video want ads for snowmobiles, then some kind of school crap with Everett Walsh that nobody wants to see over and over, and then you. I stayed up watching you until three o'clock this morning." He gave me that brilliant smile. "You're a competitor all right. I just wasn't sure you realized it yourself. And I never would have said something like that to you if I didn't consider you a true friend."

I put my mitten over his glove and squeezed. I wasn't sure whether he was hinting at a relationship or not. I hoped, if we were this big as people, we could be even bigger, and could take another shot at getting together. But I was thankful just to count him as a friend.

We slid off the lift and boarded down to the top of the half-pipe. The bell-ringing crowd had moved to the sides and bottom of the course. It seemed to have grown.

Nick pulled his goggles down over his eyes and nosed his board to the edge of the slope.

"Good luck," I called. "And be careful."

"Are you kidding? I do yoga to stay limber, so I won't get hurt. I did thirty minutes of Sun Salutations this morning."

He balanced on the deck, then sped down into the bowl and up the opposite side, momentum flinging him high into the blue sky. Six times, he executed simple but perfect tricks with incredible height. He might just beat me. If I fell in my BOY TOY jeans, I was toast. Very soggy toast.

But whether I won or not, I looked forward to my run. A half-pipe course was the best part of my day, an unbelievably decadent treat, like white cake with white icing that said CONGRATULATIONS HAYDEN! Sliding forward for my turn was like taking that first bite of sugar rush.

Following Nick's path, I raced down one wall and up the other. The slopes were crowded enough today, and enough kids had already gone through the pipe that morning, that the fresh powder had been worked into perfection for a smooth, fast run. I threw a few respectable tricks, then pulled out my specialties: back-to-back sevens, a McTwist, and my beloved nine. I hated for it to end. I would have loved to lay down just one more 720, but I ran out of pipe.

I slid straight across the flat toward the crowd and pulled up in front of them, strategically sending a wave of powder over the boys. The girls were already cheering for me and ringing their bells wildly (so cute!), but when I sent that powder flying, their cheers hurt my ears.

"You're neck and neck!" Daisy called from where she stood with the other judges. "Hayden destroyed this one!"

The huge pack of boys moaned. "What about Nick's massive air?" Gavin called.

"Hayden landed a 900," Chloe retorted. "That's bananas!"

I was happy I'd tied Nick, at least so far. I certainly wasn't going to hang around and gloat about it—not when I was about to get shown up in the big air comp. I was following Nick around the edge of the crowd to take the ski lift again when Daisy boarded over to me.

She put her head down and talked quietly, so only I could hear her above the excited crowd. "You've got this nice, quiet, compact style that competition judges are going to *love*, and then you add a nine? That's sick. The only thing we're going to work on in your lessons is height, because judges want to see that too. If you can land a nine going as low as you do, imagine what you'll put down when you're going huge like Kelly Clark. You're on your way, girlfriend. And you're mine!"

"Hooray!" I exclaimed. Never mind that I'd developed my compact style precisely because I didn't want to go too huge and lose my balance. Daisy and I locked forearms and jumped up and down together excitedly, or as well as we could manage with boards on. Then I high-fived Chloe and Liz as I passed them in the crowd, and I followed Nick.

When I boarded even with him, I asked, "Did you get all that with me and Daisy?"

He laughed. "I got enough."

"No pressure." We both cracked up.

But through our laughter, I thought I heard someone calling Nick. I touched his arm and nodded to the deck of the ski lodge. "It's your dad."

"Oh God," Nick said under his breath. "Not just my dad but his corporate partners. Beer before lunch is never a good thing. Come with me and save my ass."

I definitely did not want to talk with Nick's dad and two other men in the most expensive skiwear, drinking beer around a snow-covered table. But Nick needed me. We stopped at the wooden railing.

"Nick!" they called in big, strong, Manly Corporate Partner voices.

Nick nodded, wearing his own Big Man On Campus grin. "Dad, you remember Hayden. Mr. Jeter, Mr. Black, this is my girlfriend, Hayden."

I smiled sweetly at them and shook hands with them when they stood and extended their arms over the rail. This took my mind off the fact that my face was as red as my hair (Nick seemed to have that effect on me a *lot*) and the fact that NICK KRIEGER HAD JUST CALLED ME HIS GIRLFRIEND!

"You let a girl beat you?" one of them asked Nick with a twinkle in his eye. I think he meant this to be charming. "Must be true love."

If my face had turned red before, now it was probably turning purple. I was glad I couldn't see it. At least my freckles were obscured for once.

"Oh, no sir," Nick said. "I didn't let her beat me. Hayden's so much better than I am, she's in a different league. She's going pro soon."

"Then why'd you challenge her?" Mr. Krieger asked. His

words went along with the jovial banter of the moment. But behind the words, I heard his tone, the same bitter tone he'd used to talk about Nick when Doofus and I had crashed into his living room. He wanted Nick to win, no matter what, and Nick would hear about this again when he got home.

"Oh, he didn't challenge me," I piped up. "I challenged him, and Nick is always so supportive. He wants me to be the best I can be." This was all the corporate lingo I knew.

"But Mr. Jeter," Nick said, "about it being true love, you're absolutely right." He turned to me.

He kissed me on the forehead.

In front of his father and two corporate partners.

"Nice to see you, gentlemen," Nick said formally. Then he slid away. Rather than standing there dazed, I scrambled to follow him.

As soon as we were out of their earshot, he bent toward me. "Hayden! Good schmoozing!" he crowed.

I think he was referring to my handling of his dad's partners. However, I was still thinking about his soft lips on my forehead. I said, "I'll say."

"I hope I set a good example for my dad," Nick said. "He's flying down to Phoenix tonight for a Valentine's date with my mother."

"Nick, that's so great!" I squealed. Wait a minute. It was great that Nick's parents were making an effort to get back together. But did Nick mean that's the only reason he'd kissed me? That was not great at all!

The crowd had paused when we stopped to talk to Nick's dad, but now they moved with us toward the jump. I noticed a couple of film crews had arrived, probably from the resort and the local TV station. No pressure.

An out-of-control Chloe barreled out of the crowd, dragging Liz by the hand. They threatened to run me down. Nick caught Chloe by the hand as she slid past, and Liz was able to swing them both around in front of me.

"We'll go up the lift with you for moral support, Hayden," Chloe said. "We'll coach you off the jump."

"Great. Thank you!" I said, shaking imaginary snow out of my hair. I couldn't give Liz a meaningful look through my goggles, but I hoped she would get the message. I did not want Chloe's "help." Not today.

"Let's wait for her at the bottom, Chloe," Liz suggested. "That way we won't distract her, and we can hug her when she wins. Come on!" They followed the rest of the crowd sliding toward the bottom of the jump, leaving Nick and me to go up the lift alone.

As soon as the chair left the ground, he said quietly, "I'm going to give you the speech the football coach gives us."

I sniffed a long noseful of cold air. "Okay."

"Everything up until now has been practice," he said.

"Regardless of how good or how bad you've looked in practice, you're starting over now. The game is what matters. And a single game has never meant more than this one means to you."

"True." Going off this jump might make the difference between my career as a professional snowboarder and my life in a convent.

So I should have been focusing on the trick I was about to do, *not* on the warmth of Nick beside me, soaking through my BOY TOY jeans and long underwear and into my thigh. I wondered whether kissing my forehead and calling me his girlfriend and talking about true love were really all just examples for his father, or whether Nick had meant them.

"Speaking of starting over," he said quietly. "Hayden, can you and I start over?"

I looked up at him in astonishment.

He grinned, and I wished I could see his eyes behind his goggles. "I would rather walk across hot coals than go through seventh grade again, I have to tell you. I mean, can we say that everything up until now between you and me has been practice?"

Staring up at his superhero jaw, I enjoyed the tingles spreading across my chest and savored the moment. These were the words I'd waited for him to say since he'd sat next to me in the hall eight days before. I scooted toward him as well as I could with my board hanging heavily from my feet. "Absolutely. I'm ready to play this game with you."

He kissed me, his warm mouth on my mouth. This didn't work very well with his goggles hitting mine, so he pulled up mine and I pulled up his, and we kissed more deeply. It wasn't the most private kiss we'd ever shared, or the longest, or the most romantic. But it mattered the most. Our connection mattered. When we reached the station and boarded off the lift, my heart was racing like I'd just finished the slalom.

We couldn't stop grinning at each other as we returned downhill to the jump. We pulled up, adjusted our goggles, and gazed down the long slope at the white ramp jutting into the clear blue sky. Beyond that, way down the hill, the crowd was even bigger than it had been at the half-pipe. They were very far away, but I thought I recognized my parents' ski clothes, which they didn't pull out of storage very often. They must have gotten back from Boulder and come out to support my comp—what great parents! And ever so faintly, I could hear Josh rapping to his posse's beat. I couldn't make out most of what he was saying, but I thought I caught the word *prepubescent*.

"Do you want to go first?" Nick asked me.

"No, I want you to go first." I wanted to see what trick

he landed. Might as well pile as much pressure on myself as possible.

And, truth be told, I wanted to know that I could do this jump all by myself, without him up here coaching me.

"Okay, pep talk before I go." He put his gloves on my shoulders and squeezed. "Don't look at the crowd down there. Don't think about the jump at all. Concentrate on the sick trick you'll do when you go off." He pressed his goggles to my goggles. "Feel the 900."

"900!" I scoffed. "I'm feeling the 1080."

He let me go and stood back, eyeing me. I could tell he didn't want to say anything to destroy my confidence, but he was afraid he'd created a monster.

"Don't worry. I'm ready to play the game." I nodded solemnly.

"One more thing," he said. "If you do fall—"

I cringed. Some pep talk!

"—if something terrible happens, you still won't lose everything. Now you have good friends, and nothing will ever change that. You're *not* that girl."

"Oh, Nick." I threw myself at him, literally. He wrapped me in his arms and brushed my hair aside to kiss my forehead again.

I squeezed him hard, then drew away and punched him on his padded arm. "Go ahead, and *don't* break a leg."

Without fanfare, he steered onto the slope and sped off the jump. A nice 540, or possibly even a 720! I couldn't see his rotations when he disappeared over the edge. Anyway, all that really mattered to me was that he landed safely. I boarded a few feet to one side and leaned over until I saw him downhill, sliding to a stop, upright. The crowd all waved their arms, and faintly I heard their bells and voices.

My turn. I could do this. I inhaled through my nose and felt my lungs fill with air. My blood spread the life-giving oxygen throughout my body.

I exhaled through my mouth and felt gravity pull the energy from my heart down through my legs, through my boots and snowboard, through the snow, to the rocks below. I was one with the mountain.

I touched my remaining lucky earring.

Then I pressed all my weight forward for speed and raced toward the jump, the white edge, the blue sky beyond, the town below, the mountains in the distance. I went off.

Dancing at the Poser concert had been fun at first, but then Josh and his posse pulled Nick and me into the mosh pit. We needed a break. While Nick snagged us a lawn chair on the ski lodge deck above the concert, I bought us a couple of hot chocolates—and passed Gavin and Chloe at the teller machine. She rubbed her gloves together gleefully, then held them out while Gavin counted the cash into her hands.

"Hayden!" she exclaimed as I walked up, but her eyes didn't leave the money. Clearly, she didn't trust Gavin. "I went ahead and bought us tickets to be safe in case the concert was sold out, and now Gavin is paying—me—back—ha!" She tapped his cheek playfully with the stack of bills. He closed one eye against the attack.

"*Not* that you thought I would lose or anything," I said suspiciously.

She innocently fluttered her eyelashes at me. "Of course not!"

"We shouldn't have doubted you," Gavin said. "I have never seen anybody short of a pro ride the pipe like that."

I glared at him. Because the words were coming from his mouth, I expected them to be sarcastic. But his face was friendly and open. For once, he seemed genuine.

"And a 1080 off the jump?" he went on. "That was savage."

Chloe widened her eyes at him. "Why are you being nice? Has your body been taken over by aliens?"

"You'll find out tonight, baby."

I stopped the tickle fest I felt coming on between them

by handing them each a hot chocolate. "Hold this. My phone's beeping." I took it out of my pocket and peered at the text message.

Nick: Do u want 2 b n people?

"*People*," I murmured as if he could hear me. "As in the magazine?" I peered up onto the deck and saw him standing next to our lounge chair, talking with a group of adults with cameras. "Oh my God, paparazzi? No way!"

"Way," Gavin said. "I saw them talking to Daisy Delaney earlier. They must have followed Poser here, then realized there were more celebrities they could milk."

"Nick isn't that kind of celebrity," I said.

"I'll bet they want him for a special theme issue," Chloe suggested. "How the richest bachelors in America spent Valentine's Day."

I glanced dubiously toward the mosh pit. Then I looked toward Nick again and strained to hear what he was saying over the Poser tune.

"Are you here alone?" one of the men asked him. "Are you seeing anyone?"

"Yes, I'm seeing someone," Nick said, standing beside them but hardly acknowledging them. He was watching for my answer on his phone.

"For how long?" a woman asked.

About an hour, I thought. Or did we officially start seeing each other on the ski lift this morning? *Ten hours.* I smiled, remembering the sunny afternoon we'd spent boarding with Daisy Delaney and her boyfriend. Or . . . what did "seeing each other" mean, anyway? If nearly making out in the sauna counted, we'd been seeing each other for five days.

"Four years," I heard him say.

"Aww!" I squealed. Then I turned to Chloe. "Do I want to be in *People?*"

"No," she said firmly. "Nick is hot."

Gavin frowned and poked her in the side. "Hey."

She ducked away from his finger. "Facts are facts. Nick is hot, and when girls read *People* and see he's dating you, they will call you a skank ho. You and I have mooned over Prince William. We know the deal."

"True." When Nick glanced slyly down at me, I shook my head no.

For a few more minutes, I talked with Chloe and Gavin, and we all watched Liz and Davis swaying romantically to a rare slow song from Poser. What a happy Valentine's Day. Then, when the paparazzi had cleared out, I climbed the steps to the deck and handed a cup of hot chocolate to Nick. He sat down in the lawn chair and unzipped his parka. I settled back against his warm shirt.

"I bought you a Valentine's Day present," he said in my ear, sending shivers through me despite all my layers. He rocked to one side in the chair and pulled something from his back pocket.

I took it in my gloved hands and peered at it in the dusky light from the stage and the stars. It was a sew-on patch with a black diamond in the center, the symbol for a dangerous ski slope. "Nick, that's so cool! I love it!"

"That's not all." He rocked to his other side and pulled out another patch. This one had a four-leaf clover. "To replace the luck you're missing."

"Nick." I stared at the patches in my mittens, trying not to tear up. "This is sweet of you."

"I really like you in those 'boy toy' jeans," he said, "but this needs to go on top of 'boy.'" He took the black diamond from me and shook it. "And the clover goes on top of 'toy.'"

"Deal." I slipped the patches into my coat pocket. Then I sipped my hot chocolate and sighed, enjoying his warmth behind me. "We've been dating for four years, huh? I don't think Fiona will like that answer."

"You've always had my heart." He kissed my earlobe— the one without a bandage. The one that was still lucky. "You know, you're going to be in *People* anyway when you make the Olympic snowboarding team. ESPN will ask you, 'Hayden O'Malley, you came from nowhere at age seventeen. Where have you been?' And you'll answer, 'Oh, I had a few acrophobic issues to work through.'"

Laughing, I poked him for his embarrassingly accurate imitation of my Southern drawl.

He continued in my voice, "'Then one night my boyfriend was being an ass and I challenged him to a comp. I had to do a front 1080 off a jump just to show him up, and the rest is history.'"

"I hope so."

"I know so." He kissed my cheek.

I reached back to run my fingers through his long hair. "Right now I want to lie low, have a normal life, and hang out with my boyfriend. I'll meet you in *People* in a few years."

He chuckled, making my insides sparkle with anticipation. "It's a date."

About the Author

Jennifer Echols is the author of the romantic comedies *The Boys Next Door* and *Major Crush* and the teen drama *Going Too Far*. She lives in Alabama with her family, no snow, and a vivid imagination. Please visit her on the Web at www.jennifer-echols.com!

The Twelve Dates of Christmas

prologue

It had seemed like the perfect plan—get my boyfriend to fall for another girl, and I'd be free. No muss, no fuss, no guilt or bad feelings.

I'd approached it logically, like the scientific person I am. I'd identified the problem. I'd come up with a hypothesis. I'd set up an experiment.

And now the results were sitting across the warm, garlic-scented, holiday-bedecked room from me. Or, rather, getting up and walking out of said room, namely Manfredi's, my hometown's fanciest restaurant.

Cam glanced over toward me as he was helping his new girlfriend, Jaylene, with her coat. He smiled and waved.

I returned the smile weakly and wriggled my fingers in return.

"What are you looking at, Lexi?" My date, Andrew Cole, stopped talking about himself just long enough to notice I wasn't hanging on his every word. He looked over at the door just in time to see the happy couple depart. "Oh." He shrugged, then shoveled in a mouthful of lasagna before returning to his favorite topic. "So anyway, like I was saying, the admissions guy from Northwestern told me that if I applied, he was positive I'd get in, and . . ."

I picked up my fork and poked at my pasta. But my stomach recoiled at the thought of actually eating it. I'd lost my appetite the second I'd walked into the restaurant and spotted Cam and Jaylene together.

Andrew had, in his efficient, overachiever way, procured us a great table by the front window. It was tinted with fake frost and draped with garlands of holly and ivy, but that wasn't enough to block my view of Cam and Jaylene as they emerged onto the sidewalk outside. I watched them out of the corner of my eye, not wanting to see any more but unable to resist. Call it scientific curiosity.

It was early December and the temperature out there was normal for late evening in our part of Wisconsin—in other words, frigid. A few snowflakes drifted lazily down, lending the perfect touch to the scene. Seeing that we were in Claus Lake, that scene could be summed up in one word: Christmassy. The whole town was crazy for Christmas. Red and green lights twinkled up and down the poles of the streetlights, across the facades of all the shops on Elf Street, and even on the parking meters and stop signs. Holly and mistletoe were everywhere.

Jaylene huddled in her baby blue, fake-fur-trimmed, not-really-warm-enough-for-Wisconsin jacket, laughing at something Cam had just said. Then she let out an elaborate shiver and cocked her little blond hatless head up to say something to Cam, who was almost a foot taller than her. I couldn't hear them through the window, but I imagined her saying something like, *We-all don' have this heah wh-aht stuff fallin' outta the skah awl the tah-yam back home in Jaw-ja.*

Okay, so maybe her Southern accent isn't quite *that* bad. But it's close.

Anyway, whatever she said made Cam laugh. Now, a lot of people can laugh wickedly or sarcastically or wearily or even just politely. But not Cam. His whole face always lit up with pure joy whenever he smiled or laughed, like a little boy's on—well, okay, Christmas.

So he laughed, and then he put his arm around her. She snuggled up against him with another shiver, wrapping both her white-mittened hands around his waist.

She smiled up at him. He smiled down at her. A second later she was standing on tiptoes, and he was bending down toward her.

Their kiss sent an electric shock through me. A spontaneous kiss on a snowy evening, not knowing or caring who might see—since when had Cam become such a romantic?

And more important, since when did I *care*? After all, this was all totally my idea, my plan, my fault.

But maybe I need to backtrack a little. Begin at the beginning. See, it all really started a few months ago at the big last-day-of-freedom party at the lake the night before my first day of senior year. . . .

one

"Hold still."

I froze on command. A second later my best friend, Allie Lin, smacked me soundly on the forehead. "Ow!" I yelped.

"Mosquito," she explained succinctly.

I rubbed the spot. "Oh. Thanks."

She slapped herself on the arm, then shifted positions on the big old scratchy pine log where we were sitting. Her gaze drifted to a group of beefy-looking guys in Bermuda shorts over near the bonfire. They were pounding beers and talking football. Their loud, excited voices blended with the hip-hop music pouring out of the speakers of the battered old Chevy sedan parked on the rocky lakeside beach. The dark, still water of Lake Claus lapped gently against the car's front tires.

"I can't believe school starts tomorrow and I still don't have a boyfriend." Allie glanced from the football guys over to a couple making out furiously on the next log. "If I don't have a guy of my own before the Ball, I swear I'm going to give it up and become a nun."

In Claus Lake, there was only one thing people meant when they said "the Ball." That was the town's big Christmas Eve Costume Ball, held every year at the fireman's hall. It was a fund-raiser for some local charities, but more important, it was the social event of the season. The Christmas season, that is. And in Claus Lake, the Christmas season was the only season that counted. It lasted for a good four months, and people talked about it all year long.

"You can't become a nun," I reminded Allie. "You're not Catholic."

"Thanks, Logic Girl." She made a face at me. "My point is, I really, really, *really* don't want to go to the Ball stag this year."

I didn't see the big deal. The Ball wasn't a big date-night thing like homecoming or the prom. Lots of people went as couples, but plenty more went on their own or with their whole families or a bunch of friends or whatever.

It wasn't important who you went with; it was just important that you *went*.

But I knew Allie didn't want to hear it. For the past three years, she'd gone to the Ball with me; my boyfriend, Cameron Kehoe; and my cousin Nicholas. However, last year Nick's girlfriend, Rachel, had been part of the gang too, suddenly making it feel much less like a group thing and more like a double date plus one. I guess Allie hadn't liked the feeling, because she seemed determined not to let it happen again this year.

"Senior year," she mused. "It hardly seems possible, does it? It seems like two seconds ago that we were all scared, stupid freshmen."

"What hardly seems possible is that I'll ever get everything done this fall." I stretched out my long legs, accidentally kicking over an abandoned beer bottle with one flip-flopped foot. "I need to finish up my college applications, sign up for the SATs, interview for the Simpson Scholarship—"

"It's not like you have to worry about that last part," Allie interrupted, slapping another mosquito on her neck. "You have the Simpson Scholarship in the bag."

"Don't be so sure. Andrew Cole could weasel in there and get it instead of me, especially if I screw up the interview."

I frowned slightly at the thought. Every year, the Simpson Scholarship went to Claus Lake High School's most accomplished senior. Just having the highest GPA—which I did—was no guarantee. The committee was headed by Mrs. Alice Simpson, the town's wealthiest citizen, as well as one of its oldest at ninety-three and counting. Grades and academic achievements were very important, but so were extracurriculars, charity work, and who knew what else. Then there was the personal interview. That could make or break you with the committee—especially Mrs. Simpson.

Andrew had had the second-highest GPA in our class for the past three years running. He was also kind of charming in a geeky-nerdy, Clark Kent-y, sucking-up-to-adults kind of way. If he ended up winning that scholarship, I would probably have to reconsider my choice of colleges. And that would definitely be a total disaster.

See, I had my whole life pretty much planned out. My one-year plan was to win the Simpson Scholarship and get into a top East Coast university. Five-year plan: Earn a degree in biology and acceptance to the med school of my choice. Ten-plus-year plan: Begin fabulous career in medical research, complete with exciting big-city lifestyle.

I could hardly wait. But for now here I was, sitting with my best friend, listening to a good song, on a nice—albeit rather buggy and muggy—early September night. Not such a bad place to be, really. At least for the moment.

Reaching back over my head, I grabbed two fistfuls of my thick, springy auburn hair, lifting it up off the nape of my neck to take advantage of the slight breeze coming in off the lake. Even though the sun had set, it was hot and sticky. Sitting so close to the fire wasn't helping matters. If I hadn't known it was biologically impossible, I might have suspected I could melt into a puddle at any moment.

If the heat was affecting Allie the same way, she wasn't showing it. Her glossy dark chin-length hair was pulled back into a tiny ponytail at the back of her head, and her heart-shaped face was sweat free. As a new song came on the car radio she started bouncing and wriggling on the log, tapping her toes and shaking her slim shoulders in time to the music.

"Sit still, will you?" I complained. "You're making me sweat just watching you."

"Can't," she said, a little breathless from all the seat dancing. "The Crazy Legs Theory, remember?"

That's another thing about Allie. She was always coming up with all these psychological theories, mostly about love and romance. She planned to write self-help books someday—you know, the kind with titles like *Visualize Your Way to a Hot, Happening Love Life* or *It's Not You, It's Him*. It was pretty much her life goal to get on *Oprah* with one of her bestselling tomes.

And now that she mentioned it, I did remember this particular theory. It was one of her favorites, one she'd trotted out on numerous occasions. It posited that if a girl wriggled and toe-tapped as if she were dancing right there in her seat, a guy would be more likely to come over and ask her to dance.

"Oh, right," I joked. "The Crazy Legs Theory. How could I forget? Isn't that the one we disproved at the prom? And then at Mary Zimmer's party? And then again at your aunt's wedding last month?"

"It only has to work once." Allie smiled serenely as she boogied down on the log.

I grinned. I was always amused by Allie's endless parade of new theories. That didn't mean I actually *believed* most of them—I was too much of a hard-science girl for that sort of thing—but luckily Allie was a good sport and didn't seem to mind that I often couldn't resist applying the scientific method to her so-called data.

The bonfire was dying down by now, and the crowd was starting to thin out. The football guys wandered down to the water's edge to throw rocks or something. Meanwhile couples had been slipping off into the darkness together for a while. Last chance for some carefree romance before the daily grind started up again.

That reminded me: I hadn't seen Cam in quite some

time. However, it only took a quick glance around to locate him. He was over on the far side of the fire, picking up empty cans and bottles and tossing them into the public recycling bin near the fire pit.

Yeah. Way romantic. Then again, that was kind of the way things had been going with us lately.

I guess Allie heard my sigh and followed my gaze toward Cam. "What's wrong?" she demanded. "You're not still worried that you and Cam are losing your spark, are you?"

"Maybe a little," I admitted.

It was true. The closer we got to senior year, the more I thought about what came next—after high school. And the more I looked forward to my carefully planned out, totally fabu future, the more I realized there was one thing I hadn't taken into account while making those plans. Namely, my almost-four-year relationship with Cam.

Don't get me wrong. Cam was a great guy. Everybody said so, from Allie and Nick to my parents to the little old ladies whose groceries Cam helped bring in every weekend. Yeah, he was that nice.

And maybe that was part of the problem. I wasn't one to psychoanalyze myself or anything, but I couldn't help wondering if there was something missing between me and Cam. I guess those thoughts might have started when Nick got together with Rachel. From the beginning the two of them couldn't keep their hands off each other. They were always hugging or kissing or just walking along all intertwined. Once I noticed that, I started noticing that a lot of other couples were the same way. Touchy-feely. Staring into each other's eyes. That sort of thing.

Cam and I weren't like that. I wasn't sure we'd ever been like that. Did that mean we were missing something? Or had our relationship run its course? Had we grown apart without really noticing? Were we just stuck now in a state of stasis? My scientific mind was pretty sure it had a strong hypothesis about that, and it was getting harder to ignore the evidence.

Allie was staring at me. She'd even forgotten to keep up her seat dancing.

"You realize you're nuts, right?" she said. "Cam is *such* an amazing guy. One of a kind. And you two are perfect together." She shook her head so vigorously that a strand of hair came loose from her tiny ponytail. "All this crazy talk about breaking up is probably just fear of success or something." Her eyes lit up. "Hey, I like that! I could call it the Scared to Splitsville Theory."

I rolled my eyes. "Please," I said. "Since when do I have a fear of success? I *love* success. I embrace it. I seek it out and coddle it and call it pet names."

"I'm not talking about school and stuff." The song

on the car radio changed, and Allie suddenly seemed to remember her dancing. She started bouncing in time to the beat again while she talked. "Everybody has some kind of fear of success. Maybe yours has to do with love. Like, you didn't choose Cam through some scientific theorem, so you're not convinced that your relationship should work as well as it does, and now you're trying to sabotage it to prove yourself right. Ooh!" She looked even more excited; she always gets that way when she thinks she's figured someone out. Usually me. "That totally makes sense. You're used to always being right—you know, with the good grades and stuff—and so this has been eating you up inside and made you *want* to be wrong this time."

Before I could point out all the flaws in that reasoning, Bruce Janssen came loping over to us. Bruce was one of Cam's best guy friends, though I wasn't sure why, since he was pretty much Cam's opposite in every way. He was the type of guy who thinks other people are truly impressed that he can fart the first two bars of "The Star-Spangled Banner." He was probably planning to put that on his college applications.

He skidded to a stop in front of us. "Hey, Michaels," he greeted me.

I automatically drew in my legs as his pale-green eyes slid down them. Bracing myself, I waited for his sleazy compliment of the day. What would it be this time? Maybe how he'd dreamed about my legs last night. Or how just once before he died he wanted to know how it felt to bury his hands in my wild, luxurious hair. Even Cam had rolled his eyes the first time Bruce came out with that one. Then again, maybe he'd just call me "Sexy Lexi" and try to grope me—after all, everyone loves a classic.

However, this time Bruce turned toward Allie. "Lookin' good, Lin," he said, tossing his too-long blond hair out of his eyes. "Wanna dance?"

"Sure!" Allie bounced out of her seat.

I hid a smile. It was obvious that Allie was so excited that her Crazy Legs Theory had finally worked, she'd forgotten all about another of her favorite theories: the Never Dance with Losers Theory.

I watched as she and Bruce made their way over to a smooth spot on the beach where a few other couples were dancing. Allie immediately went from slapping mosquitoes to slapping Bruce's hands away from everywhere they weren't supposed to be.

Just then I saw Cam coming toward me. I guess he'd finally noticed the romantic mood. Or maybe he'd just seen me sitting alone and his Mr. Nice Guy side had kicked in automatically.

"Hey," he said, sitting down on the log beside me.

"Hey back," I replied, taking in that familiar sweet, handsome, square-jawed face, and his kind eyes and broad shoulders. Maybe Allie was right. Maybe I was silly to question being with a guy like that. I put my hand on his knee and squeezed, figuring a little romantic moment of our own might help chase the anxious thoughts away. "Having a nice time tonight?"

"Sure." Cam smiled, but he looked kind of distracted. He glanced around. "Hey, did you meet that guy Mike from Dornerville? Tall guy in the red T-shirt? I was talking to him a few minutes ago, and it turns out his mom works at the financial aid office at the campus over there. He thinks she can put in a word for me. Nice of him, huh?"

That brought me back to earth with a thud. Cam wasn't really the ambitious type. He seemed perfectly content to attend the nearest state university satellite campus to study culinary arts and business. He expected to use that education to get a job as an assistant chef somewhere, with the idea of someday opening his own restaurant right there in Claus Lake. We didn't talk about it much, but I hadn't been able to miss the fact that those plans didn't mesh too well with my own big-career, big-city dreams.

Cam finally seemed to notice my hand on his knee. He covered it with his own hand, rubbing my palm with his thumb.

"But listen," he said softly, wrapping his free arm around me and pulling me closer, "why worry about school on our last night of freedom, right?"

I did my best to push aside my worries once again. The future wasn't here yet. Maybe I could wait one more night to worry about it.

"Uh-huh." I turned and swung my legs over his lap, then leaned closer. My shoulder fit into the crook of his arm in its usual familiar way, and I could smell mint on his breath as his lips found mine.

The sound of squealing tires interrupted our kiss. I pulled back and glanced over Cam's shoulder toward the parking lot.

"Hey," I said in surprise, recognizing the car that had just peeled in and screeched to a zigzaggy stop across a couple of empty spaces. "Looks like Nick came after all."

That was unexpected. My cousin's girlfriend was a year older than the rest of us, and she was leaving for the University of Michigan the next day. Nick had spent the whole past week planning a big, romantic night that was supposed to tide them over until the first weekend visit.

But now here he was, climbing out of his car with his sandy hair standing on end and his polo shirt askew. Even in the dim light of the crescent moon and the fading bonfire, I could tell from his face that something was wrong.

Cam had turned to look by now too. "Whoa, he looks upset." Gently shoving me off his lap, he stood up and hurried toward Nick.

I was right behind him. When we reached Nick, I could see he was even worse off than I'd thought. He was practically hyperventilating—very un-Nick-like. Normally Nick is the type of guy who would smile in front of a firing squad and ask for a cigarette. And he doesn't even smoke. I'd known him since birth—we'd grown up next door to each other, more like sister and brother than cousins—and I'd never seen him lose his cool like this.

"Lex," he choked out. "Cam."

"What is it?" I grabbed his arm, resisting the urge to shake him. "Is someone hurt? Is it Mom or Dad? Or *your* mom or dad? What? *Who?*"

Nick waved his hand around vaguely. "No. No. Nothing like that. Everyone's fine."

"Then what?" I demanded.

"Lexi . . . ," Cam murmured soothingly.

Nick shook his head. "No," he croaked. "It's just . . . just . . . just Rachel."

Cam and I traded a confused look. "What do you mean, buddy?" Cam asked gently. "What about Rachel? Is she okay?"

Nick squeezed his eyes shut for a second, then opened

them and stared at us bleakly. "She dumped me," he said hoarsely. "Just now. Said she—um, she didn't want to see me tied down when she was off, you know, living her new life in college."

Cam probably said all the right things after that—he usually does—but I was so shocked that I couldn't react at first. Nick and Rachel had seemed like the perfect couple from day one. I'd thought those two would be together forever. *Everyone* had thought that. Well, everyone but Rachel, apparently.

So what did "together forever" really mean, anyway?

two

"*Actuate*," Allie said. "Definition, please. I'll give you a hint—it's a verb."

I took a sip of my strawberry milk shake, then drummed my fingers on the paper place mat in front of me. "Actuate," I said. "To move or incite into action."

"Very good. Now use it in a sentence."

I glanced around the crowded Elf Street Diner for inspiration. "Um, I need to actuate myself into deciding what to do about me and Cam."

Allie had just popped a french fry into her mouth. She frowned, then quickly chewed and swallowed. "Very funny," she said. "You're not still thinking about that, are you? I figured that was just end-of-summer doldrums or something."

It had been a little over a week since the bonfire, and Allie and I had been way too busy since then to sit around discussing my relationship. School had started, and the teachers seemed determined to head off any early bouts of Senioritis by assigning boatloads of homework. On top of that, my mom and aunt were both on the committee for the Christmas Eve Costume Ball again this year, which meant that Nick and I, plus all our friends, were automatically drafted into service as well. Joy to the world.

"I don't know," I told Allie with a sigh. "I keep trying to look at it logically, you know?"

Allie shoved away her list of SAT vocabulary words, almost pushing it into the water ring her soda glass had left behind on the table. "Okay," she said. "If you want to get all science-nerdy about this and do the whole pro-con thing, think about it this way. Isn't it nice not having to worry about who you're going with to the homecoming dance? Or the Ball? Or the prom?"

"No argument there," I admitted. "It's definitely easier not having to worry about those things. Especially since Cam is still always fun to hang out with. No complaints there." I shrugged and played with my straw. "But is that enough reason to stay with someone? Is it fair to either of us?"

"Of course it is!" Allie exclaimed. "You guys care about

each other. That's all that matters. Love conquers all, right?"

"Does it?" I leaned forward, gazing at her across the table. "Seriously, Allie, think about it. After this year, I'll be off to college at least, like, eight hundred miles away. Meanwhile Cam is probably going to wind up staying right here in Wisconsin."

"So what?" Allie's lower lip jutted out stubbornly. "Lots of people have made that kind of thing work."

I shrugged. "Okay, granted. But trying to keep up a long-distance relationship through four years of college is bad enough. What happens after that? Our goals and visions of life are just so different."

"Right, and that's what I've always said makes you guys so perfect together," Allie said. "Opposites Attract Theory, remember?"

Fine. If she was going to start throwing her theories in my face, two could play that game.

"Okay, then what about the Testing the Waters Theory?" I asked her. "You know, the one you came up with a while back that says nobody should just glom on to the first guy or girl who ever asks them out on a date. Neither Cam nor I have ever had any other serious relationships. How do we know the grass isn't greener somewhere else?"

"Oh, please." Allie rolled her eyes. "That theory doesn't apply to you guys."

"Why not? Besides, most relationships end at some point, especially for people our age. I'm sure there's plenty of statistical evidence about that. Why should I expect to be the exception?"

She frowned. "Why do you have to be so logical about everything?" she said. "Anyway, if you want to break up with Cam, just do it already. I can't stop you." She stuffed another fry in her mouth, then mumbled, "Even if I do know for a fact that it would be the hugest mistake of your life."

I didn't bother to argue with her usage of the term *fact*. I already knew that would be pointless.

"It's not that I *want* to break up with him," I said instead. "I just think it's probably inevitable, that's all. Sad, but necessary." With that, I decided to back off. It was obvious that Allie was getting kind of upset. She could be pretty sensitive about that sort of thing. "Anyway, give me another word, okay? The Simpson Scholarship won't help much if I blow the verbal on the SAT."

That much was logical enough not to allow any argument. I knew I could ace the math part of the test even sound asleep and with one hand tied behind my back. However, I was a lot weaker on vocabulary. Luckily Allie is a word whiz. Must be from reading all those self-help books she loves so much. They probably have to get pretty creative to keep coming up with new ways to tell women how to land their dream guys.

"Fine." Allie pulled the vocab list toward her again and scanned it. "Here are a few words for you. I offer you my sincerest adjuration to abrogate this abstruse and abhorrent aberration. Quit being so contumacious about it, or I shall have to berate you."

I was still puzzling through that one when the jingle bells hanging on the door started jangling. Glancing that way, I saw Nick dragging himself into the diner. His face wore the hangdog, depressed look that had become all too familiar over the past week.

"Nick!" Allie waved at him. "Over here."

He blinked and then shambled over. "Hey," he said. "What's up?"

"I'm just trying to talk Lexi out of doing something really stupid," Allie informed him.

Nick flopped into the booth beside me. "So what else is new?" he said with a shadow of his old humor.

"Don't listen to her." I shot Allie a warning look. Now didn't seem to be the time to involve Nick in a debate about me and Cam. He was depressed enough already. "We're just running some vocabulary words. Want to join in?"

"Sure." He shrugged. "Might take my mind off—well, you know."

"That's true," Allie said. "I have a theory about that, actually; I'm calling it the Broody Brain Theory. The idea is that if you're filling your mind with new knowledge, you won't have any brain cells left for moping over your love life or whatever."

I laughed. Normally Nick would've joined in. He loves making fun of Allie's theories almost as much as I do.

But not today. He just sighed deeply and picked at the edge of the table. "It'll take more than a few vocabulary words to take my mind off Rachel," he mumbled.

I winced. *Pathetic* used to be the last word anyone would ever use to describe Nick. But these days, sadly, it fit him perfectly. I wished there was something I could do to help him snap out of it, but so far he only seemed interested in wallowing.

That brought my mind back to Cam again. It had been bad enough thinking about breaking things off with him before. I hadn't been sure I'd have the heart—or the guts—to actually ever go through with it. If I did, I knew it would take some real finesse. Even if we weren't meant to be a couple, I knew for certain that I always wanted us to be friends. Besides, I didn't want to mess up our tight little group—Allie and Nick would never forgive me if I did. I'd never forgive myself.

But now, watching Nick brood over his ex, the idea of breaking up with Cam seemed even harder to imagine.

Nick was really devastated; who knew how long it would take him to get over Rachel? And he wasn't anywhere near as sweet and sensitive as Cam. How could I possibly put Cam through that kind of heartbreak? How would I ever be able to stand watching him go through that?

"Lexi, are you even listening to me?" Allie's annoyed voice broke into my thoughts. "Because I really didn't think that *ruminate* was that hard a word."

"Sorry. Um, *ruminate* means to think something over."

"Right," Allie said.

Nick glanced over at me. "Way to ruminate your way through that one, science geekette," he said, once again sounding almost like his old self for a second. "Maybe you'll be able to get that verbal score within two hundred points of the math one after all."

I laughed, doing my best to push all ruminations about Cam out of my head, at least for the moment. What was the hurry, anyway? This wasn't a bio lab with a time limit. Just because I'd identified a possible problem didn't mean I had to rush out and solve it right away.

One afternoon a couple of weeks later, Cam came over to help me prep for my Simpson Scholarship interview, which was scheduled for the following day. I have to admit, I was a little tense about it. Verging on hysterical.

"What if I screw this up?" I asked him for about the tenth time, pacing back and forth across my living room. "What if I don't get the scholarship?"

He was splayed out on the big squishy beige couch. My parents were both out, so we had the place to ourselves aside from Blitzen, the family cat, who was sleeping on the couch beside Cam. Sitting up carefully to avoid jostling the cat—she could be cranky when awakened suddenly—Cam gave me that easy smile that always made me feel a little calmer.

"Chill out, Lexi," he said. "You're going to do great tomorrow. Mrs. Simpson will love you."

"But what if she doesn't?" I argued, still pacing. "I might, you know, forget myself and accidentally blurt out the F-word or something."

He laughed out loud at that. "Right," he said with a twinkle in his eye. "I'm sure that's really likely to happen."

"Okay, maybe not." I sighed and ran both hands through my hair, even though I knew that always made me end up looking like Bozo the Clown. "This is just so important, you know?"

"I know."

I stopped pacing and stared down at him. "Do you?" I asked. "I mean, you never really seem to think about the future much. Where do you see yourself in five years?"

"We've talked about this before, Lexi." He reached for my hand and pulled me down until I was sitting beside him. Blitzen woke up and shot me a baleful look before slinking off. "I'll get my degree, then probably look for a job where I can learn the restaurant business from the bottom up. Maybe open a little place of my own someday."

"Okay," I said slowly, "but have you ever noticed that your goals and mine—well, they don't exactly match?"

"I guess." He didn't sound terribly concerned. "But why worry about that before we have to? The future will take care of itself. We just need to try to be happy now and figure out the rest when it comes."

I gritted my teeth. "Are you kidding?" I cried. "That sounds like one of Allie's crazy theories or something. What if the future *doesn't* work itself out? What then?"

He just shrugged. "I don't know. It always does, though."

Almost everything about Cam was great. But that default attitude of his—*oh well, it'll work itself out*—always made me crazy, even when he was just talking about finding a parking spot or something. But this time it was much worse. This time he was talking about our whole future. *My* whole future. How could he be so infuriatingly casual about it?

"Did I ever tell you how I decided to go into medical

research?" I asked, determined to make him understand for once just how important this was.

"Sure." He shifted in his seat, slinging one arm across the couch behind me. "It was when your mom got sick when you were a kid, right?"

"That was part of it." I nodded. "When I was six or seven Mom had a cancer scare, and our whole family traveled to the Mayo Clinic to have it checked out."

"Yeah, I remember now." Cam reached down and squeezed my upper arm. "That must have been really scary for you."

"Uh-huh, I guess." I stared blankly at the mirror over the fireplace across the room, barely feeling his hand as I thought back to that time. Back then I hadn't even really understood exactly what cancer was. I'd just known it was something bad. "Anyway, it turned out to be a false alarm, thank God. Everything was benign; Mom was fine. But while we were at the clinic and she was getting her tests done and stuff, there was this one doctor who was supernice to me. He kept an eye on me while Dad was distracted, and even took me on a tour of his lab and let me play with his ultrasound machine."

"Nice of him," Cam said.

I nodded. "I'm sure he was busy. All those docs always are. But he took the time to watch out for me, and I always remembered that, even though I don't even know his name. Ever since then I've known I wanted to do what he did. I asked Mom and Dad recently if they remembered who he was so I could mention him in my college application essays, but they don't remember either. So I just wrote the essays without the name."

"That's a great story," Cam said. "I bet the college admissions people will love it."

"I hope so. But that's not my point. I know we all kid around about how driven I am, how I plan out everything in my life and stuff. I guess I'm trying to tell you just how much those plans mean to me."

He reached over and gently pushed a lock of auburn hair out of my face, smiling down at me fondly. "I get that," he said, his fingers tracing the outline of my forehead. "I always have, Lexi. It's part of what makes you, you."

His expression was so caring and happy that I didn't have the heart to go on. I did my best to tamp down my own frustration, but it wasn't easy. If he really *did* understand, wouldn't he be a little more worried that our futures were so completely mismatched?

three

"So when do you find out about the scholarship?" Nick asked, carefully threading a cranberry onto a piece of fishing line.

"Weren't you listening? She already said she doesn't know." Allie grabbed a pair of scissors from the floor and snipped off the end of the cranberry garland she'd just finished. "But it doesn't matter, anyway. It sounds like she totally blew them away at the interview. That scholarship is so hers."

"Don't jinx me," I warned her. "Yeah, I think I did pretty well in that interview. Still, Andrew might've done even better. You never know."

But my focus wasn't really on the Simpson Scholarship anymore. I'd done all I could; from now on it was up to the committee, and I was trying not to stress over it too much. Besides, I had other things on my mind.

I grabbed another handful of cranberries. The three of us were sitting on the floor of Nick's roomy, yellow-walled basement rec room, stringing garlands. Nick's mom, my aunt, was head of decorations for the Ball that year, and even though it was still September, she already had us hard at work. There was a ton to do before December 24. At least she'd left us with plenty of soda and popcorn to help us through the day's task. Then again, maybe we were supposed to turn the popcorn into more garlands. If that was true, she was going to be sorely disappointed when she returned home from that day's round of committee meetings.

"Listen, guys," I said to my friends, grabbing another handful of popcorn out of the almost-empty bowl. "I want to talk to you about something. About Cam, actually."

Allie's head shot up, and she almost cut her own finger off with the scissors. "What?" she demanded. "You're not still actually thinking about ending things with Cam?"

"Sort of," I admitted. "I just keep going back and forth on it, you know? It's driving me nuts. On the one hand, Cam is great."

"As I've been telling you all along," Allie put in with a frown.

"I know. And you're right." I shook my head. "But on the other hand, where are Cam and I headed, realistically speaking?"

"Homecoming," Allie put in. "The Ball. The prom."

"Right. But then what?"

Nick looked a little confused. He'd been so deep into his own heartache that I guess he wasn't fully up to speed on my love life issues. "Wait," he said. "You're not thinking of stringing Cam along until you're ready to leave for college and then ripping his heart out with your bare hands, are you?"

He sounded a little suspicious. And a lot bitter. Who could blame him?

"Definitely not," I assured him. "That's why I'm thinking about this now instead of putting it off. If Cam and I are going to end up going our separate ways next summer, why prolong the inevitable?"

"Because you guys are in love, that's why!" Allie exclaimed.

I barely heard her. All this time, I'd been moving inexorably toward the only logical conclusion. No matter how many times I went over the facts, checked the variables, ran the numbers, the result was always the same.

"There's only one answer." I took a deep breath, ignoring the floppy-fish feeling in the pit of my stomach. That feeling was irrelevant to the facts. "Cam and I need to break up."

Allie gasped, her scissors clattering to the floor. Even Nick looked kind of shocked.

"Dude," he said. "Are you sure? Seriously, it'll kill him if you dump him out of the blue."

"Don't worry, I'm not planning to dump Cam at all." I smiled slowly as a great idea popped into my head. Who says scientists can't be creative? "No, I've just realized there's a much kinder, gentler way to handle this. I'm going to get *Cam* to break up with *me*!"

"Huh?" Allie looked perplexed. "What are you talking about, Lexi?"

"Yeah." Nick set down his threaded cranberries and peered at me suspiciously. "Since when do you play those kinds of games? You've always been a straight shooter."

I raised an eyebrow at him. "Actually, you were the inspiration for this plan."

"Me?" Nick blinked. "You're pinning this on *me*?"

"Yeah. Just look at you—Rachel dumped you almost a month ago, and you're still a mess. And you guys were together less than a year." I shook my head. "No way do I want to do that to Cam. It'll be way easier on him if I let him make the decision to end things."

"I hope you're not in a hurry," Allie said dubiously.

"I'm not," I replied, tossing a piece of popcorn into my mouth. "I won't rush it. These things take time."

"No." Allie shook her head. "I mean, I hope you aren't counting on Cam suddenly deciding to dump you anytime this century. Because it's not going to happen."

"She's right, Lex." Nick stretched out his legs and flicked a stray cranberry off the knee of his jeans. "The dude has it bad for you. He never even *looks* at other girls. Not even superhot, half-naked ones." He licked his lips. "Mmm, half-naked girls," he Homer Simpsoned.

I rolled my eyes. Maybe there was a glimmer of light at the end of Nick's tunnel of heartbreak after all.

"Anyway," he went on, "if you're really set on ending things, you should just go ahead and do it. Cam is going to be totally devastated either way."

"Not if I do this right," I countered, the plan forming more fully in my mind even as I spoke. "All I have to do is set things up so he falls for another girl. That way, he'll realize for himself that we've been growing apart and then *he'll* break up with *me*." I shrugged. "He's too honest to do anything else once he's seen the light. And that way, no one's heart gets broken. If I handle it right, we can totally stay friends and enjoy the rest of senior year together without all the complications and wondering where our relationship is going and stuff. It's win-win. Totally foolproof!"

"You're nuts, Lexi," Allie said. "I'm telling you, it'll never work. Cam adores you."

"And I adore him." I sighed as they both stared at me with skepticism written all over their faces. Just because I was able to look at the situation logically, it didn't mean I didn't have feelings or that this wasn't tearing me up inside. "Listen, you guys, I wish I didn't have to do this. But I've been over all the options, and it's the only way. Cam and I are just too different. That's okay in high school, but we won't be in high school much longer. That means it's time for some tough choices. Like it or not."

Nick rolled his eyes. "Oh, please," he said, reaching for the popcorn bowl. "If you keep this up, you'll have to quit the Science Geekettes of America and join the drama club."

I reached over and gave him a shove. "I'm serious, smart guy," I said. "If you can think of a better idea to handle this, then spill it."

"I can think of a better idea," Allie put in. "Stay with Cam. Figure things out. Live happily ever after."

That was Allie for you. Hopeless romantic. "I already told you, that won't work," I said patiently. "How are we going to live happily ever after when I'm running a lab in Boston or New York or Atlanta and Cam's running a kitchen right here in Claus Lake?"

"But you guys are such a great couple!" Allie actually looked as if she might burst into tears. "I mean, okay, maybe you're not that much alike. But that's kind of what makes it work!"

"She's right, Lex," Nick agreed. "If you ever hooked up with someone as logical and ambitious as yourself, you'd drive each other crazy."

Yeah. He had a point. Then again, it wasn't really *the* point.

"Plus you guys have always been so happy together," Allie said. "You barely ever even fight or anything."

"I know we seem happy enough now," I said. "But we'll probably both be even happier once we've moved on. And it's not like we can't stay friends, like I said. In fact, I can't imagine not having Cam in my life one way or another."

That, as it turned out, was quite literally true. As I sat there, I tried to imagine it. Not having Cam around. Never talking to him, never hanging out together. Maybe never seeing him again after graduation.

But it didn't work. My mind couldn't seem to put together that kind of scenario. It just Did. Not. Compute.

I shrugged it off, deciding it didn't matter. If my plan worked out the way I was picturing it, there would be no need for me to imagine Life Without Cam. We could stay good friends, hang out for the rest of senior year and all next summer. Then when I went off to college, he'd still be there for me just like Allie and Nick, supporting me from a distance, giving me one of his patented pep talks as I dove off the high board of life into my exciting new future.

Meanwhile he would be free to figure out how to put his own future in motion. He could find himself a girl who would be perfectly content to stay in Claus Lake all her life, maybe hostessing at Cam's future restaurant and serving on the refreshments committee with him for the Ball. There were tons of girls at our school who would dream of nothing more, especially if the plan involved an amazing guy like Cam.

"I don't know, Lex." Nick still seemed dubious as he methodically scarfed down the rest of the popcorn. "Maybe you should think about this some more."

"Yeah," Allie agreed. "Don't forget about the Fast and Furious Theory. The quicker you try to make big moves or decisions in a relationship, the more likely it is to end in anger or heartache."

"You know, that theory actually *almost* makes sense," I said. "But it doesn't apply to me. Not unless almost four years counts as a quick move."

"You might as well give it up, Allie," Nick put in. "This is Lexi Michaels you're talking to, remember? Once her mind is made up, that's that. No turning back. Mule city."

I made a face at him. "Very funny," I said. "Why don't you just come out and call me stubborn?"

"I thought I just did." He shrugged. "But here you go, Ms. Literal. You're stubborn."

I laughed. Now that I'd finally made my decision, I was feeling a little better already. It was always kind of comforting to have a course of action, a plan to follow. No more looming uncertainties. Just a problem to be solved, sort of like an especially challenging and complex bio lab. Now that I had the gist of how to approach it, I just needed to nail down the details and I'd be all set.

"Okay, you guys." I leaned over to grab the last few pieces of popcorn before Nick could polish them off. "So help me out here. It's time to set up a little social experiment. I need to get my boyfriend another woman!"

four

Getting Cam a new girlfriend turned out to be a lot harder than I'd expected. In fact, for the first few weeks I wasn't sure I'd be able to pull it off after all.

For one thing, none of the girls at school seemed quite right for him. When I'd first concocted the plan, Claus Lake High School had seemed to be bursting with vaguely appropriate potential girlfriends for Cam. But once I got specific, it seemed every girl I considered had some fatal flaw. Carla Myers talked too much—if he ended up with her, poor Cam would never get a word in edgewise. Amalia Rozin was too quiet and passive. Cam wasn't the type of person who wanted to do *all* the talking and planning in a relationship. Patti Amundson was rumored to have cheated on her last boyfriend, and there was no way I was going to risk fixing Cam up with someone who might betray him. No, if this was going to work, I was going to have to find just the right girl. The perfect girl. The girl Cam deserved.

"What about Talia Lund?" Allie asked one day at lunch. She was still dragging her heels on this whole breaking-up-with-Cam thing. But at least she seemed to be trying to help.

I glanced across the school cafeteria at a pretty blond girl talking and laughing with her friends and shook my head. "You mean little miss peppy-peppy cheerleader?" I picked up my sandwich. "Ugh. I don't think so. Cam doesn't go for that type."

"Right." Allie rolled her eyes. "Funny how none of the girls we know seem to be good enough for Cam. Maybe this is the Maybe Not Theory in action? You know, you don't *really* want to go through with this, so you're sabotaging your own efforts?"

"Sorry, guess again." I paused to take a bite of my sandwich. "I'm just trying to be scientific about this," I added after I'd chewed and swallowed, "to give my plan the best chance to work. That means narrowing it down to the absolute best candidate before proceeding."

"Right." Allie pursed her lips and sort of smirked.

* * *

"Check it out," I said to Cam. "There's Margie Mendenhall. She looks really pretty in that outfit, doesn't she?"

He barely looked up from the pine garland he was attaching to a lamppost outside the fireman's hall. "Huh?" he said, glancing briefly at a girl walking her dog farther down the block. "Oh. I guess. But listen, that reminds me—we should start thinking about our costumes for the Ball soon. You know the good ones always go fast. What do you say we go as reindeer this year?"

"Maybe," I said. "But listen, did you know Margie's a really good cook? I heard she won some kind of recipe contest in some magazine last year. Maybe we should go ask her about it."

"Not right now, okay, sweetie?" Cam's tongue poked out of the corner of his mouth as he bent lower, totally focused on what he was doing. "Your aunt will kill us if we don't get these garlands up today."

Glancing down the street, I saw Margie round the corner and disappear. Maybe it was just as well Cam hadn't taken that particular bait. Sure, the two of them had that cooking interest in common. But while Margie was really sweet, I wasn't sure her sense of humor would mesh with Cam's that well.

I leaned back against a parking meter and shoved my hands in the pockets of my parka as I watched Cam finish hanging the garland. There was a definite nip in the air these days—October was almost half over, which meant the town's holiday preparations were in full swing. In Claus Lake, the arrival of October didn't mean it was time to put up the Halloween decorations, the way it probably did in most places. Nope, the only nod to All Hallow's Eve was maybe a witch's hat on the giant Santa outside the used car lot and some pumpkins mixed in with the mistletoe. It was pretty much Christmas-Christmas-Christmas from October 1 straight through the New Year.

Nick's mom being in charge of decorations for the Ball meant she was involved in decking more than just the hall. Before long there wouldn't be a square inch of Claus Lake that wasn't bedecked and holly jolly.

Helping out with that was keeping me pretty busy. So was my mom, who was cochair of the food committee and counting on me to help keep her organized and halfway sane. Then on top of that there were the SATs, my college applications, and of course the usual daily grind of schoolwork and so forth.

With all that going on in my life, was it any wonder my plan seemed to be stalled before it had begun?

* * *

One Sunday afternoon in late October, I answered the door expecting to find Mrs. Abernathy from next door, who was late for the food committee meeting currently taking place in the glassed-in sunroom at the back of the house. Instead I found Allie standing on the front porch, wrapped in her favorite down jacket and a long purple scarf.

"Come on in," I told her. "You're just in time to help me make coffee for Mom's committee. I can use the help, too. They're all caffeine fiends."

She grimaced, but came in anyway. "Listen, I can't stay long," she began, unwinding her scarf.

"Likely excuse," I joked. "Would it sweeten the deal if I told you there are cookies?"

She laughed. "No, I'm serious," she said. "Tommy gets home from soccer practice in, like, half an hour, and I told Mom I'd be there to meet him." Tommy was Allie's eleven-year-old brother. He was pretty much a computer freak. If someone wasn't there watching him, he'd spend all his time on the computer, to the exclusion of food, sleep, homework, and possibly breathing. "But first I really need to talk to you," Allie went on. "You know that girl Jaylene who lives across the street from me, right?"

"You mean the Southern belle of Willow Street?" Jaylene was a chatty, giggly bleached blonde whose family had moved to town over the summer from somewhere south of Scarlett O'Haraville. "Yeah. What about her?"

"Well, you know she's still kind of new in town." Allie followed me into the kitchen, where the coffeepot was bubbling. The sounds of Mom and the rest of the committee chattering and laughing drifted faintly through the sliding glass doors in the breakfast nook. "So she doesn't know that many people yet."

"Really? She doesn't exactly seem like the shy type." Jaylene was a year behind us in school, but juniors and seniors shared the same lunch period. I'd noticed Allie's neighbor flirting with every guy in sight on numerous occasions. She was one of those people it was hard not to notice—and apparently the male population of Claus Lake High School agreed.

"Okay. But still, she's going to that fund-raising banquet for the new high school over in East Lake next weekend, and she asked me to help her find a date. She wants someone classy who looks good in a suit and tie." Allie shrugged. "So I thought of Nick. I've been worried about him—he's still really down about the whole Rachel thing. I thought maybe this would be a way to help him start moving on. But I wanted to check with you first to see if you think it's a good idea before I say anything to either Nick or Jaylene."

"Nick will never do it. He hates getting dressed up and

sitting around listening to speeches," I said automatically, though I wasn't really thinking about my cousin. I'd just had one of those flashes of inspiration that usually only hit me in the lab. "But I have a better idea—what about Cam?"

"What about him?" Allie looked genuinely confused for a second. Then her face cleared, and her eyes widened. "Wait, what? Are you serious?"

I shrugged. "Sure, why not? Cam will take her to that banquet if I ask him to. And who knows? Maybe spending the evening with another girl will be enough to finally jump-start my plan."

"Are you sure you're thinking of the right Jaylene?" Allie asked. "She doesn't really seem like his type. Besides, Cam hates sitting still for that long just as much as Nick does."

"I know, I know." I grabbed several coffee mugs out of the cabinet and lined them up on the counter. "Cam will be bored to death. And Jaylene is all wrong for him. But it doesn't matter. He hasn't picked up on any of my hints about more appropriate girls. So maybe the important thing is just to get him out there, spending time with someone else. Being on a date with a girl other than me. That way, he might get used to the idea and maybe want more. You know, kind of like Pavlov's dog."

"I don't know, Lexi." Allie sounded troubled. "This is Cam's life you're talking about here, not some science experiment. He's not going to suddenly decide he wants to date another girl—especially a girl like Jaylene—just because he's stuck with her for a few hours."

"You never know." I reached for the coffeepot and shot her a sly look. "What about that old Opposites Attract Theory you're always throwing in my face?"

She groaned and I chuckled, suddenly sure this was the right move. Okay, so Allie was right—there was no way Cam was going to suddenly fall for someone like Jaylene. She was giggly and prissy and high-maintenance and pushy and loud and maybe a teensy bit trashy, with her pink mohair sweaters, high heels with jeans, and baby blue eyeshadow. In other words, exactly the kind of girl Cam *didn't* like.

Still, I knew he would agree to the date as long as I made it sound like he was doing Jaylene a big favor. He was like that. So what did I have to lose?

"A banquet?" Cam sounded dubious.

But I was prepared for that. "I know it's a drag," I said, reaching over to squeeze his hand. Not wanting to waste any time, I'd hurried over to his house as soon as I could get away from Mom's Merry Minions back at the committee meeting. "If you really don't want to do it, that's okay, but I promised Allie I'd ask. She's just worried that since Jaylene is new in town, she won't be able to find anyone to go with and might just decide to stay home."

"No, it's okay," Cam said immediately—just as I'd known he would. "I don't mind, if you're sure *you* won't feel weird about it." He smiled and squeezed my hand. "You know, me out with another woman . . ."

Okay, so maybe I was already feeling a teensy bit weird. But I wasn't about to let *him* see that. Instead, I just waved one hand airily.

"Don't give that a second thought," I assured him. "It's totally cool with me. Listen, I'd better get back home before Mom notices I didn't load the dishwasher yet. Here's Jaylene's number. I'll have Allie tell her you'll call."

I pulled my hand away from his and dug into my pocket for the paper with Jaylene's phone number on it. Tossing it at him, I hurried off before either of us could change our minds.

The next week flew by. I was so busy with all the usual stuff that I hardly had time to obsess over Cam's Big Date. Well, not more than an hour or two a day, anyway. Allie had promised to fill me in as soon as she heard from Jaylene, and she showed up at my house bright and early on Saturday morning.

I hustled her upstairs before my father could spot her. Dad was busy typing up the notes from the latest Christmas Ball committee meeting on the den computer, and I knew he was probably looking for any excuse to take a break. If he spotted Allie, he was likely to start some long-winded discussion about how the Packers were doing this year. Allie was a casual football fan at best, but since Mom and I had no interest at all, Dad would take whatever he could get. And I didn't want to waste any time before getting the scoop.

"Well?" I asked as soon as we were safely in my room. "Did you talk to her?"

"Uh-huh." Allie wandered over to my desk and picked up the framed photo of Cam and me that stood there. "Have you talked to Cam yet?"

I shook my head. "Mom's been on the landline for the past hour, and my cell is recharging. So spill! Was it a total disaster, or did they both survive the experience?"

"Well, Jaylene said that Cam was a total gentleman last night."

"Yeah. Big surprise there." The cat was sleeping on my bed. I carefully pushed her over so I could sit down. "Did she mean it as a compliment or an insult?" I grinned. "I'm not sure Jaylene would appreciate the gentlemanly type."

"Think again," Allie said. "Actually, she told me she thinks Cam looks supersexy in a suit and tie."

"She's right. He does."

I suddenly felt a flash of concern. What if Jaylene really fell for Cam—and why wouldn't she?—while he was just being polite? I hadn't really considered that possibility. I didn't know Jaylene all that well, but I certainly hadn't intended to break her heart or anything. I also hadn't wanted to complicate Cam's life by forcing him to deal with that kind of awkward situation.

"So, did she say anything about how the two of them, you know, got along?" I asked.

Allie nodded. "She's convinced that Cam really got a kick out of her, um, out-there personality. And her, you know, *earthy* sense of humor."

"Really?"

"Really. Apparently they stopped off somewhere for coffee after the banquet and talked for over an hour." She took a deep breath. "Basically, Lex, it sounds like they *both* had a really great time."

five

I have to admit it, I was stunned. For a while there, I'd started to assume that my little get-Cam-a-new-girlfriend project could take all year.

But I shook it off. After all, this was exactly what I'd wanted. Okay, so maybe I hadn't expected it to happen right now, or with this particular girl. Then again, Alexander Fleming probably hadn't expected to discover penicillin when he'd noticed that mold in his petri dish. And just look how that turned out.

"That's great!" I told Allie. "If they really do like each other, that means it's time for the *real* work to begin. It's not like Cam is just going to suddenly kick me to the curb because a cute girl smiled at him and he kinda liked it." I shook my head fondly. Gentlemanly indeed! "No, we're definitely going to have to push this along if we want it to have any chance of sticking."

"What do you mean, *we?*" Allie frowned. "Uh-uh, no way. Don't include me in that. I did my part by setting up the Jaylene thing, and I feel weird enough about that."

"Okay, chill. You're right; you did your part. You're off the hook for the rest." I knew that if push came to shove, she'd back me up on whatever I needed. That was what friends were for. But she was such an incurable romantic that I knew I shouldn't be surprised if she wasn't exactly jumping for joy at the thought of helping Cam move on.

She nodded, then cleared her throat. "Um, so what do you have in mind, anyway?" she asked cautiously.

I held back a smile. Allie was incurably curious, too.

"Well, I hadn't really thought about it yet," I said, my mind already clicking into high gear as it worked through the next stage of this plan. "But Cam already volunteered to be on Mom's food committee. So I guess I can start by getting Jaylene on the committee too, so they'll have to spend lots of time together. . . ."

Nick swung the roll of snowflake-print wrapping paper like a golf club, connecting with a pudgy little tube of silver ribbon and sending it flying into the rec room wall with a solid *thwack*. He nodded with satisfaction as the ribbon unraveled its way to the floor, then turned to face me.

"Okay, let me get this straight," he said. "You want me to have a man-to-man talk with Cam about how he should dump you?"

"Sort of." I tied off the bow on the empty box I'd just finished wrapping. Nick and I were supposed to be working on the fake gifts that would go under the town's Christmas tree, though he wasn't working on them very hard at the moment. "You'll need to be way more subtle about it than that. Just remind him that he should never be afraid to go for what he wants or do what's best for him. That kind of thing. You know, guy stuff."

"Yeah." Nick snorted. "Guy stuff. Got it. 'Cause we guys just love a nice chat about relationships and feelings and that sort of thing. Maybe we can sip some chamomile tea and have our nails done while we discuss it."

I grinned. "Hey, whatever works for you. Remember, this is all for Cam's own good." I set my gift-wrapped package aside and reached for another box. "I've been dropping hints for the past week and a half since their date, so your little chat is just a way to make him think about things so he can't blow it off and pretend nothing's different."

"Hints? What kind of hints?"

I shrugged. "You know. Mentioning how I hope that whatever happens with college and stuff next year, we'll always stay friends. Turning my head or coughing whenever he looks like he's thinking about kissing me. That sort of thing." I took a deep breath. "And tonight, I'm going to call and cancel on him for next Friday. I'll tell him I need the time to finish up the last of my applications or something."

"What?" Nick looked startled. "You mean you're backing out of your traditional day-after-Thanksgiving date?"

I wasn't surprised by his reaction. Over the past three years, Leftover Turkey Day had been sacrosanct. Cam and I always spent the entire afternoon eating cold turkey sandwiches, snuggling on the couch watching movies, and just enjoying each other's company.

"Yeah. I have to." I sighed. It wasn't going to be easy to purposely miss my last chance at that particular tradition. But what choice did I have? "Blowing him off for Leftover Turkey Day is guaranteed to get his attention even if nothing else does."

Sure enough, Cam sounded shocked when I called him to pull out of our post-Thanksgiving date. "You're joking, right?" he said, sounding so plaintive that I almost changed my mind about the whole thing. "But we always get together for Leftover Turkey Day."

"I know." I clenched the phone tightly, glad that I hadn't tried to do this in person. "I'm really sorry. But maybe a rain check? Say, Saturday night? I should definitely be all finished by then. We could go see the Candy Cane Carolers concert down by the lake."

"Um, all right. Saturday night it is, then." There was a long pause. "Good luck with those apps." Cam still sounded disappointed and a little confused. Most guys probably would have pointed out that I could have planned to finish my applications on Saturday night instead so we could keep our Friday-afternoon date. But Cam wasn't most guys; he knew me too well. He probably assumed I had the application process planned out down to the minute. And he was far too caring and respectful to ask me to change that just in the name of tradition.

"Great, thanks. You're so understanding, Cam. A really good friend," I said. "That's the thing I've always appreciated about you the most, you know. Your friendship."

"Uh-huh, me too. Listen, maybe on Saturday we can talk about our costume for the Ball," he said. "Nick and I were talking the other day and I asked him to pick up the reindeer costume just in case, but if you don't want to do that, then we only have a month left to figure something out. And you know the good ones always go early. . . ."

"Sure, maybe. There are a few things we should probably talk about on Saturday, actually. Oops! I think I hear
Mom calling me. Gotta go."

I hung up quickly. Whew! That had been harder than
I'd expected. Images were flashing through my mind—me
and Cam laughing over leftover turkey last year, and the year
before, and the year before that . . . Me and Cam dancing
together at the Ball last year, and the year before, and the
year before that . . .

But I did my best to push all that aside as I picked up
the phone again. Reaching into my pocket, I pulled out
Jaylene's number and then dialed. When she answered, I
took a deep breath.

"Jaylene, hi!" I said cheerfully. "It's Lexi Michaels.
Listen, what do you have planned for Saturday night?"

And just like that, the deed was done. I arranged for Jaylene
to attend that Saturday night concert as well, convincing
her that a very special surprise blind date would be meeting
her there. The annual Carolers show was pretty informal—
just bleacher seating on the lawn in Lakeside Park near the
ice-skating inlet. I figured Cam and Jaylene would spot
each other once they were both there. Like I said, Jaylene
tends to be pretty hard to miss.

Still, I was a bundle of nerves as I paced back and forth across my room, watching the clock hanging over my desk. It was six forty-eight. The concert started at seven.

Allie was there too, lying on my green checkered bedspread, tickling Blitzen under the chin. That cat hated just about everyone and everything else in the world, but she always tolerated anything Allie did to her, even breaking out in a raspy purr once in a while.

"There's still time to change your mind, you know," Allie said. "You could call and tell Cam you're running late. Then we could go down there, explain to Jaylene that her date got held up . . ."

I shook my head. "I've come this far. I can't wimp out now."

Taking a deep breath to settle the squirrels doing backflips in my stomach, I picked up the phone and hit the speed dial button for Cam's number. He answered on the second ring.

"Lexi? Is that you? Where are you?"

"Cam!" I shot a glance at Allie. For half a second I was tempted to take her advice and change my mind. But I fought the feeling. This was for the best. For *both* of us. "Um, are you at the lake?"

"Of course. The show starts in, like, five minutes. Are you on your way?"

"Not exactly. I'm so sorry, Cam. I don't think I can make it tonight after all. Something came up."

"Are you serious? You're not coming?" It takes a lot to irritate Cam, but I thought I detected a note of irritation in his voice now. I certainly couldn't blame him—I hadn't exactly been Girlfriend of the Year lately—but it still made me feel kind of bad.

"Sorry," I said again. "Um, I have to go. I'll explain later. Sorry."

When I hung up, Allie was staring at me with a frown. "So that's it?" she said. "That's your great master plan? What if he just decides to leave?"

"He won't." I set down the phone and collapsed into my desk chair. "By now the singers will be setting up. He won't want to leave in front of them—it would be rude."

Allie couldn't argue with that. She's known Cam a long time.

"Okay," she said. "But how do you know he'll end up hanging out with Jaylene just 'cause you stood him up? There are probably lots of other people there he could hang out with instead."

"She's not exactly the bashful type, remember? Even if she doesn't end up assuming he's her blind date, she's sure to spot him and go over and say hi, especially after all the time they've been spending together lately on the food committee and everything." I grabbed the phone again. "Besides, I have a spy there to make sure it all happens like it should." I hit a different speed dial button.

"Yo," a familiar voice answered. "Lex? Mission accomplished. Was that you who called him a minute ago? I saw him answer his cell."

"It was me." I mouthed Nick's name at Allie to let her know who was on the line. "So he's with Jaylene now?"

"Uh-huh. She spotted him as soon as she came in and made a beeline straight for him. They've been sitting together for, like, ten minutes."

"Great. So where are you? You have to make sure Cam doesn't spot you, or he'll definitely invite you to hang with them, or—"

"Relax, Lexi." Nick chuckled into the phone. "Leave that to me," he added, lowering his voice and putting on an atrocious attempt at a British accent. "Remember, I am Michaels. *Nick* Michaels."

"What?" Allie whispered as I rolled my eyes. "What's he saying?"

"In case you haven't noticed, my dear cousin is actually a ten-year-old boy," I told her. "He's living out his James Bond fantasies."

"Hey, who are you talking to?" Nick asked.

"Just Allie," I said into the phone. "Listen, call me if anything happens, okay? I'll be here all night."

"Ten four." Nick hung up, and I did the same.

Allie still looked kind of confused. "So I still don't get why Jaylene would assume that Cam's her date," she said. "I thought you convinced her you'd set her up with some hot mystery guy."

"Right. But I dropped just enough hints for her to assume that guy might be Cam."

This had been the trickiest part of the plan. Jaylene knew that Cam and I were a couple, of course. But I was counting on the fact that she hadn't been around long enough—or paid enough attention—to realize just how serious a couple we were.

This was how I'd figured it would go. Thanks to my hints and the lack of other eligible guys wearing a striped scarf at the concert, Jaylene would think that Cam was her mystery date and assume that I'd set the two of them up on purpose. If I knew Cam—and I did—he would figure out the mistake quickly, but would be far too polite to tell Jaylene the truth. He would naturally assume that she'd been stood up by her real date and wouldn't want her to feel hurt and rejected. Besides, there wouldn't be much time for explanations before the concert started.

So he would play along, planning to figure out a way

to let her down easy at the end of the evening. But Jaylene liked Cam—I already knew that. And she wasn't the least bit shy. . . . If she assumed I'd set them up on purpose, I figured that the good feelings left over from their earlier "date," along with the friendship they were building on the food committee, would take care of the rest. It was sort of like mixing chemicals in chem lab. If you put the right ones together in exactly the right proportions, you got the result you wanted.

Now all I could do was sit and wait to see whether or not I'd measured those chemicals right.

Nick finally called at around ten thirty. I'd forced Allie to stay and help keep me distracted from what might or might not be going on down at the concert. We'd spent the first part of the evening working on her college essays, and when she'd gotten bored with that we'd switched to listening to music and then to playing Monopoly. When the phone rang, I jumped up so fast that I knocked the game board off the bed. Playing pieces, dice, and fake money scattered everywhere. Blitzen, who had been napping on the rug, woke up just long enough to bat the thimble under the bed.

"Nick?" I said into the phone. "Is that you?"

"It's me." He sounded weirdly somber. "I can't believe

it, Lexi. I mean, I know you can do anything you set your mind to. But I can't believe you actually pulled this off. It's almost kind of . . . I don't know, *eerie*."

My stomach did a funny little loop-de-loop. "What?" I demanded. "What happened?"

"It was just like you predicted," he said. "They sat together for the concert."

"And?" I prompted.

Even through the phone, I heard him take a deep breath. "Well, you know that Jaylene chick isn't, you know, the bashful type," he said. "Plus it's pretty cold out here tonight, and I think she's still wearing her Georgia wardrobe. So she started, like, snuggling up to Cam about halfway through. And she sort of grabbed his arm and put it around her, and he left it there."

I winced. Yeah, it was what I had wanted to happen, more or less. That didn't make it any easier to hear. Or to imagine.

"What?" Allie whispered, clearly reading the expression on my face.

"He was probably just afraid she'd freeze to death," Nick added quickly. "Like I said, her jacket wasn't really the kind of thing most people would wear to sit around outside in Wisconsin at the end of November. And her skirt was pretty short too, so her legs were . . . Well, anyway.

They didn't actually kiss or anything like that. At least not that I saw. But they were both laughing and talking when they were walking out just now, and she kept kind of squeezing his arm . . ."

"I get the picture." I didn't particularly want to hear any more details. "Thanks, Nick. Now I guess I just have to wait and see what happens next. I've done what I could—it's up to Cam now."

I hung up and told Allie what Nick had reported. She looked stricken. "Oh, Lexi," she cried. "I'm sorry!"

"Don't be." I steeled myself, doing my best to get the big picture back in focus. "This is what has to happen, remember? It's the best thing—for everyone."

On Sunday morning, Cam turned up on my doorstep bright and early. His face was haggard and conflicted, and the deep shadows under his eyes made me wonder if he'd slept at all.

"Lexi," he blurted out. "We need to talk."

"Come on in." I stepped back, and he followed me into the foyer. Luckily my parents were both out, so we had the house to ourselves. "What's up?"

He took a deep breath. "Last night," he blurted out. "Um, the concert?"

I could tell this wasn't easy for him. "Uh-huh," I said.

"Did you stay and watch? Did you run into anyone you knew there?"

"As a matter of fact, I did." The words came slowly, as if each one had to be dragged up out of his toes with a rusty fishhook. "Um, it was that girl Jaylene? You know, from the banquet? And the food committee?"

"Oh, sure!" I said, doing my best to sound normal. As if I didn't know what was coming. I had to be strong—for both of us. "She seems really cool. And you guys have been getting along really well on that committee, right?"

"Yeah. And actually, we—we sort of got along pretty well last night, too." He gulped, his face turning red. "I think she, you know, likes me. And—and you and I . . . well, I feel like we haven't really been communicating lately. Like you're not that into, you know, *us* anymore."

"Oh." I forced myself to stop there. I didn't want to throw him off.

"So anyway, I was thinking." He paused and took another deep breath. "What do you think if we, you know, take a break for a while. See other people? I—I think that might be for the best, you know? What do you think?"

He gazed at me with those earnest, puppy-dog eyes of his, and I almost lost it. Yes, he was kind of digging Jaylene right now. And no wonder. She was fun-loving and interested and available. All the things I *hadn't* been lately.

But I knew Cam well enough to tell that he believed that maybe this was what I wanted, and that he wanted to save me from having to do it. I also suspected that all it would take was for me to tell him that it *wasn't* what I wanted, and Jaylene would be out of the picture just like that.

But I didn't say it. I couldn't let myself. If I backed down now, all the hard, painful work I'd done would be for nothing. And nothing would have changed. The facts would still be what they were. I couldn't let my emotions overcome logic.

"You may be right, Cam," I said softly, not quite daring to meet his eye. "Things haven't been the same between us lately. And I understand. I really do. We can still be friends, right?"

"Of course!" His hand twitched, as if he'd started to reach out to me and then caught himself. I pretended not to notice.

"Great." I made my smile as sincere as possible. "That's the important part anyway, right? So consider us officially friends from now on, okay? And as a friend, I hope you and Jaylene will be really happy together. Really."

six

After Cam left I had that same sort of breathless, almost out-of-body feeling I always got whenever I aced a big test or won an academic award. Cam always jokingly called it the "rush of success."

This time, though, it was undercut with a feeling of sadness. Even more than I'd expected, actually. It had been a good four years—*really* good—and it was hard to believe it was over. But I tried not to dwell on that. Instead, I focused on the positive. That rush. I'd done it, against all odds! Now I could relax and look forward to the future without the constant, nagging worry over what would become of us next year. I could stop worrying about hurting Cam and know that he was going to be okay.

Allie let out a wail when I called and told her. "I can't believe he did it!" she cried. "I never thought this would actually happen. I mean, I know you said it was going to happen, and so I believe it because you're usually right about stuff. But still, I never thought it would actually happen!"

"I know. You're a hopeless romantic," I said. "But this is all for the best. You'll see."

"Hmm." She didn't sound convinced. "So what now?"

"What do you mean?"

"Are you going to start dating right away?"

I hadn't really thought about that. "I guess there's no reason to wait," I said. "I mean, Cam already has someone. Knowing him, he'll probably feel all guilty and weird if he thinks I might be lonely without him." I nodded, switching the phone to my other hand. "You know, you're right, Allie. That's very logical of you! I definitely should start dating other people right away."

"That's not what I meant," she protested. Then she sighed. "Okay. But don't forget about the Rebound Guy Theory."

"Remind me on that one?"

"Your rebound guy should be someone as different as possible from your ex," she said. Then she sniffled. "I can't believe Cam is now your *ex*. . . ."

"Focus, Allie!"

"Okay, sorry. Anyway, so Mr. Rebound should be totally different, but nobody you would ever be serious about long-term. He's like the palate-cleansing sorbet you have between the courses of a good meal."

I laughed. She really did have a way with words sometimes. Maybe she'd make that bestselling book happen after all.

"Okay," I said. "Well, if you think of anyone that fits the bill, let me know. I'm a little rusty on this whole dating deal. I mean, the last time I went out with anyone but Cam, I still had a nine thirty curfew, and a peck on the lips at the end of a date was cause for gossip and scandal."

"Aw, that's true. You and Cam have been together for so long. Too bad it had to end now."

I rolled my eyes. "Look, I feel bad enough about this as it is," I said. "Enough with the guilt trip, okay?"

"Sorry." She sounded a bit wounded. "But I'm kind of glad to hear you admit that you feel bad. It's kind of hard to tell sometimes."

"Whatever." I didn't feel like getting in a fight with my best friend today of all days, even if she was practically accusing me of being a robot. "Sorry for snapping at you. I guess maybe I'm a little touchy right now."

She immediately sounded more sympathetic. "No, *I'm*

sorry," she said. "You're allowed. I know this has to be rough—you know, getting dumped." She paused, then couldn't help adding, "Even if it was, you know, all your idea."

"Thanks." I smiled, knowing she was trying. "Listen, I should go call Nick and let him know."

"Okay. Call me if you need me."

I'd barely hit the button to hang up when the phone rang in my hand. "Hello?" I said.

"Lexi? Yo, it's me. Bruce. So I hear you're swinging single these days."

I winced. News travels fast in a small town. Still, Cam's buddy wasn't the first one I'd expected to call to offer his sympathies.

"Um, that's right," I told him. "As you probably heard, Cam met someone else. I'm really happy for them."

"Cool. So you're over it already?" he said. "Then how about going out with me? You know what they say—you're supposed to get right back on the horse, right?"

I wasn't sure if that was one of his sleazy little jokes or just a bad choice of words. But it didn't really matter. Now that I thought about it, maybe I shouldn't have been so surprised to hear from Bruce. He'd been obviously lusting after me for years. I'd always thought he was at least half joking with all the little innuendos and lingering glances—after all, he'd never hesitated to do all that stuff right in front of Cam—but then again, maybe not. Okay, so maybe most guys probably wouldn't have asked me out within an hour of the breakup. But I'd always known that Bruce wasn't like most guys.

And maybe that was perfect. Allie's Rebound Guy Theory floated through my head, and I smiled. Complete opposite of my ex? Check. Nobody I'd ever be serious about? *Double* check.

"Sure, why not?" I said. "Sounds like fun."

"Great!" Bruce actually sounded a little surprised. "You won't regret this, Lexi. What should we do? Dinner? Dancing? A candlelit evening at my place?"

I shuddered. There was rebounding, and then there was *rebounding*. "I have a better idea," I said quickly. "How about the North Pole? The first is only a few days away."

December 1 at the North Pole Theater was another of Claus Lake's holiday traditions. That was always the date of the old-fashioned movie house's first annual showing of *It's a Wonderful Life*. The theater served eggnog and Christmas cookies in the lobby, the whole place was draped in tinsel, and a barbershop quartet provided the preshow entertainment. It was quite the Xmastravaganza.

"Okay, sure, whatever turns you on," Bruce agreed. "Pick you up at six thirty?"

"I'll be waiting with jingle bells on," I joked.

As soon as I hung up, I wondered if I'd just made a big mistake. Rebound Guy Theory or not, was it wrong to go out with someone just to help make sure my plan stuck? Especially someone like *Bruce*?

But my logical mind soon overruled the twinges of guilt. Bruce wasn't exactly the sensitive type, and he was certainly used to getting plenty of rejection from me. Yes, he was as good a way as any to ease my way back into the dating stream.

"Whoa, it's packed! I hope we can get a parking space." Bruce leaned forward and peered out through the windshield of his battered old Mustang.

I shot him a look. "Yeah, it's always like this on the first. Haven't you ever been before?"

"Nah. Not really my scene."

We were driving slowly toward the north end of Pine Street. Traffic was bumper to bumper with cars lined up to get into the old movie theater's parking lot. I glanced out the window as we drove past the building. There was a wreath draped on the big old-fashioned red-and-white barber pole out in front that had given the place its name. People were lined up on either side of the pole waiting to get in.

Unlike Bruce, I'd come to the North Pole on almost every December 1 of my life—the last three of them with Cam. It felt strange to be arriving with someone else.

We finally reached the alley leading back between the theater and the Laundromat next door. The narrow parking lot behind the buildings was almost full, but Bruce found a spot between a pickup truck and a tree.

"Here we are," he said, turning off the engine and looking around at the dozens of people hurrying toward the theater from all corners of the lot, most of them huddled inside heavy coats and parkas. "Along with half the town, looks like."

We climbed out of the car and joined the migration. A dusting of snow had fallen the day before and the weather was chilly and dry. The steamy air drifting into the parking lot from the back of the Laundromat hit my face like a damp washcloth, and I could almost feel my hair frizzing. And at that precise moment, I noticed a familiar green Volvo parked in the first row just behind the theater. Figured he'd arrived early enough for a good spot.

Bruce saw the car, too. "Hey, looks like Cam is here," he said. Then he glanced over at me. "Oops. *Awk*ward."

"It's no big deal." I pulled my gaze away from the car. "Cam and I are still friends. Anyway, like you said, half the town is here tonight."

"Whatever you say." Bruce put one hand on the small of my back to guide me around a puddle of snowy mush. I almost acted on instinct and slapped the hand away, but then I reminded myself that we were on a date. And he seemed to be trying to be a gentleman so far. Still, his touch felt oddly heavy and foreign even through my heavy wool coat.

I spotted Cam as soon as we rounded the corner. He was standing in front of the barber pole, digging into his pocket for something. Jaylene was beside him, clinging onto his arm and laughing. She looked cold in her fashionable little baby blue jacket.

I froze. The logical part of my mind knew that if Cam had broken up with me to be with Jaylene, that meant I was likely to see him, you know, *with* Jaylene. And considering the size of our town, that was bound to happen sooner rather than later.

But I still wasn't prepared for how it felt. Seeing them together. Her hand on his arm, her cute little round face peering up at him. Him looking back at her and smiling. Cam. *My* Cam.

The logical portion of my brain struggled to regain control. It did its best to remind the other parts that Cam wasn't *mine* anymore. . . .

"You okay?" Bruce had dropped his hand from my back by now, but he stepped over and nudged me with one shoulder. "We could go do something else if you want. Grab some dinner or drive out to the mall to see a real movie."

"No, it's okay." I struggled to focus on the positive. This was what I wanted. My plan had worked. "Thanks. I'm fine. Come on, let's go say hi."

Cam saw us coming when we were still a few yards away. His whole face sort of crumpled, but then he forced a smile.

"Hey, guys," he called out. "What's up?"

Jaylene looked up too. "Lexi!" she exclaimed in her Southern accent, which made my name sound more like "Lake-sie." Weirdly, she seemed genuinely happy to see me. Then again, maybe it wasn't so weird. After all, she thought I was the one who'd hooked her up with Cam. "Isn't this fun? Ah can't believe Ah'm about to see *It's a Wonderful Life* in a theater instead of on TV. Ya'll really know how to do Christmas around here, that's for sure!"

"Yeah, that's Claus Lake for you." I tried to return her smile sincerely. After all, this ridiculously awkward moment wasn't *her* fault. No, it was pretty much, well, *mine*. "Um, Jaylene, have you met Bruce?"

"Oh, sure thang. We had a nice chat when he came to pick up Cammie after one of our committee meetins last week." Jaylene snuggled up against Cam, one of her arms sneaking around his waist.

Cam smiled weakly. I could tell he was more than a little uncomfortable with Jaylene's public display of affection. That wasn't just because I was there, either. Cam hated that kind of touchy-feely stuff.

At least I thought he did. He didn't do a thing as Jaylene gave him a squeeze, then started playing with the sleeve of his coat. Maybe he was just too nice to protest and embarrass her. Or maybe he didn't mind it that much after all.

For one crazy second, I had the urge to leap forward and shove her away from him. But I did my best to repress it, just repeating my mantra. This was all for the best. All for the best.

Wasn't it?

The next day was Saturday, and the mall was packed. The noise, smells, and body heat of hundreds of frenzied shoppers dashing among dozens of overstocked stores hit me as soon as I pushed in through the heavy glass doors. Everywhere I looked, bright red and green signs screamed about the fantastic holiday savings. But I ignored them all. I wasn't there to shop.

Dodging through the crowds, I headed for the high-end department store in the west wing of the mall. Allie had a part-time job there wrapping gifts for the holiday season.

It paid better than being one of Santa's elves, as she'd done the previous year, and involved far fewer sticky little-kid hands and runny noses wiped on your shirt. Aside from those dubious advantages, it didn't look like much more fun to me.

"Lexi!" Allie looked up from wrapping a decorative candle for a bored-looking preteen boy and his father. Her dark hair was flopping in her face, totally uncontained by her perky candy-cane-striped headband, and her expression was frazzled. "Hi! What are you doing here?"

"Sorry to bother you at work. I was hoping to talk to you about something. But it looks like you're kind of busy, so . . ."

"Hold that thought." Allie finished her wrapping job with expert speed, handed the package to the boy, then checked her watch. "Hey, Rhonda!" she called to the stout gray-haired woman at the next table, "I'm going on break, okay?"

"You betcha." The woman barely glanced up from the picture frame she was encasing in sparkly silver paper. "But be back by the lunch rush, all right, hon?"

We hurried away from the gift wrap area. "So what do you want to talk about?" Allie asked curiously.

"I'll tell you in a second," I replied. "Want to go sit down? I'll buy you a coffee."

"Okay. I could use the caffeine." Allie fiddled with her hair while we walked, trying to get her headband to hold it back out of her face.

It was still early, and the food court was relatively quiet. It only took a few minutes to get our coffees from the dough-nut stand. Black with one sugar for me, and cream and three sugars for Allie. We found an empty table and sat down.

"I went to the North Pole with Bruce last night," I began.

"Oh, right." Allie wrinkled her nose. "How was it? Did he sprout eight extra hands as soon as the lights went down?"

"Well, sort of. But that's not what I wanted to talk to you about." I took a deep breath, wrapping my hands around my steaming coffee cup. "I ran into Cam there. With Jaylene."

"Oh, Lexi!" Allie exclaimed sympathetically. "Sorry. Was it totally weird?"

"Yeah. Weirder than I expected." I hesitated, not sure how to say what I wanted to say next. "You know, all this time I've been really sure I was doing the right thing. But last night, just for a second, well . . ."

Allie didn't even wait for me to finish. "So you're having second thoughts about this crazy breaking-up-with-Cam plan?" she exclaimed, bouncing in her seat so vigorously that she almost tipped over her coffee. "Oh my God, Lexi. I thought you'd never come to your senses!"

"Now, hold on," I said. "I'm not saying I've changed my mind. Not really."

"But you have, haven't you?" She stopped bouncing and gripped the edge of the table, staring at me intensely. "You've got to do it, Lexi. Just this once, go with your heart instead of your brain. I'm sure you can still get Cam back. It's not too late—not yet."

She had a certain demented gleam in her eyes. I recognized that gleam. It meant she was in the midst of formulating a new theory.

"Okay, let's hear it," I said.

"What?"

"You know what. The theory." I raised an eyebrow at her. "You *do* have a theory that applies to this situation, don't you?"

She smiled. "As a matter of fact, I do. It's a new one. I'm thinking about calling it the Dozen Dates Theory." She tapped the stirrer from her coffee on the table. "See, I've sort of been thinking lately about how relationships get started. And how some of them last, and some don't. And just how important those early days are to a new couple as they get to know each other and stuff."

"Okay, Dr. Freudina," I said. "So what does this have to do with me and Cam?"

"I'm getting there. See, the idea behind the Dozen Dates

Theory is that by the time a new couple has gone out a dozen times, their relationship is pretty much set." She shrugged. "There's more to it than that, of course. I mean, I'm thinking this one could make a whole book if I work it out right." She pushed her coffee aside and leaned forward. "But for your situation, Lex, the key point is this: You need to move fast."

"Huh? What do you mean?"

"I mean this is the grace period," she said. "The honeymoon. You know, for Cam and his new woman. That means you still have a chance to get him back. There's still time. But not much." She stared at me seriously. "Because if you let Cam and Jaylene get a dozen dates under their belts, that's it. You can kiss any hope of rekindling your own romance good-bye."

seven

The Dozen Dates Theory sounded just about as wacky as the rest of Allie's long line of theories. But for once, I wasn't in the mood to pick it apart bit by unscientific bit.

"Two dates, twelve dates—it doesn't matter," I told her, shoving my coffee away. "I mean, this is what I wanted—Cam happy with someone else and me free to move on into the future without worrying about him. I just had a moment of weakness, that's all. You know, because of seeing them together like that. I'll just have to suck it up and get used to it."

Allie looked disappointed. "Wait, but I thought you

said you weren't sure this was the right thing anymore. You should always go with your instincts."

"My instincts tell me to use my brain," I said. "And my brain has been telling me for months that I have to figure out a way to solve the problem of me and Cam before it's too late and we end up like Nick and Rachel."

"That would never happen to you guys," she insisted. "It only happened to them because of Rachel deciding she didn't want to bother with a long-distance relationship."

I stared at her, suddenly feeling as if we were speaking different languages. Specifically, I was speaking Logic and she was, as usual, fluent in Ridiculously Impractical Emotion. How many times did I have to point out the facts to her? It felt as if I were trying to convince her that two trains heading in opposite directions were totally safe, while she kept insisting hysterically that they were sure to crash into each other at any moment.

Thinking about that made me feel a little more settled. I was just going to have to get a handle on my emotions for a while—just until I got used to the new world order. Seeing Cam with Jaylene would get easier with time and exposure. It had to.

"Thanks for talking it through with me," I told Allie, sitting back in my seat. "I think I'm back on track now. Even your Dozen Dates Theory helped."

"Really?" She looked hopeful. "You mean it helped you see that you've got to get back together with Cam before it's too late?"

I shook my head. "I mean it helped me see that I only have to wait them out for, like, nine more dates before I can stop worrying about Cam. You know, if we count that banquet and the concert as their first two dates, and then the movie as number three."

She looked disappointed. "But—"

"So!" I interrupted brightly, deciding we could both benefit from a change of subject. "Any progress on your own love life lately? Sorry I've been so wrapped up in my own thing that I haven't asked."

"It's okay. And not really." She glanced at her watch. "But listen, let's talk about that later, all right? I'd better head back now."

I walked Allie back to work, then browsed through the department store for a few minutes looking for gift ideas for my family. But I couldn't seem to focus on the cases and shelves full of jewelry and clothes and perfume and everything else under the sun. Finally I gave it up and headed back toward the mall.

I was still deep in thought as I stepped out of the hushed, tasteful interior of the department store back into the din of hurrying feet, screaming kids, and the Muzak version of "I Saw Mommy Kissing Santa Claus." It was a moment before my ears adjusted and I realized that someone was calling my name.

To my surprise, it was Andrew Cole. He had just stepped out of Radio Shack holding a shopping bag. His polished leather loafers squeaked on the tile floor as he hurried toward me.

"Lexi, hi," he said, straightening the collar of his long-sleeved polo. "Doing a little shopping?"

"Something like that." I tried to remember the last time Andrew and I had spoken to each other. Despite having been in most of the same classes for the past twelve years, we weren't what you'd call close, except maybe in the way that the Green Bay Packers and the Chicago Bears could be considered close. To put it another way, we'd been fierce academic rivals since before either of us could spell *fierce academic rivals*.

"Hey, I was sorry to hear about you and Cam splitting up," Andrew said. "Uh, but I heard you're already dating again."

Oh, great. So Bruce was already bragging about that. I wondered what exactly he'd been telling people. Then again, knowing Bruce, I probably didn't want to know.

"Yeah, sort of, I guess," I said, drifting into a private little fantasy of shoving Bruce's wandering hands up his own butt.

"Great. Then how about we go out sometime?"

That snapped me back to reality. "What?" I blurted out. "Uh, we? You mean you and me? Going out on a date?"

"Sure, why not?" Andrew shrugged. His lower lip was twitching slightly. "Hope it's not too soon. I just don't want to miss my chance again."

"Again?"

He winced, looking as if he wished he could take it back. "Well, yeah," he admitted. "I thought about asking you out once before. Back in eighth grade. I wanted to ask you to the Christmas Ball, but you and Cam got together before I could."

Wow. That was so out of the blue I didn't know what to say for a second.

"Um, okay," I said at last. "Sure. That would be . . . nice."

"Great! Are you free tonight? How about dinner at Manfredi's?" Weirdly, he had that same triumphant gleam in his eye that he got on the rare occasion he received a higher grade than me on a test. I could only imagine what kind of theory Allie would come up with to explain that.

"Sounds good," I said, trying to sound normal. "I love that place."

"Fantastic. I'll pick you up at six."

You could call it bad luck. You could call it a statistical improbability. Or you could just call it what it was—life in a small town. Whatever the terminology, I could hardly believe my eyes when Andrew and I walked into Manfredi's that evening and I saw Cam and Jaylene sitting at one of the tables for two along the cozy little restaurant's back wall.

Date number four, I thought, Allie's Dozen Dates Theory flitting across my mind. *But who's counting?*

Cam looked up and spotted me. He froze in midchew. I didn't have to look to see what he was eating: fettuccine carbonara. That was what he always ordered at Manfredi's.

We stared at each other for a second. Then his expression relaxed into sort of a sad smile. He lifted one hand in a wave, and I waved back, feeling as awkward as humanly possible. I mean, what were the odds? Even in Claus Lake? I was still waving when Jaylene glanced around curiously. She waved back cheerfully, then leaned forward to say something to Cam.

Andrew had just turned after giving our name to the maître d'. Following my gaze, he took in the sight of the happy couple. I had to hand it to him—he was as cool as a cucumber. Only a slight twitch of the lower lip gave away that he'd noticed anything. Without acknowledging the situation at all, he reached out and put an arm around my shoulders.

"Come on, Lexi," he said. "I think our table is ready."

I was so distracted as we walked across the tightly

packed restaurant that I'm surprised I didn't trip over a table leg and land in someone's soup. When we reached our table by the front window, the maître d' stepped forward as if to pull out one of the chairs for me. But Andrew blocked him neatly, steering me to the other chair—the one with no view of Cam's table.

"Uh, thanks," I mumbled, still trying to wrap my head around what was happening here. Was I doomed to spend the rest of my senior year running into Cam and Jaylene everywhere I went? And if so, would it ever get easier to see them together?

I lurched into my seat, somehow managing to half miss and almost fall on my butt. Putting out my right arm to catch my balance, I accidentally set it down right on the lit candle in the center of the table.

"Ow!" I yelped, yanking my hand away from the flame and in the process almost falling off my chair again. Smooth. Really smooth. This was rapidly turning into a how-not-to manual for making a sexy impression on a first date with a new guy. Not to mention playing it cool in front of an ex and his new squeeze. Too bad Allie wasn't there—she could have been taking notes for her next bestseller.

My face burned as several nearby diners glanced over in surprise and Andrew stared at me as if I'd just sprouted a second head. He reached out and righted the candle before it could set the little holly-and-ivy wreath surrounding it aflame.

"Are you all right?" he asked.

"Fine." I stuck my singed finger in my mouth to soothe the burn. Then, realizing that wasn't helping make me look any more sophisticated or in control of the situation, I quickly removed it and surreptitiously wiped it on my pants beneath the table.

Fortunately the waitress appeared at that moment with a pitcher of ice water and our menus. I was able to hide my face behind the menu until I felt my cheeks start to return to their normal color.

Somehow, I survived the next half hour or so. I even managed to avoid peeking over my shoulder to see what Cam and Jaylene were doing. The trouble was, I couldn't seem to control my mind nearly as well. It kept drifting away from whatever Andrew was saying. Not that you could blame me too much for that. The guy only had one topic of conversation: himself. His choice of colleges. His predicted SAT score. His grades and extracurriculars. Oh, sure, once in a while he interrupted his autobiographical lecture to ask me a question about myself. I would grunt out some distracted, monosyllabic response, and then the Story of Andrew would continue. Of course, there *was* that one totally awkward moment when he mentioned something about wondering when the Simpson Scholarship would be announced already and then caught himself and stopped talking abruptly, apparently remembering that his primary competition for said scholarship was sitting across the table from him. His cheeks had sprouted little red spots for a moment, then he'd shrugged and changed the subject. Back to himself, of course.

I was relieved when he excused himself to go to the restroom. As soon as he was gone, I slumped in my seat and stared at my burned finger. It still stung a little and looked kind of red. I hoped it wouldn't swell up and make it hard to type. I still had a few applications to finish.

"Lexi?"

I glanced up, but I already knew who I'd see standing there beside the table. I'd recognize that voice anywhere.

"Oh—hi, Cam," I said, quickly tucking my finger away out of sight within my fist. "Having a nice time?"

This time I couldn't resist glancing over my shoulder at his table. Jaylene was nowhere in sight.

He saw where I was looking. "Jaylene just went to the bathroom," he said. "Um, I mean the little girls' room." He smiled faintly. "That's what she calls it."

"Cute." I wasn't really in the mood to hear every little adorable thing about Jaylene. But I did my best to keep smiling as if it didn't bother me in the least.

"Anyway, I just wanted to come over and make sure you're okay." Cam gestured toward my hand. "It looked like you burned yourself pretty good."

"Oh." I was touched. "Yeah. I'll be all right. Thanks."

"You sure? Good." He looked down at my plate. If he noticed I'd barely touched my food, he didn't say anything. "Having the tortellini, huh? That's one of your favorites."

"Yeah. And let me guess—you got your usual fettuccine?"

"Believe it or not, no," he said with a slightly sheepish laugh. "Jaylene talked me into trying the lasagna." He shrugged. "It's pretty good. Maybe not as good as the fettuccine, but good."

"Oh." Were we still talking about Italian food? I wasn't quite sure.

Cam shot a glance across the restaurant, suddenly looking a little uncomfortable. "Well, I'd better get back. Enjoy the rest of your dinner. And I hope your hand feels better too."

"Thanks."

He headed back to his seat. I watched him weave his way among the other tables. What a nice guy! Everyone always said that about him, of course, myself included. But until that moment, I wasn't sure I'd ever stopped to think about what the phrase *really* meant.

"I'm back!" Andrew announced as he returned to our

table a minute or two later. He sat down and reached for his water glass. "So where were we? Oh yeah—I was just telling you about that weird essay question for the application to . . ."

I pasted a smile on my face and stared at him, still lost in the thoughts Cam's little visit had brought up. Andrew was exactly the kind of guy I probably *should* be with. He was smart and driven and likely to succeed and all sorts of other things I generally admired.

But was he "nice"? No, not really. Not like Cam.

A few minutes later Cam and Jaylene finished their meal and got up to leave. I watched them out of the corner of my eye as he retrieved her silly little baby blue coat from the hooks near the door and helped her put it on. As she fussed with her blond hair, pulling it out from beneath her fur-lined collar, Cam glanced over and saw me looking. He smiled and waved. I returned the smile weakly and wriggled my fingers in return.

"What are you looking at, Lexi?" Andrew interrupted himself. He looked over just in time to see Cam open the door for Jaylene. "Oh." He shrugged, then shoveled in a mouthful of lasagna before returning to his favorite topic. "So anyway, like I was saying, the admissions guy from Northwestern . . ."

As the door swung shut behind the happy couple, I

picked up my fork and poked at my pasta, feeling a little sick. Would this ever get any easier?

I couldn't resist peeking out the window as Cam and Jaylene emerged onto the sidewalk just outside. She said something. He laughed and put his arm around her. She snuggled up to him, her little white mittens sneaking their way around his waist. Smile, smile, kiss . . .

And this is where we came in. Their spontaneous, romantic kiss hit me like a punch to the gut. What had I been thinking all these weeks? All this time, the idea of Cam—*my* Cam—with another girl had seemed somehow speculative and theoretical. Like a science hypothesis waiting to be proved or one of Allie's crazy theories being tested in a double-blind study.

But now that the result was standing right there in front of me, kissing on a snowy evening beneath the twinkling holiday lights, I somewhat belatedly realized the truth.

I was still in love with Cam.

Yep, there was no denying it any longer. Stuck in a rut, opposites attract and all, I still loved him. All the logic in the world couldn't change that. Which meant, of course, that I'd just made the stupidest mistake of my life.

Was it too late to fix it?

eight

I'm not sure how I survived the rest of my date with Andrew. For one thing, I was already calling him Annoying Andrew in my head—I had to be really careful not to slip and say it out loud. Somehow, I didn't think he would have the sense of humor to handle something like that very well.

But that was far from my worst problem. Being with Andrew, and with Bruce before him, had only showed me what I would be missing if I couldn't figure out how to make things right with Cam. Okay, so maybe that spark had faded a bit over the years between Cam and me. But I couldn't imagine ever feeling the spark at all with those two guys. Or with anyone else, for that matter.

No, the grass definitely wasn't greener for me. But what about for Cam? Based on that kiss I'd just witnessed, I wasn't too sure.

"Here we are." Andrew pulled to a stop at the curb in front of my house. As I unhooked my seat belt, he leaped out of the car and raced around the front of it like a demented rabbit, slipping a little on the rapidly freezing slush on the road. Then he opened my door with a flourish.

"Thanks," I said, climbing out without taking the hand he held out to help me. I didn't want to give him any ideas.

Unfortunately, he already seemed to have them. After he'd closed the car door behind me, he hurried to catch up as I headed up the front walk. He slung one arm around my shoulders, squeezing a bit.

I resisted the urge to elbow him in the ribs. Instead, I waited until we reached the porch steps and then scooted up them quickly, managing to extricate myself from his arm in the process. He was a smart guy, and I hoped he'd take the hint.

But no. He climbed the steps after me and watched as I fished my house key out of my purse. My mind wandered back to a similar but oh-so-different wintry evening about four years earlier. Cam and I had just returned from our first real date—skating on the lake—and I'd been digging in my coat pocket for my key. It had been an amazing evening, and I hadn't wanted it to end. Cam and I had skated and talked and laughed and had a great time. I still remembered the tingle I'd felt, even through my wool gloves, when he'd shyly reached over to hold my hand as we'd glided along side by side across the ice and everything had felt so romantic and new. . . .

"This was fun," Andrew said, snapping me back to the here and now. "We should do it again sometime."

"Sure, maybe." I finally found the key and pulled it out. "Although with the holidays and all, I'm sure we'll both be kind of busy, right? Anyway, thanks for dinner."

"You're very welcome."

I glanced up to say good-bye. My eyes widened in alarm as I saw his eyes sort of squeeze half-shut and his lips go all poofy and start moving toward me like a heat-seeking missile. Yeah, so much for picking up my hints. He was going in for the good-night kiss.

I quickly turned my head, deflecting him just in time. The kiss landed on my cheek instead of its intended target.

"Well, good night, then," I said as cheerfully as I could manage, stepping back and reaching for the door.

He opened his eyes and licked his lips, looking startled. "Oh," he said. "Um . . ."

But I didn't wait around to hear any more. Quickly stepping inside, I shut the door behind me without looking back.

The next day my mom asked me to run out to the mall to pick up some stuff she needed for her next food committee meeting. While I was there, I stopped in at the department store to see if Allie had time to talk. To my surprise, she wasn't there. Normally she worked every weekend day between Thanksgiving and Christmas Eve. The place was packed, and her coworkers were so frantic in their quest to wrap snowflake-print paper and curly red ribbons around everything in sight that I didn't even bother trying to ask them why Allie wasn't working. Instead, I just stopped off at her house on my way home.

"Hi, Lexi," Allie's mother greeted me when she opened the door. Mrs. Lin looked exactly like Allie would probably look in thirty years, right down to the tiny ponytail. "Nice to see you. Have you heard anything about that Simpson Scholarship yet? Allie tells me you'll probably win it this year."

"No, no word yet. You know how it is—Mrs. Simpson always likes to keep everyone in suspense for a while." I chuckled along with Mrs. Lin. "Um, is Allie home?"

"Oh, sure." She waved me inside. "She and Nick are in the den."

I blinked, a bit surprised to learn that my cousin was there. Allie and Nick hung out all the time, of course, but usually only when I was around. It was kind of like I was the oxygen atom in our water molecule of friendship.

"They're working on the decorations for the kiddie room at the Ball," Allie's mother added, ushering me toward the cozy den at the back of the house.

That explained it, then. Sure enough, when I entered the den it looked as if one of Santa's elves had exploded in there. Red and green paper scraps covered every available surface, from the burgundy carpet to the leather couch to Allie's shiny black hair. I wondered how Nick—or more likely, Nick's mom—had suckered her into helping with this one. Every year, while everyone over the age of twelve danced the night away in the main room, the younger kids gathered in the upstairs section of the fireman's hall under the supervision of a fleet of paid out-of-town babysitters for an evening of Christmas cookies, sing-alongs, naps, stories, tantrums, and games. They also had their own decorations up there, mostly consisting of paper garlands, Christmassy cutouts, and other nontoxic-if-eaten-or-licked items. Preparing that stuff for a bunch of sugar-hyped sprogs wasn't anyone's favorite task on the decorations committee.

Allie and Nick were bent over a sheet of construction

paper together. They both looked up in surprise when I walked in and said hello.

"Lexi!" Allie exclaimed, jumping to her feet and brushing her hair out of her face. "What are you doing here? I mean, I was going to call you and see if you wanted to come help us with this stuff, but I figured you had that date last night and probably wanted to sleep in, plus I know you've got that last application essay to finish and then that paper for history class, so . . ."

She was babbling, probably out of sheer boredom. Or maybe the Elmer's glue had gone to her head. Either way, I brushed aside her torrent of explanations.

"I'm glad you guys are both here," I said. "I need to talk to you about something. It's important."

"Uh-oh," Nick joked. "The last time you said something like that, you'd decided to break up with Cam. Let me guess—this time you're breaking up with the two of us, right?"

"Very funny." Even though my mind was pretty much filled to capacity with my own problems, I couldn't help realizing that he sounded almost back to normal lately. At least Rachel hadn't broken him forever. "But I'm serious. I think I've made a colossal mistake."

Allie cocked her head. "Wait. Did you end up going out to dinner last night with Andrew?"

"Uh-huh." I'd scooted back into the department store the afternoon before to let her know about that invitation. "Let's just say it didn't go well. In more ways than one . . ."

Flopping down onto the leather sofa, I quickly filled them in on the whole evening. Nick let out a low whistle when I told them about seeing Cam and Jaylene at the restaurant, and Allie gasped with horror when I (briefly) described their kiss.

"So anyway," I finished, "I realize now that I was wrong. Cam is the guy for me. I never should have decided to end things with him." I took a deep breath. "So go ahead. Say it. You told me so, right?"

"Well, now that you mention it . . . ," Nick began.

Allie shut him up with a punch to the upper arm. "Don't," she said. "You know Lexi. She doesn't admit she's wrong very often, mostly because she *isn't* wrong very often. We don't want to make her feel any worse about being so, so, *so* wrong this time." She smiled at me. "But anyway, why are you here telling us about this? You should be at Cam's house right now getting back together with him!"

"What? It's not that simple."

"Sure it is," Nick urged, leaning back against the edge of an overstuffed armchair. "Cam's a reasonable guy. So you throw yourself at his feet, tell him you were an idiot, then kiss and make up."

Allie nodded vigorously. "Just be honest with him, and see if he'll consider trying again. I'm sure he will."

I sat up so fast that the sofa squeaked. "Are you insane? I can't tell him the truth about all the idiotic stuff I did to make this happen." I grimaced, feeling my cheeks go hot as I thought about all the deceptive tricks I'd pulled over the past couple of months. How could I have been such a fool? "He'd never understand," I added sadly. "He's so honest and straightforward—he'd probably never forgive or respect me ever again if he found out how I finagled the end of our relationship. Then I wouldn't even have him as a friend anymore, let alone anything more. And I *really* couldn't stand that."

"But you can't give up, Lexi!" Allie cried. "You have to get him back."

"Yeah," Nick said. "It's not like you to give up, Lex. That's why Dad always calls you the family go-getter."

"Don't worry, I'm not giving up," I told them. "I'm just saying I need to figure out the best way to handle this."

Allie looked dubious. "Well, you'd better hurry up and figure it out soon," she said. "Dozen Dates Theory, remember?"

Nick let out a snort. Clearly he'd heard about Allie's latest theory as well.

Allie shot him an irritated glance. "Anyway, I still

think you can do it. Right now you've still got time on your side. See, I've been working out more of the theory lately, and there's something I'm calling the Nostalgia Footnote. That means that, as the recent ex, you still have the advantage of all the memories you two have together. But the closer you get to that dozen dates mark, the less weight that kind of thing—"

"Hold it," I interrupted, tapping my fingers on the arm of the sofa. "I think you might be on to something there with the nostalgia thing, Allie."

"Really?" She looked surprised and kind of delighted. And no wonder. That was probably the most enthusiastic response I'd ever given to one of her theories. "Well, I mean, sure I am. So if you just confess everything to Cam right now, his memories of your past together should totally overcome any weirdness about, you know, your methods."

"No, that's not what I mean." I leaned forward and gazed thoughtfully at my cousin. "Hey Nick, I just realized your birthday's coming up in, like, a week."

"Let me guess. This is your way of warning me to expect an IOU instead of a real present again this year?"

Poor Nick was always getting shafted on the whole birthday-present thing. I guess that happens when your big day is too close to *the* big day. And like I said, in Claus Lake the entire autumn season is probably too close. Oh, and just in case it's not obvious, that's how Nick got his name. After all, being born in December in Claus Lake, what other name could he have?

"Don't worry," I told him. "Your birthday gift is already wrapped and waiting in a secret location in my house. But I was just thinking, shouldn't we all do something special to celebrate?"

He cocked one eyebrow suspiciously. "Why do I have the feeling this idea *isn't* coming from a genuine burst of cousinly love?"

"Of course it is." I grinned. "Then again, I've always been a multitasker, right? See, I was just thinking, how about if you invite the whole gang out ice-skating on the lake next weekend?"

"Hmm." Nick picked a sparkly bit of paper off his sleeve and flicked it across the room. "Could be fun, I guess. Plus that way nobody will be able to forget my birthday for once. But what's in it for you? You realize I'll have to invite Jaylene, too, right?"

I shrugged. "That's okay. She's from Georgia—she probably can't even skate. With any luck she'll spend most of her time drinking hot chocolate on shore and Cam and I can reminisce about the first time we went skating together."

"Ooh, I remember that." Allie smiled. "It sounded totally romantic."

"It was. So maybe being out there on the lake together will remind Cam of that night—you know, get that nostalgia thing working for me. If you guys are right and he wants me back too, that could be all it takes to kick-start a reconciliation—no messy confessions required." I shrugged. "If I play my cards right, Cam and I could be a couple again in plenty of time for the Ball. We can wear the funny front-and-back-halves-of-a-reindeer costume he picked out, and everything will be back to normal."

"Okay, what the hell. Let's do it," Nick said. "I'll start calling people tonight."

"Call Cam first, okay?" I urged. "There's not much point if he can't make it."

Nick snorted. "Right. No point at all."

Allie giggled. "Don't worry, Nick, she's crazed with jealousy—she doesn't know what she's saying." She turned to me. "But Lexi, even if this works, you're right back where you started. You know, that fabulous mismatched future you were so worried about before . . ."

That had been nagging at the back of my mind too. But I was trying to keep it back there for now.

"I know," I said. "But I'll just have to worry about that once I'm back with Cam."

nine

"Brrr," Bruce complained. "Nick, dude, why'd you have to have your birthday at the coldest time of the year?"

"Don't be an idiot." I looked up from lacing my left skate, quickly tucking my bare fingers into my armpits in a vain attempt to thaw them enough to lace up the other skate. "If his birthday was in July, we wouldn't exactly be celebrating with an ice-skating party, would we?"

Still, he kind of had a point. It was cold. *Really* cold. Not that it's ever exactly balmy in Wisconsin in December, but it's usually not Siberia, either. But just my luck—a front had rolled in the night before and it was downright frigid, with a bitter wind gusting in and howling around the edges of the lake, shaking the latest snowfall off the tops of the pines. At the moment we were all still huddled around the benches and snow-covered pathways by the skating inlet, even though most of us had arrived at least ten or fifteen minutes earlier. Nobody seemed too eager to leave the relative shelter of the shoreline and hit the open ice.

But the weather wasn't the main reason I was feeling kind of tense. Cam hadn't even arrived yet, and I was already wondering if this had been a stupid idea. Nick hadn't been able to reach Cam on Sunday night. He'd tracked him down as soon as he could in school on Monday, but the best he'd been able to get from Cam was an "I'll let you know." Cam hadn't given him an answer until Tuesday morning, which meant Nick hadn't been able to start asking other people until after that. By then a large chunk of the guest list already had plans for Saturday afternoon. Then a few more had canceled because of the weather. Wimps.

So that left a pretty small group. Me. Nick. Allie. Bruce. Two giggly girls from Nick's music class. And finally, Cam and Jaylene—if they ever showed up. Now, normally Cam wasn't the type of guy to cancel at the last minute. If he committed to be somewhere, he was there, come hell, high water, or subzero windchill factor. But now that Jaylene was in the picture, I was starting to wonder if he was still as predictable as I'd always thought. After all, I never would have expected that impulsive, snowy kiss the other night, either. . . .

Ripping my mind away from that unwelcome image, I stood up, brushed some snow off my black Polartec pants, and surveyed our paltry group. When I'd come up with this idea, I'd envisioned Jaylene lost in crowds of people out on the ice, giving me free rein to zero in on Cam and work the nostalgia angle. After all, Nick had tons of friends, which meant his parties normally resembled New Year's Eve in Times Square. But with only eight of us, it wasn't going to be so easy to cut Cam loose from the herd. Still, Allie and Nick had promised to run interference for me if they could. I was just going to have to make the best of it.

I finished my laces, then sat up and pulled my warmest gloves back on. That made my hands feel a little less like blocks of ice, though it didn't help my face, which had gone numb. Who needs Botox when you have an Arctic air mass?

Nick already had his skates on. He was swinging his arms back and forth, trying to stay warm as he waited for the rest of us to finish getting ready. "Hey Bruce," he said, "where's your man Cam? Thought he said he'd be here."

Good question. I wanted to check my watch, but it was hidden under three or four layers of clothing.

Bruce was sitting on a bench playing snowplow with his skate blades in a handy drift. "Yeah, he'll be along. Probably late though. That new girlfriend of his takes forever getting ready to go out." He stood up and sidled over to me. Even with a frozen face, he could still leer. Amazing. "Guess she's not the natural woman type like you, eh, Lexi?"

Before I could answer, I heard a car door slam. I glanced over toward the parking lot, my heart jumping. But it was only Allie. She'd been changing into a borrowed pair of Nick's extra-warm wool socks in his car.

But behind her, I finally saw a familiar car pulling into the lot. "Cam's here," I hissed at Nick.

Bruce spotted the car at the same time. "Finally. Here they are."

He headed over to greet the newcomers. The rest of us drifted along after him, walking awkwardly across the snowy lawn in our skates and guards.

Cam climbed out of the car first and waved. Then he hurried around to the other side to let Jaylene out.

"What, is she incapable of opening a car door for herself?" I muttered to Allie.

She shot me a sympathetic glance. "Be fair," she said. "You can't blame Jaylene because Cam's a gentleman."

"Oh yeah? Just watch me." I scowled as Cam bent over the passenger side door.

A moment later Jaylene emerged. My frozen eyeballs bulged as I got a look at her. Sure, technically what she was wearing could be considered appropriate for skating. But only if the skating in question was in the Ice Capades. She was dressed in a snug Irish wool sweater, a flippy little lavender miniskirt, and shiny white tights. To top it off, a navy-and-white striped scarf was looped jauntily around her neck. At least she was wearing a hat today. It matched the scarf perfectly.

"Oh mah gosh, y'all!" she called out to us, laughing in little bursts that were visible in the cold air. "Ah guess Ah may be kind of underdressed fer this shindig."

Cam swung his battered old hockey skates by their laces, looking sheepish. "She thought we were going to an indoor rink," he explained. "I guess I should have been more specific when I told her about this—she's still not used to, you know, being in the north."

Jaylene waved her hands, which were as usual encased in cute but awfully thin-looking white mittens. "No, Ah'll be fine," she insisted. "Of course, Ah might need a little help to stay warm, if ya'll know what Ah mean!" She grabbed Cam and snuggled up against him.

"Aw, young love," one of the music class gigglers called out. "Aren't they adorable?"

"Sweet," Bruce agreed. "Yo Jaylene, how is it you can

look freezing cold and smokin' hot at the same time?"

Jaylene giggled, swinging her hips a little so her skirt danced. "Oh, Bruce. You're such a nut!"

I gritted my chattering teeth. The worst part was, Bruce's obnoxious comment was true. The outfit Jaylene was wearing was totally inappropriate for the occasion. But she *did* look ridiculously hot.

Still, I figured in that getup Jaylene wouldn't last long on the ice. I was glad I'd brought plenty of hot chocolate— it was already bubbling away in Mom's portable party beverage dispenser, which was plugged in in one of the little cement picnic shelters nearby. With any luck, Jaylene would give up on skating within minutes and camp out in there to stay warm. All I had to do was distract Cam enough to keep him from following her in there. If it was awkward watching her cling to him now, I didn't want to think about catching a glimpse of them making out or something.

"Come on, everybody," I called out with forced cheer. "Why are we all standing around here? We'll be a lot warmer once we get moving."

"She's right." Nick waved an arm toward the lake. "Let's skate!"

I felt a little better once I was out on the ice. My parents and aunt and uncle started taking me and Nick skating as soon as we were old enough to stand up on our own, and I still loved it. The ice was solid in the inlet, though I knew it was probably still a little iffy farther out in the deeper parts of the lake. I forgot about everything else for the moment as I swooped forward, doing some big loopy circles and figure eights to work out the kinks.

The rest of us had left Cam and Jaylene putting on their skates. After a few minutes, I glanced over to see how they were doing. I was just in time to see Cam lead a wobbly-looking Jaylene down the slight incline and onto the ice.

Allie swooped over to me, executing a neat T-stop. "Think she knows how to skate?"

"Nick asked Cam about that," I replied, not taking my eyes off the pair. "Apparently she's skated a few times, but she's not very good."

We watched as she pushed off, clinging to one of Cam's hands with both of hers. Two or three strokes in, her left skate skidded out from under her, quickly followed by the other. She would have fallen if Cam hadn't been holding onto her. Once he'd set her on her feet again, she collapsed against him, laughing.

"Oh mah gosh!" her giddy voice floated across the lake. "This is even harder than Ah remember!"

But before long she was upright and sliding along with tiny, choppy, tentative strokes like a little kid. Cam practically had to skate backward to stay with her at that (lack of) speed.

Nick glided over to Allie and me, both hands tucked into his jeans pockets. "Looks like Cam's doing some baby-sitting," he said in a low voice. "It's going to be hard to peel her off of him."

"Tell me about it," I said. "But you guys promised to do what you could, right?"

Allie nodded. "Come on, Nick. You taught beginner lessons that one winter, right? Why don't we go offer your expertise to poor Jaylene?"

My friends are brilliant. Within minutes, they'd commandeered Jaylene, pushing Cam out to watch as they took Jaylene by each arm and taught her some basics. I waited until Jaylene looked good and distracted, then skated over to Cam.

"Hey," I greeted him, doing a little backward circle on the ice in front of him. "Having fun?"

"Sure." He smiled at me. "It's kind of cold, but hey, what's a little frostbite when it comes to a friend's birth-day?"

"Huh? Oh, right." I'd almost forgotten that we were all supposed to be there for Nick. "So anyway, it looks like Jaylene is learning fast now that those two have ahold of her."

"Yeah. I just hope she doesn't get too chilled." He looked worried. "I really should have warned her we'd be skating outside."

Personally, I thought he was being way too hard on himself. What kind of Southern-fried nutjob expects indoor skating in December in a town located on the shore of a huge frozen lake? But I didn't bother to point that out.

"I'm sure she'll be fine," I said. "Once you start moving around out here, it's not so bad. Speaking of which, want to take a spin around the inlet while she's having her lesson? You know, for old time's sake."

"Sure, I guess." Cam shot another glance at Jaylene, who had just slipped again and was clinging to Nick's waist while Allie tried to haul her back to her feet without skidding out herself. I wasn't sure Cam had even caught the "for old time's sake" bit in my invitation.

"Let's go, then," I said as cheerfully as I could. "Last one to the swimming platform's a rotten egg!"

In summer, the skating inlet became the swimming inlet. There was an ancient, half-rotted wooden platform that had been out there since sometime before my parents were born. It was pretty much unofficially condemned at this point—kids only ever climbed on it as a dare. But it still floated out there, making a handy end point for racing whether the water was frozen or not.

I took off toward it, pushing out faster and faster to work up speed. After a moment I glanced back over my shoulder. Cam was a few yards back. I could tell he wasn't going anywhere near full-out—he always let me win, no matter how many times I scolded him about it, saying it was sexist.

I skidded to a stop once I reached the platform, spinning around and waiting for him to catch up. When he got there he was smiling, his cheeks showing the two rosy little spots he always got when he exerted himself.

"You win, as usual," he said. "I should know better than to even try."

That sort of comment used to annoy me a little. After all, it wasn't as if I needed him to let me beat him at speed skating. It was one thing for my dad to do that when I was five, but Cam was supposed to be my boyfriend—my equal.

Only he wasn't my boyfriend anymore, and somehow that made it seem more sweet than annoying. That Nostalgia Footnote thing was obviously working on *me*.

"Winner and still champion," I said lightly. Suddenly remembering one of Allie's older theories—the Touchy-Feely Theory—I reached over and punched him lightly on the arm. "How about a rematch? Shore and back?"

"Maybe later." His gaze had wandered back across the

ice toward where Nick and Allie were still guiding their pupil along. "I should probably go back and check on Jaylene."

My heart sank. So much for trusting in those theories.

"Okay," I said, feeling a little desperate. "But wait, first you've got to see my new move. Double axel."

"Really?" He turned back to me, looking impressed. "I had no idea you'd been practicing that, Lexi."

The truth was, I hadn't. I'd only seen skaters do it on TV. But what did I have to lose? I could do a single axel in my sleep. If I pulled off a double on my first try, yay me. If not and I wiped out, Cam would have to rush to my aid. Right? With any luck I'd be injured and he'd be stuck nursing me while the others rushed to call 911. . . .

I was so lost in that wacked-out little fantasy that it took me a moment to notice that he was sort of drifting back in the direction of the others. It was now or never.

"Here I go!" I sang out, not stopping to think about what I was about to attempt. At least if I broke both my arms and legs, my college applications were already finished.

I pushed off, picking up speed quickly, aiming toward a broad patch of smooth ice toward the north end of the inlet. Faster. Faster. I raised one leg and got into position. My heart pounded as the sane part of my brain screamed at me to stop. The uninhabited wooded shoreline over there was getting closer, and I had to go soon or else give up and turn back.

Thinking of Cam, I went. I might have closed my eyes for a second. Then I pushed off—and spun. Once around. Twice. A second later I felt the blade of my landing skate connect cleanly with the ice. I'd done it!

"Whoa!" I heard Bruce call out from over near the shore. "Did you guys see that? That was amazing, Lexi!"

But I didn't care what *he* thought of it. I glanced back toward Cam. He was smiling. But then his expression switched over to one of alarm.

"Lexi, look out!" he called. "You're heading straight for the—"

SPLASH!

The ice collapsed beneath me. *"Aaaah!"* I screeched as I sank into freezing-cold water up almost to my thighs.

It was only then that I recognized my mistake. The spring. We'd all had it pounded into us since we were kids: *Don't skate too close to the spring.* The water there bubbled up from underground, constantly moving, and therefore it was the only part of the inlet that never fully froze, even in the coldest depths of February.

And what had I done? I'd skated right into it. Brilliant. It was a good thing old Mrs. Simpson hadn't been there to witness my stupidity, or that Simpson Scholarship would have been Andrew's for sure.

Luckily the water isn't very deep that close to shore. By the time my friends reached me, I had clambered my way onto dry—well, make that *snowy*—land with soaked legs, chattering teeth, and bruised ego.

"Lexi, what were you thinking?" Allie exclaimed. "You know better than to get so close to the spring!"

Jaylene arrived only a moment after the others, so her lessons must have been working. "What happened?" she cried. "Oh mah gosh—skating outside is so *dangerous*!"

The cold was seeping into my bones, giving me an overall feeling of numb pessimism. I expected Cam to rush over and give Jaylene a detailed topographical lecture on Lake Claus. But instead he shrugged off his ski jacket and draped it around me.

"Come on," he said. "We've got to get you dried off."

Nick reached into his pocket and pulled out his keys. "Stick her in my car," he said, tossing the keys to Cam. "It has the best heater. Also, I think there's a pair of sweats in the back."

Cam caught the keys and put an arm around my shoulders. "Come on, Lexi."

My teeth were still chattering, which was probably a good thing. Otherwise I probably would have been grinning like a fool. I shot Allie a quick, triumphant look.

Who needs nostalgia theories when good ol' hypothermia works even faster? I thought as I allowed Cam to pull me back onto the ice and across the lake in the direction of the inlet park.

Soon I was huddled in the passenger seat of Nick's car, dressed in Nick's faded old sweatpants, my bare feet propped up on the dashboard to get them closer to the heat vent. Cam's jacket was still around me; it smelled faintly of his aftershave.

Meanwhile Cam himself was in the driver's seat. He fiddled with the heat blowers, pointing all of them in my direction.

"Feeling okay?" he asked. "Can you wriggle your toes? Do you think you have frostbite?"

"I'm okay." I wriggled my toes to show him. "I was only in the water for a few seconds."

"Good." He glanced out the car window.

"So," I blurted out, guessing that he was thinking about heading back out there to where Jaylene was surely waiting for him, "this reminds me of our very first date."

"Huh?" He blinked at me. "What do you mean?"

I laughed. "Um, not the frostbite and stuff," I said. "I mean the skating. Remember? Our first date, the two of us out there on the lake . . ."

He shook his head, his brow furrowing slightly. "Skating

wasn't our first date, Lexi," he said, suddenly sounding kind of sad. "It was our second. Our first date was the Christmas movie at the North Pole."

Oops. Now that he mentioned it . . .

"Oh, right," I said. "Sorry. Um, must be frostbite of the brain."

His smile looked wistful. "You know, I'm starting to think maybe you were right all along. I wasn't sure this—this breakup was the best thing. But it could be that we're better off as friends, you know? Even if I didn't want to accept it at first . . ."

No! My brain stalled out, and I could almost feel Nick and Allie perched on my shoulders, like the little angel and devil figures you see in sitcoms and comic strips sometimes. Only they were both on the same shoulder, poking me in the head and yelling, "Tell him the truth! Tell him the truth!"

And at that moment, I wondered if maybe they were right. I'd made a big mistake playing games with our relationship in the first place. Was it time for the games to stop?

"Listen, Cam . . . ," I began.

Just then there was a knock on the driver's side window. A moment later the door opened and Jaylene stuck her cheerful face into the warm car.

"Ya'll okay in here?" she asked brightly. "Lexi, Ah hope you didn't freeze your little toesies off, fallin' in that freezin' cold water like that!"

I forced a smile. "No, my toesies are all still attached."

Cam was already climbing out of the car. "I think you'll be okay, Lex," he told me as Jaylene latched onto his arm like a five-foot blond leech. "You might want to stay in the heat for a while, though. Maybe drink some hot cocoa to help warm up."

"Thanks, doc," I said, that fake smile still plastered on my face.

But as soon as they were out of sight, I closed my eyes and blew out a frustrated sigh. So close and yet so far . . .

ten

"The More Than Friends Theory," Allie said.

"What?" Nick and I both looked up from our burgers.

The three of us were sitting in one of the deep, private window booths at the Elf Street Diner, eating dinner and talking over that afternoon's disastrous skating party. A reggae version of "God Rest Ye Merry Gentlemen" was rolling softly out of the speaker over our table, doing a pretty good job of drowning out the conversations of the other customers and the rattles and clinks of the cooks and waitresses at work.

"It's just what it sounds like." Allie reached for a french fry from the communal plate in the center of our table.

"We all agree that what's needed here is to remind Cam of what he's missing by being just friends, right?"

"Sure, I guess," I replied. Nick shrugged.

"Okay," Allie went on. "Then the More Than Friends Theory states that you have to *show* him what he's missing by being 'just friends.' You know, by being sexy. Seducing him. That kind of thing."

Nick laughed. "Yeah, right," he said sarcastically, looking me up and down. "That's going to happen."

"Shut up." I had to admit I wasn't exactly looking the part of seductress at the moment, dressed as I was in a pair of plaid flannel pants and one of my dad's shabby old University of Wisconsin sweatshirts. But that wasn't really the point. "He's kind of right, though, Allie. That doesn't exactly sound like me. Or like Cam, for that matter."

Allie dipped her fry in ketchup. "That's what you said about him liking Jaylene. Anyway, desperate times call for desperate measures. How many dates are they up to now, anyway?"

"Five," I said before I could stop myself. "Um, but who's counting? Anyway, I'm still not convinced on this Dozen Dates thing in the first place, or— What?" I interrupted myself as Allie's eyes widened.

"Five? But that means the next date is number six."

"And people say *I'm* good at math," I teased.

She shook her head. "No, listen, Lexi. I've been working some more on the Dozen Dates Theory. According to the Halfway Point Addendum, your task gets harder from date six on. Um, you know, exponentially."

"Expressing your theories in mathematical terms now, are you?" I commented with a laugh, reaching for the salt. "I guess it's always important to know your audience. Did you learn that from Oprah?"

Nick chortled, but Allie didn't even crack a smile. "I'm serious, Lexi. You need to do something."

I stopped laughing. "Do you think I don't know that? It's killing me to think that I might have messed things up with Cam for good. You know that."

"I know." Her expression softened. "But see, that's exactly why you need to be willing to try whatever it takes to get him back. And we all know that guys think mostly with their hormones." Ignoring Nick's snort, she went on, "So our best bet is to let him see you in some supersexy outfit that will remind him of just how attracted he is to you."

"What, do you want me to wear some lacy little number from Victoria's Secret to school on Monday? Then again, why be subtle? Maybe I should just show up on his doorstep stark naked."

"You're right, showing up at his house is probably too obvious." She chose to ignore the rest of my suggestion, which was just as well. In her current state, she might actually think I was serious. "No, you might have to work it right in front of Jaylene on this one. In fact, maybe that's better anyway. Let him see exactly what he's given up to be with her." She nodded, looking pleased with herself. "Okay, so that means we have to find out when and where their next date is."

Nick grabbed another fry. "I already know," he said. "Cam was talking about it at the lake today. They're going bowling tomorrow night."

"Hmm, bowling. That doesn't sound very sexy." Allie tapped one finger on her chin. I could almost see the little gears in her brain turning. "But never mind—I'm sure we can still come up with an outfit that will turn his head. Is Cam more of a leg man or a boob man?" When I shrugged, she turned to my cousin. "Nick?"

He looked a bit startled. "How should I know?"

"Isn't that what you guys talk about? You know, in the locker room and stuff?"

He rolled his eyes. "If we do, I'm not about to start discussing it with the two of you." Setting down his half-finished burger, he wiped his hands on a napkin and stood up. "In fact, all this talk of boob men and sexy outfits for my cousin makes me think it's a good time for a nice long game of pinball. See you."

He scooted off toward the line of arcade games along the side wall. "See that, Allie?" I reached across the table, peeled the pickle off Nick's burger, and popped it into my mouth. "You made him lose his appetite. That's not easy. Congratulations."

"Now that he's gone, let's get down to business." Allie shoved her plate away and leaned forward. "What are you going to wear to the bowling alley tomorrow night? How about your purple cami? I'm working on a theory about how guys really notice the color purple."

"Um, I don't think so. In case it's slipped your mind, it's December. If I show up in something like that, Cam won't think I'm sexy; he'll think I've gone insane." I wiped my pickley fingers on my napkin. "No, I'm thinking maybe I'll wear my green V-neck sweater. Nick always compliments me on that one. Says it brings out the gold in my eyes."

She looked disappointed. "Okay, I guess that'll have to do. So let's talk strategy. Maybe you can, like, lure him off by himself somewhere and then pretend you have a cramp in your leg, and ask him to rub it for you."

"Are you kidding?" I laughed. "I'm not going to do that."

"But the Dozen Dates Theory . . . ," she began urgently.

I shook my head. "I know, I know. There isn't much time. I get that. But even so, I think I just need to keep things simple. Cam isn't the type of guy to fall for anything too obvious. And plotting and scheming is what got me into this mess to begin with."

"That's true," Allie agreed, reaching for her iced tea. "Okay. But you're not just going to, like, stand there, right? Let's talk about the little things you can do to catch his attention."

"Like what?"

"Don't look so suspicious," she said. "I just mean stuff like smiling at him. Touching him on the arm whenever you get the chance. That sort of thing."

I felt as if I should be taking notes. It hadn't required nearly this much effort to win Cam over in the first place, and I felt kind of foolish having to work so hard at getting him back now. Still, I figured I had to do whatever it took to undo what I'd done.

Walking into the bowling alley all by myself felt weird. For one thing, I'm not much of a bowler. I'd probably only ever been there four or five times total in my life. Plus it's really the kind of place people normally go as part of a big group. To top it off, Allie had twisted my arm until I'd agreed to put on a little extra makeup before I went. I guess that was to make up for the fact that I'd continued to insist on wearing jeans and a sweater rather than the leather bustier and hot pants she probably thought would be much more ideal.

As soon as I got inside, I heard an ear-splitting screech of laughter. Glancing that way, I saw Jaylene dancing around giddily in her adorable lemon yellow minidress, giggling loudly as the gutterball she'd just thrown ambled its way down the lane. Cam was watching her from the scorekeeper's seat, with his long legs splayed out to one side and his arm draped casually over the seat back. But he spotted me a second later and sat up straight.

"Lexi?" he called out, sounding surprised. No wonder. As I mentioned, I'm not exactly the bowling queen of Claus Lake.

Jaylene looked over too. "It *is* Lexi!" she cried, waving at me. "C'mon over here, Lexi!"

I obeyed, ducking around the molded orange plastic chairs to enter their seating area. "What a surprise," I said. "So you guys are doing a little bowling tonight, huh?"

"Yeah." Cam stood up, looking kind of awkward. "Um, what are you doing here?"

I had my cover story ready, of course. "Oh, I was supposed to meet Nick here on my way home from shopping. He was in the mood for bowling—you know how he gets ideas in his head sometimes."

Cam chuckled. "Uh-huh." He glanced at Jaylene. "If

Nick decides he wants to do something, it's easier just to go along with it. Otherwise he'll hound you until you give in."

"Right." I smiled weakly, trying not to calculate exactly how many lies I'd told Cam by now. "But anyway, he just called my cell to say he has a flat tire and can't make it after all. So I ducked inside for a few minutes to warm up before I head home."

"Oh, y'all don't have to go home," Jaylene said brightly. "Why don't you join us? It'll be fun!"

On the one hand I was relieved, since getting invited to hang with them was the point of the whole plan. On the other hand, couldn't Jaylene at least seem a *teensy* bit threatened at having Cam's ex crash their date?

"Well . . ." I pretended to think it over for a second. "Sure, I guess that would be fun. Thanks."

"Hey, check it out—Sexy Lexi's here!"

I spun around. "Bruce?" I blurted out in surprise. He was walking toward us from the direction of the snack bar, the usual cocky grin on his face and a plastic tray of nachos and sodas in his hands.

"That's right," Jaylene told him. "Lexi's going to join us."

"Cool." Bruce dumped the food on the scoring table and brushed off his hands on his pants. "Now I won't be a third wheel anymore. Or at least I'll have a cute fourth wheel keeping me company." He stepped closer and slung one arm around my shoulders, giving me a squeeze.

I somehow managed *not* to punch him in the head in return. This was definitely not part of the plan. How was I supposed to work on Cam with Bruce drooling all over me?

Still, it seemed too late to abort the mission now. So I trooped over to trade in my Skechers for a pair of smelly red, white, and blue bowling nerd shoes. And for the next hour, I pretended to have a good time while simultaneously fending off Bruce's wandering hands and watching Jaylene giggle and bounce and kiss Cam on the forehead every three seconds and generally be exactly the kind of girl that I wasn't. And yet Cam didn't seem to mind, though I did catch him shooting me weird looks every so often, as if wondering what I was doing there. No wonder. I was wondering that myself.

Still, I did my best to keep hope alive. I kept waiting for that magic moment when Jaylene and Bruce would both wander off to the restroom or the snack bar at the same time, leaving me alone to wow Cam with my irresistible charm and wit.

Finally, after one too many gutter balls, Bruce decided his bowling shoes were at fault and stomped off to the counter to get a different pair. At the same time, Jaylene drained her soda cup.

"Think Ah'll get another pop," she said.

Cam immediately stood up. "I'll go," he offered.

But she waved him off. "It's okay, sweetie," she said. "Ah can go mahself. Be right back!"

She strolled off toward the snack bar. Cam glanced at me. He looked kind of uncomfortable. I knew how he felt. Being together used to be so easy, so natural. Now it was as if just hanging out with Cam had turned into the world's hardest school assignment, a test I desperately needed to pass but hadn't studied for nearly enough.

"Um . . . I think it's your turn, Lexi," he said.

Setting down my soda cup, I stood up and took a step toward the little ball-return thingy. The ball I'd been using all evening, a blue one with green swirls, was right at the front of the line. One of the extras, on the other hand, was sitting at the other end of the machine. It was a little smaller than mine, with gold speckles on a black background. I stared at it, realizing that if I went to grab it instead of the other one, it would force me to lean over Cam's legs, which were sprawled out into the path as usual. My leg might brush against his. Or my hand might rest briefly on his knee to balance myself as I picked up the heavy ball. It was even possible that my thick, curly hair—the hair he'd always loved and complimented—would fall into his face. It would be easy to make it all happen. All I would have to do is reach for that other ball, claim that my old one was cramping my game, like Bruce with his shoes. Or that the old one was pinching my fingers. Or any other number of excuses. It would be so easy. . . .

I knew what Allie would have advised. I knew what someone like Jaylene would have done as instinctively as she drew in a breath one second and blew it out the next.

Somehow, though, I just couldn't do it. After all the trickery I'd pulled, the lies I'd told, it just seemed like one step too far somehow. Call me stupid—I suspected even in that moment that my friends certainly would. But I just grabbed my regular ball and stepped up to the lane. My fingers were shaking a little as I shoved them into the holes.

"Straight and steady, Lexi." Cam leaned forward to watch me. "Don't think about it—just do it."

That made me smile. It was just so . . . Cam.

I glanced at him over my shoulder. "Remember who you're talking to here," I joked. "Since when does it ever work to tell me not to think?"

He grinned. "Good point. Okay, so pretend it's a trig problem or something then, and just throw the ball straight!"

I laughed and threw the ball. It wobbled halfway down the lane, then rolled into the gutter.

"Rats! So much for that trig scholarship to MIT," I said.

Cam laughed. I did too. And just like that, the awkwardness between us dissipated. For that moment, it was as if nothing had changed.

Unfortunately, the moment only lasted, well, a moment. Then Bruce came stomping back, a satisfied look on his face and a pair of identical-looking bowling shoes on his feet.

"You should have seen the soles of those things," he announced, blasting into the seating area and grabbing for his ball. "No wonder I couldn't anchor my throws! You guys had better look out now. . . ."

My brief-lived moment of contentment flickered out. What had I been thinking? I'd just squandered my chance to rekindle things with Cam on stupid trigonometry jokes and actual, you know, *bowling*. It wouldn't have taken some stupid flirty move like switching balls to make things happen. All I'd needed to do was talk to him. Remind him of what we'd had together. Maybe tell him I missed him.

Promising myself I wouldn't waste a second chance, I settled in to wait for it. But it never happened. Instead I eventually found myself alone in the bowling pod with Bruce while Cam was getting more drinks and Jaylene was powdering her nose.

It was Bruce's turn to bowl, but he stayed planted on the seat next to me. "So Lexi," he began. "I meant to ask you at the lake yesterday, but I forgot when you decided to turn it into a swimming party." He grinned and waggled his thin, pale eyebrows up and down. "How about we go out again sometime? The Ball's coming up in just a couple weeks if you don't have a date yet. . . ."

"Oh. Um . . ." I shot a look at Cam to make sure he was out of hearing range. "I don't know. I was sort of planning to just go with Nick and Allie. You know, Nick's still kind of bummed about Rachel, and, well, you know."

"Aw, c'mon, beautiful." He reached over and stroked my cheek. As if *that* was going to be a selling point, especially since his fingers reeked of Cheez Whiz and jalapeño peppers. "Just this once, I want to have a date lined up for the Ball before the Cam man does."

"You mean Cam isn't going with Jaylene?" I tried to keep my voice casual, though it wasn't easy.

Bruce shrugged. "I dunno. Probably," he said. "But as far as I know, he hasn't asked her yet. Maybe he wants to keep his options open. I mean, the poor dude was tied down for a loooong time, you know." Suddenly realizing what he'd just said, he grinned apologetically. "Hey, you know what I mean. No offense or whatever."

That made me feel much less uncomfortable about turning him down. "Now that you mention it, I feel the same way. So that's definitely a thanks but no thanks on the Ball. No offense or whatever."

Cam and Jaylene both returned at that moment. "So whose turn is it?" Jaylene chirped. "Lexi? Aren't you up next?"

I stood up and checked my watch. "Actually, I think I'd better head out," I said. "It's been fun, but it *is* a school night, and I have a physics test tomorrow."

"Aw, you sure?" Jaylene actually looked disappointed. I wasn't sure whether to be flattered or insulted.

"We were only going to bowl one more frame anyway," Cam put in.

"Sorry." I was already reaching for my coat. "You guys will just have to finish without me."

eleven

"So what kind of costume do you want to get?" I asked Allie as we stepped into the mall the next day after school.

The place was busy for a weekday. Cheery holiday tunes poured out of every storefront, competing with each other and with the equally cheery holiday music playing constantly in the concourse. Hurried-looking shoppers went dashing from store to store or lined up at the coffee place to fuel up for more shopping.

Allie smiled at a little kid racing past us toward the Santa pavilion in the fountain court. "Not sure," she said. "Just something Christmassy and cute, I guess."

I realized she hadn't been talking much lately about her goal to land herself a boyfriend before the Ball, though now that I thought about it, I wondered if it was a lingering hope that she'd be going as part of a couple that had made her wait so late to get herself a costume. But I kept quiet about that. Allie was a pretty chipper person in general, but the one topic that could get her bleak and gloomy like no other was her love life—or lack thereof. I didn't want to bring her down by making her focus on her single status.

Instead I returned to our previous topic of conversation. *My* love life. Or lack thereof.

"So anyway," I said as we strolled down the bustling mall concourse toward the costume shop, "the one interesting thing that came out of that disaster of a 'double date' at the bowling alley was this: Bruce mentioned that Cam hasn't asked Jaylene to the Ball yet."

"Really?" Allie glanced over, brows lifted in surprise. "That *is* interesting. I wonder if he's afraid she'll say no if he asks her too soon. I came up with a theory about that once—it's called the Delayed Date Theory. It helps explain why guys are so lame about stuff like asking girls to the prom before the last possible second."

We turned the corner and immediately had to dodge an empty baby stroller being pushed kamikaze-style down the mall by a wild-eyed toddler. Barely escaping with our kneecaps intact, we hurried down the concourse and ducked into the costume shop. The song selection there was a jazzy instrumental version of "Deck the Halls." Or "Deck the Malls," as Cam had always jokingly sang it to me whenever we'd heard it under similar circumstances.

"But never mind that," Allie continued. "What we need right now is to get back to the More Than Friends Theory. Just because it didn't work out on the first try doesn't mean you should give up."

"I don't know, Allie." I stepped over to the closest rack and started flipping absentmindedly through the costumes. I'd been pondering the whole Cam situation all day, with only a brief break to focus on and pass my physics test. "I'm starting to wonder if maybe I'm trying too hard."

Allie was pawing through the costumes too. "Wow, the pickings are pretty slim here. I guess most people already have their costumes. Hey, but this one is cute." She grabbed a sparkly white Christmas Angel costume and held it up. "Come on, I want to try it on. You can come with me and explain exactly what the heck you're talking about with the 'trying too hard' stuff."

We headed toward the dressing rooms at the back of the store. "I just wonder if I'm panicking for nothing, that's all," I said as we pushed our way between two racks of Santa suits. "I mean, Cam can't really be happy with someone like Jaylene long-term, can he? What if I just wait it out? After all, if he hasn't even asked her to the Ball yet, maybe he's only with her because he thinks that's what *I* want."

"What?" Allie looked alarmed. "Lexi, no! Think about what you're saying here. I mean, maybe you're right. But he's too special a guy to take that kind of chance. If you let that blond little Southern-fried—"

She let out an audible gulp as we rounded the corner into the dressing-room aisle. For a second I thought she'd stepped on a pin or something.

Then I saw what she'd seen. Or rather *who* she'd seen.

"Well, hi there!" Jaylene exclaimed, her face brightening as she spotted us. She was standing in front of the big full-length mirror on the wall opposite the individual dressing room stalls. "Y'all are just in time to give me your opinion. What do y'all think of this outfit?"

She twirled around in front of the mirror, showing off the costume she had on. It appeared to be meant to represent some kind of elf, though I couldn't imagine any living creature surviving North Pole temperatures with that much flesh showing. The strapless green satin top laced up the front like a corset, hugging her curves and showing an impressive amount of décolletage. The flouncy little skirt—with the emphasis on *little*—was striped like a candy cane, with a hem that appeared to have been dipped in glitter. Jingle bells chimed on the perky hat atop Jaylene's blond curls and the pointy toes of her slippers. Elbow-length satin gloves, a green velvet choker, and green fishnet stockings completed the look.

"They call it the Naughty Elf," she explained with a giggle. "Isn't that adorable? Ah'm just so glad they had mah size."

"Um, it's . . . cute?" Allie seemed to be struggling for the right words. "Doesn't look very warm, though. You know, for December."

Jaylene twirled around and craned her neck to check out the back view. "Oh, Ah'm not worried about that," she said. "Ah'm sure once Ah'm out there dancin' with Cam, Ah'll be plenty warm enough."

"Oh! So Cam asked you to the Ball?" Allie asked, sneaking me a quick look.

Jaylene nodded, making the bell on her hat jingle. "Last night when he dropped me off after our date." She smoothed down her tiny skirt. "He tells me everyone dresses up for this thing, so Ah didn't want to waste any time gettin' started shoppin' for a costume and miss out on all the good ones. Ah bet he'll just love this outfit, don't y'all think so?"

I couldn't quite seem to respond. Seeing Jaylene there

in the flesh—*lots* of flesh—in her sexy elf costume had apparently robbed me of the power of speech.

Luckily Allie wasn't similarly afflicted. "Well, since you asked," she said, "I'm not sure that outfit is, um, exactly Cam's cup of tea. He's more the fuzzy reindeer or snowman type of guy. Right, Lexi?"

"Yeah," I blurted out, trying not to stare at Jaylene's cleavage. "He's kind of, you know, conservative that way."

"Oh, come on, y'all!" Jaylene shimmied in front of the mirror, smiling blissfully as she took in her own reflection. "What self-respectin' man *wouldn't* love a cute lil' costume like this? Ah think Ah'll get it. Thanks a bunch for the input, though, y'all!"

She jingled off back to her dressing room stall. Allie grabbed my arm and yanked me into an empty cubicle nearby.

"That was close!" she hissed into my ear. "Do you think she heard us talking about her when we were coming in?"

"Didn't seem like it. That corset she's wearing probably cut off the blood supply to her ears."

"Shh!" Allie looked alarmed. "Let's not talk until— you know." She tilted her head in the general direction of Jaylene's dressing room stall.

She hung the angel costume on the door and started peeling off her clothes. I slumped on the hard triangular seat in the corner of the stall and waited, staring off into space. I was fine with not talking for a few minutes. Maybe that would give me time to figure out whether I'd really known Cam as well as I thought I did.

Allie was adjusting the halo on her outfit when a tap came on our door. "See y'all later!" Jaylene called in to us.

"Bye," Allie and I called back.

We waited until we were pretty sure she was out of earshot. Then I let out a long breath of frustration. "Listen, Allie," I said. "Do you think I wasn't trying hard enough with Cam?"

"Make up your mind—are you trying too hard, or not hard enough? Anyway, what do you mean?" Allie tugged at the hem of her white skirt. "Like, last night at the bowling alley? I already told you, I—"

"No, not that." I sat up straight and stared at her. "I'm just starting to wonder if Cam was actually as happy in our relationship as I always assumed. Is he really just a conservative, fuzzy-reindeer-costume kind of guy? Or would he maybe have appreciated a little more excitement, a little more naughty elf or whatever, and I wasn't trying hard enough to see that?"

Allie's eyes widened. "Oh, Lexi . . ."

"No, really. We thought he'd never go for someone like"—I glanced cautiously toward our cubicle door—"um, you-know-who. But look at them now! Maybe that's what he likes about her. She keeps him on his toes, gives him something fresh and new and sexy and different. Instead of me, who just sort of took him for granted."

"So what are you saying? You're not giving up, are you?"

"No way. Since when do I back down from a challenge?" I smiled grimly. "No, I'm going to do exactly what you've been telling me to do. Pull out that More Than Friends Theory. Give it a real test. Starting with finding my *own* sexy costume for that Christmas Eve Ball."

Allie looked dubious. "Um, are you sure?" she said. "I mean, I know I've been telling you to do the More Than Friends thing. But I'm not sure a head-to-head sexy competition with Jaylene is, you know, the best way to do it. That naughty elf costume was, well . . . and she has, um, you know . . . I'm just not sure how you're going to top that, okay? Maybe it's better if you stick to being yourself."

"What, you mean dress up as a test tube or something?" I grinned to let her know I wasn't insulted. "Anyway, that angel costume looks great on you. So get it off and come out and help me find one for myself."

Despite her doubts, Allie loyally helped me dig through the racks of Christmas costumes. Unfortunately, we didn't have much luck. All that was left in my size were frumpy

Mrs. Claus dresses and a snowman costume that would have made me look like the Michelin Man.

Biting my lip, I glanced toward the clearance rack at the back of the store. That was where the leftover Halloween stuff hung, dusty and forgotten amidst all the Yuletide frenzy.

"Come on," I said grimly, heading that way. "Let's see if there's anything we can use over there."

Allie trailed after me. "Maybe you could go as a vampire and try to scare Jaylene back to Georgia," she joked halfheartedly as I dug into the costumes.

"Hey, look at this." I pulled out a shimmering pair of emerald green see-through harem pants. I held them up against my long legs, casting a critical eye downward. "Looks like they'll fit."

"What is that, a genie outfit?" Allie asked. "That doesn't have anything to do with Christmas."

"And here I thought you were supposed to be the creative one," I said. "All we need are the right accessories. . . ."

A few minutes later I was in the dressing room, twirling around in our creation. In addition to the translucent green harem pants, which billowed gauzily around my legs and allowed free view of my (thankfully clean and hole-free) white panties, I was wearing a green vest with red and white trim that we'd taken from a boy's-sized Santa's-helper outfit. It ended several inches above the waistband of the harem pants and didn't quite close across my chest, so I was also wearing a wide candy-cane-striped headband as a makeshift tube top underneath. Oh, and a festive Santa hat just to top it all off. At first I felt a little queasy at the thought of going out in public with so much of me exposed, but I reminded myself it really wasn't any different from walking around the community swim club in a bikini.

"Ta-da," I announced, twisting around to check out the back. "We can call it a Christmas Genie."

"More like a Rated-Xmas Genie," Allie commented wryly. "Or better yet, a Triple-Xmas Genie."

"I don't care what you call it." I stared at my reflection, trying to imagine what Cam's reaction would be when he saw me in it on Christmas Eve. Jaylene wasn't the only one who could make his life fresh and exciting. "All I care about is that it works."

twelve

The sales clerk at the costume shop seemed a little dubious as she rang up the various parts of my costume. But I didn't care. This was going to work—it had to.

"So what's your plan?" Allie asked as we headed back out into the mall concourse with our shopping bags. "Are you just going to show up in that outfit at the Ball and see what happens?"

"Yeah, I guess so." I bit my lip, realizing I hadn't really thought this through. That wasn't like me. "Um, maybe when I get there I can go over and ask Cam to dance, and then . . . Oh, who am I kidding?" I cried, tossing my bag onto a nearby bench and then flopping down next to it.

"This is never going to work. You're right—I can't compete with Jaylene when it comes to this sort of thing. She's all cute and flirty and sexy without even trying, and that's so not my thing. I can't even imagine going out in public wearing this trashy thing!" I poked at the bag containing the costume.

Allie sat down and patted me on the knee. "Don't freak out, Lexi. It'll be okay."

"How can you say that?" I glared at her. "You're the one telling me I only have a dozen dates and then Cam is gone forever. Maybe all this scheming and planning is just a big stupid waste of time. Maybe I should just call him up right here and now and come clean about the whole mess—throw myself on his mercy and beg him to take me back."

I reached into my purse and grabbed my cell phone. It would be so easy to hit that speed dial button. . . .

Allie looked excited. "Oh, that's a fantastic idea!" she exclaimed. "Do it, Lexi. Call him. Tell him the truth. He'll forgive you—I know he will. It's just like my Candid Couple Theory. Even when times are difficult or someone has messed up, being honest is usually the best way to fix your relationship, even if it sometimes makes things seem even worse for a while."

That brought me back to earth with a thud. I stared at my phone.

"Yeah," I said slowly. "Being honest usually fixes things. Except when it makes things even worse *permanently* because the trust is gone. Am I really willing to take the chance of losing Cam forever once he hears how crazy and deceitful I've been about all this? He'll never be able to look at me the same way again."

"But this is you and Cam we're talking about," Allie said. "Of course he'll forgive and forget. That's the way he is."

"How do you know that? What if he doesn't?" I shoved the phone back into my purse. "Sorry, but I can't take the chance. If he decided never to talk to me again . . ." I dropped my head into my hands, feeling self-pity envelop me like a thick, stifling cloak.

"It's okay, Lexi." Allie's moment of hope and glee had passed, and now she just sounded kind of tired. "We all know how you are. You trust your head more than your heart. I'm sure Cam realizes that too."

I barely heard her. "All this time, I just wanted to save both of us from a little pain and suffering by being practical," I moaned. "But now it seems like I just made things worse on both of us." I paused and frowned. "Well, worse on myself, anyway. Cam doesn't exactly seem to be suffering now that he's with Miss Naughty Elf."

Allie sighed and stood up. "Come on, let's hit the food court. I suddenly feel the need for some serious caffeine."

* * *

By the time I got to school the next morning, I had formulated a new plan. I found Cam at his locker. Fortunately he was alone, with Jaylene nowhere in sight.

"Hi, Cam," I greeted him in what I hoped was a normal tone of voice. "Listen, I was just organizing my room over the weekend and I realized I still have a bunch of your CDs and stuff. Do you want to stop by this afternoon and pick them up?"

Cam blinked. "Oh," he said, sounding kind of subdued. "Um, sure. I guess I could do that."

"Great." I smiled, relieved that the pieces were falling into place so easily. "Why don't you stop by around four? I'll be ready for you."

"Okay."

As I hurried away, my heart was pounding at the thought of what I was planning to do. Could I actually pull this off?

Well, one thing's for sure, I thought as I headed down the hall toward my homeroom. *When Cam stops by this afternoon, he definitely isn't going to find the same old boring Lexi who always took him for granted!*

I tucked the phone between my ear and shoulder, leaving both hands free to fiddle with the waistband of my harem pants. I rolled it down carefully, exposing even more of my bare belly.

"So I decided to ditch the vest," I told Allie, who was on the other end of the line. "I mean, why be subtle here, right?"

"If you say so. I just hope you don't give Cam a heart attack."

Giving one last tug at the pants, I then reached up and carefully tweaked my headband/tube top to allow for maximum exposure. Then I took the phone in my hand and switched ears. "Oh, and I'm wearing a thong under the genie pants. Cam always said I have a cute butt." I giggled, trying to keep my nerves under control. "Anyway, Allie, you should see this outfit. If you thought it was triple-X before . . ."

I surveyed myself in the full-length mirror on the back of my bedroom door. It was a good thing both my parents were out for the afternoon. There was no way they'd let me leave my room looking like that, let alone answer the door.

And answering the door was the plan. When Cam arrived to pick up his stuff at four—right on schedule, as he always was—I was going to "accidentally" answer the door in my Triple-Xmas Genie get-up. I would pretend I'd forgotten about our appointment and thought he was Allie coming over to see the costume. Oopsie! Blush, wink, wriggle . . . and as Jaylene herself might say, what man could resist that, y'all?

"There's the doorbell," I told Allie, glancing at the clock as I heard a chime from downstairs. "He's a little early—it figures. I'll call you later and let you know how it went."

I hung up and tossed the phone onto my bed. Then, with one last glance at my reflection and a quick adjustment to my Santa hat, I headed for the stairs, walking carefully in my mom's tallest spike heels.

When I reached the door I paused, closed my eyes briefly, and took a deep breath, doing my best to calm my nerves. Then I opened my eyes and flung open the door.

"Hi," I said brightly. "I—uh—oh."

I froze. And not only because it was about twenty degrees outside and I was practically naked.

No, it was because there were three people standing on my front porch, and none of them was Cam. I stared in horror from my school principal to ninety-plus-year-old Mrs. Simpson in her wool coat and pearls to some gawky twenty-year-old kid holding a camera.

"Er, good afternoon, Miss Michaels," Principal Jamison stammered, his startled gaze wandering briefly downward before snapping up to my face again. "We're, uh, here to surprise you with the news that you've won the Simpson Scholarship this year."

It worked. I was *definitely* surprised.

thirteen

Actually, to say I was surprised is an understatement. Stunned was more like it. The gawky kid with the camera had looked kind of bored when I'd opened the door. But now his eyes were practically bulging out of his face. He lifted his camera and quickly snapped a few shots. That jolted me back in action.

"Stop that!" I blurted out, ducking behind the door.

"Sorry." He smirked. "Just doing my job. I'm with the *Claus Lake Courier*."

Mrs. Simpson was peering at me through her spectacles. "Perhaps we should come back at another time, my dear," she said in her quavery voice.

"No, wait!" I said, not wanting to give them the chance to change their minds about that scholarship. "Um, wait here a second. Please. I'll be right back."

I swung the door shut behind me and raced for the coat closet, almost tripping over my own feet in those stupid spike heels. Flinging open the closet, I grabbed my dad's oversized camo-print hunting coat. When I shrugged it on, it came down past my knees. Perfect. Wrapping it around me until nothing showed south of my neck, I headed back toward the door.

"Um, okay," I said, stepping out onto the porch and hoping my face wasn't as crimson as it felt. "Sorry about that . . ."

I'm not sure how I survived the interview that followed, though I do vaguely remember promising the young reporter-photographer to e-mail him a picture of me wearing normal clothes. I tried not to think about where those photos he'd taken of me might end up, but made a mental note to stay off the Internet for a few days just for my own sanity.

We were all still there on the porch when Cam's car pulled into the driveway, right on time as always. He looked confused as he climbed out and took in the sight of me in the camo coat and Mom's heels. "Er . . . Lexi?" he said uncertainly, coming closer.

"Hello there, Mr. Kehoe." Principal Jamison seemed a lot more comfortable now that I was no longer dressed like a stripper. He sounded downright jovial as he greeted Cam. "We're just here bringing Lexi some good news. She's this year's recipient of the Simpson Scholarship."

Cam smiled up at me from the bottom of the porch steps, shoving his hands into his coat pockets. "Congratulations, Lexi," he said. "I knew you could do it. Um, and maybe I should come back another time, to, you know . . ."

"Thanks, Cam." I could only watch helplessly as he gave me a wave and then turned and hurried back to his car.

"What about Sugarplums?" Nick said, glancing across the street as he emerged from the steamy interior of the local dry cleaner's shop. "I know we just picked up pledge forms there last week, but they always get a ton."

"Good call." Allie stepped around a slushy puddle on the sidewalk. It had been a sunny and relatively warm day, and some of the snow that had fallen earlier that week had melted, but now the sun was setting, the wind was picking up, and the slush was starting to harden into ice once again. "Plus while we're there, maybe we can stop and have a hot chocolate or something. I'm freezing!"

I switched my backpack over onto my other shoulder. It was getting heavy. The three of us had been assigned to

walk around Claus Lake's main business district that afternoon and pick up the pledge forms that people had been
leaving at all the shops and restaurants. The Christmas Eve
Costume Ball was a charity event, and in addition to buying tickets and contributing at the Ball itself, townspeople
could pledge additional money while they shopped or ate at
sponsoring businesses throughout the holiday season. And
people seemed to be in a giving mood, judging by the number of pledge cards we were collecting. With less than two
weeks to go until Christmas Eve, Claus Lake was reaching
a fever pitch of festive spirit, as usual.

But I couldn't seem to focus on any of that. Not this
year. Ever since that embarrassing moment on my front
porch the other day, I had been fighting a sense of impend-
ing doom. It seemed that every time I tried to win Cam
back, something got in my way. And even though I'd never
put that much stock in Allie's theories before, I couldn't
stop thinking about the Dozen Dates Theory. What if it
was true?

I was busy pondering that for the fifty-millionth time
as we crossed the street to Sugarplums, the town's most
popular ice cream and sweets shop. In fact, I was so deep in
thought that I bumped into Allie as she came to a sudden
stop in the doorway.

"Hey, what's wrong?" I gave her a poke in the back.

"Keep moving—my frostbite is getting frostbite out here."

"Um, I was just thinking." Allie turned and pushed me back a step or two. "I'm not really in the mood for hot chocolate after all. Maybe we should go over to the diner instead."

"What's the matter with you? You love hot choc—" I stopped short. I'd just gotten a look past her at the interior of the sweets shop. Cam and Jaylene were seated at one of the tiny round tables for two, their heads close together as they dug into a shared ice cream sundae.

Their backs were to us, so they didn't see us. While we stood there gawking, Jaylene reached up and wiped something off Cam's cheek. He smiled, and she leaned her blond head against his shoulder for a moment before continuing to eat.

Nick grabbed me by the arm. "Come on," he said. "Allie's right. Suddenly the diner looks like a much more appetizing idea."

Soon the three of us were down the block at the Elf Street Diner, sliding into our usual booth, me on one side, Allie and Nick on the other. My mind was still whirling with what we'd just witnessed.

"If I'm counting right and haven't missed anything, that's date number eight they're on right now," I said. "I've been trying to figure it out mathematically. At the rate they've been going, there's a high probability that the Ball will be date number twelve."

"Oh, Lexi." Allie's expression was anxious and sorrowful. "I wish I'd never even told you about that theory. It's making you too crazy."

"Yeah. Since when do you believe in her nutty theories, anyway?" Nick said. Shooting Allie a glance, he added, "No offense."

The waitress approached at that moment bearing menus. "We don't need those," Nick told her. "We'll just have three hot cocoas and a basket of fries."

She shrugged. "You got it, hon." After quickly scribbling a note on her pad, she bustled off again.

"Anyway," Nick said to me, "no matter what Allie says, there's nothing magical about date number twelve. It's not like Cam's going to turn into a pumpkin or something."

"I know." I ran my hands through my hair, not even caring for once about Bozo-ing myself up in public. "I know that. Of course I know that. But it's not really the point, is it?"

"What do you mean?" Allie asked.

I stared at her. "Twelve dates, thirteen . . . at some point, that theory of yours is going to be right. They're going to be a real couple, and it'll be too late for me to get him back." I bit my lip. "And then I may spend the rest of my fabulous, exciting, big-city life wondering if I let my one true love get away."

Allie and Nick exchanged a glance. "Look, Lex," Nick said. "There's a really easy solution to all this angst."

"Don't tell me to just talk to him," I warned.

"But you have to!" Allie cried, leaning forward over the table. "Just tell him the truth already. What's the big deal? You've always been honest with the rest of us."

"Yeah," Nick added. "Even when we didn't ask for it. Like when you made me get rid of those ratty old cargo pants I used to wear all the time."

"Or that time back in middle school when you were the only one who told me my new haircut looked terrible and I should get it fixed," Allie put in. "I was kind of hurt at first, but you were sooo right, and I would've been way more embarrassed if I'd walked around like that for weeks without realizing the truth."

"Oh, and then there was the summer after sixth grade when you convinced me to confess to breaking old Mr. Miller's window," Nick said. "Yeah, he was mad at first, but he was so impressed with the way I took care of his lawn to pay him back that he hired me to mow for the next three summers. So you were right to make me 'fess up."

I held up both hands as Allie opened her mouth again. "Okay, enough. I get the picture. Honesty is the best policy, blah blah blah." The waitress was returning with a tray of water glasses by now, so I paused until she'd set one in front of each of us and then hurried off again. "But this is different," I went on, wrapping both hands around the cool, slick surface of my water glass. "I've dug myself in too deep already. If Cam and I *do* get back together, he can never know what a devious psycho I truly am." I stared at them both. "That means you guys can never tell him either. Promise?"

"Whatever you say, Lexi." Allie sighed and tugged at the loose strand of hair that had fallen out of her ponytail.

"Yeah, Scout's honor and all that." Nick lazily crossed his heart with one finger. "But if you're not going to tell him the truth, how exactly *are* you planning to win him back?"

"Good question." I gulped down half my water, then set down the glass and tapped my fingers on the table, thinking hard. "I definitely can't just beg him to give me another chance. Way too random and pathetic, especially after I spent so much time practically shoving him at Jaylene. No, getting back together has to seem like *his* idea."

"Are you kidding me?" Nick shook his head. "That sort of thinking is exactly what got you into this mess in the first place, remember?"

But I barely heard him. What I'd just said had sparked

something. Not a real answer, not quite . . . but the feeling that an answer was just around the corner somehow.

"Throwing myself at Cam isn't going to work," I mused aloud. "I had to practically staple Jaylene to his lap to get him to break up with me." For the first time in, oh, about five or six dates, I felt a flicker of real hope and confidence. "After all, I convinced Cam to decide to break up with me when you guys swore it couldn't be done. It can't be impossible to convince him to decide he has to have me back. All I need is the right plan. . . ."

fourteen

We were halfway through the basket of fries before I finally hit on a promising idea. "It was one of your theories a while back," I told Allie. "Something about being jealous—Jealous Jumping Beans or something?"

"You mean the Jealousy Jump-Start Theory?" she guessed.

"That's the one. It was something about how a guy who's on the fence about asking a girl out is more likely to do it if he thinks another guy is about to swoop in and snag her."

"Yeah, that's basically it." Allie licked some ketchup

off her fingers. "But that theory is really meant for new couples, not your kind of situation. Plus Cam isn't the competitive type like a lot of guys."

Nick nodded. "True. Otherwise he would've decked his buddy Bruce long ago for slobbering all over you every chance he gets."

"That's different," I said. "Cam knew I never had any interest in Bruce. But think about it. It took me seeing him with Jaylene to truly realize what I was losing when we split up. Maybe if he sees me with another guy—a *real* guy, a hot, mysterious guy, not anyone like Bruce or Andrew—he'll have the same kind of epiphany."

"You know, that *almost* makes sense." Allie sounded dubious, but there was a hint of interest in her voice too. "I guess it could work. Maybe. It would definitely be an interesting expansion of that theory."

"Kind of sucks for your decoy boy if it does work, though," Nick put in. "Are you really going to use some poor dude like that, Lex? Get him all hot and bothered over you, dump him like a bad potato, and then go running back to Cam?"

"Of course not!" I retorted.

To be honest, I hadn't gotten that far yet. But now that I thought about it, I realized my cousin was right. I couldn't treat any guy like some lab rat, no matter how important it was to get Cam back. Maybe a little of Cam's niceness had rubbed off on me over the years after all.

"No," I said thoughtfully, reaching for another french fry, "the other guy will have to be in on the plan." I smiled as the perfect guy popped into my head. "Hey! How about your friend Charlie?"

"You mean Charlie Welles from baseball camp?" Nick asked.

"Yeah. He's perfect—he's good-looking, he's smart, he has a sense of humor, and you're always saying he's kind of a player when it comes to women. And most important, Cam has never met him." I smiled at Nick hopefully. "Think he'll go for it?"

Nick shrugged and reached into his pocket for his cell phone. "I can ask him. Actually, it kind of sounds like the type of crazy plan he'll think is a riot."

"Wait," Allie said before Nick could punch in Charlie's number. "Even if this Charlie guy is willing, how are you going to make sure Cam sees you guys together?"

"That's easy." My mind had already worked out that next step while we were talking. "I'm betting I know what their next date is. Holiday Harmonies is this weekend."

Allie's eyes widened. "Of course! I bet you're right. Everybody goes to that."

The Holiday Harmonies concert was another of the

town's myriad annual holiday events. It was a fund-raiser for the Claus Lake Fire Department, traditionally held on the Friday before Christmas. As Allie had said, just about everyone in town attended to socialize with their neighbors, discuss the upcoming Ball, and listen to various local musical groups and soloists do their thing. I figured there was roughly a ninety-nine percent chance that Cam and Jaylene would be there.

"Okay, then." Nick lifted his phone. "Let's see if we can get you a fake date for Friday night."

I looked out the window as Charlie maneuvered his Saab into the last remaining parking space on the block. Dozens of concertgoers were hurrying toward the fireman's hall, most of them with their hands in their pockets and their shoulders hunched against the cold wind gusting in off the lake, which was blowing around the snow that had been falling steadily all day.

"Hang on." I dug into my purse as Charlie cut the engine. "I have the tickets in here somewhere. Let me find them before we get out in the cold."

When I pulled out the tickets, Charlie held out his hand. "Let me hold on to them both until we get inside." He winked. "That's what a *real* date would do, right?"

So far Nick's friend really seemed to be enjoying this

whole scheme. Maybe almost *too* much. I couldn't really complain, though. He was just as good-looking as I'd remembered, with mischievous blue eyes, tousled dark hair, and a rakish grin.

"Okay, Prince Charming." I handed over the tickets. "Ready to go in?"

"Can't wait, my love."

Soon we were among the people rushing through the cold and snow. Charlie put one arm around my waist as we walked and reached over and took my hand with his other hand. It felt like overkill, but I didn't complain. It was warmer that way.

"See your ex anywhere yet?" he murmured into my ear as we entered the hall. "Be sure to point him out so I know who my audience is."

I glanced around at the sea of familiar faces. Nick and Allie were just coming back from the coat check window. When they saw me, they hurried over. Nick immediately started into some elaborate high-five ritual with Charlie, but Allie grabbed my arm so tightly it hurt.

"They're here," she hissed. "Over by the snack table."

Looking that way, I saw them. Cam was leaning against the wall, looking casually handsome in cords and the Nordic print sweater I'd bought him for his birthday the previous year. Jaylene was totally overdressed for the occasion in a sparkly midnight-blue dress and high heels, though she didn't appear at all self-conscious about the fact that most of the other female concert-goers wore something closer to my own attire of nice black pants and a sweater. The two of them were chatting with several girls from Jaylene's class.

"Come on," Nick said. "Let's go over and say hi, shall we?"

"Absolutely." Charlie reached over and took my hand. "Shall we, my princess?"

"Sure. Just remember, we're supposed to be on, like, our second date, okay? Don't go overboard with the princess thing."

"Got it." He winked. "Just having a little fun."

The other girls drifted away as we approached. "Well, hi there, y'all!" Jaylene greeted us with her usual enthusiasm. "Cam said the whole dang town comes to this concert, but Ah guess Ah didn't believe it until Ah got here."

"Yep, we never miss it. We're all addicted to Christmas." Nick gave Cam a friendly slap on the shoulder. "Isn't that right, buddy?"

"Definitely." Cam smiled at him. But I was pretty sure I saw his eyes dart curiously toward Charlie.

Jaylene's curiosity was much more open. "So Lexi," she said with a coy smile. "Who's your handsome friend? Ah don't think we've met." She held out a hand toward Charlie. "Ah'm Jaylene."

"Charlie." He shook her hand. "Nice to meet you, Jaylene. Any friend of the lovely Lexi is a friend of mine."

I tried not to wince. So much for not going overboard. "Charlie, this is, um, my other friend, Cam. Cam, this is Charlie. My—my date."

"Good to meet you, Cam." Charlie held out his hand. Cam took it. "Likewise."

I tried to watch him without letting on that I was doing it. Was it my imagination, or had his jaw clenched slightly when he'd taken Charlie's hand? I wasn't sure.

"So how did you two meet?" Jaylene asked, snuggling up against Cam until he put his arm around her.

Charlie slung one arm around my shoulders and squeezed. "It's a cute story, actually," he said with a chuckle. "I live over near Dornerville, but I was here in Claus Lake one day last week doing some Christmas shopping. When I stopped at the red light on Elf Street, I looked over and saw the most gorgeous girl I'd ever seen in the car next to me. It was our Lexi, of course." He squeezed again and bent to give me a kiss on the top of my head. "I tried to get her attention, but just then the light changed, and she drove off without even looking over. I was heartbroken."

"Aw, so sweet!" Jaylene cried. "Then what happened?"

Charlie shrugged. "I followed her, of course. What else could I do? I'd been struck by Cupid's arrow." He put his free hand to his chest. "I knew I had to meet her. So I forgot all about my shopping and followed her. I had to run a red light at one point to keep from losing her, and a traffic cop pulled me over. But when I explained, he let me go—he said Lexi Michaels is well known to be the most beautiful girl in town, so he couldn't blame me for chasing her."

If I could have muzzled him at that moment, I would have. Or better yet, strangled him. I'd conveniently forgotten that the main reason Charlie was friends with Nick was because they shared that wicked sense of humor.

"He's just kidding," I said quickly. "He didn't really get stopped by the cops."

Charlie squeezed again. "You don't have to be modest, baby," he said. "Anyone with eyes can see that you're gorgeous. Aren't I right, guys?" He nudged Nick.

Nick coughed. "Uh, she's my cousin, dude."

"Oh, right. Well, I'm sure Cam here agrees with me." Charlie turned and beamed at Cam instead. "Back me up here, buddy."

Cam looked uncomfortable. He shot me a quick glance, then shrugged. "Sure," he said quietly. "Lexi's beautiful."

I felt a pang. How many times had he told me that over the past four years? Somehow, though, I'd never fully appreciated the compliment until right now.

"Sure she is," Jaylene put in happily. "And that's *such* a sweet story, Charlie!"

"Not as sweet as my Lexi." Charlie reached over and chucked me under the chin. "That red light was the luckiest thing that ever happened to me. It was fate, you know?"

I shot Nick a helpless glance. He shrugged at me.

"Um, so did anyone catch the Packers game last weekend?" he spoke up. "Kind of a heartbreaker, wasn't it?"

"The only heartbreaker for me is Lexi," Charlie put in. "It would break my heart if I couldn't be with her."

Things were rapidly spinning out of control. There was no way Cam would believe this guy was for real. Maybe it was better to 'fess up now, admit that Charlie and I were just friends, and play the whole thing off as some kind of joke. . . .

Before I could decide, a buzzer went off to call people into the hall. The concert was about to start.

"Come on, guys," Allie said, sounding relieved. "We'd better go find our seats."

Charlie and I had seats near the middle of the room on the aisle. Nick and Allie were sitting together across the way. Cam and Jaylene were a few rows ahead of them.

"What's the deal with that ridiculous how-we-met story?" I hissed at Charlie as soon as we were sitting down. "Where did you come up with that, some bad romance novel? There's no way anyone would believe that's really how we hooked up."

He leaned back in his seat and grinned at me. "Oh, I don't know. Fact is stranger than fiction, right? Anyway, I think they bought it."

I blew out a sigh. "Well, just cool it a little, okay? Try to keep things more believable."

"Sure, sure. Hey, don't look now, but your pal Cam is looking this way. Let's give him something to look at."

Before I could respond, he leaned over and planted a kiss right in the middle of my forehead. Then he grabbed me and hugged me, running his hands up and down my back.

"Okay, enough." I shoved him back into his own seat before he could get carried away. "This is a family event, you know."

I shot a look toward Cam out of the corner of my eye. He was turned away from me, talking to Jaylene. Had he really looked over and seen me and Charlie just now? Or had that just been another one of Charlie's little jokes?

The house lights started to go down. Just then, I saw Cam turn and look over. His face was somber. When he saw me looking, he immediately turned away again.

My eyes widened even as the place went dark. Was I imagining things, or had he actually looked a little bit . . . jealous?

No way, I thought with a sudden flare of hope as the first singer stepped out onstage. *Could this goofy act of Charlie's actually be working after all?*

I had plenty of time to ponder it over the next hour or so. Finally the last act before intermission came on: a kids' choir. As they began their first song, "I Saw Mommy Kissing Santa Claus," I had a brainstorm. I leaned closer to Charlie.

"Listen," I whispered, "are you up for a little kissing?"

"Anytime, anywhere, my love," he whispered back, his teeth gleaming in the dark as he grinned at me. "As long as it's you I get to kiss, and not some fat guy in a red suit."

"Good. Let's see if we can get out of here fast at intermission. If we time it right, maybe we can make sure we have an audience for our first kiss, if you know what I mean."

"Reading you loud and clear."

As soon as the lights came up, I dashed across the aisle to where Nick and Allie were sitting. "Get Cam outside," I hissed in Nick's ear.

Then Charlie grabbed me by the hand, and we darted up the aisle and into the lobby. Once there, we immediately headed for the door.

"Wait a second, can't we do this inside?" Charlie complained as I pushed open the door.

"Don't worry, we're not going all the way out." There were two sets of doors leading into the main lobby. In between was a sort of outer lobby, really just a small space with a bulletin board for local announcements and a little table full of safety pamphlets. "I don't want to do this in front of the entire town."

He grinned and stepped closer. "Why not? You ashamed of me?"

"Maybe." There was a window in the door leading inside, and I caught a flurry of movement on the other side. "But never mind that. Kiss me!"

I didn't need to tell him twice. Just as the door swung open, he bent down, wrapped both arms around me, and pulled me to him.

I'd been expecting a first-kiss type of peck on the lips. But what I got was more like a the-world-is-about-to-end-so-kiss-me-dammit type of kiss. I'm talking full contact make-out move. I was so taken by surprise that I just kissed him back. He was actually a pretty good kisser, as far as I could judge—after all, I hadn't really kissed anyone but Cam in a long time.

"Oh, my!" Jaylene's voice broke in with a giggle. "Are we interruptin' something?"

Finally Charlie and I broke apart. I was feeling a little breathless and discombobulated. Glancing over, I saw Nick,

Allie, Cam, and Jaylene standing in the doorway. Nick looked amused. Jaylene looked delighted. And Cam . . . well, I couldn't quite tell how Cam looked. Usually he's as easy to read as a large-print book. But at the moment his face wasn't giving anything away.

"Whoops! You caught us." Charlie grinned with a total lack of shame or sheepishness. "Can you blame me for wanting to sneak off for a little of this?" He reached down and patted me on the butt.

I felt like smacking him. Instead, I forced a smile. "Um, sorry," I said. "Guess we got a little carried away. Come on, Charlie. Let's head back inside."

I didn't quite dare look at Cam again. Was this going to work? Or had I just made a big fool of myself?

Once we were back in the lobby, Jaylene excused herself to go to the ladies' room. Allie went with her. That left me standing there with Nick, Cam, and Charlie.

I shot Nick a pointed look. He caught the hint.

"Hey, Charlie," he said. "I was thinking of going to grab some drinks at the snack table. Want to come along?"

"No, thanks." Charlie put his arm around me. "I'm not thirsty."

I debated whether stomping on his foot or elbowing him in the ribs would give him the hint more clearly. Before I could decide, Cam cleared his throat.

"Listen, Charlie," he said. "Er, would you mind if I borrowed Lexi for a minute? I—I need to talk to her about something."

My heart leaped into my throat. Well, not really. That would be scientifically impossible. But *something* funny started happening inside of me. Cam wanted to talk to me? That could only mean one thing, couldn't it? My crazy plan must have worked!

"Sure, Charlie doesn't mind," I said quickly, trying to head off any more goofing around. "Right, Charlie?"

Charlie shrugged. "Sure, I guess," he said. "But you have to promise to give her back, okay, buddy?"

"Sure." Cam put a hand on my arm to steer me away from Charlie and Nick. It felt warm and familiar.

We ended up in a quiet corner of the lobby behind the big glass display case full of firefighting suits and stuff. When Cam turned to face me, his expression was still unreadable.

"Sorry to drag you away from your—your date like that, Lexi," he said.

"No, it's okay," I said quickly, my heart beating a little faster. "What is it?"

"I just wanted to tell you something." He shoved his hands in his pants pockets, looking uncertain. "See, ever since we—we broke up, you've been telling me it's for the best. That you loved seeing me with Jaylene, and that sort of thing."

"Yes?" I held my breath.

He shrugged. "Well, even so, I still felt kind of, you know, guilty. And worried about you too—being alone, while I had someone new. You said it was okay, and that you were happy just being friends now, but still . . ." Pulling one hand out of his pocket, he rubbed his head the way he always did when he was trying to figure out how to say something. "Anyway, I know you're good at hiding your emotions sometimes, and I just wasn't sure I'd done the right thing. For both of us. For a while there . . ." He hesitated, then shook his head.

I resisted the urge to reach out, grab him by the collar, and yell *Get on with it!* Instead, I just stood there looking at him in what I hoped was an encouraging manner.

"But never mind all that." Cam smiled uncertainly. "Now I can see that I didn't need to worry. You've moved on. I guess we both have." He shrugged again. "So it seems like this really was meant to be, you know? I have to admit, it was pretty weird to see you kissing another guy like that. But at the same time, it was like a huge weight off my shoulders." He reached over and squeezed me on the arm. "Now I don't have to worry anymore about whether we've done the right thing. I'm glad you and Charlie found each other, Lexi. I hope you'll be really happy with him."

No. My mind refused to take this in. This definitely wasn't what was supposed to happen. . . .

"There y'all are!" Jaylene appeared around the corner of the display case with Charlie right behind her. "Charlie said Ah'd find y'all over here. Come on, they're already shooin' us back in for the second half of the show."

She grabbed Cam's arm. Charlie stepped forward and took mine.

"Yes, we'd better go back in too, darling," he said. "We wouldn't want to miss anything."

I went along with him, my mind completely numb. I didn't even bother to push him away when his arm snaked around my waist again. My eyes and every fiber of my being were fixed on Cam, who was walking with Jaylene just ahead.

I wouldn't have believed it was possible. But it seemed I'd just managed to make things even worse. *Again*.

fifteen

"Cheer up, Lexi," Allie said with an anxious smile. "You can't just give up."

"Why not?" I glared at her across Nick's dining room table. It was Saturday morning, and the three of us were sitting there wiring together a bunch of fresh evergreen garlands. "In case you've both forgotten, the Ball is less than a week away. The fateful twelfth date."

Nick flicked a juniper berry at me. It bounced off my forehead. "Since when do you have so much faith in her wacked-out theories, anyway?" he demanded. "Usually you're the first one pointing out all the ways they don't make sense. But you're acting like this Dozen Dates thing is, like, the periodic table of elements or something."

I sighed. "I don't need a theory to tell me that things are looking hopeless. All I need are my own two eyes. And my own two ears hearing Cam tell me how thrilled he is that I've finally hooked up with someone so he can fa-la-la-di-da off into the sunset with Jaylene, guilt-free."

Allie and Nick shared a concerned look. "Are you sure you don't want to try talking to him?" Allie suggested tentatively.

"What's the point?" I frowned at the stack of pine fronds in front of me. "I told you, if he finds out everything I've done, he'll totally write me off. I'm sure of it."

"Well, then I have another idea," Allie said. "Want to hear it?"

I shrugged apathetically. "Why not? What do I have to lose? I've already lost Cam, my self-respect, my dignity. . . ."

"This one is called the Heartbreak Charm Theory," Allie said. "I don't think I've told you about it before. But the idea is that guys have a strong protective instinct, and if they think you've been hurt by another guy, that will come out. So for instance, if Cam were to find out that Charlie just dumped you in some totally harsh way, it'll rile up his sympathy and protective impulses. And if you play it right, that could lead to you two getting back together."

"Sounds to me like you should call it the Pity Party

Theory." But I couldn't help a glimmer of interest. If any guy would fall for something like that, it was Cam. "Do you really think it could work?"

"Like you said, what do you have to lose?" Nick reached for another evergreen branch. "Want me to see if Charlie's up for a big public breakup scene?"

"No thanks. I've had enough of Charlie's acting skills. Besides, there's not enough time for that." I smiled. "I have a better idea. . . ."

Later that afternoon, Allie sat on my bed next to the cat and watched me put on a pair of gold hoop earrings. I was already dressed in a pair of nice black wool pants, a warm but attractive wool sweater, and the brand-new pair of snazzy high-heeled boots I'd bought earlier that week with the Christmas money my grandfather in Florida had sent.

"You look nice," Allie said.

"Thanks." I smiled at her, a shiver of nervousness passing through me. "Hand me the phone, will you? It's time to call."

Allie tossed me my cell. I caught it and punched in Cam's number. While it rang, I took a deep breath and closed my eyes. I'd already planned out what I was going to say. The only question was, could I pull it off?

"Hello?" Cam's familiar voice answered after a couple of rings, sounding a bit rushed.

"Cam! I'm so glad I caught you." I put a note of panic into my voice.

"Lexi? What is it?" He was instantly on alert, his voice worried. That was Cam for you. "Is something wrong? You sound funny."

I shot Allie a thumbs-up. "I—I'm really sorry to bother you." I did my best to put a little sob into my voice. "But I didn't know who else to call. Allie and Nick aren't answering their phones, and I need to leave for the ceremony soon . . ."

"You mean the tree-lighting ceremony?" he asked.

"Yeah."

The town's annual tree-lighting ceremony was the keystone of my plan. Like everything else having to do with Christmas in Claus Lake, it was kind of a huge deal. Everyone in town gathered in front of the town hall, the newspaper showed up to take pictures, and the local Girl Scout troop served hot cocoa and cookies and sang carols. Basically, it was the last big public gathering before the Ball.

As that year's Simpson Scholarship winner, I had the honor of placing the big fancy antique star at the top of the tree. Traditionally, the star-placer got all dressed up— well, as dressed up as you could be and still (a) climb a ladder; and (b) not freeze your butt off—and brought along a helper whose job was to hit the switch as soon as the star was in place. That way the newspaper's photographer could get a good shot of the whole shebang while the star-placer was still atop the ladder. A few times in the past, star-placers had brought along a parent, sibling, or best friend to serve as the light person. But since we were talking about high school seniors here, most of them brought a boyfriend or girlfriend as their helper.

In all the commotion over the whole Cam situation, I'd almost forgotten about the ceremony until my conversation with Nick and Allie that morning. On the few occasions it had crossed my mind before then, I'd sort of vaguely assumed that Cam and I would be back together in time for him to go with me.

"Were—were you planning to go to the tree-lighting tonight?" I asked Cam. I threw in a sniffle. Allie nodded approvingly.

"Um, sure," Cam replied. He hesitated. "I'm meeting Jaylene there later. She's going to be a little late, but I was planning to get there in time to see your big moment."

"Oh." I sniffled again. "Look, I normally wouldn't ask, especially at the last minute like this, but like I said, I can't reach Nick or Allie, and my parents already left, and I don't know what to do—" Calling upon my honest feeling of desperation at the thought of losing Cam forever, I dredged up another somewhat dishonest sob. "See, Charlie just— just—just *dumped* me!"

"Oh, Lexi!" He sounded genuinely distressed. "I'm so sorry. You guys seemed so happy last night."

"That's what I thought," I moaned. "But I was sitting here waiting for him to pick me up for the ceremony, and then he just called, like, five minutes ago and said he decided I wasn't what he was looking for after all."

I felt more than a twinge of guilt at the bald-faced lie. Somehow, it seemed even worse than most of the previous semitruths and vague manipulations. But I tamped down the feeling and plowed on. After all, I was in it this far. What was one more thing to keep from Cam if I ever did win him back?

"So now I don't have a partner for the ceremony, and if I show up alone I'll feel like the world's biggest loser, and so I just thought . . . Is there any way you could flip that switch for me? You know, for old time's sake?"

I held my breath. For a second he didn't answer. I shot a glance at Allie, who was hanging on every word of my end of the conversation. She held up both hands to show me that all her fingers were crossed.

"Um . . . ," Cam said at last. "Wow. I can't believe he did that to you, Lexi. He doesn't even know . . . Well, anyway. I guess—I guess it would be okay. You know, if Jaylene is okay with it, of course."

"Of course." I made my next sniffle especially pathetic. "Do you think she'll let you do it?"

"Let me call her. Like I said, she's going to be late— some relatives are visiting from down South, and they're all having dinner together. So I'm sure she won't mind. I'll call you back in a second, okay?"

"Okay. Thanks."

"Just hang in there, Lexi. It'll be okay." He hung up.

I hung up too, then stared at Allie. "He's calling Jaylene."

Allie looked sort of worried. "Do you think she'll say yes?"

"Why wouldn't she? She's never seemed the least bit threatened by having me around Cam before." I shrugged and set the phone on my desk. "Besides, she's totally clueless about all our weird Claus Lake traditions. She won't have any idea how seriously everybody takes this one, either."

"But Cam does."

"Right. With any luck, I'll be able to use that to my advantage. And by the time poor Jaylene shows up, it'll be too late."

* * *

At first everything went perfectly. Cam showed up looking ridiculously handsome in dark pants and a sweater with a shirt and tie underneath, smelling pleasantly of balsam and soap. We walked down the roped-off pathway to the tree area arm in arm while everyone we knew watched and clapped. It felt so much like old times that for a second I wondered if I'd imagined all the rest—my stupid plan, the breakup, Jaylene . . .

We stopped at the base of the tree, an impressive fir draped with hundreds of ornaments and countless ropes of lights just waiting to be set aglow. There was a couple of feet of snow on the ground thanks to the Alberta clipper that had rolled through earlier in the week, but it had been pushed back from around the base of the tree into several large drifts, which only added to the holiday ambience. A podium was set up near the bottom of the tall ladder that stood waiting for me to do my thing. Mrs. Simpson, Principal Jamison, and various other town bigwigs were lined up beside the podium, and Cam and I took our places at the end of the line.

"Congratulations, Miss Michaels," Mrs. Simpson called over to me in her quavery voice. Apparently she'd forgiven me for that scandalous encounter on my front porch. Or maybe she was just senile enough to have forgotten about it. I could only hope. Meanwhile the reporter from the local paper—the same guy who'd documented my earlier shame, by the way—was snapping photos of the whole festive scene. By the way he smirked at me, I could tell *he* hadn't forgotten.

The mayor stepped up to the podium, straightened his candy-cane-print tie, and began his usual speech about the meaning of Christmas in Claus Lake. I didn't really need to listen. Like just about everyone else there, I'd heard it every year of my life. I glanced around quickly, wondering where Nick and Allie were hiding. They'd promised to keep out of sight until after the lighting, just in case Cam had any notions about handing off his duties to one of them.

But at the moment, he appeared content to stand there beside me. "Doing okay?" he murmured as the mayor rambled on, his voice just loud enough for me to hear.

"A little better. Thanks."

"Good. Try not to think about . . . you know." He smiled at me sympathetically. "Hey, remember when Jason Phillips did the honors two years ago?" He chuckled quietly. "He was so terrified of heights that we were all glad there was plenty of snow on the ground in case he fainted and fell off the ladder. I think some of the guys were taking bets on whether he'd make it."

I smiled at him. I could tell he was trying to keep my spirits up, and I loved him for it.

"I remember," I said. "Listen, Cam. Thanks again for doing this. I know it was a lot to ask."

"Not at all." He reached over and gave my hand a squeeze. "That Charlie guy doesn't know what he's missing."

"Thanks." I squeezed back. "Anyway, I'm kind of glad it's you here with me, Cam. It feels right somehow."

"I know what you mean." He didn't take his hand away. "It's weird, but I guess I just always assumed we'd be here together this year for you to do this, you know?"

I nodded. "Me too."

The mayor was winding up his speech by now. For once, I sort of wished he would ramble on even longer. Cam and I seemed to be making some real progress. Maybe if I could get in a bit more reminiscing time with him before Jaylene showed up . . .

"And so, without further ado," the mayor announced, "I present this year's Simpson Scholarship winner, Miss Alexis Michaels. Come on up here, Lexi!"

I gave Cam's hand one last squeeze. Then I dropped it and hurried over to the base of the ladder. Everyone was clapping, and I gave a self-conscious little wave before grasping the sides of the ladder. It felt weird to have everyone staring at me. But I tried not to think about that as I got ready to climb. As I lifted my boot to the first rung, I glanced over to make sure Cam was in place. He was standing by the switch box. When he saw me looking, he gave me a smile and a thumbs-up. I waved back. Then I turned, accepted the star from the mayor, and started to climb.

It was a little tricky climbing the ladder while also holding the star, which was about the size of my head—hair and all. Only a few rungs up, I realized that the high-heeled boots had probably been a bad idea; they got caught up in the rungs with practically every step. But that hardly seemed worth worrying about. My heart felt lighter than it had in weeks as I thought back over my conversation with Cam.

It really does feel right, us being here together, I thought. *I must have been crazy ever to have thought there were no sparks left between us. He had to be feeling them just now too, right?*

Just then I reached the top. Leaning over carefully, I set the star in place on the clip someone had attached to the tip of the tree. A cheer went up from the crowd below, and the Girl Scouts burst into an enthusiastic if slightly ragged rendition of "O Tannenbaum." Then the lights all over the tree flickered on, bringing more oohs and aahs and cheers from the spectators. I smiled as the newspaper photographer lifted his camera and fiddled with the flash. Cam had done his job.

I glanced down at him. He was still standing by the switch. But this time he wasn't looking at me. He was looking off to the side at . . . Jaylene?

My heart sank like a stone as I saw her appear at the edge of the crowd, leaping giddily through the snow in a pair of ridiculously inappropriate pumps. She flung herself at Cam, grabbed his face in both hands, and planted a big juicy kiss right on his mouth.

No! I couldn't believe it. It wasn't fair. How could she just run in, kiss him like that, and erase everything that had just happened between us?

I guess I must have sort of lunged toward them. I'm not sure why, except that maybe I thought I could peel them apart or something.

But all I really succeeded in doing was losing my balance, being that I was still at the top of the ladder. Oops.

"Whoa!" I cried, forgetting about Cam and everything else for a second as I felt myself sway. My glove slipped off the side of the ladder, and I flailed helplessly in the air for a moment, probably looking like something out of an old Road Runner cartoon. I tried to catch myself with the other hand, but the damp sole of my boot slipped and the heel got caught up in the rung, throwing me further off balance.

Somehow, I managed to hold on with one gloved hand as I slid partway down the ladder. Cries of alarm and surprise were rising from the crowd as people started to notice what was happening. But it was too late for anyone to try to catch me, and I couldn't seem to catch myself. Out of the corner of my eye, I could see the photographer snapping away. Bastard.

I closed my eyes as I felt myself lose my grip on the ladder entirely. My whole body tensed, waiting for the impact. When it came, it was softer than expected but very, very cold. Also, very wet.

If several people hadn't rushed over to pull me out, I would have been happy to lie there in that snowdrift forever. Because just at that moment, it seemed significantly better than the alternative.

sixteen

My embarrassing tumble off the ladder into the snowbank was pretty much the last straw for me. How many times was I going to insist on publicly humiliating myself before I gave up? What was the point? Cam and Jaylene were as tight as ever. If anything, my behavior seemed to be driving them closer together. Cam was probably relieved to finally have a normal girlfriend instead of being stuck with an exhibitionist nut who had no sense of balance.

"But you can't just give up," Allie insisted as we assembled canapés in my family's kitchen the day after the ceremony.

I shook my head and sighed. "You're such an optimist, Allie. It's sweet. But come on, we need to be practical. The Ball—and that twelfth date—is only three days away." I rested my head on my hand. "Maybe this is fate telling me I was right in the first place. I had good reasons for thinking Cam and I should split up, remember? So why am I second-guessing myself now?"

"Because you and Cam belong together!" Allie looked as if she might cry.

I stuck a caper on a piece of frozen shrimp. "That's what I used to think," I said. "But maybe I was wrong. Maybe we weren't that well-suited after all, and it was just inertia keeping us together all this time."

Over the next couple of days, my mind kept worrying over that. Cam and I were so different. Everyone had always remarked on that. My friends had always insisted that was a good thing—opposites attract, balancing each other out, and all that. But now I wondered. Were we good for each other?

I was pretty sure that Cam had been good for me. He'd helped me relax and not take myself quite so seriously. He'd showed me how to balance out my natural inclination for hard work with a little fun and relaxation. But had any of me rubbed off on him?

In any case, I eventually realized that it didn't matter.

Whatever our relationship had been in the past, it was naive to think that it could ever be that way again. Too much had happened over the past few months. I'd reached a sort of critical mass of untruthfulness. Even if I could scheme my way into getting us back together, would I really be able to go on knowing how many lies and secrets I was keeping from him? No, I wasn't sure I'd be able to handle that very well at all. Not with Cam, who was honest and sincere to a fault. It would feel almost like cheating on him. So what was the point, really?

The afternoon before Christmas Eve, I was perched on the edge of the tub in Allie's bathroom. I was supposed to be helping her figure out what shoes and accessories to wear with her angel costume, but my mind kept wandering. When she hurried back to her bedroom at one point for another pair of shoes, I found myself staring at the twin sinks in the room. The one on the right was Allie's. It was mostly tidy but completely random, with not only the usual toiletries occupying its edges but also loose change, several pens and pencils, scrunchies in every imaginable color, and even a paperback book. The other sink was her brother's. It only had a few items sitting on its edges—toothbrush, toothpaste, comb—but it still looked like a mess, encrusted with old smears of Colgate stuck with loose hairs. In my current mood, it seemed like some kind of metaphor. The sinks were paired up, but totally mismatched. Just like me and Cam.

"What about these?" Allie hurried back in wearing a pair of strappy ivory sandals. She stuck out her foot and stared at herself in the full-length mirror that stood between the two sinks. Then she let out a frustrated sigh. "None of these are working at all. I really need some new shoes to go with this costume, but I spent my whole paycheck already." She glanced at me. "I wish we wore the same size. Those white mules you have would be perfect."

"Maybe you could stuff the toes with tissue paper or something," I suggested halfheartedly.

She giggled. "No way! I want to be able to dance the night away." She twirled in front of the mirror, making the skirt of her costume flare out.

Her chipper mood was wearing on me a little, though I was trying not to let it show. After all, it wasn't Allie's fault that I was feeling so low. No, the blame for that lay squarely on me, myself, and I.

Allie glanced at me in the mirror. Then she turned around to face me.

"Hey," she said. "You're wallowing again, aren't you? Stop that. All we need is the right theory, and maybe you and Cam will be together by the end of the Ball tomorrow. Have we talked about the Hot and Cold Theory yet? Or maybe the—"

"Enough with the theories, okay?" I snapped, finally too fed up to hold in my inner grinch any longer. "All this theorizing doesn't seem to have landed you a date to the Ball, so why should I trust it either?"

I regretted the words as soon as they were out of my mouth. Like I said, Allie could be awfully sensitive about her love life.

In fact, she looked slightly wounded. "Fine," she said. "If you don't want my help, just say so."

"I'm sorry, Allie." I stood up and took a step toward her, a little sick to my stomach. I wasn't sure I could handle it if I messed up another important relationship in my life right now. "I didn't mean that. It was a rotten thing to say. Please forgive me?"

She hesitated, then shrugged and giggled. "Well, okay," she exclaimed, grabbing me and hugging me so tightly that it made her angel wings crinkle. "How can I not forgive you? It's Christmas!"

I hugged her back in relief. All the Claus Lake Christmas cheer was obviously going to her head and making her even giddier and happier than usual. I was glad about that, even if I wasn't feeling it at all this year myself.

"Thanks." I stepped back, and as I smiled at her, I reached a decision. "And listen, I have an idea about your costume. Why don't you scrap the angel thing and wear my Xmas Genie outfit instead? If we roll the hem so the pants aren't too long, it'll look great on you."

Her eyes lit up with interest. But then she frowned. "Wait," she said. "If I wear that, then what will you wear? Your reindeer costume?"

I shook my head. I'd almost forgotten that the outfit Cam and I had picked out way back when was still sitting around in the back of my closet.

"No," I said. "Actually, I think I'm going to skip the Ball this year."

Allie gasped and took a step back. "What?" she exclaimed. "But you can't skip the Ball! Nobody skips it— JoAnn Garson even dragged herself there last year when she had the flu, remember?"

"I know. But I'm really not in a Christmas kind of mood. And I'm even less in a party kind of mood." I stared at her, willing her to understand. "I just think it's better this way."

She stared back. Her dark eyes looked troubled. But finally she nodded.

"Okay," she said quietly. "If that's really your decision, I guess I know better than to try to talk you out of it. It won't be the same without you, though."

"Thanks." I smiled at her, welling up a little as I thought about what a good friend she really was. For a second I almost changed my mind—maybe I could still go, just hang out with Allie the whole time . . . But no. It was better this way. "So how about it?" I asked her. "Want to wear the genie costume?"

"Oh!" She shrugged, looking a little sheepish. "Well, if you're sure you really won't need it . . ."

"I'm sure."

"All right. I'd hate to see the Triple-Xmas Genie go to waste." She giggled, her joyful mood already seeping back. "I might tone it down to a single X, though. I could ditch the vest and wear my gauzy red beach cover-up over the candy cane thing instead. Oh, and I think I'll wear tights under those see-through pants, too—otherwise my parents will probably disown me." She giggled again. "What do you think?"

"Sounds perfect. You'll have to take lots of pictures, okay?"

Christmas Eve dawned bright, clear, and cold. My parents were in a frenzy of last-minute preparations all day, so I barely saw them. When they finally came home to get changed for the Ball, I told them I had a stomach virus and wouldn't be going. They were surprised but didn't argue. After all the work they'd put in all autumn long, they were totally focused now on going and enjoying the results.

By the time they came downstairs, dressed as a gingerbread cookie (Mom) and a glass of milk (Dad), I was wrapped in my shabby old Polartec robe on the couch watching a rerun of *Rudolph the Red-Nosed Reindeer*. "Looking good, guys," I called to them.

My mom hurried in, pulled off her gingerbread glove, and put her hand to my forehead. "Are you sure you'll be okay here all alone?" she asked.

"Totally," I said. "It was probably just something I ate. I'll be fine."

"Come on, Mellie." Dad toddled in, his legs looking skinny in their white stockings sticking out under the bottom of the milk glass costume. "Lexi's a big girl. She'll be fine. Just call us if you need us, okay, sweetie?"

"Sure, Dad."

The doorbell rang. "That'll be Laurie and Hal," Mom said, hurrying to answer.

Sure enough, Nick's parents were standing on the porch. They were dressed as a lumberjack and a decorated Christmas tree. My uncle was the tree. His ornaments jingled beneath his L.L. Bean parka.

"Lexi! Nick said you weren't feeling well, but I was hoping you'd recover in time to make it to the Ball after all," my aunt said as she entered and spotted me.

"I don't think so," I told her. "I'm going to have to sit this one out."

She tsk-tsk'd a bit. "What a shame. Well, never mind. There's always next year."

There's always next year. I felt a flash of premature nostalgia as I watched my parents and aunt and uncle acting all eager and merry, preparing to go out and have a good time enjoying the fruits of all their labor. No, there wouldn't be a next year for me. Not really. Oh, sure, I'd probably come back to Claus Lake for Christmas and go to the Ball itself. But it wouldn't be the same. The whole extended holiday season was such a part of life in Claus Lake. What would it be like to spend next autumn someplace else—someplace where people probably didn't start humming Christmas carols right after Labor Day? It was a weird thought.

"Oh! I almost forgot." My aunt had been saying something to my mother, but now she turned to my uncle. "Harold, did you remember to bring over the package?"

"What package?" my dad asked as he pulled on his coat. It looked pretty funny trying to stretch over his costume.

My uncle reached into his voluminous jacket pocket and pulled out a brown-paper-wrapped package about the size of a large book. "It's for Lexi. It got delivered to our house a day or two ago by mistake," he said, tracking snow all over the floorboards as he hurried over to me. "In all the commotion, we didn't notice until just now."

That sort of thing was always happening. Even though

the same mail carrier had been delivering to our neighborhood for years, our two houses were always getting each other's mail. I suppose that's what came of having two families with the same last name living next door to each other.

"Thanks, Uncle Hal." I took the package without looking at it. "Have a great time tonight, you guys. Have some eggnog for me."

"That's a promise." Dad gave me a wink. "Come on, gang. Let's party!"

They all bustled out, talking and laughing. As soon as they were gone, the house felt a whole lot emptier.

I sighed. Not a creature was stirring. "Merry Christmas to me," I muttered, feeling sorry for myself.

Not particularly interested in Rudolph's TV antics, I glanced down at the package in my lap. I'd expected it to be a gift from one of my out-of-state relatives. But to my surprise, I saw Cam's name and address on the return label!

I ripped open the package. Beneath the brown shipping paper were a gift-wrapped item and a cream-colored envelope.

My mother had taught me to open the card before the gift. So that was what I did, slitting open the envelope. Inside was a holiday card with a picture of a sprig of holly on the front and Cam's familiar slanty, pointy handwriting inside.

Dear Lexi, it read. *I hope you don't think this is weird. But I came up with the perfect gift for you ages ago, before we broke up, and I still wanted you to have it even if we're not together anymore. I thought it might help inspire you once you get to college. Merry Christmas. Your friend always, Cam.*

Curious now, I grabbed the gift-wrapped package and ripped it open. It was one of those double picture frames. One half held a framed photo and the other a handwritten note. For a second I wasn't sure what it was supposed to be.

Then I gasped as I recognized the sharp-chinned, wild-haired little girl staring out toward the camera. A cheerful, slightly portly man in a white lab coat stood beside her, one hand resting paternally on her shoulder.

"It's me!" I exclaimed aloud to the empty house, grasping the frame in both hands and staring intently at the pair. "And—and is that the doctor from the Mayo clinic?"

My head spun as I tried to understand what I was seeing. It was like gazing directly into the past. Over the years, I'd pretty much forgotten what he looked like. But now it all came back. The horn-rimmed glasses. The good-natured smile. The wisps of graying hair around the edges of his otherwise bald head.

"But how . . . ?" I whispered.

I looked at the note framed beside the photo. The writing was unfamiliar.

Dear Lexi, it said. *I was so touched and honored when your boyfriend contacted me and told me your story. I'm retired now, but naturally I immediately remembered the bright little girl who was so interested in my lab all those years ago. I'm so glad to know that your mother is still doing well, and am especially thrilled to hear that you intend to pursue a science career yourself! I hope you will enjoy this photo—I don't know if you recall, but one of the nurses snapped it that day just by chance. When I retired a few years back, she included it in the scrapbook they all made me. And now I want you to have it. Always stay curious, and please don't hesitate to contact me if you ever need anything. Best wishes, Dr. William J. Ericsson.*

Tears filled my eyes as I read the note a second time. I couldn't believe Cam had done this. How long had it taken him to track down the right doctor? I couldn't imagine how he'd managed it.

My emotions were going crazy as I thought about it. I was so touched by his thoughtful, personal, caring gift that it gave me a sudden surge of new energy—and a new idea. . . .

seventeen

A few people turned to stare as I walked into the festively decorated fireman's hall a short while later. And no wonder. I was dressed as a reindeer—hind end only. I'd hitched up the extra fabric of the costume with Dad's Christmas suspenders, which were decorated with little wreaths.

The Ball was in full swing. At one end of the hall, a live band dressed as elves was playing a rousing version of "Deck the Halls," and tons of people were dancing and singing along with the "fa la la la la" parts. The walls were draped with the garlands and swags we'd all worked so hard for the past couple of months to make, the ceiling dripped with mistletoe and blinking holiday lights, and the squat blue spruce behind the band was so heavily decorated, there was hardly a needle in sight. The bar and refreshments area was doing a booming business; Mom's shrimp canapés seemed to be a particular hit, since I saw at least three people enjoying them within the first thirty seconds after I arrived. People had been creative with their costumes as usual—in addition to the expected elves, snowmen, and Santas, I spotted an icicle, a potted poinsettia, and a couple of wrapped gifts.

But I took all that in only peripherally, with the detached, perpetually observant part of my mind. Most of my focus was on finding Cam. I looked around for him, but it was hard to see very far in the dense crowd.

I took a few steps farther into the room. "Hi, Lexi," someone said from nearby. "Merry Christmas!"

"Same to you," I replied, glancing over and recognizing my ninth-grade history teacher, who was standing with her husband. They were dressed as what appeared to be a Victorian-era Santa and Mrs. Claus. Or maybe it was Elizabethan era. History was never my best subject. Either way, I gasped as I suddenly caught sight of a couple dancing a few yards beyond them. "Um, would you excuse me?"

I rushed past them and over to the other couple, so shocked by what I was seeing that all thoughts of Cam, the future, and everything else had been wiped out of my mind, at least for the moment. Because that other couple was Allie and Nick. They were dancing together, which was no huge surprise. But they were also *kissing*!

"Hey!" I blurted out, skidding to a stop in front of them. "What's going on?"

Okay, so it wasn't the most tactful approach. But I'd had a rough day. Make that a rough couple of months.

They sprang apart as if I'd hit them with a Taser. "Lexi!" Allie cried, her face immediately going bright red.

Nick kept his composure a little better. "What are you doing here?" he asked. "I thought you were, ahem, 'home sick.'"

"I was. I mean, I— Don't change the subject!" I exclaimed. "I saw you guys—you were totally making out!"

"Would you believe us if we blamed the mistletoe?" Nick asked, squinting upward.

I crossed my arms over my fuzzy reindeer chest. "Try again."

"We're so sorry we didn't tell you, Lexi," Allie cried, grabbing my arm. She looked totally adorable as the Xmas Genie, by the way. The costume suited her much better than me. "We didn't mean to keep secrets. But you were so bummed out about the whole Cam thing, and then once a few weeks had gone by, it just seemed kind of awkward. . . ."

"Wait, *what?*" I was really having trouble taking this

in now. My scientific mind had already started plugging the strange little scene I'd just interrupted into a logical sequence. They'd come to the Ball, neither with another date; they'd danced together, gotten a little carried away . . . But no. It sounded like there was a lot more to it than that.

Nick took a deep breath. "Okay, here's the deal," he said. "Allie was really cool to me after Rachel and I broke up. Especially since, um, a lot of people were, you know, kind of distracted by other things."

I felt a pang of guilt. Come to think of it, I hadn't really paid that much attention to Nick's heartbreak after the first week or two. Not only had I been distracted by the whole Cam situation, but also by the SATs, the Simpson Scholarship, my classes at school . . .

"Anyway, we started getting kind of, you know, close," Allie picked up the story. "Then a while ago, the two of us spent a lot of time together working on the kids' room decorations, remember? That's when we realized we were starting to like each other as, um, more than friends."

"Oh." I blinked. "Wait. So like, that time I stopped by your house when you guys were making the paper chains . . ."

I paused as Allie giggled and shot Nick a glance. He grinned.

"Yeah, that was interesting timing," he told me. "If

you'd barged in about thirty seconds earlier, you would've interrupted our first kiss."

"Really?" I thought back, trying to remember the details of that day. I'd been pretty wrapped up in my own stuff at the time, what with having just survived that disastrous dinner with Andrew and realizing how colossally wrong I'd been to let Cam go. Even so, how had I missed the clues? If I'd been paying more attention, would I have caught them sooner?

Allie was peering at me with concern. "Are you mad at us for not telling you?" she asked. "We wanted to. But we weren't sure you were ready to deal with it. You know, considering your state of mind with the Cam thing and all."

"Yeah," Nick said. "We figured it would be better to wait until you and Cam were back together." He shrugged. "Who knew it would take so long?"

I wasn't sure what to say. My cousin and my best friend, a couple . . . I was awed and confused and surprised and a little weirded out by this unexpected romance that had happened right under my nose without my ever noticing. So much for my observant scientific nature. Not to mention my worries about not wanting anything in our tight little group to ever change.

"Oh," I said. "Um. Well, I can't say I'm not surprised. But I'm pretty sure that once my brain is working again,

I'll think this is a good thing." I smiled. "Congratulations. I'm happy for you two. And I might forgive you for keeping this secret if you promise to tell me everything now. Or, rather, a little later. Right now I have something I came here to do."

"Really?" Allie shot a look at Nick. He raised his eyebrows curiously. But neither of them asked any questions. That was a couple of really good friends for you.

I gave them a wave and moved off through the crowd. My shock at what I'd just found out was fading a little, and my mind was getting back to the reason I was here.

It only took another minute or two to locate Cam and Jaylene. They were standing at the edge of the dance floor, watching the action out there and nibbling at a shared plate of snacks. Cam was dressed as a very handsome Nutcracker. Jaylene looked even more incredible in her Naughty Elf costume than she had at the store. Seeing them standing there together, totally wrapped up in each other, I almost lost my nerve. But I shoved that aside, took a deep breath, and walked right up to them.

"Hi, Lexi! Merry Christmas." Jaylene scanned my half-reindeer getup, looking a little confused. "Uh, cute outfit."

"Thanks. Yours too," I replied. "Um, can I borrow Cam for a sec? It's important."

"No problem, Lexi." Jaylene seemed as unperturbed by

my presence as usual. "Ah was just going to visit the little girls' room anyhow."

She wandered off. I grabbed Cam by the arm and dragged him away, barely allowing him enough time to set his plate down on a table nearby.

"What is it, Lexi?" he asked. "And what happened to the other half of the costume? If you thought I still had it, I brought it over to your house weeks ago, remember? Although it's really made for *two* people, so I don't know if—"

"No, it's not that." I turned to face him. We had just left the main hall and were now in a quiet hallway that led back to some dark and empty offices. "I only wore the bottom half of the costume on purpose. That's because I realized I've been a real ass lately."

"Huh?" He looked startled.

"It all started a few months ago at that big last-day-of-freedom party at the lake the night before our first day of senior year . . . ," I began.

And then I proceeded to tell him the truth. About deciding we would be better off splitting up. About setting him up with Jaylene. About all the crazy things I'd done since then trying to win him back.

"So basically, I've been a total moron," I finished. "But it's all because I didn't really appreciate what I had with you until it was gone."

He hadn't said a word all through my confession. By the end he looked as stunned as someone who'd just been run over by Santa's sleigh, including all eight reindeer.

"Wow," he said at last, his tone and expression completely blank. "I can't believe it."

My heart sank. Had I just blown it? Judging by the look on his face, I was afraid my earlier fears had been right. Now that he knew everything, it could very well be the end of any chances we might have had.

eighteen

But then: a Christmas miracle. Cam smiled.

"Wow," he said again. "I know how hard that must have been for you."

"Huh?" I said. "You mean being apart from you?"

He chuckled. "No," he said. "Well, okay, maybe that too. But I was talking about how tough that must have been just now—you coming out like that and admitting your mistakes. And your fears about the future. And your lack of control."

Okay. So maybe he did know me pretty well.

"Um, yeah. Kind of. Maybe," I admitted, realizing it was true. All this time I'd been using his own honesty as an excuse not to tell him the truth. And that really had been part of it. But maybe another part had been not wanting to admit I was wrong. I'd been a straight-A student for a long time. I wasn't used to making many big mistakes.

He gazed at me, still smiling. "A lot of people probably don't realize how cautious you can be about some things, Lexi," he said. "You're so direct, it's easy to assume you never have any doubts or fears about anything. But I've seen the way you can sort of hide behind that directness, you know?"

I didn't, actually. At least not until he said it. But again, I realized he was right. Maybe sometimes I did just plow ahead when I might be better off admitting I didn't know what the heck I was doing. I would have to think more about that later.

"I didn't want you to know what I'd done," I told him, not ready to let myself off the hook just yet. "I figured you'd be shocked and horrified by how I'd been so manipulative and dishonest and stuff."

"Horrified, maybe." He winked. "But actually, now that I'm clued in, I can't say I'm really all *that* surprised. Science geek or not, nobody can say you're not creative!"

I laughed a little, finally starting to relax as I realized he really wasn't going to hold this against me. But then my nervousness returned as I realized we were still dancing around the main point.

"So," I said, calling up that directness he'd just been talking about. "I guess I'm asking you to make a choice here, huh?" I swallowed hard, trying not to picture Miss Sexy Elf waiting for him back in the other room. "Me or Jaylene."

He glanced down at the floor for a moment. Lifting one hand, he ran it over his face and up through his hair, dislodging the little soldier's cap from his Nutcracker costume. I felt queasy. This was it—after he answered, I would know my fate for sure. If he chose Jaylene, I only hoped he'd let me down easy. . . .

Then he looked up again and met my eye. "Don't be an idiot," he said, his voice suddenly hoarse and low. "That's no choice at all, Lexi. It's you. It's always been you and only you for me."

I gasped, relief flooding through me so violently that my knees wobbled and I was afraid I might have to sit down. "Really?"

"Of course. These past few weeks have driven that home more than ever." He blew out a loud sigh. "It was killing me to think things might really be over between us. The only reason I went along with the whole Jaylene thing in the first place is because she was so totally different from you in every way. I thought maybe that would distract me a little once I got to be pretty sure you were pulling away."

He smiled rather wanly. "See? I can pick up a hint. And I knew if you'd decided you didn't want to be with me any-more, there was no point trying to change your mind."

"That sounds just like what Nick and Allie keep telling me," I murmured. "Am I really that stubborn?"

"Let's just call it determined. Anyway, I figured it was better to let you go with some dignity if you'd made up your mind. That way I figured at least maybe we could still be friends."

"Yeah. I always definitely wanted us to stay friends too. I couldn't imagine not having you in my life." I gazed at him thoughtfully. "But listen, Cam, if you really thought I was making a mistake or treating you unfairly or whatever, you should have said something. It may seem like I want to make all the decisions all the time, but I don't. Especially not if it means you might be unhappy."

He bit his lip. "I hear you. Guess maybe I need to stand up for myself a little more from now on?"

"Yeah." I smiled at him. Okay, so maybe we both had a few things to work on. But it was worth it if it meant being together.

That reminded me . . .

"Oh," I said. "Um, so who's going to break it to Jaylene?"

"I don't know." Cam sounded dubious. "I mean, she has those long fingernails, and I'm pretty sure her dad owns a shotgun. . . ." Seeing the startled look on my face, he laughed. "Kidding! I'll take care of it. As long as *you* promise never to put us through anything like this again."

I quickly crossed my heart with one finger. "That's a promise I'm happy to make." My heart leaped with something—tidings of comfort and joy, maybe?—and I was itching to grab him and kiss him just to make it all official. But I had a feeling he wouldn't be comfortable with that quite yet. Not until he'd settled things with Jaylene. He was that kind of guy, after all.

"Be right back," he promised.

"I'll be waiting."

He hurried off. As soon as he was gone, I dug into the waistband of my reindeer butt and fished my cell phone out of the pocket of the pants I was wearing underneath. I was bursting with my good news and couldn't wait to share it, but I also wasn't ready to go out there and risk running into Jaylene at the moment. So I quickly sent a text message to Allie's phone.

She texted back within seconds. Her message was so full of exclamation points that I could hardly decipher it. I guessed that meant she was happy for me.

It was only a few minutes before Cam returned. "Well?" I demanded.

"She took it pretty well, actually. Guess that means I

wasn't the man of her dreams after all." He smiled wryly. "In fact, she's already comforting herself by dirty dancing with Bruce."

Easy come, easy go. That seemed to be how Jaylene viewed her love life. Then again, maybe there was something to Allie's Dozen Dates Theory after all. . . .

Cam saw me smiling. "What?" he asked.

"Nothing," I said. "I'll tell you later. Right now, I'm still trying to figure out why it took me so long to just be honest with you. Maybe—maybe it's because I wasn't being honest with myself when I decided I needed to break up with you."

"What do you mean?"

"I mean I might be a little more nervous than I wanted to admit about that fabulous future I have planned for myself." I shot him a sheepish glance. "I know I always talk about how I'm looking forward to going away to some great school, living in a big city . . . but it's going to be a huge change, you know?"

He nodded. "I know. But you're going to be great. I'm sure of it."

"Thanks. But if I'm out there and you're still here—"

"It won't matter," he put in. "Lexi, nobody can predict the future. We'll just have to take it as it comes. But I can promise you one thing—I would never make you choose between going after your goals and being with me." He shrugged. "I know I talk about that little restaurant on Elf Street. But you have to understand, my heart isn't set on that the way yours is on your career stuff." He reached for my hand and smiled that open, honest, easy smile of his. The smile of a kid on Christmas. "Nope, the only thing my heart is set on is being with you. Whatever it takes, we'll work it out."

Stepping forward, I wrapped my arms around him. I felt his encircle me in their familiar way, strong and gentle at the same time. He bent his head toward me, and as soon as we kissed, I knew he was right. Whatever it took, we could do it. Together. It was Christmas Eve in Claus Lake, all was right with the world, and the future could wait.

When we finally came up for air, Cam smiled down at me. "Hey," he said, "I almost forgot. Did you get my present? What did you think of it?"

"I loved it," I answered truthfully.

But as he bent to kiss me again, I couldn't help thinking happily that all I'd ever *really* wanted for Christmas was him. It was a good thing I'd finally figured that out—just in the Old Saint Nick of time.

About the Author

Catherine Hapka has never dressed up as a Christmas Genie, but she always enjoys the holiday season nonetheless. She has written more than one hundred and fifty books for children and young adults. In addition to reading and writing, she enjoys horseback riding, animals of all kinds, gardening, music, and traveling. She lives on a small farm in Chester County, Pennsylvania, with a couple of horses, three goats, a small flock of chickens, and too many cats.

Love winter romances,
but ready for something sizzling?

Here's a peek at

endless
SUMMER

by Jennifer Echols

Sean smiled down at me, his light brown hair glinting golden in the sunlight. He shouted over the noise of the boat motor and the wind, "Lori, when we're old enough, I want you to be my girlfriend." He didn't even care the other boys could hear him.

"I'm there!" I exclaimed, because I was nothing if not coy. All the boys ate out of my hand, I tell you. "When will we be old enough?"

His blue eyes, lighter than the bright blue sky behind him, seemed to glow in his tanned face. He answered me, smiling. At least, I *thought* he answered me. His lips moved.

"I didn't hear you. What'd you say?" I know how to draw out a romantic moment.

He spoke to me again. I still couldn't hear him, though the boat motor and the wind hadn't gotten any louder. Maybe he was just mouthing words, pretending to say something sweet I couldn't catch. Boys were like that. He'd just been teasing me all along—

"You ass!" I sat straight up in my sweat-soaked bed, wiping away the strands of my hair stuck to my wet face. Then I realized what I'd said out loud. "Sorry, Mom," I told her photo on my bedside table. But maybe she hadn't heard me over my alarm clock blaring Christina Aguilera, "Ain't No Other Man."

Or maybe she'd understand. I'd just had a closer encounter with Sean! Even if it *was* only in my dreams.

Usually I didn't remember my dreams. Whenever my brother, McGillicuddy, was home from college, he told Dad and me at breakfast what he'd dreamed about the night before. Lindsay Lohan kicking his butt on the sidewalk after he tried to take her picture (pure fantasy). Amanda Bynes dressed as the highway patrol, pulling him over to give him a traffic ticket. I was jealous. I didn't want to dream about Lindsay Lohan or getting my butt kicked. However, if I was spending the night with Patrick

Dempsey and didn't even *know* it, I was missing out on a very worthy third of my life. I had once Googled "dreaming" and found out some people don't remember their dreams if their bodies are used to getting up at the same hour every morning and have plenty of time to complete the dream cycle.

So why'd I remember my dream this morning? It was the first day of summer vacation, that's why. To start work at the marina, I'd set my clock thirty minutes earlier than during the school year. Lo and behold, here was my dream. About Sean: check. Blowing me off, as usual: noooooooo! That might happen in my dreams, but it wasn't going to happen in real life. Not again. Sean would be mine, starting today. I gave Mom on my beside table an okay sign—the wakeboarding signal for *ready to go*—before rolling out of bed.

My dad and my brother suspected nothing, ho ho. They didn't even notice what I was wearing. Our conversation at breakfast was the same one we'd had every summer morning since my brother was eight years old and I was five.

Dad to brother: "You take care of your sister today."

Brother, between bites of egg: "Roger that."

Dad to me: "And you watch out around those boys next door."

Me: (Eye roll.)

Brother: "I had this rockin' dream about Anne Hathaway."

Post-oatmeal, my brother and I trotted across our yard and the Vaders' yard to the complex of showrooms, warehouses, and docks at Vader's Marina. The morning air was already thick with the heat and humidity and the smell of cut grass that would last the entire Alabama summer. I didn't mind. I liked the heat. And I quivered in my flip-flops at the prospect of another whole summer with Sean. I'd been going through withdrawal.

In past years, any one of the three Vader boys, including Sean, might have shown up at my house at any time to throw the football or play video games with my brother. They might let me play too if they felt sorry for me, or if their mom had guilted them into it. And my brother might go to their house at any time. But *I* couldn't go to their house. If I'd walked in, they would have stopped what they were doing, looked up, and wondered what I was doing there. They were my brother's friends, not mine.

Well, Adam was my friend. He was probably more my friend than my brother's. Even though we were the same age, I didn't have any classes with him at school, so you'd think he'd walk a hundred yards over to my house for a visit every once in a while. But he didn't. And if I'd gone to visit him, it would have been obvious I was looking for Sean out the corner of my eye the whole time.

For the past nine months, with my brother off at college, my last tie to Sean had been severed. He was two years older than me, so I didn't have any classes with *him*, either. I wasn't even in the same wing of the high school. I saw him once at a football game, and once in front of the movie theater when I'd ridden around with Tammy for a few minutes after a tennis match. But I never approached him. He was always flirting with Holly Chambliss or Beige Dupree or whatever glamorous girl he was with at the moment. I was too young for him, and he never even thought of hooking up with me. On the very rare occasion when he took the garbage to the road at the same time I walked to the mailbox, he gave me the usual beaming smile and a big hug and acted like I was his best friend ever . . . for thirty heavenly seconds.

It had been a long winter. *Finally* we were back to the summer. The Vaders always needed extra help at the marina during the busy season from Memorial Day to Labor Day. Just like last year, I had a job there—and an excuse to make Sean my captive audience. I sped up my trek across the pine needles between the trees and found myself in a footrace against my brother. It was totally unfair because I was carrying my backpack and he was wearing sneakers, but I beat him to the warehouse by half a length anyway.

The Vader boys had gotten there before us and claimed

the good jobs, so I wouldn't have a chance to work side by side with Sean. Cameron was helping the full-time workers take boats out of storage. He wanted my brother to work with him so they could catch up on their lives at two different colleges. Sean and Adam were already gone, delivering the boats to customers up and down the lake for Memorial Day weekend. Sean wasn't around to see my outfit. I was so desperate to get going on this "new me" thing, I would have settled for a double take from Adam or Cameron.

All I got was Mrs. Vader. Come to think of it, she was a good person to run the outfit by. She wore stylish clothes, as far as I could tell. Her blond pinstriped hair was cut to flip up in the back. She looked exactly like you'd want your mom to look so as not to embarrass you in public. I found her in the office and hopped onto a stool behind her. Looking over her shoulder as she typed on the computer, I asked, "Notice anything different?"

She tucked her pinstriped hair behind her ear and squinted at the screen. "I'm using the wrong font?"

"Notice anything different about my boobs?"

That got her attention. She whirled around in her chair and peered at my chest. "You changed your boobs?"

"I'm *showing* my boobs," I said proudly, moving my palm in front of them like presenting them on a TV commercial. All this can be yours! Or, rather, your son's.

My usual summer uniform was the outgrown clothes Adam had given me over the years: jeans, which I cut off into shorts and wore with a wide belt to hold up the waist, and T-shirts from his football team. Under that, for wakeboarding in the afternoon, I used to wear a one-piece sports bathing suit with full coverage that reached all the way up to my neck. Early in the boob-emerging years, I had no boobs, and I was touchy about it. Remember in middle school algebra class, you'd type 55378008 on your calculator, turn it upside down, and hand it to the flat-chested girl across the aisle? I was that girl, you bi-yotch. I would have died twice if any of the boys had mentioned my booblets.

Last year, I thought my boobs had progressed quite nicely. And I progressed from the one-piece into a tankini. But I wasn't quite ready for any more exposure. I didn't want the boys to treat me like a girl.

Now I did. So today I'd worn a cute little bikini. Over that, I still wore Adam's cutoff jeans. Amazingly, they looked sexy, riding low on my hips, when I traded the football T-shirt for a pink tank that ended above my belly button and hugged my figure. I even had a little cleavage. I was so proud. Sean was going to love it.

Mrs. Vader stared at my chest, perplexed. Finally she said, "Oh, I get it. You're trying to look hot."

"*Thank* you!" Mission accomplished.

"Here's a hint. Close your legs."

I snapped my thighs together on the stool. People always scolded me for sitting like a boy. Then I slid off the stool and stomped to the door in a huff. "Where do you want me?"

She'd turned back to the computer. "You've got gas."

Oh, goody. I headed out the office door, toward the front dock to man the gas pumps. This meant at some point during the day, one of the boys would look around the marina office and ask, "Who has gas?" and another boy would answer, "Lori has gas." If I were really lucky, Sean would be in on the joke.

The office door squeaked open behind me. "Lori," Mrs. Vader called. "Did you want to talk?"

Noooooooo. Nothing like that. I'd only gone into her office and tried to start a conversation. Mrs. Vader had three sons. She didn't know how to talk to a girl. My mother had died in a boating accident alone on the lake when I was four. I didn't know how to talk to a woman. Any convo between Mrs. Vader and me was doomed from the start.

"No, why?" I asked without turning around. I'd been galloping down the wooden steps, but now I stepped very carefully, looking down, as if I needed to examine every footfall so I wouldn't trip.

"Watch out around the boys," she warned me.

I raised my hand and wiggled my fingers, toodle-dee-doo, dismissing her. Those boys were harmless. Those boys had better watch out for *me*.

Really, aside from the specter of the boys discussing my intestinal problems, I enjoyed having gas. I got to sit on the dock with my feet in the water and watch the kingfishers and the herons glide low over the surface. Later I'd swim on the side of the dock upriver from the gasoline. Not *now*, before Sean saw me for the first time that summer. I would be in and out of the lake and windy boats all day, and my hair would look like hell. That was understood. But I wanted to have clean, dry, styled hair at least the *first* time he saw me, and I would hope he kept the memory alive. I might go swimming *after* he saw me, while I waited around for people to drive up to the gas pumps in their boats.

The richer they were, the more seldom they made it down from Birmingham to their million-dollar vacation homes on the lake, and the more likely they were complete dumbasses when it came to docking their boats and finding their gas caps. If I covered for their dumbassedness in front of their families in the boats by giggling and saying things like, "Oh sir, I'm so sorry, *I'm* supposed to be helping *you*!" while I helped them, they tipped me beyond belief.

I was just folding a twenty into my back pocket when Sean and Adam came zipping across the water in the boat emblazoned with VADER'S MARINA down the side, blasting Nickelback from the speakers. They turned hard at the edge of the idle zone. Three-foot swells shook the floating dock violently and would have shaken me off into the water if I hadn't held on to the rail. Then the bow of the boat eased against the padding on the dock. Adam must be the one driving. Sean would have driven all the way to the warehouse, closer to where they'd pick up the next boat for delivery.

In fact, as Sean threw me the rope to tie the stern and Adam cut the engine, I could hear them arguing about this. Sean and Adam argued pretty much 24/7. I was used to it. But I would rather not have heard Sean complaining that they were going to have to walk a whole extra fifty yards and up the stairs just so Adam could say hi to me.

Sean jumped off the boat. His weight rocked the floating dock again as he tied up the bow. He was big, maybe six feet tall, with a deep tan from working all spring at the marina, and a hard, muscled chest and arms from competing with Adam the last five years over who could lift more poundage on the dumbbell in their garage (Sean and Adam were like this). Then he straightened and smiled his beautiful smile at me, and I forgave him everything.